# THE BAIT

ALSO BY ROBYN DELVEY

*The Seven*

# PRAISE FOR THE AUTHOR

## Writing as Michelle Davies

## For *Gone Astray*

'[A] stunningly accomplished debut . . . deserves to shoot to the top of the best-seller lists. I read it in a single sitting.'

*Daily Mail*

'A full-bodied police procedural thriller from start to finish – with a whirlwind plot and sensational sub-stories, it's a real binge-read kind of book.'

*Stylist*

'A clever but all too believable crime thriller that's right on the money when it comes to creepy, twisted plots.'

*Fabulous*

*'A tense thriller that kept us guessing.'*

*Heat*

'I couldn't put it down. Every single character in *Gone Astray* has a strong and unique emotional story to tell.'

Rachel Abbott, author of *Only the Innocent*

*'I read it in one sitting.'*

*Erin Kelly*, author of *He Said/She Said*

## For *Wrong Place*

'Gripping.'

*Sun*

'Cleverly plotted.'

*Daily Express*

'Full of twists and turns.'

*Good Housekeeping*

*'I loved it . . . A brilliant, compelling read.'*

*Debbie Howells, author of The Bones of You*

*'Gritty, no-nonsense.'*

*Red*

*'This all-too-believable thriller is full of plot twists.'*

*Essentials*

*'A gripping debut novel.'*

*Bella*

*'[A] compelling, twisty debut crime novel.'*

*Dead Good Books*

## For *False Witness*

'Gripping, thought-provoking and expertly plotted – a cracking read.'

Katerina Diamond, bestselling author of *The Teacher*

# THE BAIT

ROBYN DELVEY

This is a work of fiction. Names, characters, organizations, places, events, and incidents are either products of the author's imagination or used fictitiously. Any resemblance to actual persons, living or dead, or actual events is purely coincidental.



Published by Thomas & Mercer, Seattle

www.apub.com



EU Product Safety contact:
Amazon Publishing, Amazon Media EU S.à r.l.
38, avenue John F. Kennedy, L-1855 Luxembourg
amazonpublishing-gpsr@amazon.com

ISBN-13: 9781662521959
eISBN: 9781662521942

Cover design by Dan Mogford
Cover image: © cobalt88 © Zenobillis © stocker1970 © DinkeyDoodle © Sentavio © Vandathai / Shutterstock

Printed in the United States of America

*For Sophie*

# Prologue

## EVE

Gripping her upper arm, he pulled her across the two lanes of Victoria Embankment, weaving deftly in and out of the traffic. There was a cycle path on the river side, and both jumped as a rider streaking past yelled at them to get out of the way. His grip loosened for a second and Eve twisted on the spot to pull away, but he grabbed her tighter again. He didn't care that he was hurting her. All he cared about was getting her up on that bridge. Nothing and no one would stop him.

She struggled to catch her breath as they climbed the stairs to reach the brow. It was still so hot and her chest was constricted with fear. Twice she tripped and fell on her knees; twice he pulled her to her feet again like she was a rag doll. She no longer pretended the sedative was still having an effect, because he didn't care either way.

They were on the bridge now. His expression terrified Eve. It was like he wasn't there. But while his eyes were vacant, he moved with purpose. She was under no illusion – he was going to hurt her. She choked back a sob. Why hadn't the others managed to find her yet? Surely the nearest bridge would be the first place they'd check . . . unless they hadn't realised yet that she was no longer in the club? She had to believe they had, and that they were now frantically trawling the streets near and around the club looking for her. She prayed they wouldn't be too late.

Metal railings ran along both sides of Waterloo Bridge. Like mini ladders, each railing had three rungs that were all too easy to climb. He yanked Eve towards the nearest one. She was crying openly now, any hope she had of trying to talk him out of his plan long evaporated. Then he grabbed her hair at the scruff of the neck and forced her to look over the edge. The drop was so high it made her head spin. She reared back but he forced her forward again. This time she saw the river was flowing beneath the bridge at a frightening speed. She'd never be able to swim against that current.

'Climb,' he ordered.

'I can't.' Her head was spinning so much she wanted to throw up.

He yanked her hair harder. 'I said, climb.'

She shook her head even though it hurt to do so. She could hear people approaching – they were telling him to get off her.

Then, to her shock, a voice she recognised rang out.

'Let Ms Wren go.'

Her attacker spun round, pulling Eve with him.

Approaching them with his hands held out in front of him, like he was trying to calm a wild animal, was the man who'd caused her so much distress over the past few months. She let out a sob. Never had she been so pleased to see someone that she'd never wanted to clap eyes on again.

'I've called the police,' he was saying. 'They'll be here any minute.'

In the distance, sirens wailed, coming closer.

'You need to let Ms Wren go now.'

But her attacker's reaction was to grip Eve's hair tighter and pull her head back so hard she screamed. Shouts went up from the crowd that had now formed a cordon around the three of them. Traffic was at a standstill too, with drivers and passengers climbing out of their vehicles to see what the hold-up was.

Her rescuer inched forward. 'You can see there's no escape now. You're surrounded. You must let Ms Wren go.'

Eve was yanked backwards again. Her side slammed into the metal railings and she lost her footing. Terrified, she kicked out, trying to scramble away from her attacker, but he hooked his arm around her throat and pulled. Screaming at the crowd to get back, he climbed over the railings, his back now to the river. Eve grabbed the top rung with both hands and tried to hold on with all her might, but his chokehold squeezed the breath from her and she let go to claw at his arm.

Through half-closed eyes she could see her rescuer looked panicked. Eve wanted to scream at him to stop, that he was making things worse. The sirens were getting louder. She tried to speak. 'Leave it to the police—'

Suddenly she was in mid-air. Her attacker had stepped backwards off the bridge – pulling Eve over the side with him.

# PART I

## FOUR MONTHS EARLIER

# Chapter One

## EVE

During the forty minutes Eve Wren had waited in the restaurant, she'd come up with a stream of excuses for why her date, Harry, hadn't shown yet. He'd been held up at work. He was stuck on the Tube. He'd had an accident or was helping someone else caught up in one. His phone battery had run out, so he couldn't message ahead. Or maybe there was nothing to worry about, and any second now he'd arrive, eager to see her and apologising for being late.

Eve sipped the wine she'd been nursing since her arrival, one eye on her phone, the other on the entrance. This wasn't their first date. They'd matched on Hinge a month previously and had been out an average of twice a week since. Their last date, three nights ago, had gone so well, in fact, that Harry had stayed over at her flat in Old Street afterwards. Had it been too soon? Eve hadn't thought so at the time but now, feeling exposed as her fellow diners filled the air around her with laughter and chatter, she wished she'd waited a bit longer.

She hated feeling this vulnerable. Especially since she'd had to be talked into dating in the first place. She'd only signed up for the app because her friends had decided that three years was long enough for her to be single following her broken engagement.

To make matters worse, tonight was supposed to be a celebration to mark their month 'anniversary' – Harry's idea. Eve had joked it was too early in their timeline for an evening of contrived romance, but he had insisted it would be fun. The restaurant he'd picked was certainly romantic enough, tucked in the basement of a building near the Strand and festooned with fresh flowers and candlelight. But it felt more like a prison waiting room now, Eve the only inmate without a visitor.

Fed up, she tapped out a final text message.

*I'm leaving. I've been waiting long enough.*

But as she pressed send, she noticed Harry's profile picture change from a smiling headshot to a greyed-out avatar. And instead of the usual two delivery ticks, there was just one, also grey. Frowning, Eve clicked through to his profile – only to discover it was no longer visible.

Her mouth dropped. He'd blocked her.

'You pig,' she exclaimed.

'Excuse me?'

Startled, Eve turned to her right. The next table was occupied by a couple around the same age as her, late twenties. The man was staring at Eve, but his companion, an attractive blonde, was scrolling on her phone, the bowl of mixed seafood pasta at her place setting barely touched.

'Oh, sorry,' said Eve hastily. 'That wasn't aimed at you.'

The diner grinned and nodded, his mop of brown curls bobbing. The shadow cast by the candle on his table gave him a slightly wolfish air.

'I should hope not,' he said. Then his eyes narrowed. 'Do I know you?'

'I don't think so,' Eve replied stiffly.

'Really? I'm sure I recognise you from somewhere.'

Eve caught the waiter's eye to ask for her bill. She hoped he'd be quick with it. She didn't want to have the conversation she feared was coming – because, chances were, the diner had indeed recognised her.

It was all Madeleine Farmer's fault. Madeleine was an actress who'd been the star witness at the Old Bailey trial of a group responsible for bombing a black-tie event in London almost two years ago. Madeleine had been injured in the blast, while Eve was the lawyer for the Crown Prosecution Service who'd been brought on to the case at the last minute to conduct an evidence review. Her work had ensured the conviction of every person responsible.

A few weeks ago, Madeleine had singled Eve out for praise in a *New York Times* interview, saying that without her diligence and hard work, she and the other survivors and the victims' families might have been denied justice.

Eve knew Madeleine had namechecked her with the best of intentions, but the spotlight it put on her had been unpleasant to deal with. A British tabloid had followed up the article with a profile, and before Eve knew it, her name and picture had gone viral as 'the hotshot lawyer who'd saved the Novus Theatre trial from collapsing'. Since then, she'd been recognised a few times in public, which had mortified her and forced her to set all her social media accounts to private to block trolls. But worse than that, she now had an unwelcome admirer in the form of a true-crime fan called Frank Tooley. He seemed desperate to befriend Eve, and his emails and calls to the CPS headquarters in Victoria had become a daily bother.

So she was definitely hoping the curly-haired diner wouldn't make the connection. But instead, he persisted. 'What's your name? I'm definitely sure we've met.'

Eve politely ignored him. Tonight was bad enough without him working out who she was and then firing questions at her about Patrick Nye, the cult leader who'd headed the Novus attack. He was all people wanted to talk about.

The diner suddenly slapped his forehead. 'I remember now – you're Leah's flatmate. Eve, isn't it? I'm Jamie. I work with Leah at St Bart's.'

Eve gave him a blank look, her recall failing her. He didn't look at all familiar.

'I was at her birthday drinks the other month?' he nudged. 'At the George in Shoreditch?'

'You're a junior doctor too?' Eve asked.

He nodded, curls bobbing again. 'For my sins.' He gestured to his companion. 'This is my sister, Tilly.'

Tilly looked up briefly from her phone, flashed Eve a smile, then lowered her gaze again.

'Boyfriend troubles,' Jamie whispered. 'I've brought her out to cheer her up.'

Judging from Tilly's dour expression, it wasn't working. Eve was relieved when the waiter appeared with her bill and placed it in front of her with a flourish.

'You're going? But you haven't eaten anything,' said Jamie.

'My date's been held up. Work emergency, apparently,' Eve bluffed. 'I've got an early meeting I need to prepare for as well, so it's no bad thing.'

That wasn't a lie. Tomorrow morning Eve was due in a team meeting about a contentious case and was dreading it.

'That's a shame.' He paused, eyeing her shrewdly. 'More fool him.'

Eve appreciated the comment, but she'd had enough now. She wanted to go home, change out of the dress she'd borrowed from Leah – she usually wore trousers or jeans, and regretted making the effort now – pour herself an obscenely large glass of wine, then pretend tonight had never happened. She settled her bill then rose to leave.

'Bye then,' said Jamie. 'Nice to see you again.'

She nodded, even though she still couldn't remember meeting him. But the pub had been packed for Leah's birthday, so maybe she just hadn't noticed him among the crowd.

'Enjoy the rest of your evening,' she said.

He side-eyed his sister, then smiled. He had a nice smile, Eve noted, then she dismissed the thought just as quickly. It would be a long time before she'd consider dating again after tonight's humiliation.

Climbing the steep stairs to the restaurant's exit, Eve felt her mood lift. Sod Harry. She'd chalk it up as a narrow escape – and delete Hinge from her phone. Online dating really wasn't worth the effort.

Out on the street, Eve shivered against the bitter wind. Her mum had texted earlier to say the Shropshire town where she and Eve's dad lived was blanketed by snow, and the forecasters were saying London might get some too. Eve could believe it – the temperature was already at freezing and would plummet even lower overnight.

She pulled her collar up and shoved her hands deep into her coat pockets. The nearest Tube station was only a short walk away, but Eve headed to a bus stop on the Strand. She'd avoided using the Underground after a colleague had been pushed down an escalator during the Novus trial. The incident had left her with a fear of falling from a height and now presented as full-blown acrophobia. Travelling by bus wasn't so bad, it just took longer.

She was scanning the board to check which one she needed when she felt a tap on the shoulder. 'Hello, Eve.'

For a split second she thought it was Harry finally showing up, but when she turned round to see who it was, she jolted with alarm.

'What are you doing here?' she stuttered.

Eve had never met Frank Tooley in the flesh, but she recognised him straight away from his picture, which she'd looked up on his true-crime website after he'd started bombarding her with messages asking her to call him.

Tall, grey-haired, with a dense beard that covered most of his cheeks and all of his throat, he was swaddled in a bulky bright blue anorak that looked more suitable for an Arctic exploration than a stroll through Covent Garden, with a navy, thick woollen hat pulled down low over his ears. His nose, however, was crimson with cold – had he been waiting outside the restaurant all this time to follow her?

'You're a hard woman to get hold of, Ms Wren,' he said. 'It's taken me three trains and two buses to get here.'

His broad Scottish accent was recognisable from his voicemails, but she knew he lived in Northampton now. His tone also unnerved her. She wasn't going to thank him for making the trip to ambush her in the street, but he was clearly expecting a response along those lines. Rattled, she took a step backwards.

'I appreciate you're keen to speak to me, Mr Tooley, but not like this . . .' She trailed off, anxious not to say the wrong thing. Prior to joining the CPS, she'd worked in private practice as a criminal defence solicitor and had once defended a client accused of stalking. It had alarmed her how much the client had deliberately misconstrued comments made by his victim as words of encouragement, and Eve wasn't surprised the jury had convicted him. Frank Tooley might turn out to be harmless, but her gut told her to proceed with caution.

'But you haven't returned any of my messages. What was I supposed to do?' he said haughtily.

Eve knew from his website that Tooley was in his late fifties; a former building control officer who had taken early retirement on medical grounds. Divorced, without children, he spent his days obsessively researching unsolved true-crime cases. His keenness to talk to her now was baffling: the Novus trial had concluded and its instigators were behind bars. There was nothing unsolved about it.

'I can't talk to you now,' she said. 'Here's my bus.'

The double-decker heading towards the stop was too far away for Eve to make out the route number clearly, but she didn't care where it was going. She was getting on it regardless.

To her shock, Tooley grabbed her arm. 'Now wait a minute, young lady. I haven't come all this way to be given the brush-off. It's important that we talk.'

Eve started to protest and pull away, but his grip was firm.

'Ms Wren, I need you to listen—'

A male voice cut between them. 'Eve, there you are. I thought I'd missed you. I've got you a taxi.'

She whipped round to see Jamie, the diner from the restaurant, by the kerb. Beside him a black cab idled, its rear door open. With a final wrench, she yanked her arm from Tooley's grasp and darted towards the vehicle.

Tooley bellowed after her, telling her to wait.

'You go,' said Jamie. 'I'll deal with him.' He instructed the driver to head to Old Street. 'She'll give you the full address on the way.'

'Thank you,' said Eve hoarsely.

As the cab drove off, Eve knew it wasn't the cold making her shiver uncontrollably. Tooley had frightened her, turning up like that. His voicemails might have been uncomfortably persistent, but she could still ignore them when they were just a click away from deletion. But now he was harassing her in public she might have to act. She looked out of the back window as the taxi sped on. Jamie was still standing by the kerb, but Tooley had stepped on to the road to watch her go, his face contorted with what Eve could only describe as white-hot fury.

# Chapter Two

## GEMMA

Reece sighed. 'You may as well get off, Gem. I can handle this crowd on my own.'

Gemma stopped wiping the inside of the pint glass. 'Are you sure?'

'I don't think we'll be troubled by any drunken congas through the bar tonight, do you?' her manager deadpanned.

Gemma grinned. The only people present besides them were two elderly men engaged in a quiet conversation over two half-pints of stout. They weren't even hotel guests – just locals who preferred drinking in The Compton's dated bar to anywhere else in town.

'I'll need you in nice and early, mind,' said Reece. 'We've got that coach party from Perth checking in, and the rooms will need going over again in the morning.'

Gemma couldn't imagine what would compel anyone to book a break in Bridlington in February, much less stay at The Compton. The hotel was a dump, its decor untouched since the eighties, its star rating only a two. The owners lived in Tenerife most of the year, leaving Reece to run the show, and Gemma didn't blame them. If she had the money, she'd live somewhere hot and sunny too. She'd leave Bridlington and never look back.

She promised Reece she'd be in at eight. Then she left before he changed his mind and decided her company was better than sitting in silence watching the pensioners sip their ale.

Bridlington was a coastal town in the East Riding district of Yorkshire, and looked out over an unforgiving North Sea. Gemma headed down to the harbour. Black slush covered the pavements from where it had snowed days before, and she slipped twice, the soles of her trainers struggling for purchase. At the harbour she pulled her thin coat tightly around her slight frame as the icy wind whipping across the shore cut through to her bones. Like her trainers, the coat was inadequate against the cold, but she couldn't afford to upgrade that either. Virtually every penny Gemma earned went on bills.

Home was a small, detached house she shared with her mum, situated further along the seafront, past the promenade. Setting off in that direction, she didn't pay attention to the group of youths at first. They were leaning over the sea wall, catcalling a passing jogger on the beach below. Then one of them spotted Gemma hurrying along, and nudged the others. Like a swarm of bees, the group peeled away from the wall as one; a mass of bodies suddenly blocking her path.

'Look everyone, it's Gemma Berk.'

The girl who said it was front and centre of the swarm, her lip curling with disdain as she looked Gemma up and down. Kira Maybank. She'd been in the same year as Gemma at secondary school and had made sure every moment was a living hell for her. By their final year, Gemma had bunked off so much to avoid Kira that she'd only sat two GCSEs – history and food tech. She'd missed too many lessons to confidently sit her other subjects. Her lack of maths and English qualifications was the reason she only made minimum wage at The Compton. Kira, on the other hand, earned a decent salary working in the office of a haulage company in Leeds, or so Gemma had heard.

'It's Kirk, not Berk,' she shot back. 'I'm off home, so leave me be.'

Kira stepped towards her. The swarm swayed from side to side as it followed suit. There must've been twenty of them in all. Some of the faces were recognisable to Gemma from school, the rest were strangers.

'No, it's Berk,' said Kira nastily. 'Gemma Berk. What's the matter, don't you know your own name now?'

'Look at the state of her,' sniggered one of the strangers, a male teen with a greasy curtain fringe and bulbous nose.

'It's 'cos she spends the day cleaning other people's shit out of hotel toilets,' sneered a girl's voice. Gemma recognised it as belonging to Maura Keegan, Kira's best friend. She was somewhere at the back of the swarm, not visible.

Gemma itched to say that at least she had a job. Last she'd heard, Maura had been sacked from Lidl for nicking a bottle of gin. But backchatting would most likely earn her a slap, and she didn't fancy the odds of one against twenty.

Kira suddenly switched tack. 'Is that your bag?'

Her anxiety rising, Gemma hugged the shoulder tote closer to her.

'What's in it?'

'Nothing.'

'Nothing?' crowed Kira, while the swarm laughed. 'What's the point of carrying it, then? Come on, give us a look.'

Gemma swallowed hard. She could no longer feel the cold. Her cheeks were flaming hot, and her insides were roiling with fear. The only way to get past the group was to either run into the road or jump down on to the beach.

Kira took another ominous step forward. 'I said, give us a look.' Her eyes bored into Gemma's. 'Did your mum bring it home from the scrapheap with that coat?'

Maura and the others from school burst into peals of laughter. The strangers, unaware of the subtext, looked confused. Gemma burned with shame.

Without warning, Kira sprang forward and made a grab for the bag. Gemma ducked sideways but accidentally caught Kira's foot with her own, sending Kira sprawling to the ground. The swarm yelled in outrage. Gemma looked left and right, hesitating for a second. Then she heaved herself over the seafront wall. She landed heavily on the sand below but managed to stay upright. Ignoring Kira's screams that next time she'd get her, Gemma started to run.

The house was in darkness when Gemma arrived back a few minutes later. Terrified that Kira and her mates might catch up with her, she'd sprinted the entire way. She let herself in, panting slightly, and flicked on the light in the hallway. The first thing she saw was the bulging black bin bag blocking the foot of the stairs, and her heart sank.

'Mum? Are you in?' she called out.

She heard a creak upstairs, then footsteps. Her mum, Mel, appeared on the landing, wrapped in a towelling robe. 'Keep it down, love. I'm trying to sleep.'

'It's seven thirty, Mum. If you go to sleep now, you'll be up in the night again.' She paused. 'What's in the bag?'

'Don't you go touching it,' cried her mum from the top of the stairs, clenching her fists rhythmically. 'It needs to stay where it is.'

Fighting back tears, Gemma edged forward, careful not to nudge the rows of precariously stacked crates lining the hallway.

One false move would send a tsunami of crap tumbling down on her head. She reached the door to the front room and stuck her head round it. Every inch of space inside was occupied. Piles of second-hand clothes, at least eight broken dining room chairs that didn't match, multiple kitchen appliances, and even more crates filled with everything from broken Barbies to jigsaws that didn't have all their pieces. Coiled on the only area of carpet still visible were reams of electrical leads that didn't match any of the appliances present.

Across the room, the sofa was blanketed by newspapers the same shade of yellow as the net curtains hanging in the bay window, headlines proclaiming news that was years old now. Gemma had been ten when she last remembered sitting on it. Her dad, Dennis, had vainly attempted to clear up so she could invite her friends for a birthday sleepover, but their reaction to the state of Gemma's home had ensured it was the first and only time she ever did. Dennis had moved out later that same summer.

She eased back into the hallway. Despite the mess, she could tell nothing new had been added to the front room. It was just the bin bag in the hallway – unless more surprises awaited her in the kitchen.

'We should keep the stairs clear, Mum. I don't want you tripping.'

Her mum looked fretful as Gemma moved the bag to one side. She was thirty-nine but looked at least a decade older, worn down by her chronic compulsion to hoard. It had robbed her of her looks, her marriage, her self-worth, her ability to hold down employment and her ability to parent. Inheriting the house outright from her late parents was Mel's only saving grace, meaning Gemma didn't need to find money for rent on top of their other bills. Solid red brick, three bedrooms, and a decent-sized back garden, it was prime property overlooking the sea. Yet now it was the shabbiest on the road, years of neglect earning it sore-thumb status.

'See? It's fine here,' said Gemma. But she knew when she came down in the morning that the bag would be back in its original position. It was the dance they did every time her mum went rummaging, either at the local tip – the scrapheap Kira had referred to – or in the town's charity shops. Her mum would put her latest bin bag of 'treasure' down in an inconvenient spot in the hallway, then Gemma would try to move it. Eventually – sometimes it could take weeks – her mum would relent, and the contents of the bag would be decanted around the house to join the rest of the rubbish. To make room for it, Gemma would then secrete a small bag of other junk out of the house to throw away. It was an endless and exhausting battle, and no way for either of them to live.

She wearily climbed the stairs. 'Go back to bed, Mum. It's fine. I can see you're tired.'

Her mum pecked Gemma on the cheek. Her lips were dry and cracked and her breath smelled of stale coffee. 'I'll see you in the morning, love.'

It would be earlier than that, though. It was usually around four in the morning that Gemma was woken by her mum prowling outside her bedroom, a piece of junk in her hand. Like with the bin bags, they followed the same script night after night: Gemma would open the door, and her mum would try to come inside to deposit the item, saying she couldn't sleep until she knew it was safely stored in Gemma's room. Last night it had been a broken plastic kettle.

But Gemma's bedroom was the one place in the house that was out of bounds to her mum's hoarding, and Gemma always held firm, even though she knew it caused her mum mental anguish that she couldn't act on her compulsion to fill the space. Gemma had to have somewhere private and tidy for herself. She'd never cope otherwise.

She waited until her mum was back in bed before she entered the passcode into the combination lock fitted on her bedroom door. Extreme behaviour called for extreme measures. Slipping inside and shutting the door behind her, she exhaled softly. Her room was the smallest of the three and only able to accommodate a single bed, narrow wardrobe and small chest of drawers. She used to have the middle bedroom, but her mum had made her give it up when Gemma was twelve because she wanted it for storage. Small though her current bedroom was, at least it was clean and – more importantly – pristinely neat.

Sitting down on the bed, she pulled her phone from her bag and fixed it to the tripod on the chest of drawers. Next to the tripod was a ring light. It had taken her months to save up to buy both.

She slid open the top drawer and pulled out a make-up bag and mirror. Her cosmetic collection was sparse – again, she'd saved hard for every item, which was why she never wasted it on work – but it was enough to transform her tired face. Finished, she smiled back at her reflection, then untied the messy bun she'd secured her peach-blonde hair in for work. She gave it a brush so it settled in waves to her shoulders. She smiled at her reflection again. She was ready.

Making TikTok videos was Gemma's escape. Her content was mainly sarky monologues about celebrities in the headlines. In the three months since setting up her account she'd attracted a thousand followers, which she found astonishing. People actually liked watching her. Then again, her online alter ego @Gemz1026 was everything she wasn't: relaxed, sassy, confident. @Gemz1026 would never have run away from Kira and the swarm. She'd have stood up to them.

Batting the thought aside, Gemma readied her phone to record. Excitement bubbled up inside her. Switching on the camera meant switching off from her shitty, miserable existence. It was only for a few minutes at a time, but it was all she had.

# Chapter Three

## EVE

The meeting was at deadlock.

Eve glared at Ashley across the table. Ashley glowered back. The rest of the review team shrank back in their seats. They couldn't break the impasse, and had given up trying. Let these two argue it out.

'Ashley, think about it. If you're so sure this is the right decision, it makes more sense for you to tell Hazel yourself,' said Eve. 'You'll explain it far better.'

'No, I want you to do it,' Ashley snapped back, her face flushing. 'I've been here longer, so I get to pick. We must all do tasks we don't want to do,' she added primly.

Eve simmered with frustration. 'You're missing the point. I am not trying to get out of anything. I just don't think it's a good idea for me to sit that poor woman down and explain a decision I am opposed to. If she and her lawyers get a whiff that not everyone here is behind it, they could push for a judicial review. That would be a disaster for us.'

'Eve's right,' said Janani, leaning forward and clasping her hands. 'The task of telling Hazel that we're not charging Walker shouldn't be done by the one person on the team who thinks it's wrong.'

Eve was grateful to Janani for speaking up. Janani was senior to everyone in the meeting and should've been leading it herself, but their team manager, Beverly, had put Eve and Ashley in joint charge instead. She thought that working closely together might dispel the tension between them. It was a nice idea but, as the current stalemate proved, hopelessly misguided. The more time they spent in proximity, the more they wound each other up.

The animosity wasn't Eve's doing. Well, it hadn't been at first. During her first few weeks working at Petty France – the Brutalist building in Victoria where the CPS was based – she and Ashley had rubbed along okay. Then, one night after work, over more glasses of wine than was wise, Eve had confided in her colleague how she'd been sacked from a private City law firm after being wrongly blamed for a senior partner's mistake. Not only did Ashley tell everyone, but she used it as a stick to undermine Eve, remonstrating with her to check her work for mistakes every opportunity she got. There had been no let-up even after Eve was lauded for her contribution to the Novus trial. If anything, that had made Ashley even more combative. It was a running joke in the office that if Eve said the sky was blue, Ashley would disagree.

Ashley cast Janani an annoyed look, then addressed Eve again. 'You need to get on board with the decision.'

'I am on board. I just reserve the right to believe it's the wrong one.'

Ashley huffed and rolled her eyes. Eve could tell from the others' expressions that they also wished she'd just shut up and accept their majority decision. But the Walker case had got under her skin in a way she couldn't shake.

Zayn Walker was a Met detective constable who had infiltrated an eco-activist group as part of an undercover operation. Pretending to be an activist himself, he'd embarked on a relationship with one of the group's members, Hazel Mackett. This was despite him knowing relationships were discouraged during covert assignments because of a public inquiry probing officers' relationships while UC between 1968 and 2010. He'd then lied to his Met handler about it. By the time Walker's real identity had come to light four years later, Hazel had given birth to their son.

Hazel was distraught at having been duped. Her political and social beliefs meant she'd never have knowingly got involved with a police officer – much less one sent to spy on her and her friends. She and her army of supporters had since mounted a legal challenge to get Walker charged for rape, fraud, and the emotional and physical exploitation of her and their son.

Eve and the others had spent the past two months combing through the evidence to see what charges the CPS could bring against Walker. For Eve, it was a no-brainer. Walker had violated Hazel's trust and her body. Hazel couldn't have consented to sex with someone who didn't really exist, and Eve had argued that Walker's undercover role should not mitigate his actions. At a minimum he should've been charged with misconduct in public office.

However, after 'careful examination of the facts', the rest of the team had agreed there was no public interest in prosecuting Walker because there wasn't a realistic prospect of securing a conviction. Despite the history of undercover Met officers being accused of similar behaviour, which had sparked the public inquiry, clandestine relationships still weren't considered unlawful. As such, the CPS couldn't set a legal precedent with Zayn Walker. Eve was disappointed to have been outvoted, which is why she didn't want to be the one to tell Hazel. The fundamental role of the CPS was to support victims, and this decision felt the opposite of that.

'Look, I get why we're not prosecuting,' she said. 'But this is going to devastate Hazel. We've all read her statement: she feels violated that Walker had sex with her under false pretences. Every time she looks at their son, who's his spitting image, she's reminded of what he did. How awful must that be for her as a mother?'

For a moment her mind strayed to Harry. She'd only slept with him once before last night's humiliation, and that was bad enough. The level of duplicity Walker had employed to trick Hazel into a sexual relationship was, in her view, diabolical.

'We've been over this, Eve,' said Janani patiently. 'We cannot set a legal precedent. Hazel has the option of bringing her own private action against the Met, like others have.'

Eve crossed her arms defiantly. 'Well, I'm not telling her. Someone else can.'

'She's going to be here in five minutes,' said Owen nervously. Sitting on Ashley's side of the table, he was a newcomer to the division, with a sharp mind for data analysis and an aversion to confrontation. 'Maybe we should ask Beverly to decide.'

Eve looked out of the window and across the way to the glass-walled office that was their boss's. She wasn't at her desk though, and Eve was grateful: Beverly would not welcome being called upon to settle a squabble. Then, as if on cue, Hazel and her legal team walked into the department, led by an admin who must've been sent to greet them.

Hazel Mackett had the pinched expression of a woman on guard. Dressed in an oversized pea coat and sturdy boots, her eyes darted nervously from side to side as she and her counsel came further into the room, like she was braced for someone to leap out at her. Seeing how anxious Hazel was changed Eve's mind on the spot. Better she relayed the news with compassion than let Ashley deliver it with all the emotional heft of someone reading aloud from a shopping list.

'Okay, fine. I'll tell her,' said Eve. 'Everyone clear out so I can use this room.'

Relieved, the others rose quickly to their feet. Ashley flashed her a smug smile on her way out, which she ignored. She might've won this time but Eve would not give her the satisfaction of acknowledging it.

# Chapter Four

## EVE

Hazel took the news as badly as Eve had expected. She cried, cursed and railed against the Establishment for conspiring to protect one of its own.

Eve kept her counsel throughout the meeting, knowing that if she tried to defend the CPS's decision not to prosecute DC Walker, her comments would end up in a national newspaper; Hazel had threatened as much.

She still felt wretched for the woman though, who asked her over and over, 'What am I supposed to do now?' Eve could not provide an answer, but she hoped the poor woman's lawyers would. If she were them, she'd be pushing hard for that judicial review.

Eve stayed in the meeting room after Hazel and her legal team had departed, to gather her thoughts. The outcome grated on her, because what she loved most about working at the CPS was the sense of being on the right side of justice and being an advocate for victims. Of course, not every person brought to trial was guilty, but in cases like Walker's, Eve found it hard to justify the CPS declining to bring charges. Even if they couldn't make the rape accusation stick, proving misconduct in public office should've been straightforward.

With a sigh, she gathered up her papers and laptop and left the meeting room. Beverly was back at her desk, so Eve headed over to share Hazel's reaction. She also wanted advice on how to deal with Frank Tooley – his ambush on the Strand last night had left her rattled and she'd slept fitfully, waking up a few times convinced someone was trying to get into the flat.

As she approached Beverly's office, Eve saw her boss lift a tissue to wipe her eyes, which were visibly bloodshot. She slowed to a halt. The times Beverly had shared her feelings on personal matters that didn't relate to work could be counted on one hand, so to see her openly crying was a shock.

Eve didn't want to intrude on a private moment but neither did she want to ignore her boss's obvious distress; if something bad had happened, she might need some support. She hoped it wasn't something to do with Beverly's husband. Beverly and Ronnie had been married a long time, more than thirty years, and it was just the two of them. Eve didn't know why they'd never had children and had never felt it was her place to ask.

She rapped softly on the glass door. Beverly looked up with tear-filled eyes, then nodded.

Eve let herself in, and shut the door behind her. 'I was just coming to tell you about the Hazel Mackett meeting, but, um . . . are you okay?'

Beverly bit down on her bottom lip and shook her head. 'I've just had some terrible news.'

'Can I do anything to help?' Eve didn't want to come right out and ask what had happened in case it came across as prying.

'No, thank you.' Beverly plucked a fresh tissue from the box on her desk. 'It's just – I can't even . . .' She gulped down a breath. 'My goddaughter drowned last night.'

Eve's fear of overstepping evaporated. 'God, I'm so sorry. How did it happen?'

Beverly motioned for Eve to sit down. As she did, Eve noticed Ashley hovering outside the office with another colleague, Sarah. They must've seen Beverly crying and were angling to find out why.

Eve pretended not to notice them. Put all her focus on Beverly.

'The police say she committed suicide jumping off Southwark Bridge in the early hours,' said Beverly, her voice cracking. 'She drowned before the river rescue crews could pull her out.'

'I'm so sorry,' Eve repeated, desperately meaning it.

'She wasn't suicidal though, Eve. I know she wasn't. She came to ours for dinner last week and was as right as rain. She didn't leave a note either. It makes no sense she'd take her own life.'

Eve didn't want to state the grim truth: those closest to the deceased were often the last to know how desperate they had been feeling.

'Were there any witnesses?' she asked Beverly gently. If anyone had spotted her goddaughter on the bridge and saw her jump, it might provide clarity.

The question triggered fresh tears. 'No. The police are claiming she waited until she was on her own.' Beverly raked her grey hair back from her face, her devastation raw.

'Are City dealing with it?' Eve asked.

Even though the Met had responsibility for the wider capital, the City of London Police had sole jurisdiction for an area known as the Square Mile, which stretched roughly from Barbican to Tower Gate and Inner Temple Gardens to Liverpool Street. The 1,355-strong force also policed the five bridges within the Square Mile, including Southwark.

'Yes, they are. I've spoken to a contact there and they're already discussing the case being passed straight to the coroner.' Beverly stifled another sob. 'She was only thirty-three, Eve. I really don't believe she intended to take her own life. There has to be another explanation.'

Eve considered for a second how freezing it must've been in the water in the early hours. February had been particularly bitter so far. Beverly's goddaughter wouldn't have stood a chance against the temperature or the strong current.

'I've only just found out,' Beverly continued. 'Becca's mum just called me. We've been best friends since middle school. Grew up together in a village near York.'

'That's her name? Becca?'

'It's Rebecca Farrow, but everyone calls her Becca. I doubt it'll be long before her name's public,' said Beverly tightly. 'We know how these things work.'

Eve knew that was a nod to her own public unmasking. Beverly had shared her dismay at the way Eve's name and image had been plastered all over the internet after Madeleine's interview. Eve hadn't appreciated how much she valued her privacy until it was taken from her, and she appreciated Beverly's acknowledgement of it.

'Where did she live?'

'In Balham. She worked in Farringdon though, for a tech start-up. She was head of people culture, which is a fancy name for HR.' Beverly snivelled into her crushed tissue. 'From what she told us last week she'd been doing really well.'

Eve felt wretched for her boss. 'Maybe you should go home, be with your husband?'

'I'm about to. Becca's parents are on their way down from Yorkshire to identify her body and they're going to stay at ours for a few days. I'm going to ask Sol for some time off to be with them.' Solomon 'Sol' Archer was the Director of Public Prosecutions, head of the CPS. 'Jackie's in pieces,' Beverly added tearfully. 'I don't know how she'll get through this.'

Eve presumed Jackie was Becca's mum. 'Is there anything I can do here while you're off?'

'There is one thing. My contact has given me the details of the investigating officer. This is her number.' Beverly handed a scrap of paper to Eve. Printed on it was a mobile number, under the name DC Alix Quinn.

Eve caught movement in her peripheral vision and turned to see Ashley and Sarah still outside, ostensibly in conversation but clearly craning to read what was on the note. Hiding it from view, Eve cleared her throat to alert Beverly. Her boss, on seeing their audience, wiped her eyes again and gathered herself.

'The police are going to write Becca off as just another bridge jumper,' she said darkly. 'But there was no history of depression, and she wasn't on any medication. Other than wishing she could meet someone to settle down with, her life was sorted. I want you to call this DC Quinn to find out what she knows.'

'Isn't it better that she talks to Becca's parents directly?'

'You and I both know that families are often kept in the dark over lines of inquiry, and me being Becca's godmother puts me in that same bracket as far as the police are concerned. But if you call her with your CPS hat on, you might get more out of her.' She paused. 'Leave it until tomorrow though, after the formal ID's been done.'

Eve nodded. She'd happily chase DC Quinn if it meant one less thing for Beverly to worry about.

'I know in my gut that Becca wasn't suicidal, Eve, and I don't want the police to just dismiss her death with a bit of box-ticking and that's that. I need you to stay on their case to make sure they don't.'

# Chapter Five

## EVE

It wasn't until Beverly had left the office to meet Becca's parents that Eve remembered she still had the problem of Frank Tooley to contend with.

He'd crossed a line in surprising her in public and she needed to put a stop to his unwelcome attention. She just wasn't sure how. Feeling it would be inappropriate to bother Beverly about it until she was back in the office, Eve decided to seek advice from the one other person at the CPS she trusted to give her a straight answer.

John Horner was at his desk, holding a document aloft and reading it to himself – lips moving wordlessly as he did so. With his spare hand he absent-mindedly pushed his trademark wire-rimmed glasses back up his nose before they slid again; something they were in the habit of doing frequently. Eve had suggested contact lenses might be preferable to readjusting his glasses every thirty seconds, but he couldn't be swayed. Horner didn't care for such fripperies and was perfectly happy with the glasses he had, thank you very much.

'Hey, have you got a minute?'

He looked up from the document, but instead of his usual smile, Eve was greeted by a frown.

'Not really. Why?'

The unfriendliness threw her. 'Um, I have an issue with something, and I was hoping I could get some advice,' she replied cautiously.

He pushed his glasses up again. 'If you've come to complain about Ashley—'

'No, I'm not. It's nothing to do with her.'

'Well, I'm busy right now, so it'll have to wait,' he said, and he returned to his reading.

For the second time that morning, Eve found herself asking a senior colleague if they were okay.

Horner's head shot up again. 'Why wouldn't I be?'

'You're just a bit, well, snappy. It's not like you.'

'I have a headache,' he said tetchily.

Eve caught the look on his face. He might sound irritated, but he appeared worried.

Something shifted in the back of her mind, a recollection. 'Didn't you go home with a headache last week?'

For a moment she thought he was going to snap at her again, but instead he nodded. 'I did. I've been having them off and on since Novus. But they're getting more frequent.'

It took Eve a few moments to join the dots. If he'd been having headaches since the Novus trial, that meant only one thing: 'Since you were pushed down the escalator? Why didn't you tell me?'

'You sound like Lizzy,' he grumbled, referring to his wife. 'She's been on my case for not telling her as well.'

'Well, what does your GP think?' She caught his sheepish look. 'Don't tell me you haven't been to see them about it? John, you suffered a head injury and now you're having headaches. You need to get it checked out.'

'I keep going to make an appointment, but you have to ring at eight on the dot, and I'm usually on the Tube then.'

'Maybe you should go to A&E and ask for a scan?' said Eve worriedly.

'It's not an emergency, it's just a headache.' He fingertipped his glasses into place again. 'I'm sorry I snapped. What do you need help with?'

Eve recognised deflection when she saw it, but she also knew Horner well enough to know that badgering him to make the appointment wouldn't bear fruit.

'A member of the public who lives in Northampton has been leaving multiple voicemails for me since that Madeleine Farmer interview went viral. Last night he turned up here, in London, when I was out for dinner. I was on the Strand waiting for my bus home when he just appeared.'

Horner frowned. 'How did he know where you'd be?'

'I guess he followed me. It's a bit stalkerish, isn't it?'

'There's no "ish" about it, Eve. Have you kept all the communications he's sent?'

'He's only called so far. The voicemails were on my work line and I deleted them to free up space. He doesn't have my mobile number, at least.'

'Can you tell me the gist of his messages?' Horner was now taking notes, his headache seemingly forgotten.

'Just that he saw my name in relation to Novus and he wants to speak to me. The messages aren't aggressive in tone,' she admitted, 'just persistent. I've done a bit of digging and he's a true-crime fan with a particular interest in unsolved cases. I don't know why he wants to talk to me about Novus though.'

She and Horner shared a knowing look. He'd been the CPS's lead advocate on the case.

'The messages I could handle, him grabbing me in the street, no,' she added.

'He grabbed you?'

'Yes. He got hold of my arm when I tried to walk away. I know he just wanted me to listen, but he was being aggressive and I felt intimidated.'

Horner frowned. 'I want you to write a statement of everything that happened so it's on the record. We've had cases before where advocates have been stalked, and there are measures that we can put in place, like giving you a personal alarm and making sure your home is secure, installing cameras and the like. It might also be worth varying your route to and from work for the time being. Speak to Beverly when she's back.'

Eve had come to Horner for reassurance, but their discussion had become the unsettling opposite of that.

'I was thinking someone could just have a quiet word, to tell him to back off.'

'A verbal intervention from anyone here could be viewed as making threats against him, and that's the last thing you want. The police would recommend logging everything for now, so that's what you should do. If it escalates, we'll take it further.'

Eve knew he was right. She needed to establish a trail of evidence, so logging every communication was sensible. Just in case.

'Thank you. I was going to talk to Beverly but she's, um, left for the day.' Eve didn't think she should tell Horner why Beverly had gone home early, but in the next beat he made it clear that he knew about Becca.

'Tragic business. Beverly's friends must be devastated.'

'She's asked me to keep tabs on the investigation. Ever had any dealings with a City of London DC named Alix Quinn?'

'Nope. Why?'

'She's leading Becca's case. I'm calling her tomorrow.'

'It's not a criminal matter.'

'I know. I'm doing it as a favour to Beverly.'

Horner nodded.

With Beverly now off on compassionate leave, Eve left the office on time for once. It wasn't that she demanded her team always work late, but Beverly did tend to check in as the day was winding down, so they would be drawn into discussions about cases just when it was time to leave. But with no debrief required of her today, Eve left on the stroke of six. From Petty France she walked to St James's Park to catch the first of two buses that would take her home to Old Street.

She'd have the flat to herself tonight because Leah was on call at St Bart's. She had her evening all planned out: she'd reheat the Bolognese sauce she'd batch-cooked at the weekend, slap it on a jacket potato topped with cheese and, unless Leah had drunk them all, wash it down with a cold beer. Then she'd catch up on the US version of *The Traitors*.

A concierge manned the foyer of the modern block Eve's flat was in, which sounded fancier than it was. Darrel was more like a security guard. He was a giant of a man who on sight you wouldn't want to cross, but when you got to know him – as Eve had – he was gentler than a baby's bath water.

'Evening, Eve. Got something for you,' he called out as she entered the building. 'It was dropped off at lunchtime.'

Part of Darrel's job was to sign for residents' parcels. This was a padded envelope though, bigger than A4. Intrigued, Eve took it from him. Her name and address had been written on the front in block capital letters with a thick black pen, but there was no stamp or postage label attached. In the top-right corner where they would usually be, someone had written 'By Hand'.

Eve flipped the envelope over and quailed. In matching handwriting across the back was 'From: Frank Tooley', followed by his address. Another 'By Hand' was written in the bottom left-hand corner.

She dropped the envelope on to Darrel's counter like she'd been stung. He cocked an eyebrow. 'Something the matter?'

'Did you see who delivered this?'

'Yeah. Older geezer. Fifties. Wearing a massive coat, like he was expecting snow or something.'

Panic seized Eve's throat. Frank Tooley. He knew where she lived.

Darrel looked concerned. 'I'm taking it from your face that this geezer isn't a welcome visitor.'

'No, he's not,' said Eve unsteadily. The shock made her feel feverish. She dropped her bag to the floor then shed her coat. 'He's been calling me at work, leaving messages, and now he's come here.' Hot tears pricked her eyes. Her home was her safe space. How dare he invade it.

'Noted,' said Darrel. 'I'll make sure he doesn't set a foot in this building again.'

'But what about when you're not here? You don't work twenty-four-seven.'

'True, even I need my sleep,' he smiled. 'But we've got CCTV everywhere. You'll be safe.' He eyed the envelope on the counter between them. 'Don't you want to check what's in it?'

'Can you open it?' asked Eve, her voice tremulous. 'Or should we call the police and get them to do it?'

Darrel gave her a searching look. 'Has he made any threats to harm your person?'

'No.' A voice in her head silently added *not yet.*

'In that case, I'll give it a butcher's.'

Darrel carefully peeled back the envelope flap. He lifted its contents out: a blue foolscap folder about an inch thick, with a typed letter paper-clipped to the front of it. He scanned the letter.

'The letter says it's an unsolved case file. And he'd like you to look at it.'

Eve was relieved that was all it was, but she couldn't get past the fact that Tooley had delivered it by hand. 'How did he know where I live?'

'You ever met him?'

Eve told Darrel of the previous evening's encounter, right up to and including how Tooley had stood in the road to watch her leave. 'Do you think he got in a cab to follow me?'

'Like they do in the films? Nah, my guess is he heard that Jamie bloke tell the cab driver to take you to Old Street, and he looked you up afterwards on the electoral roll. It's easily done.'

Eve trembled. Darrel's theory sounded plausible. Jamie had done a nice thing in coming to her rescue with the taxi, but in doing so he'd inadvertently led Tooley to her door.

'You want me to bin this?' Darrel was still holding the folder.

'No, I should take it. If I need evidence . . .' She trailed off tearfully.

Darrel bent his huge frame until he was eye level with her. 'Eve, you are safe in this building.'

'What if he follows someone inside after they've activated the door?'

'I'll get a message sent to all the residents with his description, warning them to be on their guard. He might have snuck in once, but I'm telling you, he won't get so lucky again.'

# Chapter Six

## VALERIE

The DC hotel wasn't Valerie's favourite. Her preference was a boutique guest house in Berkley, close to the Kreeger Museum and away from the tourist traps. But this one was right in the heart of Washington's sightseeing district, and what it had going for it was its view. Walk out of the entrance and face left and there, directly across the road, on the other side of Lafayette Square, was the world's most famous political residence, 1600 Pennsylvania Avenue – the White House.

To Americans, a symbol of power, ambition, freedom.

To Valerie, potentially her next workplace.

She unzipped the small carry-on suitcase and laid out its contents on the double bed. One navy skirt suit to carry her through tomorrow's back-to-back meetings. One cream silk blouse to wear beneath it. One calf-length fit-and-flare dress, in sage green, for tomorrow's dinner. One pair of subtly platformed cream heels that went with both and wouldn't leave her feet crying for mercy at the end of what would be a very long day.

She hung both outfits in the wardrobe and stowed the shoes beneath them. Then she reappraised the outfit she'd changed into after checking in. Smart indigo jeans, white shirt tucked in, multicoloured silk scarf knotted at her throat to hide the scar, navy blazer, laced white trainers. Her mainstay off-duty look, perfect for catch-up drinks with an old friend. She peered at her reflection, smoothed down flyaway strands of fresh highlights, and inspected her make-up for flaws. Long-haul flights dried out her skin, and in her haste to pack she'd stupidly left her favourite moisturiser at home in London. The summons from the White House had given her less than two hours to prepare.

When the President called, you hurried.

The powder she'd set her foundation with had settled in the deep lines around her eyes and between her nose and mouth. She rubbed at the areas with her fingertip. Why was it that the older you got and the more you needed to fill in the cracks, the less effective make-up was? All it did was accentuate the ageing process. Valerie rubbed harder. The change in her face now she was fifty-eight depressed her. Everything had gone south. Peering closer still, she lifted the skin beneath her chin with the back of her hand. Was it time to go under the knife? The thought of having her skin sliced into appalled her, but presentation was key when you were a woman in politics and held to a higher standard than men doing lesser jobs.

Valerie left her room and headed down to the hotel's lobby bar. She scanned the alcoves but couldn't see Glenn seated in any of them. She did recognise a few other patrons though; the bar was renowned for attracting power brokers from the Hill. It was the kind of discreet place where people knew to look the other way as deals were being cut.

Approaching the maître d's station, she knew her presence would be noted. Those in DC's political circles were aware the post of Deputy Secretary of Commerce was vacant within the White House administration and that Valerie, the Minister Counselor for Business Affairs at the US Embassy in London, would be a good candidate to fill it. Her arrival in town would be common knowledge by the end of the evening.

The maître d' smiled. 'Good evening, ma'am. Do you have a reservation?'

'Yes. It should be in the name of Valerie Aspen. If not, check under Glenn Threfell.'

Glenn was an old college friend and a senior advisor to the Secretary of State, the number three position of power behind the President and Vice President. It was Glenn who'd suggested she apply to work in Commerce, one of fifteen departments responsible for the administration of federal government.

The maître d' scanned the screen on his station and smiled. 'Ah, yes. Mr Threfell hasn't arrived yet, but your table is ready, Ms Aspen. Please, follow me.'

The table was in a prime position, tucked into one corner but with a one-eighty view of the rest of the bar.

The maître d' asked if she'd like to order or wait for her guest to arrive. 'I can send someone over with the drinks menu,' he said.

'No need. We'll take two whisky sours, straight up.'

In London, Valerie usually stuck to drinking wine. It was the culture there, particularly among women – 'a large glass of, please' when 'wine o'clock' came round at the end of each working day – but back home in the States, she always ordered hard liquor. And she knew Glenn would want the same. It was a habit they'd developed while studying law at the University of Chicago: drink hard or go home.

He arrived as their drinks were being set down on the table.

'Great timing,' he extolled.

Valerie got to her feet and hugged him. He smelled of sandalwood, his signature scent, and she drank it in, revelling in the familiarity. But that was all it was. The sexual attraction that had drawn them together at Chicago had long dissipated, and in its place was an enduring friendship. Glenn knew almost everything about Valerie, and vice versa. Their closeness had been a bone of contention at times for their respective spouses, but Mark, Valerie's husband, had trusted her when she'd said there were no feelings in play any longer and hadn't been for years. Glenn's wife, Claire, had been less reassured and was often aloof towards Valerie, but she tolerated the friendship because it mattered to her husband.

They disentangled themselves and sat down. Both had changed considerably since college – she had been a natural brunette and 20 lbs heavier back then, while Glenn had had hair and an athlete's build – but when they caught up it was like time rewound. She almost forgot the crushing weight of responsibility that came with her job, alongside keeping her marriage functioning and supporting Bradley, her twenty-four-year-old son, while he decided what he wanted to do with his life. In Glenn's company, Valerie was an idealistic young student again, with a plan to conquer the world of politics in the back pocket of her ripped jeans and a defiant disregard for the obstacles she would face getting there.

Two drinks later, her sides hurting from laughing so much, she tried to inject some solemnity into the evening. 'I need some water. I can't get drunk tonight, tempting though it is,' she said. 'I also need to crash soon. It might be only six here but my body's reminding me it's eleven p.m. in London.'

'Much as I would love to get blasted too, I agree,' said Glenn. He motioned to the waiter. 'Can't have you breathing whisky fumes for your meet-and-greet with the President.'

The meeting was scheduled to last ten minutes, beginning on the dot at 11.30 a.m. It would not overrun. Nor would it take place in the Oval Office – it had been scheduled in another room in the West Wing.

Those ten minutes could make or break Valerie's future. She'd sailed through the early stages of vetting, but if the President didn't warm to her there and then, he wouldn't nominate her for approval by the Senate.

'Is Mark coming round to the idea of moving back?' asked Glenn, after requesting a bottle of sparkling water and two glasses.

'Kind of. He appreciates that it's an amazing opportunity for me, but his business is doing well out of London, so moving to Washington will take some juggling,' she said. 'I keep reminding him of the contacts he'll be able to make back on the Hill, and I'm hoping he comes round. Well, if I get the position.'

'What about Bradley? Is he on board?'

'He is,' she said cautiously, her fingers automatically reaching for the scarf that covered her scar. Glenn's gaze followed. He knew exactly how she'd come to get it.

It had been the ugliest confrontation she and Bradley had ever had, taking place a couple of months after they'd relocated to London from her last posting, in Prague. Mark had been away for work and Valerie came home late one evening to find Bradley chopping out lines of coke in the kitchen with some friends from his new college. She'd gone ballistic, ordering the friends to clear out. When they'd laughed in her face, too wasted to give a damn, she'd seen red and tried to manhandle them to the front door. In the commotion, Bradley had shoved Valerie, sending her flying into the console table in the hall. She'd caught her throat on a vase of flowers and the glass had smashed, leaving a gouge. The doctor who'd stitched her up said she was lucky it hadn't been any deeper or she might've bled out.

'Does Bradley appreciate what's at stake if you do get the job?' asked Glenn sternly. 'That he needs to behave himself and knock the drugs and partying on the head?'

'He does. He's talking about applying to do a master's at Georgetown if we do come back.' She grabbed his hand. 'Can we talk about something else? Please?'

They'd spent too many hours over the years discussing her son's foibles, which had also included racking up huge debts on their credit cards without their realising.

Glenn's frown slackened into a smile. 'Sure.'

They spent the next half-hour running through the questions Valerie was likely to face the next day. Then Glenn excused himself to use the restroom.

Valerie checked her phone in case Mark had messaged. They'd spoken briefly when she'd landed but nothing since. There was nothing from him, but there were a few notifications from the news apps loaded on her phone. She idly opened the first one, then froze.

*No, no, no.*

She clicked through to the article, her heart thwacking against her ribcage. She could barely focus on the details, but what she did manage to take in made her sick to the stomach.

'Val? Are you okay?' Glenn had returned to their booth without her noticing. She couldn't meet his eye.

'I'm sorry. I've got to go back to London.'

'What?'

'There must be a red eye I can get on,' she said frantically. 'It won't take me long to pack.'

Bewildered, Glenn slid into his seat. 'Valerie, what are you talking about? You can't fly back to London tonight. You're meeting the President tomorrow.'

She shook her head vehemently. 'I can't do it. I'm withdrawing from the process.'

'Is this because you're nervous? Look, I get that it's a big deal, but you know you've got this.'

Valerie faltered. Could she burden him with this? Would that be fair?

'What the hell is going on? Tell me.'

'It's Bradley. I think he's in trouble again. I need to go back and sort it out.'

'What kind of trouble?'

She swallowed hard. 'The Prague kind.'

'Are you serious?' Glenn had paled with shock.

'I hope I'm wrong.' She grabbed his hand. 'I'm sorry. I'm so grateful that you backed me for this.'

She let go of him. Her hands shaking, she shoved her phone into her bag and stood up. 'Get them to put the drinks on my room.'

'Val, you walk out now and you're kissing goodbye to any chance of being considered for another job in the administration. You'll stay stuck where you are. I don't get it. Why screw your career like this?'

She fought back tears. 'I don't have a choice.'

'There's always a choice, Valerie,' Glenn said sternly.

Not for her there wasn't. The last time she'd been faced with a choice like this she had made the wrong call and lived to regret it. She couldn't make the same mistake again.

# Chapter Seven

## GEMMA

Gemma's alarm went off at seven. She had a small window in which to shower, dress, eat breakfast, then walk to The Compton for her 8.a.m. shift. She usually made it with ten minutes to spare. Today, however, she couldn't drag herself from her bed.

Frustration pinned her to the bottom sheet, which was threadbare and bobbly from years of washing. The video she'd uploaded last night had received only thirty likes overnight, and none in the twenty minutes she'd been scrolling on TikTok since waking. Why weren't people liking it?

Lying on her side, she watched it again with a critical eye. The sound was okay – she'd seen far worse – and her monologue, about an incident at the recent Grammys when the best pop album winner had slipped on stage while accepting his award, was amusing, with a strong punchline. She scrolled to the comments to see what people were saying and, to her embarrassment, they were overwhelmingly negative.

*Way too try-hard.*

*My grandma's funnier.*

*Yawn. This has been done to death.*

The last commentator was right, she had to admit. The fall had been picked over a million times online and even the singer had posted a Reel taking the mick out of himself. There was nothing original about her content.

Maybe she should just give up, Gemma thought huffily. Find some other way to make some money to escape Bridlington, because the influencer route wasn't going to make her rich.

She dragged her pillow out from under her and stuffed it against the wooden slatted headrest so she could sit up. What could she do instead though? She'd need to re-sit maths and English to get a better job, but she couldn't afford to stop working and go back to school because how would they cover the bills? Her mum, for reasons Gemma had never been able to get her head round, refused to apply for benefits. They were entitled, Gemma had checked, but Mel still wouldn't entertain the idea. 'No handouts' was her mantra.

But that was alright for her, when she wasn't the one whose body ached most days from all the scrubbing, folding, vacuuming and mopping. The Compton had thirty rooms, and Gemma was its only chambermaid. It wasn't too bad now, during the winter season when bookings were sporadic, but in summer, when the hotel was full every night, it was backbreaking work.

Gemma's careers teacher at school had said she was bright enough to go to university. That had been in year nine, before her truanting became chronic. She had been predicted top grades. She'd had an aptitude for science and had quite fancied idea of studying chemistry with a view to working in the food industry. Gemma had always liked the science of cooking, which was why food tech was one of the only two exams she'd bothered to sit.

Her dad, Dennis, had triggered her interest in food. He had been a professional chef at a restaurant in Leeds when she was little. Before he left, when their kitchen wasn't as unusable as it was now, he'd taught Gemma to cook. By age six she could chop an onion with the skill of a kitchen veteran, blade zipping through the tart flesh like a guillotine. She had loved the alchemy of mixing herbs and spices to create different flavours like he showed her, and had developed a palate for strong tastes. By eight she could make restaurant-worthy beef birria. Now, she never cooked. The cooker and hob were no longer accessible, buried beneath piles of rubbish, so dinner was usually instant noodles. On the days she couldn't find the kettle she had to use hot water from the tap.

If she had a functioning kitchen, she could film cookery segments to post on TikTok. She'd thought about asking Reece if she could use the hotel's kitchen, but another stumbling block was not having money for ingredients. She was hardly going to rack up tens of thousands of followers showing how to rehydrate chow mein from a sachet.

She closed the TikTok app and checked the time. It was seven fifteen: if she didn't get a move on, she'd be late. Still, she was confident Reece wouldn't sack her for not being on time for once, because he'd struggle to find a replacement prepared to accept her pitiful salary. The Compton's owners were far too tight to increase it.

Confident she had at least ten minutes' grace, she opened the search engine on her phone and began to scroll its news feed. There must be something happening that she could make a video about that wasn't celebrity-based, but would still get people liking and commenting. Something a bit controversial, but not political, because she had, like, zero interest in government stuff. Politicians just took your money and made life far harder than it needed to be. Gemma thought they were all as bad as one another.

Nothing in the main headlines grabbed her, until she scrolled down a bit further. The story leapt off the screen at her.

> *CPS REFUSE TO CHARGE UNDERCOVER POLICE OFFICER WHO TRICKED WOMAN INTO HAVING HIS BABY*

Gemma read the article, her disgust mounting with each passing sentence. Some poor woman called Hazel Mackett had found out the man she was in a relationship with was really a fed sent to spy on her. She'd even had a son with him, thinking he was a decent sort. Hazel wanted the fed, who wasn't named, to be put on trial for deceiving her, but the CPS – the people who decided who went to court – had said no. Gemma re-read the article, a spark of excitement taking flight in her tummy. A video of her sharing her outrage on Hazel's behalf would be great content. How dare that copper get away with abusing an innocent woman like that. And what about the son! Then Gemma bit down on her lip, unsure. Maybe she should read a bit more about the case first, to make sure she knew what she was talking about?

*No, don't prepare*, a voice in her head told her roundly. An off-the-cuff video would be far more engaging than some dry speech she'd written out. *Just do it.*

Gemma threw back her duvet and leapt out of bed. No time for a shower now, she'd just touch up the make-up she hadn't bothered removing last night and film it.

The only thing Gemma double-checked before pressing record was the woman's name, Hazel Mackett, and what 'CPS' stood for. The rest she ad-libbed.

Five minutes later the video was done and uploaded.

By the time she arrived at The Compton at eight fifteen, Gemma's one-woman rant had already got over a hundred likes.

# Chapter Eight

## EVE

Eve had slept terribly. The slightest noise had her shooting upright in bed, wild-eyed with fear, heart pounding in her chest. The third time it had happened – triggered by the boiler gurgling in the kitchen as the heating powered down for the night – she'd risen to check all the locks were secure again.

Frank Tooley turning up at her home had rattled her even more than she could have imagined, and she couldn't bear to take a look at the file he'd left. The less she thought about Tooley the better. She wondered when she'd sleep soundly again.

When Leah got back from her shift at 7 a.m., Eve was on the sofa, wrapped in her duvet, cup of tea clenched between her hands. She'd been there since five thirty.

In the time it took Leah to set down her bag and take off her coat, she yawned five times. Eve didn't want to keep her up; she'd wait to tell her about Frank Tooley coming to the flat.

'How was your date on Tuesday?' Leah asked.

'Put it this way, I won't be seeing Harry again.'

'No? Just as well,' said Leah, her exhaustion vanishing beneath an impish grin. 'I gave your number to Jamie. He told me he'd run into you and that you were being bothered by some creep and he wanted to check you were okay. That's fine, isn't it? He's a lovely guy,' she added hastily. 'I wouldn't have given it to him if he wasn't. Everyone at work loves him.'

Eve wished Leah had asked her first, but didn't want to make her feel bad.

'He's single,' said Leah pointedly.

'Right,' Eve replied non-committally.

'You definitely don't mind I gave him your number?'

'It's fine. Now get some sleep. We'll catch up soon.'

'I'm doing nights until next Wednesday, then I've got a few days off,' said Leah. 'We can go out then.'

Eve nodded, but the thought of being alone at night for the next week filled her with dread. Until now, sharing with someone who worked a shift pattern had been a blessing. Days could pass before they were home at the same time, and she relished having the place to herself. She'd lived alone when she first moved to London – the private law firm job that had brought her to the capital had paid enough for her to rent a one-bedroom place, until she was sacked – and having a flatmate had taken some adjustment. Now, with Tooley lurking, Eve wished Leah worked normal hours so there was someone else at home overnight.

With another yawn and a wave, Leah disappeared into her room.

Eve stayed on the sofa for another half-hour, watching telly with the volume down low. Then she wearily got ready for work.

Taking Horner's advice, she took a different route into town. On the first leg, via Leadenhall Market and London Bridge, Eve got out her phone and began a mindless scroll of her apps. Except Hinge, which she'd deleted.

She opened TikTok last. She never posted on it herself but liked it for the funny videos. She also followed a few lawyers she knew. Scrolling down, she saw one of them had reshared a post with the hashtag #CPSscandal. She clicked on it, and the sound played discreetly through her earbuds.

The video was of a teenage girl talking directly to the camera. She had a strong Yorkshire accent. To Eve's shock, she opened with a precise recap of the Hazel Mackett case, then followed it with an impassioned and articulate dismantling of the CPS's decision not to charge Zayn Walker.

Concern shot through Eve. Not because she didn't agree with the video's sentiments, but because she knew how a story like this could go viral and she didn't want the scrutiny. Madeleine Farmer had unintentionally put her in the public's cross-hairs: if it came out that she'd been on the review team that had decided in Walker's favour, she might become the focus of more public attention.

She clicked on the poster's nametag – @Gemz1026. In TikTok terms the teen didn't have a huge following, but the video had garnered a few hundred views already. Eve knew that wasn't enough to count as going viral, but the video was clearly gaining momentum, the likes rising every few seconds. She wondered whether it had been picked up on other social media platforms but didn't check. If it did go viral on a wider scale, she expected someone higher up than her at the CPS would deal with it.

# Chapter Nine

## VALERIE

There was no pre-booked taxi waiting when Valerie's red-eye flight landed at Heathrow Terminal 5 just after seven. She hadn't told anyone at the embassy she was flying back, covering the £668 charge from her own pocket. The return flight in economy had been in acute contrast to her outward journey in business, when she'd sipped champagne and reclined into a relaxed slumber, but she hadn't minded being hemmed in mid-row. There was no way she'd have got a wink of sleep anyway, so a more opulent setting would've been a waste of time and money.

Instead, her mind had churned with fear for the entire flight, and she couldn't stop re-reading the article that had forced her on to the plane. She desperately wanted her suspicion to be proved wrong, but the voice in her head screaming *What if it's Bradley?* drowned out all sensible introspection.

Before catching her flight, Glenn had urged her to call the White House aide overseeing her meeting with the President to excuse herself, but she'd been too cowardly and had instead fired off a one-line email citing a family emergency. She'd waited until the exact second the stewardess asked for electronic devices to be switched to airplane mode to send it. Then she'd powered her phone down and fought the urge to cry.

Glenn was right, there would be no going back from this. She couldn't stand up the President then expect to be rewarded afterwards. She'd see out her tenure at the US Embassy in London then take a lesser role somewhere else.

But first she had to tell Mark she'd withdrawn her application.

Valerie tugged her carry-on past the line of drivers bearing placards scrawled with the surnames of passengers they were to collect. An overhead sign pointed towards the cab rank, but she headed for the escalator to catch the Tube instead. She couldn't face sitting in a car with a driver who might be in a chatty mood.

Home was a five-bedroom Edwardian rental in Putney, in the capital's south-west. A relocation consultant recruited to help senior embassy staff settle in had found it for them. Valerie's main criteria had been somewhere she could walk to work from, but the house was too far away from the embassy in Nine Elms to manage the distance on foot. It was, however, close enough to the Thames that she could catch the Clipper to work. Travelling upriver every morning had proved to be even more relaxing than walking, and now she loved her commute.

By the time Valerie emerged into daylight at Putney Bridge Tube station she'd been travelling for more than twenty-four hours. Her eyes were gritty with exhaustion, and the shirt and jacket she'd worn to meet Glenn at the hotel bar were now musty with sweat beneath her overcoat. Sleet began to fall as she set off, but she kept going, suitcase dragging behind her, until she reached her road.

As she walked, her phone beeped incessantly. Word of her return to London had spread while she'd been in the air and underground. The aide who'd arranged her meeting with the President had emailed a caustic reply to say he was deeply unimpressed by her cancelling. There was no ambiguity: Valerie was done in DC.

There were also messages of concern from some colleagues here in London, referencing the so-called family emergency. Her assistant, Langdon, had called five times. He would know what people were saying about her, but she decided his gossip round-up could wait. A couple more hours wouldn't alter the content.

Reaching the corner of their street, she stopped, suddenly overcome with panic. How was she going to handle this? What should she say? The lack of contact from Mark suggested he was unaware that she'd caught a flight home, so – she checked her watch to confirm the time – right now he'd be upstairs in his home office, firing off emails to current clients or drawing up proposals for prospective ones. How could she explain her decision to him when she could barely articulate it to herself? The online article had triggered her into thinking Bradley was to blame for this latest incident, but now, in the cold light of day, she was horrified at how hasty she'd been in thinking the worst of him. If she – his mom, for crying out loud – couldn't give him the benefit of the doubt, who could?

Her key in the lock alerted Scout, their two-year-old golden retriever, to her unexpected homecoming. With unabashed joy, the dog skidded sideways down the hallway towards her, hind legs and backside colliding with her case and sending it crashing on to its side. Moments later Mark appeared at the crest of the stairs, clearly taken aback to see his wife home when she should've been readying to shake the President's hand inside the West Wing.

'Why aren't you in Washington?'

The door to the kitchen sprang open and Bradley appeared. Her son's expression was inscrutable as he came into the hallway, but his stride was assured.

Mark descended the stairs and the two men reached the foot of them at the same time. Her peas-in-a-pod. So alike with their chestnut-brown waves – Mark's hair was mainly grey now though – aquiline noses, grey eyes and lean frames. If she hadn't carried him for nine months, Valerie would question whether there was a single molecule of her DNA in her child.

She looked from one to the other, wondering which of the men she loved with all her heart she should address first. In the end, she chose her husband. If she looked at her son for too long, she'd go to pieces.

'How do you feel about us staying in London?'

Bradley's smile slipped. Mark was visibly stunned. Then he let out a thunderous 'thank God' that made Scout whimper and shoot down the hallway into the kitchen.

'I guessed you'd be happy,' said Valerie, as her husband shot forward and hugged her. In his arms, her mind calmed for the first time in hours.

'I'm not gonna lie,' he grinned as he released her, 'I know it was the White House, but with my business doing so well here, it's much better for me if we stay put.' He looked deep into her eyes. 'Are you sure though? That job was everything you've been working towards.'

Valerie swallowed. It was an effort to. The stale air on the flight had desiccated her throat. 'I'm sure. As soon as I landed in DC, I kept thinking what a terrible mistake I'd made by going. I realised I didn't want to uproot us again. We've been in London nearly eight years but it's our fourth country in sixteen. I'm tired of moving around so much. I'm thinking a few more years here at least.'

She watched her husband's reaction carefully. She'd never told him what had happened with Bradley during her last posting in Prague, and why it was his fault they'd had to leave as suddenly as they did. Valerie had kept the truth from Mark. But would her withdrawing from the DC job prompt him to start asking difficult questions?

Mark's smile broadened, though. 'A few more years and the business should be ready to float. That'll give us the means to retire pretty damn well.'

Bradley's voice cut between them. 'What about what I want?'

Valerie turned her focus to her son. His cheeks were mottled, and for a second her heart constricted. This was her boy, the unconditional love of her life. The baby she'd carried inside her, the infant she'd nurtured, the child she'd raised and protected, and the young man whose terrible secret she'd hid.

'You can still go to DC to do your master's, bud,' said Mark. 'Just because we're staying here doesn't mean you have to.'

'Here with us would be better,' Valerie said quietly.

'Honey, you've got to cut the apron strings sometime,' Mark laughed. 'He's nearly twenty-five.'

Bradley's eyes bored into hers. 'You shouldn't have flown back, Mom. It's a mistake. You should have waited to meet with the President. You deserve that position.'

'I like the role I'm in. Don't forget, it has a lot of perks.' She elongated the final three words.

Bradley's expression flickered, then set. 'You're making a mistake, Mom.'

Mark frowned at their son. 'We need to support her decision, bud, not pick it apart.' He turned to his wife. 'You must be shattered. How about I make us coffee?'

Without waiting for her reply, he strolled into the kitchen.

Valerie didn't move. Bradley also stayed where he was, at the bottom of the stairs. She wanted to say something, but the words stuck in her throat.

'You saw the news about that woman falling from Southwark Bridge and decided it must be my fault again, didn't you, Mom.' His tone was matter-of-fact. 'I made one mistake as a kid and I've had to live with knowing what I did every day since. But you've got it wrong *again*.'

◆ ◆ ◆

The girl's name was Nadia. She and Bradley had been in their final year at the same international school. They'd been friends. One Saturday night, a group of them had attended a house party in another part of Prague, then decided to walk home across Charles Bridge. Somehow Nadia had lost her footing, fallen into the river, and been swept away. Her body was recovered two days later.

To Valerie's horror, Nadia's best friend, Leeza van der Kleji, came forward and accused Bradley of pushing Nadia. She claimed Bradley had previously asked Nadia out but she'd rejected him, saying he wasn't her type. Leeza claimed Bradley had been in a foul mood all evening and had deliberately dawdled on the bridge so Nadia would hang back to see what was wrong. When the others went ahead, he'd pushed her to her death.

The finger-pointing had devastated Bradley. He'd sworn that Nadia's death was an accident. She'd been goofing around and leaning over the side of the bridge for a joke and had pitched forward too far, losing her balance. He'd tried to grab her but wasn't quick enough. Valerie had quizzed him repeatedly but his account had never wavered. There was no argument. He'd had no reason to be angry with Nadia that night or on any other.

Despite the stress of the situation, Valerie took solace in knowing that the Czech police had no power to investigate the lies Leeza was spreading about Bradley because of her own position as a foreign diplomat. Under the Vienna Convention of 1961, she had immunity from prosecution in any country she was posted in – and so did her son and husband under its familial rules. The police could never arrest, question or charge them in relation to any crime, no matter how serious.

Leeza's claims still niggled at her though. Bradley had been a difficult child and had needed therapy, and the last thing she wanted was for that to come out and be used against him. Anxious to confirm their position, she'd sought counsel from a trusted older colleague named George Stow. To her surprise, George had urged Valerie to get Bradley out of Prague as quickly as possible. Yes, it was indeed correct that the police couldn't touch her son, but that did not make him immune from public outcry should Leeza persist in blaming him for Nadia's death. Better for the Aspens to leave the Czech Republic for pastures new and put it behind them. George assured Valerie that he would arrange it all, including making sure Leeza withdrew her defamatory accusation.

Two weeks later, Valerie and Bradley landed in London. Mark joined them a month later after wrapping up loose ends at work.

It was during the flight to London that Bradley finally told Valerie the truth. He and Nadia had argued on the bridge and he had pushed her, but he hadn't meant for her to fall. In other words, Nadia's death was not quite the accident he'd painted it to be.

Valerie was devastated he hadn't been honest with her. And she was even more appalled that he'd lashed out at a girl whose only crime was to not want to date him. Leeza had been right all along.

But Bradley had seemed genuinely distraught as he unburdened himself on the plane, begging for Valerie's forgiveness and saying he had never meant for Nadia to die. It was a heat-of-the-moment act of stupidity that he regretted with every fibre of his being, and he'd been too scared to tell the truth because he thought the police would find a way to arrest him despite Valerie's diplomatic position.

Valerie had assured him the police couldn't do that, but his distress that they might reversed her thinking that he should return to Prague to tell Nadia's parents what had really happened. What would be gained by him admitting to them something he desperately wished he could undo? It wouldn't bring Nadia back or ease their grief. So Valerie had suppressed her own guilt that Nadia's parents would never know the full story and instead focused her energy on settling them into their new life in London.

She'd continued to believe that Bradley had never meant for Nadia to drown right up until nearly six months ago, when a young woman had plunged into the Thames off Putney Bridge, a short distance from their house. She'd pored over every detail of the case looking for commonalities, and there were plenty – the main one being Bradley had met the victim on previous occasions. It had caused Valerie endless sleepless nights until eventually she confronted him. Bradley was bemused, saying he'd been in bed asleep when it happened, but still Valerie couldn't shake her suspicion. So when she'd seen the news report about the woman falling off Southwark Bridge, her mind had gone into overdrive again. What if he'd known this victim too? Now, seeing his hurt expression, she realised she might've made a terrible mistake in jumping to conclusions once again.

'Your paranoia is hurting me, Mom,' he said. 'For the record, I was nowhere near Southwark Bridge. I was here again, in bed. It kills me that you think I could deliberately hurt a woman.'

His words were a dagger to Valerie's heart. What kind of mother was she that she couldn't shake off her doubt?

'I just want to protect you,' she said feebly.

'Protect me from what?' he said despairingly. 'I haven't done anything. You should've stayed in DC, Mom. Pulling out of the interview process proves that you think I'm guilty.'

Valerie watched, shamefaced, as her son went upstairs. He was right. She had returned to London simply because she no longer trusted his innocence.

Yet ruining her White House prospects was also her way of protecting him. If she'd been offered and had taken that job in the administration, her diplomatic status would have ended and with it their familial immunity. As long as she remained working at the embassy in London, Bradley was untouchable.

# Chapter Ten

## EVE

Eve spent the morning at Petty France, tackling her caseload. Her attention span was shot though, exhaustion making her eyes swim when she tried to read. Then she'd jolt every time her mobile buzzed, or someone said her name. Frank Tooley's trip to her flat had triggered a nervousness she couldn't shake and she still hadn't opened the file. At lunchtime she went in search of Horner to update him – he was right that Tooley's behaviour needed to be acted upon – but he wasn't in. Eve hoped another headache wasn't to blame.

At 2 p.m. she called DC Alix Quinn to see if there was any update on the Becca Farrow case. The parents had formally identified the body yesterday afternoon but her name hadn't been released to the media yet.

'Why is the CPS chasing me for an update?' asked Quinn, sounding bemused. 'You don't usually get involved in suspected suicides.'

Eve decided there was no point in lying. 'My line manager Beverly Atkins is Becca's godmother, so she has a vested interest in making sure the case is thoroughly investigated.'

If Quinn was affronted by the suggestion that it might not be, she hid it well. 'There's nothing much to tell at the moment,' she replied. 'I'm gathering witness statements and talking to Becca's friends and colleagues to piece together her last movements before I pass the case to the coroner's office.'

'You've had witnesses come forward?' asked Eve sharply.

Quinn's reply was almost lost in a background cacophony of traffic noise. Eve wondered where within the Square Mile she was.

'Not yet. There's CCTV in operation at both ends of the bridge, so we've got footage of her arriving. She appears intoxicated and is weaving all over the pavement,' she said. 'The bit where she went over isn't covered by cameras, so we're putting out an appeal for witnesses, to see if anyone picked her up on their dash-cams. We're already out of luck with any buses – overnight roadworks on Upper Thames Street meant they were being diverted away from Southwark Bridge at the time she went into the water. The last bus went across at eleven thirty and the access wasn't due to open again until six. We're reliant on cars and cabs and helmet cams from motorcyclists and bikers for any sightings.'

Eve welcomed Quinn's openness in discussing where the case was at. 'My boss is adamant Becca wasn't suicidal,' she said. 'They were close, and when they met up last week, my boss claimed Becca was her usual self. So . . . did she leave a note?'

'Not that we've found so far. But I spoke to her firm's CEO this morning and he said that Becca had been under extreme pressure at work overseeing lay-offs and was signed off with stress for two weeks before Christmas. He also said she'd been drinking heavily, often coming into work smelling of booze. The colleagues she was out with the night she died confirmed that she had been very drunk when she left them.'

Beverly couldn't have known about Becca being signed off with stress, Eve noted. She would've said, given its significance.

'If she was that drunk, what's to say she didn't just trip and fall by accident?'

'The height of the balustrade means she'd have had to heave herself over it,' said Quinn soberly. 'That implies intent.'

An image of Beverly crying in her office pierced Eve's mind.

'There must still be some doubt that she meant to jump though,' she said. 'She could've clambered up on the bridge as a cry for help but then slipped.'

'Look, I get why your colleague wants it to be an accidental death. I really do,' said Quinn patiently. 'Suicide is incredibly hard on those left behind. But I can only go on what I know, and Becca was struggling with alcohol and severe stress. Just one of those might be enough to send someone spiralling. Combined, it may well have been just too much.'

Eve knew she had a point. Quinn wrapped up the conversation by telling her to call back in a couple of days for further updates.

The rest of the afternoon dragged by until, just before four, exhausted by the lack of sleep, Eve decided to slope off home. She told the colleagues seated closest to her that she felt nauseous, like she was coming down with something. It wasn't a lie either: all day she'd had a sick feeling in the pit of her stomach from thinking about Tooley's visit to her flat.

She was putting on her coat when Ashley scuttled over. 'Did you know your voicemail is full? I've just had someone come through on my line because they can't get hold of you.'

Eve had diverted the calls on her work phone to voicemail first thing, worried that Tooley might call. In her tiredness she'd forgotten she'd done it. Checking the display, she saw eighteen new messages. Suppressing a groan, she took off her coat and sat down again. She couldn't go without listening to them.

The first few were related to cases Eve was working on. Message number five was from Tooley. Eve's blood chilled to hear his voice but she forced herself to listen, aware she needed to document every interaction with him.

'Ms Wren, this is Frank Tooley. I am ringing to check you got the file I left for you. I would have given it to you in person the other evening had you spared me a few minutes of your time. Your rudeness was quite unwarranted. However, I am prepared to overlook that and move forward with discussing its contents. It's important you call me back.'

Eve swallowed down the bile rising in her throat. The comment about calling him back sounded more like an order than a request.

To her horror, message six was also from Tooley. And seven, eight, nine and ten. Left at half-hour intervals, with him sounding increasingly exasperated that she hadn't dropped everything to return his calls. The next couple of messages, eleven and twelve, were case-related, then thirteen was from Beverly, asking if she'd spoken to DS Quinn yet. But fourteen through to eighteen were Tooley again.

The last message set Eve's teeth on edge.

'How dare you ignore me,' he bellowed down the line, his accent even more abrasive with rage. 'Who do you think you are? I could get you sacked, missy. It wouldn't be the first time either, would it? Oh, I know all about you and your past, Ms Wren,' he added, spitting her name with venom. 'You should do very well to remember that. I could make your life hell.' Then, abruptly, his tone changed. 'But let's not go down that route, eh. All I want is to discuss the case file with you. So please extend me the courtesy of calling me back. If I don't hear from you, I shall try you again in person.'

Eve put the phone down and burst into tears.

# Chapter Eleven

## EVE

Like virtually all women at one time or another, Eve had been on the receiving end of unwelcome male attention before. But Tooley's felt on a different level to the usual crass jokes and sexual come-ons. His interest was insidious, threatening and unpredictable. The way he'd turned in his voicemail message – one minute furious, the next placatory – had made Eve feel vulnerable and raw, like her skin had been flayed and her muscle and tissue exposed to the world.

Even Ashley had expressed concern on seeing her distressed. Eve explained that she was feeling under the weather – which, thankfully, Ashley seemed to buy. Until she looked further into what official and practical steps she could take to make Tooley cool his attention, Eve wasn't ready to share what was going on with everyone.

Too shaky from the flood of adrenaline and shock to get the bus back to Old Street, she'd flagged a taxi. It was a journey she could do without after having to pay for the taxi following her aborted date with Harry, but it felt the safest way to get home. For all she knew, Tooley could still be in London, waiting to ambush her again. She knew he had no family or job in Northampton to rush back for.

The taxi was making good progress, the traffic still flowing pre-rush hour, when Eve saw she had a message notification on her phone. She'd put it on silent when she left the office, petrified Tooley had got hold of her number somehow, and knowing that if she answered the phone and it was his voice she heard, she'd lose it completely. To her surprise, however, it was a text from Leah's colleague Jamie, asking how she was and wanting to know if she might be free for a drink sometime.

Impulsively, Eve called him straight back. Jamie was the only person who'd seen how Tooley had been with her and he therefore might understand how scared she was. Her heart hammered in her chest as she waited for the call to connect; so used to communicating by app and text, it felt alien to be ringing a man she hardly knew.

Jamie sounded delighted when he picked up.

'Hi Eve, it's lovely to hear from you,' he said. 'How's things?'

To her utter embarrassment, on hearing his voice she burst into tears and couldn't get her words out.

'Eve, what's wrong? What's happened?'

'It's that man again,' she said in a strangled voice between sobs. 'He found out where I live and came to my flat.'

Jamie's reply was brisk and businesslike. 'Where are you now? I'll come and meet you.'

'Um . . . I'm in a cab.' Still crying, she peered out of the window to see where they were. 'We're on Charterhouse Street, just about to pass Fabric,' she said, on spotting the famous nightclub on the left-hand side.

'I'm nearby. Can you get to Barbican station? I'll meet you outside the entrance.'

'Okay. It'll be a few more minutes, I think.'

'I'll be there.'

◆ ◆ ◆

Jamie was true to his word and already waiting as the cab pulled up outside the station. He stayed put while she paid, then opened the cab door for her. Her tears had dried up but her embarrassment at Jamie hearing her cry still lingered. Yet she was angry too, Tooley the target of her ire. How dare he frighten and intimidate her. She had to put a stop to it.

There were a few awkward seconds when she and Jamie were unsure how to greet each other, both shuffling on the spot like boxers in a bout. A hug felt too familiar, a handshake too cold. Laughing, they settled on trading hellos.

'What do you fancy?' Jamie asked her. 'Coffee or a drink? I'm fine with either.'

'A drink, definitely.'

'Then follow me. There's a great place round the corner.'

Falling into step with him, Eve wondered where Jamie had been going or coming back from when she'd called, because he was smartly dressed in black skinny trousers, shiny black brogues, and a fitted grey woollen overcoat, his hands thrust deep into the pockets to stave off the biting cold.

'I'm not keeping you from anywhere, am I?'

He side-eyed her with a smile. 'I've just had a job interview. Still at St Bart's, but in the cardiology department. I'm about to complete my two-year foundation so now I'm applying to specialise.'

'I remember Leah doing the same last year,' said Eve. 'Although she stayed in emergency care.'

'I know, and she's my hero for wanting to.' He shook his head. 'I'm just not cut out for it. The pace is too relentless.'

'When will you find out if you've got the job?'

'Not sure, but hopefully not too long. If I don't get it, I'll start looking outside St Bart's. Right, here we are.'

Coming up on the right was an old-fashioned-looking pub called The Mattison Arms, with leaded windows and a battered wooden door that creaked in protest as Jamie pushed it open. The interior was more modern, with pastel-blue walls and an artisan vibe. Jamie got the first round in – a pint of craft ale for each of them – while Eve found a table. Taking off her coat, she chose the side facing the room: she wanted a clear view of the door to see who was coming through it.

'Do you want to tell me what happened?' Jamie asked. He'd taken his coat off too, to reveal a suit jacket over a white shirt. If he'd worn a tie for his interview, it had long been discarded.

Eve gulped down a mouthful of her pint. Then, with a steadying breath, she told him everything, starting with Madeleine's interview. Jamie listened intently, sipping his pint and only interrupting when she reached the part where he'd become involved outside the restaurant.

'My sister got a text from her ex begging her to meet him, so we paid up. I was heading home myself when I saw you at the bus stop. After your taxi left, that guy Tooley was really pissed off with me, but I told him he was the one who'd been out of order. After that he walked off and I got the Tube home.'

Eve hesitated to tell him that Tooley had most likely tracked her down because he'd heard Jamie say Old Street. She didn't want to make him feel guilty. But it was an important part of what had happened next, so she ploughed on.

'I'm really sorry,' Jamie said on hearing that Tooley had hand-delivered the envelope to her home. 'If I had known, I'd have been more careful.'

'This isn't your fault. He'd have found out some other way eventually,' she said placatingly. 'He showed that today when he left a string of messages on my phone at work. It's like he reckons he's entitled to my undivided attention. The last message was awful. He sounded so angry, then just like that' – she snapped her fingers – 'he was eerily calm. He said if I didn't call him back, he'd be coming to see me again, like I have no choice in the matter.' She felt embarrassed, her cheeks reddening. 'I don't normally cry like that, but the messages really got to me. I'd only just listened to them when you texted.'

Jamie looked contemplative for a moment. 'I know this isn't the point, but did you look at the file he dropped off? I mean, is it worth seeing what he wants, then telling him you can't help?'

It was a good point, and one Eve had yet to consider. She'd chucked the envelope on the desk in her bedroom after bringing it up from the foyer and hadn't touched it since.

'I guess I could do that.'

'You should also report it to your manager.'

'I would, but she's off at the moment. I don't know when she'll be back in.'

Jamie must've sensed Eve's discomfort. 'Isn't anyone covering for her?'

'It was very last-minute, so no.'

He looked even more intrigued. Eve realised there was no harm in telling Jamie. The story was in the public domain now. 'Have you heard about the suspected suicide on Southwark Bridge? The woman who supposedly jumped?'

Jamie shook his head, his pint glass in mid-air. 'Not your boss?'

'No, it was her goddaughter. My boss is off because the parents have come down from Yorkshire and are staying with her.'

'That's really sad.'

'I know.' Eve paused. 'Would she have suffered much, in your expert medical opinion?'

'I guess it depends.'

'On what?'

'The state she was in when she went into the water. If she was extremely intoxicated, for example, she might've gone under the water quickly and that was that. The clothes she had on would've dragged her down.' He grimaced. 'Drowning is a horrible way to die if you're aware that it's happening. It's human instinct to gasp for air but the only thing you're inhaling is water.'

Eve was lost in thought for a moment, letting the awfulness of his comment sink in, when her phone vibrated with a message. Her eyes widened with fear.

'It won't be him,' said Jamie reassuringly. 'He doesn't have your mobile number.'

He was right, but her hand still shook as she checked the message. It was from DC Quinn.

> *A witness has come forward – need to update you urgently. By you, I mean CPS.*

Eve frowned. What did that mean? 'Sorry, but I need to make a quick call,' she told Jamie. 'Can you excuse me for a minute?'

'Of course. Shall I get another round in?' He checked his watch. 'Although it is only five thirty.'

Eve didn't care that it was early still. Sitting in a pub getting drunk with Jamie was preferable to being in the flat on her own, terrified of every sound. 'I'm happy to stay. And I promise the next round is on me.'

Jamie smiled. 'I'll hold you to that.'

While he went to the bar, Eve went outside so she could hear better.

'I'm really glad you called,' said Quinn, sounding almost breathless. 'We've had a witness come forward, a van driver. He remembered seeing Becca on the bridge and his dash-cam recorded her. Eve, your boss was right. Becca wasn't suicidal and she didn't jump. She was pushed off that bridge – and I'm sitting here looking at the man who did it.'

# Chapter Twelve

## EVE

Jamie said he didn't mind her shooting off, but Eve got the distinct feeling as she pulled on her coat that he was just being polite.

'Let me give you some money for the drinks,' she said, gesturing to the two full pints he'd set down on the table.

He batted the offer away. 'I've paid now. I guess I'll just stay here and get drunk by myself.'

'I am sorry I have to leave so suddenly,' she said. 'There's been an important development in a case, and I really need to look into it now.'

'It can't wait until morning?'

She didn't want to tell him what the case was, or the development, or who she was going to meet. It was none of his business.

'Unfortunately not. I would stay if I could,' she said, although she wasn't sure if she meant it. There was something about the set of Jamie's expression that she found off-putting. It was like he was annoyed with her when he had no right to be. Coat on, she hovered beside the table, wondering how to say goodbye when he was no longer making eye contact.

'Well, it was nice to see you again.'

'You too,' he said coolly.

Was that it? Eve's hackles rose. This was their second meeting and not even an actual date, yet he was behaving like she'd somehow slighted him. Without another word she headed for the exit.

He caught up with her by the door, suddenly all smiles. 'I'm sorry, I'm being a dick. I'm just really disappointed we can't hang out now. You called me wanting to meet up and now you're running off.'

Eve bristled. She had no time for mood swings or gaslighting. Cute though Jamie was, and a friend of Leah's, he was definitely another to consign to the bin marked 'men to avoid'.

There was currently only one City of London Police station in operation after the Wood Street and Snow Hill sites had been sold off to developers. A new state-of-the-art station combining law courts was due to open in Fleet Street next year, but for now the entire force operated out of Bishopsgate. Eve toyed with getting a cab there, but with her phone's map app saying it would take just twenty minutes to walk and her bank app showing dwindling funds, she set off on foot.

Halfway there, Quinn sent her another text, this time with a request. Could Eve please meet her on the main concourse at Liverpool Street train station rather than at Bishopsgate. Bemused, Eve texted back agreeing and adjusted her route accordingly.

It was nearly six o'clock – peak commuter hour – when she got to Liverpool Street. The main concourse was heaving. Quinn had, however, specified that they meet on the upper balcony, outside Lush. There was an escalator, but Eve took the stairs.

The heady scent of bath bombs and handmade soap assailed her as she approached the retail outlet, but she couldn't see anyone loitering outside who might be Quinn. She moved across the walkway towards the glass barrier overlooking the concourse below, then almost immediately had to move away, her fear of falling causing a spurt of dizziness that made her stumble.

A steadying hand grabbed her arm. 'Eve?'

Her pulse juddered. She turned to see a woman with light-brown hair, casually dressed in jeans and a cobalt-blue coat. Her deep-brown eyes radiated concern.

'DC Quinn?' Eve asked.

The woman nodded. 'Call me Alix.' She paused. 'Are you okay?'

Eve was suddenly mindful of her breath smelling of beer. She pulled away, putting some distance between them. 'I'm fine. I forgot I don't like heights and went too close to the edge,' she said, jerking her head in the direction of the barrier.

'Would you prefer we went downstairs?'

There was a branch of a sandwich chain among the balcony outlets.

'Here's fine,' said Eve, not wanting to cause more fuss. She suggested they bought coffees, thinking a strong latte would hopefully mask the booze.

'Sounds good.'

A few minutes later, coffees in hand, the pair sat down at a table inside.

'Why did you ask to meet me here and not at Bishopsgate?' Eve asked.

'The investigation is going to be out of my hands soon, and if I brought you, a CPS lawyer, into the station it would raise too many questions. But I wanted you to see the footage.' Quinn, who was softly spoken, eased her phone from her coat pocket. 'I shouldn't be showing it to you like this, so please don't tell anyone.'

'I won't. You have my word.'

Quinn tapped the screen. 'I should warn you, it's not conclusive.'

Eve frowned. 'How do you mean?'

The detective passed her the phone. 'See for yourself.'

The footage was brief, no doubt reflecting the speed at which the van had been travelling when Becca was captured on its dash-cam. Quinn had slowed it down for the purposes of watching it back.

The van had been driving on the same side of the road where Becca went into the river, travelling north. Eve concentrated on the screen, waiting for the moment Becca appeared. There she was!

Quinn had been right about her weaving all over the place. She bumped repeatedly against the balustrade as she staggered along. Then, like a lightning strike, a man in a peaked baseball cap suddenly appeared in the frame, side-on to the dash-cam. He must've darted across from the other side of the bridge.

It was hard to make out their expressions clearly, but Eve could see that Becca looked confused at first. Then her mouth formed an 'O' which stretched into a silent scream as the man lifted her off her feet and pushed her over the edge.

Horrified, Eve looked up from the screen. 'How is this not conclusive?'

'I don't mean the murder itself. When I spoke to you on the phone, I said I was looking at the man who did it, but as you can see his face isn't very clear. That's what I mean by not conclusive. The techs are trying to get a clearer shot, but I don't know whether we'll get a decent enough image,' said Quinn. 'But there's no doubt now that Becca Farrow was deliberately pushed, and we're now hunting for her killer.'

◆ ◆ ◆

Quinn, it turned out, was a trainee detective. Five years older than Eve at thirty-four, she was midway through a fast-track graduate programme. Her trainee status might have a bearing on whether she stayed on the case, she was now telling Eve.

'An SIO is being appointed as we speak. I don't know who it is yet, or whether they'll want me to stay on as part of the team. I've never worked on a murder case before,' she said.

'You found the van driver,' said Eve. 'That'll count for something.'

Quinn shrugged dismissively. 'He crosses the bridge multiple times a day for work. He saw the signs we'd put out asking for witnesses to a major incident and checked his footage. It wasn't just my doing.'

'Will the case stay with City?'

Quinn's eyes narrowed. 'Why wouldn't it?'

It was an open secret in London law enforcement circles that City detectives often didn't have the experience to handle serious crime investigations like murders, resulting in their cases being passed to or shared with their Met counterparts. Sharing a case meant two senior investigating officers and lots of time-sucking conference calls, which both complicated and slowed down the process.

'Well, it's a murder case. High stakes.'

'So? Southwark Bridge is in our jurisdiction. It's our case.'

Either Quinn was too new to know about City's track record, or she did but was determined to buck the trend. Eve hoped it was the latter. It would be much easier for her to keep tabs on the investigation via Quinn if it stayed with them.

'Will you release this footage?' she asked.

'Not of the actual moment she was pushed. It would be too distressing for her family,' said Quinn. 'But my DI reckons we'll probably release a still of her approaching the bridge.'

That troubled Eve. The image wouldn't put Becca in a good light if she appeared intoxicated, and Eve knew from experience that the court of public opinion could be vicious. In the event of her killer standing trial, a good defence barrister would almost certainly use Becca's drunken state against her. Classic victim-blaming.

But, Eve rationalised, that wouldn't be her concern if it went to trial. The CPS division she worked within, London South, did prosecute cases investigated by City police, but that didn't mean Becca's murder would end up on her desk. Her line manager being Becca's godmother would make it too close to home, a potential conflict of interest.

'Can you keep me updated on when it might be released?'

Becca had died two days ago. Now that the police knew she'd been murdered, the pace of the investigation should speed up.

'The techs reckon they'll get it back to us by lunchtime tomorrow, so I expect it'll go out by end of play, presuming the SIO is in place by then and gives the go-ahead.'

'Why wouldn't they?'

'It depends on the quality of the image. If we can get a clear shot to circulate, great. If not, we'll have to trawl other CCTV in the area to see if we can pick him up before or after it happened and release one of those. I mean, we're looking at that anyway, because like Becca he can only have crossed the bridge from one of the approach roads.'

'Have her parents been informed yet of the dash-cam footage?'

'My DCI spoke to them an hour ago at your boss's house. They've agreed that we can release her name.' Quinn checked the time on her phone. 'Media notice should've gone out by now. We're keeping to the major incident line and are asking for more witnesses. We're also going to confirm her death was suspicious, to make it clear suicide has been ruled out as a cause of death.'

Eve wondered how Beverly had taken the news. Her instincts about Becca not being suicidal had been spot on, but Eve doubted that would bring her much peace now she knew her goddaughter had been murdered.

'I hope you get to stay on the case,' she said, meaning it.

'Me too. There's something so horribly brazen about the way he pushed Becca that I wouldn't be surprised if he's tried it before. Or he might do it again.' Quinn's expression darkened. 'I want to help catch him before he does.'

# Chapter Thirteen

## GEMMA

Gemma's Thursday had gone from good to great. A guest who'd checked out in the morning had generously left a twenty-quid tip for housekeeping, and Reece had let her keep the lot for once. Even better, the views for her #CPSscandal video had steadily risen since she'd posted it in the morning and were now nudging forty thousand. She was officially viral.

Buoyed by her success, instead of going home after her ten-hour shift, Gemma headed to a budget department store in Prince Street that stocked designer clothes at discount prices. She planned to splurge the money on a new top and false eyelashes to wear in her next video. Unused to putting her wants first, she pushed down her guilt that the money should go into the bills pot or be set aside for a rainy day. She never got to treat herself and for once she wanted to be selfish.

Inside the store however, Gemma's mood sank. Despite the discount prices, even the cheapest tops would swallow her entire budget – and she really wanted the fake eyelashes, too. After rejecting an Adidas hoody for being ten quid too much, she decided to try a shop in the next street. The clothes sold there were made from cheap fabric that would smell musty after only one wear, but at least they were in her price range.

Gemma was footsteps from the automatic doors to exit the department store when a security guard appeared at her side. She stopped compliantly.

'Need to check your bags, love,' he said amiably. 'Nothing personal, store rules.'

She shrugged and opened her tote bag for him. It was the same whichever store she went into. She'd read online that Bridlington had been voted one of the UK's worst seaside resorts because of its high crime and poverty rates, and the local paper had reported shoplifting was at record levels as the cost-of-living crisis pushed the town's residents to the brink.

But Gemma had never gone on the nick and never would; it wasn't worth it, when they sent shoplifters to prison these days. Plus, her mum's hoarding had taught Gemma a valuable lesson: you didn't have to steal when there was so much free stuff going to waste.

Her mum had always had a compulsion to stockpile junk, but it had worsened after her divorce. Unable to tolerate his wife's messiness any longer, Dennis had gone to live with his brother in Sheffield. He'd taken most of his belongings with him, but the little he left behind her mum had stored in her bedroom and guarded like her life depended on it. She'd yell at Gemma if she so much as looked at it.

Gradually her mum had begun adding to the pile. At first it was items that could've been gifts for Dennis, such as second-hand recipe books and old vinyl records. But once it became clear he had no intention of ever returning, her hoarding had filled every inch of the house and she sank into a deep depression. When Dennis died two years ago from cancer, her mum had pleaded with Gemma to go to his home and bring back as many belongings as she could carry, to add to the pile of his things in her bedroom. Gemma refused.

Satisfied she was empty-handed, the store security guard stood aside to let her leave.

Half an hour later Gemma was on her way home with two fitted tops – one black, one white, and only four pounds each in the sale – and a set of false eyelashes costing a quid from Superdrug. With the leftover money she decided to treat herself to some chicken and chips from a takeout place near the seafront. It was nearly eight and she was starving, and it would make a change from noodles.

Standing in the queue, she checked the likes on her video. Another thousand views since she'd last looked! Gemma beamed. She couldn't wait to record another one. She'd stick to the same topic, but make sure she moved the story on, to stay relevant.

She was about to search for 'Hazel Mackett' for updates when she caught the tail end of the conversation between the two women waiting in front of her.

'I'm telling you, that's her. The mum was a teacher at your Josh and Keely's primary. Blonde hair, big hips, ran the choir.'

'Mrs Farrow?'

'That's the one. I just saw it on Facebook. Her daughter's been pushed off a bridge in London by some bloke and drowned. A van driver saw him do it.'

The second woman gasped. 'What kind of maniac would do that?'

'On drugs, probably. You know what London's like.'

Gemma craned to hear more.

'I don't think the family lives in Brid,' said the second woman. 'I mean, it's ten years since my two were at that school, but I remember Mrs Farrow saying she had a drive to get there.'

'They live out Driffield way. The daughter moved to London for work.'

Driffield was a market town about twelve miles inland from Bridlington, on the road to York.

'He just pushed her in?' queried the second woman. 'Isn't that killing?'

'Police haven't said owt official yet. The van driver spoke to a paper. I wonder how much he got for his story—'

Gemma tuned them out then. She searched for 'Farrow' and 'bridge' on her phone, and the first link took her to the van driver's interview with a tabloid. He said his van's dash-cam had caught the man heaving his victim over Southwark Bridge at four in the morning. He hadn't spotted them at the time because he'd had his eyes on the road, but he'd checked the footage after he'd seen the initial police appeal and realised it had captured the attack in full. He hadn't been able to share the footage with the paper though because it had been seized by the police.

According to the rest of the report, the woman had been named by the police as thirty-three-year-old Becca Farrow, originally from Yorkshire. She'd been walking home to her flat near Butler's Wharf from a night out with colleagues in Cannon Street. The police had refused to comment on the van driver's account but had confirmed that Becca's parents had travelled to London to identify her body. The police were now appealing for more witnesses who'd been in the vicinity of Southwark Bridge at the time to come forward.

Gemma gripped her phone excitedly. This was what her next video would be about. Becca Farrow was from the East Riding district, her mum had worked at a Brid school – who better to speak up on her behalf than Gemma, another Brid girl? She already knew what her angle should be: while the police were busy letting their officers trick vulnerable women like Hazel Mackett into getting pregnant and the CPS were turning a blind eye, others like Becca Farrow were being violently murdered on their watch. The public should be outraged on Becca's behalf, and it was Gemma's aim to make sure they were.

'What will it be, love?' said the woman behind the counter.

Gemma hadn't noticed she'd reached the front of the queue. Her face set with grim determination, she slipped her phone into her pocket and backed out of the shop. 'Changed my mind.'

Chicken and chips could wait. Her followers needed to know all about poor Becca Farrow – and how it was the police's fault she'd been pushed off that bridge to her death.

# Chapter Fourteen

## VALERIE

The US Embassy had moved across the river from its previous location in Grosvenor Square a few months before Valerie had joined. The new building on the river at Nine Elms was a towering example of modernist architecture: a glass cube with distinctive cladding, set on a plinth and surrounded by a semi-circular pond. It was impenetrable by security standards yet had been designed to look open and inviting.

Valerie had come to love it. Her favourite time of the day was now, first thing, when she brought her coffee into the gardens for a brief break before being sucked into the relentless schedule of meetings and briefings that her job demanded. Out here, even in the cold, it was an oasis of peace. The sounds of the traffic on road and river were just far enough away so as not to intrude.

Today, however, she had come outside to escape the whispers that had greeted her when she'd arrived. Word of her aborted trip to Washington had clearly spread, and the hushed conversations and quizzical looks were already wearying. She was thankful it was Friday. Hopefully after the weekend they'd have something else to gossip about.

Even her assistant, Langdon, had tiptoed around her like he was too scared to ask what had happened. It was a conversation they needed to have, though. She'd told him about going for the Deputy Secretary role because she'd hoped he'd relocate with her if she got it. Now she was staying in London, and he deserved to know why. Not the whole truth, but her version of it.

After a sleepless night, she'd managed to convince herself that most moms would walk away from a career opportunity if they feared it would be detrimental to their child. Striving to keep her family's immunity didn't equate to her deciding Bradley was guilty – she was just being cautious.

Part of her wished she'd taken the day off – she hadn't been due back in until Monday anyway – but the atmosphere at home was dire and she'd wanted to escape it. Bradley was refusing to engage with her, which in turn had triggered a row between him and Mark, who couldn't understand why their son was reacting so strongly to her rescinding the Washington job application. In turn, Valerie was afraid that Bradley would tell his dad the real root of his upset – which would be awful because she'd never told Mark the full story of what had happened in Prague. All Mark knew was what she'd told him and what he'd learned from the police comments in newspaper reports: Bradley's friend Nadia had been messing around on the bridge and, tragically, had leaned too far over the side. Only one other person knew the full truth besides her, Bradley, and George Stow: Glenn, her old college friend, and that was only because she'd slipped up and told him one night while drunk.

It had been easier to preserve Mark's ignorance than worry him. In fact, he'd jumped at the opportunity to move his business from Prague to London, one of the world's finance capitals. He didn't need to know that Valerie had begged George to find her a new embassy position anywhere in the world. It was sheer luck that Nine Elms had an opening that needed filling immediately, and that her previous experience in trade made her the ideal candidate. She'd have moved to Mongolia if that was what had been on offer.

She took a sip of coffee, but it had gone cold. She was starting to think it was time to head indoors when Langdon appeared on the walkway. He looked pensive. Well, more than usual. He was, Valerie had decided early on in the years he'd worked for her, the most serious twenty-something she'd ever met. It wasn't that he never smiled or was humourless, far from it. But he contemplated every aspect of the job with a level of exactness that often made her feel flaky by comparison. No angle went unexamined. Sometimes it frustrated the hell out of her – sometimes you just needed a snap decision, or a task to be actioned without discussion – but mostly she admired his attention to detail. He didn't miss a trick, which is why she'd wanted him to assist her if she'd got the White House job.

'Mind if I join you?' he asked.

'Of course not.'

Hitching his suit trousers at the knee to sit down, Langdon settled on the bench next to her. He'd cut his hair overnight and now his appearance was even more pristine. She wasn't sure the shorn look suited him; she preferred it longer, with its natural wave.

'What's up?' she asked.

Langdon never usually intruded on her coffee breaks, so Valerie knew something specific had brought him outside. She presumed it was the conversation they needed to have about her not returning to the US.

'Your eleven o'clock has been pushed to twelve, so you've got a free window now to look at the Luxemburg report ahead of the four o'clock video call.'

'Thanks. I'll get on to it when I go back up.'

Langdon wasn't meeting her gaze, Valerie noted. His was focused on the ground between his evenly spaced feet and very pointedly not on her.

'What's wrong, Langdon?'

His eyes remained downcast. 'I have something to show you.'

'Okay.'

Outwardly she projected calm, but inside, her pulse accelerated like an engine revving up a gear. Had someone posted something online about her fleeing Washington before her interview? The last thing she needed was her reputation trashed publicly.

Langdon reached for the inside pocket of his suit jacket to retrieve his phone. Then he opened up the same news app that had triggered her red-eye return.

'It's about this story,' said Langdon stiffly.

She clenched and unclenched her fingers quickly to stop their tell-tale trembling before taking his phone from him. The headline confirmed it wasn't an article about her, but her relief was fleeting when she realised it was a news report about the young woman falling off Southwark Bridge. She stared at Langdon in shock, her chest tightening in panic. She could barely breathe. Of all the news stories out there, why the hell was he bringing this one up with her?

'What's a woman being pushed off a bridge got to do with me?' she asked in a strangled voice.

'Not you as such,' said Langdon tightly. 'Look at the picture the police have released of the suspect. It's towards the bottom of the article.'

Her shock magnified. The police had a picture? She kept scrolling until a grainy CCTV image filled the screen, showing a partial side view of a man in a baseball cap. His features were in shadow, but she could see enough.

'You see it too, don't you? It's the spitting image of Bradley.'

She thrust the phone back at Langdon. Clearly not expecting her to, he fumbled and almost dropped it.

'I don't know what you're getting at,' she lied.

The rev of her pulse sent blood rushing to her ears. The gut instinct that had forced her back from Washington had been right.

But she had to stay calm. A grainy image with a passing similarity to Bradley was no proof of anything.

'I think you do,' said Langdon.

'Are you serious?' she scoffed uneasily. 'It's a CCTV grab of some guy that could be anybody.'

'Except it's not. It's Bradley.' Langdon had lowered his voice, even though they were alone in that stretch of the gardens. 'You can't pretend this time.'

'What do you mean, "pretend"?' she asked, stunned.

'I was there, remember. In Prague.'

Valerie's blood chilled. She'd forgotten that Langdon had joined the US Embassy in the Malá Strana district of Prague a couple of months before her abrupt departure. He'd transferred to London himself about six months later and was appointed her assistant not long after that.

But even though their paths had crossed then, he couldn't possibly have known about what had happened on Charles Bridge. Only her colleague George knew that Bradley had pushed Nadia – and he'd since retired from ill health and passed away. When he died, Valerie had been confident the secret of why she'd suddenly transferred to London had died with him. So how the hell did Langdon know?

Seconds later, the answer slammed through her like a ten-ton truck. How could she have been so stupid as not to foresee this? Langdon knew because he made it his business to know everything. But exactly how much did he know?

Following Bradley's mid-flight confession, Valerie had called George as soon as they'd touched down in London. She'd sought reassurance that they shouldn't return to Prague to set the record straight, and George had agreed.

'There's nothing to be gained by him speaking up now. It's done. The friend's retracted the allegation, so Nadia's parents think she fell of her own volition,' her colleague had replied. 'It's not as though he pushed her with the intention of killing her.'

That closing comment had haunted Valerie ever since, and with good reason it now seemed. Langdon must have discovered that she and George had conspired to get Bradley out of Prague – or, worse still, he somehow knew that Bradley had admitted to pushing Nadia to her death. She didn't dare ask which.

'I don't know what it is you're implying, but this conversation is over,' she snapped at Langdon. 'I – I'm . . . honestly lost for words.'

He looked as though he couldn't have cared less. 'I think you know exactly what I mean,' he said. 'I just want to know what you're going to do about it.'

She stared at him. Was he saying that she should jump to Bradley's defence again? Or did he expect the opposite now, just because of that stupid CCTV image? Valerie bristled. Langdon had no right to dictate any course of action she took regarding her son.

'What I'm going to do is get up from this seat and go back to my office and get on with my work. I suggest you do the same,' she said, as she got to her feet, coffee forgotten, her moment of solitude ruined. Then she stopped. 'You know what, I was going to talk to you later, but this is as good a time as any. Even though I'm staying in my role here, I think it's time for a change,' she said firmly. 'You should start looking for a new position.'

Langdon stared up at her. 'You're firing me?'

'No, of course not,' she backpedalled, realising she could be talking her way into an unfair dismissal lawsuit and an even bigger heap of trouble, given what he knew. 'I want you to get on in your career. You've been a wonderful assistant, the best, but we both know you're capable of much more. I know you would've proved that in Washington, but now I think you deserve a bigger promotion. My friend works at the State Department in DC and he mentioned a researcher's role that I think you should go for.'

The lie scorched her tongue. She had to pray that Glenn would find something suitable for Langdon when she called him to beg for the favour.

'Wow, that would be amazing,' said Langdon, but his words rang hollow.

'I mean it. You're too good to stay as someone's assistant.'

'And in return for the State job you'd presumably like my silence?'

Valerie's body shook with anger. 'There's nothing to be silent about. You've jumped to a conclusion that's entirely wrong,' she said coldly. 'And if I ever hear you repeat it to anyone, the consequences for you will be dire. Yes, I can swing you a job at State, but I can also make sure no one ever hires you again. Don't cross me or my family, Langdon. It won't end well for you.'

His mouth dropped open, and his cool demeanour evaporated. 'You're threatening to ruin my career?'

'No, I'm making it clear that I do not respond well to my family being falsely accused, and I will take a stand against anyone who does that. I don't know what you hoped to achieve coming out here and showing me that picture, but it stops now.' Valerie's tone was tough, but inside she was quaking. If she couldn't scare Langdon into compliance, God knows how he could retaliate. Her voice grew firmer. 'My son's friend died in Prague and he has grieved her loss ever since. It was a tragic accident. Please do not make it into something it wasn't.'

Langdon looked stricken. 'I'm sorry. I shouldn't have said anything.'

'No, you shouldn't.'

Had she been too hard on him, she fretted inwardly as she left Langdon on the bench and hurried towards the embassy building. Had she made a mistake acknowledging Nadia's death like that?

Only time would tell.

# Chapter Fifteen

## EVE

DC Alix Quinn had messaged Eve just as she was going to bed the previous evening asking to meet up first thing. Eve had agreed immediately, keen to hear how the police were handling their main witness talking to the press, and whether Quinn was still a part of the investigation. She'd given nothing away in her text.

With Beverly still on leave, Eve had called Janani at the office to say she'd be late and explained why. Janani understood she was doing it as a favour to their boss and told her to take her time.

Despite a near-zero chill still enveloping the capital, they'd agreed to meet outside, in the grounds of St Paul's Cathedral. The landmark was close to Quinn's workplace and on the way to Eve's. Walking there from her Old Street flat, Eve welcomed the blast of cold – offset by the clearest, brightest blue sky of the year so far – because she'd had another sleepless night worrying about Tooley, and her mind felt fogged by exhaustion. Leah was still working nights, so Eve's ears had been pricked by the tiniest of noises. Now, approaching the side of the cathedral where the detective should be waiting for her, she was wide awake.

Quinn was already there, bundled up in her eye-catching coat and sipping from a bottle of water. She looked tired herself and greeted Eve with a wan smile. 'Want to find somewhere to sit?' she asked.

The blue skies made Eve want to keep moving. 'It's nice out for once. How about we walk across to the Tate and back?'

The world-famous art institution was on the other side of the river and could be accessed via the Millennium Bridge, a couple of minutes from St Paul's.

'Good idea,' said Quinn, screwing the cap back on her bottle and shoving it in her pocket. It wouldn't have fitted in her bag, which was a black money belt that she wore strapped across her chest like a harness.

They set off across the road and down the slope towards the mouth of the bridge. Quinn wasted no time in detailing the fallout from the van driver's decision to spill his guts to a tabloid.

'We can't stop witnesses talking to the press, but it was made clear to him he mustn't jeopardise any future prosecution. He didn't give a shit though – he just saw pound signs. The paper apparently offered him enough to cover a week's all-inclusive in Spain. If he'd been able to give them the dash-cam footage it would've been a fortnight. The cheeky sod got annoyed when we said he couldn't have it back.'

Quinn's tone was light, but Eve could tell she was aggrieved. 'I hope it hasn't come back on you,' she said.

'No, thankfully. And because my DCI has been made SIO, I'm officially on the team. My first murder case.'

'That's great. I'm pleased for you.' But not as pleased as Eve was for herself. Beverly would also be happy to know Eve had established a good contact within the investigation. 'So, why did you want to see me? You know it's unlikely I'll be allocated the case from our end, because of my boss's connection to Becca. I can only listen, I can't advise.'

'I know. I just thought you'd appreciate the update.'

'Why in person though? You could've just called. Not that I mind,' she added. 'Any excuse to delay getting to the office.'

'I thought the CPS allowed working from home now?'

'We can ask for flexible hours, but I prefer to go in. Most of the division is back full-time. It's easier for meetings, and decisions get made quicker.' Eve cocked an eyebrow. 'So? Why in person?'

'I didn't think you should come to the station.'

Eve was pretty sure she knew why but wanted Quinn to say it. 'Why not?'

'Novus.'

She should've guessed.

'What you did to help secure all the convictions was brilliant,' Quinn added, 'but some of my colleagues didn't react well when I mentioned your name yesterday.'

'It was a Met case, though. Nothing to do with City.'

'Doesn't matter. We back our own, whatever the force.'

Eve was annoyed. She hadn't asked to be put on the evidence review for Novus and she'd just been doing her job. It wasn't her fault that one of the officers on the Novus case had lost his job for concealing crucial evidence.

'For what it's worth, I think it was the right outcome,' said Quinn. 'It was a clear abuse of process. He had to go.'

'Thanks.'

They had reached the Millennium Bridge. Eve tried not to think about the height of the drop between the walkway and the water below. If they stuck to the middle, she'd be fine.

'I see the CCTV image is in circulation now,' she said.

'It was a mad scramble to get it done after the van driver jumped the gun, and it's not the best likeness because it's based only on the dash-cam footage. We're still checking for clearer images of the suspect arriving on the bridge. Got nothing so far.'

'Nothing? Does that mean he didn't travel there on foot?'

'It's possible that he used some mode of transport and stopped on the bridge right before attacking Becca.'

'I didn't think vehicles were allowed to pull over on bridges. Isn't there also a cycleway on Southwark Bridge that prevents it?'

The bridge they were on now was pedestrian only. The two of them sidestepped joggers and commuters as they walked across it.

'Yes, but who's going to stop him at four in the morning?'

'Isn't there CCTV of him pulling over?'

'Sore point. There are TfL traffic cameras at either end but not along the bridge itself.'

'Why not?'

'That's a question for the City of London Corporation. It has responsibility for Southwark, London, Tower, Blackfriars and this bridge.' Quinn waved her hand in front of her. 'There's been talk of installing more cameras above and below the bridges, but it hasn't happened yet. Instead there are signs for the Samaritans to dissuade anyone thinking of jumping off.'

'Does that mean the Met has all the other bridges covered?'

Quinn's expression pinched. 'I can't speak for the Met's CCTV network.'

'But it could be relevant, no? That he deliberately picked a bridge where he knew there was less chance of him getting caught on camera?'

Quinn appeared pensive. 'Again, it's possible. At the risk of sounding like a bloody press release, I can confirm we're examining all scenarios. Shall we stop here for a minute?'

They were midway across the bridge. Behind them was the dome of St Paul's. Ahead of them loomed the Tate. To the right, the London Eye was visible past the bend in the river, and to the left was the Shard, soaring into the flawless blue yonder. On a clear day like today, London looked magnificent.

'Can we stand here, though?'

They weren't quite in the middle of the bridge, but nor were they near the side.

'Why?'

'I don't like heights. Being too close to the edge makes me dizzy.'

Quinn nodded. 'I'm the same with spiders. If I see one, I think I'm going to pass out. Right, as I was saying, we're examining all scenarios. We're also looking into Becca's background to see if there are any disgruntled exes or co-workers that we should be paying attention to. I don't suppose your boss has mentioned anyone?' asked Quinn.

'I haven't spoken to her directly since Wednesday. What have Becca's parents said?'

'Nothing much of use. According to the family liaison officer who's in contact with them, they don't know much about her life in London beyond the basics about her job and flat. Put it this way, they couldn't name her closest friends here.'

'If I do speak to Beverly today, I will ask her.'

'Let me know if you do. We need something soon. We're getting monstered online for believing it was suicide at the outset,' said Quinn wearily.

'It comes with the territory,' said Eve. She told Quinn about the Hazel Mackett decision and the TikTok video she'd seen criticising it. 'You can't let it get to you.'

'The critics have a point though. If the van driver hadn't come forward, the case would probably have been passed to the coroner already. We might never have realised that Becca was deliberately pushed.'

Eve's gaze flickered downwards. The Thames was a churning muddy grey, the current fast-flowing. Poor Becca hadn't stood a chance.

'What if she wasn't his first victim?' she mused. 'What if other victims who've drowned off bridges have been incorrectly ruled as suicide or misadventure?'

Quinn groaned. 'Do you know how many bodies are pulled from the Thames between Dartford and Hampton Court each year? Up to forty.'

'I still think it's something your SIO should consider.'

'I thought you weren't here to give advice,' said Quinn wryly.

'I'm not. I'm just raising the possibility of more victims.'

'I know. It's just the thought of it.' The detective sighed and thrust her hands deep into her coat pockets. Then her face creased into a frown.

'Don't make it obvious you're looking, but there's an older guy standing in the middle of the bridge staring at you.'

Eve turned her head a fraction to see. Her stomach lurched. Tooley. She whipped her head back.

'Oh God. I know him. He won't leave me alone.'

'He's stalking you?'

Eve gave Quinn a hurried rundown. She didn't dare look round at Tooley again but she could feel his stare boring into the back of her.

'He must've followed you here,' said Quinn.

Eve's skin crawled at the thought. Tooley tracking her every footstep was bad enough, but given how early the hour was, she had to assume he'd stayed overnight near her flat, rather than travelling down from Northampton in time to intercept her as she left for work.

'Have you reported him?'

'I'm logging every incident but I don't know if I want to take it further. I'm worried it'll aggravate him even more.'

'If you report him and he does kick off, we can arrest him. What the hell—?' Quinn exploded so suddenly that Eve jumped. The detective pelted towards Tooley. 'Why are you taking pictures of us?'

Tooley, who had a professional-looking digital camera on a strap around his neck, appeared unflustered by the confrontation.

'It's a public place. I'm allowed,' he said haughtily.

'But you were taking pictures of us,' said Quinn. Her head jerked towards Eve, who wanted the ground to swallow her up. People walking past were slowing down to see what was going on.

'I was doing no such thing. I was taking photographs of the view.'

'Show me,' Quinn demanded.

'Give you my camera? I don't think so.'

The detective whipped out her warrant card and held it up. 'I'm DC Alix Quinn. Under the Ways and Means Act, I would like you to show me the images you just took.'

Tooley went puce, but he didn't argue. He unhooked the camera from around his neck and handed it over. Eve was desperate to see what was on it but didn't budge from where she stood. She didn't want to be anywhere near him. Instead, she focused on Quinn's face, trying to read her expression as she studied the screen on the back of the camera, her finger clicking methodically to move the digital images along.

Eventually Quinn handed the camera back. 'Delete the ones you took without our permission.'

Tooley did as he was told. Wanting to avoid eye contact, Eve made sure she looked away before he raised his head.

'If you do this again, it will constitute a course of conduct and you'll be investigated for harassment,' said Quinn. 'Understand?'

Eve didn't hear Tooley reply so she imagined he'd nodded to indicate his cooperation. A few moments passed, then Quinn returned to her side.

'It's okay. He's gone,' she said.

'Thank you for getting rid of him,' Eve replied, her voice quavering. 'I've never heard of the Ways and Means Act though. Is it a City of London by-law?'

Quinn grinned. 'No, it's made up. It's very handy to invoke when you need an excuse to tell someone to piss off.'

Eve gasped. 'Won't you get in trouble for that?'

'Only if he bothers to look it up . . . and even if he does it's still his word against mine that I said it.' Quinn's expression hardened. 'You need to escalate this, Eve. That man is bad news. I got him to delete the pictures he took of us, but there are others still on the camera and I couldn't touch them without arresting and cautioning him. But for me to do that, you need to make a complaint first that he's been stalking you. Then we can use the images to prove that he's done it repeatedly.'

'Images of what?'

'You, Eve. Every frame saved on that camera that I looked at was a picture of you.'

Horrified, Eve's legs buckled beneath her and she moved across the walkway to grab the handrail for support, her fear of heights forgotten for a moment. 'Pictures of me doing what?'

'Walking, mostly, plus there were a few of you at bus stops and going in and out of your apartment block and Petty France. Not just in the daytime – some were taken at night. Eve, he's been following you at all hours of the day and you haven't known it.'

# Chapter Sixteen

## GEMMA

Gemma worked six days a week at The Compton, including Saturdays and Sundays. Her day off was always Tuesday, which she usually spent catching up on sleep.

But not this week. Since posting her first video about Becca Farrow's murder, five days earlier, she'd barely been off her phone. She spent every snatched moment she could checking her TikTok. The likes had racked up so quickly she could barely keep track, while her followers were now running into the tens of thousands. To keep the momentum going she'd posted a second video, then a third, fourth and fifth. Last night she'd posted her sixteenth.

Each video stuck to the same theme: if the police weren't so busy trying to protect corrupt officers like DC Zayn Walker, vulnerable women like Becca Farrow would be able to walk the streets without being killed. Gemma had ramped up her criticism throughout, arguing the public should be demanding answers while the police should be giving them. She'd searched online for more stories of sacked officers, like the one who'd tried to conceal evidence from the Novus trial, and spun those into her 'the police are to blame' narrative.

There were some dissenters among those who'd commented on her videos. Gemma had been expecting that. They mostly defended the Met against her claim of neglect, pointing out that it was the City of London Police who were investigating Becca's murder, not them. But to Gemma it made no odds: police were police as far as she was concerned. Plus, it was all the same bit of London, wasn't it?

The more articulate of her critics called Gemma naive and ignorant; claiming she was drawing conclusions when it wasn't that simple. The rest had resorted to vile name-calling and threats of sexual violence. She was undeterred though. She couldn't stop now. For the first time in her life, she was making a genuine difference – and the feeling of accomplishment was addictive. She was no longer 'Gemma Berk', the girl with the weirdo mum and a house full of rubbish that stank like the tip it was ferreted from. She was @Gemz1026, the TikTok advocate for keeping women safe in the face of police corruption. Her East Riding connection to Becca had given her authenticity – in one of her videos, she'd talked about what it was like growing up there and how Becca had followed the dreams of many girls like her to work in London, only to have her life cut brutally short.

Gemma had been careful to avoid discussing the killer directly. Some of the papers had speculated over the weekend that, given the nature of the murder, it might be someone with a history of mental illness. Comparisons were being made to a case involving a serial killer who'd pushed commuters in front of Tube trains because the voices in his head had told him to. Gemma didn't want to get into a debate about the impact of poor mental health – it felt too close to home, because of her mum.

When she'd got up an hour ago, Gemma had found three new bin bags blocking the hallway. Now, standing in the kitchen, she realised her preoccupation with her TikTok content since Thursday had given her mum free rein to 'stock up' over the weekend. Besides the bin bags – two contained old clothes, the third mismatched shoes in sizes too big or too small for them both – the mess that covered the worktops had been added to with three wooden chopping boards. They had clearly been thrown out by previous owners, their surfaces stained and scored from meals eaten long ago.

Gemma, hungry for breakfast, reached for the boards to move them out of the way of the toaster.

'Don't touch them!'

She turned to find her mum in the kitchen doorway, dressed for a change – in jeans that looked like they were cut for a man's physique and an off-white sweatshirt with the slogan 'Happy Daze' printed across it in silver foil. She'd even brushed her hair, the ends looking less wispy than usual.

'They need to stay there,' her mum screeched. 'Leave them be.'

Gemma withdrew her hand from the chopping boards. She didn't have the energy to argue. Instead, she filled and flicked on the kettle. Breakfast would have to be a cup of tea.

She opened the cupboard where the mugs were kept. Behind her she could sense her mum tracking her movements.

The mugs were missing. In their place, packed to the gills, were tatty paperbacks, magazines, and packets of greeting cards.

'Where are the mugs, Mum?'

'Upstairs.'

'In your room?'

Her mum nodded. Without another word, Gemma brushed past her. Plaintive cries of 'Don't touch anything' and 'You mustn't move them' followed her all the way upstairs.

In the years since her dad had walked out, Gemma had taught herself to deploy tunnel vision as a coping mechanism, so that when she entered her mum's bedroom she could easily ignore the belongings that were once his, and the mess that had exploded around them. She went straight to the wardrobe, where eleven mugs of differing patterns and sizes were lined up on its base. It was where they'd been the last time they disappeared from the kitchen. Gemma took a chipped and stained one from the bottom of the pile, then left the rest where they were. Best to move them one at a time over the next week or so, to lessen her mum's reaction.

Turning to leave, her gaze landed on her mum's bed. The duvet had been smoothed flat and on top of it was an opened brown envelope and letter. Aware that brown envelopes rarely brought good news to the door, Gemma picked up the letter. It was addressed to her mum, and it was from the council. Another complaint had been made to Environmental Health about the state of the house. That wasn't anything new, they'd had visits from environmental health officers before, but the rest of the letter made Gemma's insides flip. The council wanted to appoint an adult care social worker to assess her mum's needs and put a plan in place to help her. If she failed to cooperate, they could carry out a forcible house clearance. Phrases jumped out as Gemma continued to read. Multi-agency protocol. Safeguarding. Self-neglect. Fire hazard. Fire service inspection. Court action.

This was bad, really bad. They'd had warnings before but none as explicit as this. Gemma hurried downstairs. Her mum was in the kitchen still, standing close to the chopping boards as though she was guarding them. Which Gemma knew she was.

'Mum, why didn't you show me this?' she asked, holding up the letter.

'That's mine. You shouldn't have taken it.'

Her mum made a grab for it but Gemma flicked her wrist to put it out of reach.

'Give it back,' her mum shrieked. She began to cry and her chest started to heave, the sign that she was on the cusp of a meltdown. They couldn't afford any more complaints from the neighbours so Gemma handed her the letter, kicking herself for not taking a photo of it on her phone first. Going on past form, her mum would hide it now and Gemma might never find it again.

'I'm sorry, Mum. I shouldn't have touched it. But I did read it and it's serious. We can't ignore it.'

Her mum's expression shuttered. She clutched the letter to her chest. 'They want to take my things.'

'No, they don't,' Gemma lied. 'They just want to help us tidy up a bit. Maybe they'll give us more cupboards, or shelves to put things on.'

Her mum's eyes lit up. 'We could buy our own. Then they wouldn't have to come.'

'We don't have the money to buy new furniture, Mum.'

'What about your wages?'

'They go on the bills. There's nothing left after that.'

Her mum pouted. 'Can't you do more shifts?'

'I'm already working six days a week.'

'But I need my things.'

Frustration clawed at Gemma. It was like trying to negotiate with a small child. 'Mum, I can't work every single day without a break. I'm doing my best to support us both but I can't do any more than I already am.'

Her mum acted like she hadn't heard her. 'We could put the new shelves over there,' she said brightly. The wall space she was pointing to was in fact the back door, which led out to an overgrown garden cluttered with Gemma's old bikes, a toddler's plastic swing and slide set bleached pale by the sun, various bits of garden furniture, ornaments, tools – all broken – and three lawnmowers whose blades had rusted up.

Gemma turned on her heel and left the room. She couldn't take any more. She was tired of having to be the grown-up. She wanted to bawl and scream and pound her pillow with her fists. She wanted someone to look after her for a change.

But back in her bedroom, door locked behind her, she got straight on her phone instead. If she gave in to her emotions and allowed herself to cry, she'd never stop. Better to lose herself online and let the dopamine hit lift her out of her despair.

It worked, too. The jump in likes and new followers just while she'd been downstairs sent a ripple of pleasure through her. She was starting to get DMs too, from followers telling her to keep up the good work.

She was halfway through checking her messages when she stopped. A user called @ConcernedCitizen911 had sent her a message.

> *I know who killed Becca Farrow and he's going to get away with it because his mother works for the US government. If you expose him, the authorities will have to act.*

Gemma frowned. It wasn't the first message she'd received from someone claiming they knew who the killer was. But there was something about this one that didn't smack of the usual tinfoil-hat brigade.

There was a link with the message. She clicked on it and it took her to the Instagram profile of someone called Bradley Aspen. His account wasn't locked, and when she looked through his grid, she saw he was a young man a few years older than her, with dark curly hair and a wide smile.

With a start, she realised that Bradley Aspen closely matched the image the police had released of their suspect. The set of his eyes, the shape of his jaw, the way his hair curled below his ears – it could be the same man.

Heart thumping, she returned to the TikTok app. She needed more info. Her reply to @ConcernedCitizen911 was blunt.

*How do you know he's the killer?*

To her delight, @ConcernedCitizen911 was online and messaged her back instantly.

*Because he's done it before. He got away with it then because of who his mom is.*

*Who is she*, Gemma messaged back.

This time the link @ConcernedCitizen911 sent was for a website profile of a woman called Valerie Aspen. It said she worked at the US Embassy in London and lived in Putney with her husband, Mark, and their son, Bradley. *It must be the same Bradley*, Gemma thought. Before she could think of a reply, @ ConcernedCitizen911 messaged again.

*She's a diplomat, which means she has immunity from prosecution – and so does her son. The police know he's killed before Becca but can't touch him.*

Gemma scoffed. Now she knew this was a wind-up. If the police suspected Bradley Aspen had killed Becca, he'd have been arrested. She was typing that out when @ConcernedCitizen911 sent another DM.

*Watch this if you don't believe me.*

This time it was a video link. It took Gemma a second to work out what was going on. The opening shot was of people dressed in black slowly walking into a church, then the video jumped to inside the church, focusing on the coffin at the altar. It was covered in flowers, and next to it, on a stand, was a large picture of a teenage girl. She was beautiful, with long dark hair. Then someone off camera spoke but Gemma didn't recognise the language.

@ConcernedCitizen911 messaged again.

> *Her name was Nadia Vinke. She was a Dutch student living in Prague and she died when Bradley Aspen pushed her off Charles Bridge in the city centre. His mom worked at the US Embassy and they covered it up to save his skin.*

Another link arrived. A newspaper article about a girl named Leeza van der Kleji. The headline said: *Second Tragic Death in Nadia Vinke Case.*

> *Leeza was Nadia's best friend. She was the one who saw Bradley push Nadia. Two days after the Aspens fled to London, Leeza was killed in a hit-and-run. They never caught the driver.*

Gemma was stunned. She couldn't believe what had just landed in her lap. Breathless with excitement, she sent a reply to @ ConcernedCitizen911.

> *I can't believe he's done it before and got away with it. That's so wrong.*

@ConcernedCitizen911 replied.

> *It really is. This is why I contacted you. You can share the links with your followers and out him as the killer he is.*

Gemma frowned. She frantically typed out a response.

*But I could get into trouble putting his name online. Why don't you post it?*

She held her breath as she waited for the next message.

*It's too risky for me but I promise there will be no comeback on you. The police will thank you for doing them a favour because him being exposed publicly should force the US authorities to lift his immunity so he can be arrested and charged. Valerie won't dare sue you because she won't want to answer questions about her killer son in court. If you do this, you'll be a hero. You'll be exposing poor Becca's killer and getting justice for her.*

Gemma still wasn't convinced.

*What if I say no?*

Another pause.

*I guess I'll have to send it to one of the other TikTokers who've been copying your videos. You started the fight for justice for Becca, but you're not the only one keeping it going. Bradley Aspen needs to be exposed one way or another. His mom knows what he did and she's using her diplomatic immunity to protect him. That makes her as bad as him. If you won't post it, I'll find someone who will.*

It took Gemma less than a second to decide. They were right – she'd started this, so she should be the one to expose Becca's killer. Plus, she might even make some money off the back of it. Enough to sort out the house for her mum and find a place of her own. She could even move to London to start a new life.

> *I'll do it. I'll record a new video and I'll run the footage and link with it.*

@ConcernedCitizen911 responded with a line of hand-clapping emojis.

> *YES! You superstar. But you need to do it now, because VA could be planning to get Bradley out of the country again, like she did from Prague. Once he's no longer in London, it'll be even harder for the police to prosecute. They both need to be stopped.*

Resolute, Gemma messaged back saying she would do it immediately and would post the video within half an hour. When she read @ConcernedCitizen911's final reply, she became even more excited. If they were right, no one would ever take the mick out of or bully Gemma again. She'd be famous.

> *You won't regret this. Becca's family will thank you and the whole world will think you're amazing for exposing her killer. Bradley Aspen has got away with murder once already – but you're going to be the person who makes sure he doesn't again.*

# PART II

## FIVE WEEKS LATER

# Chapter Seventeen

## EVE

The President was in the White House Rose Garden waiting to start a press conference with the Australian Prime Minister after the most recent round of trade talks. The two men looked ill at ease in one another's company, like both would rather be anywhere else but there.

As though trying to cover up the awkwardness, the President began throwing comments to reporters before the event started, as per his brand of soundbite politics. That was when a Sky News reporter shouted across the lawn, 'When are you going to lift Bradley Aspen's immunity?' and the President reacted like they'd lobbed a grenade at him.

'The kid said he didn't do it, and he's got a rock-solid alibi,' he shot back angrily. 'It sickens me that you'd even ask. Bradley is a proud US citizen who's been wrongly accused, so I'm gonna do all I can to protect him – and that means not lifting his immunity just because you think I should. Sure I feel sorry for that girl's family, but we're not going to throw one of our sons to the wolves just because the fake-news media says we should. He didn't do it, fair and square.'

The reporter wasn't done, though. 'What about the reports of his involvement in another girl's death in Prague?'

'Sounds made-up to me.'

Another reporter jumped in. 'Aaron Peters, CNN. Given how controversial Bradley's presence is in the UK, should the Aspen family return to the States?'

The President grew even more incensed, his face purpling as he stared down his interrogators. 'Why the hell should they? Valerie Aspen is doing a terrific job for our great nation at the US Embassy in London and I want her to continue. Nothing controversial about it. Go write some real news.'

Standing in the restroom at Petty France, Eve replayed the news clip on her phone. The President had his own dubious track record with multiple allegations of improper behaviour towards women and clearly felt he'd found a kindred spirit in Bradley Aspen. Despairing, she put her phone down on the sink unit. The cumulative effects of weeks without enough sleep stared back at her in the mirror above it. Her hair was lank, and dark half-moons underlined her eyes. She gingerly applied some more concealer to the delicate skin, blending it in with her fingertip, but it still couldn't disguise the bags. What she really needed was one unbroken night. No nightmares jolting her awake. No churning thoughts keeping her from nodding off again.

Sighing, she screwed the lid back on the concealer tube and dropped it into her handbag. Then she raked her fingers through her lacklustre hair and secured it in a scruffy bun. It would have to do.

The door to the restroom swung open and Janani walked in. She didn't head for a cubicle but, like Eve, dumped her handbag on the shelf above the sinks. She smiled at Eve's reflection.

'You off out?' Janani asked.

'Just meeting friends. You?'

'Same. It's someone's birthday so I need to show willing. Frankly I could do with going straight home.' She eyed Eve in the mirror. 'I bet you could do with a quiet night in too. How are you doing?'

Eve had been hoping Janani wouldn't ask her that. To her embarrassment, her eyes filled with tears. She tried to bat them away, waving her hand in front of her face. 'Take no notice of me. I'm fine,' she said.

'You don't have to pretend, Eve. Hang on, let me get you a tissue.'

Janani dived into one of the cubicles and yanked a few squares of toilet paper from the dispenser. She came out and handed them to Eve.

'I don't know what's wrong with me,' said Eve, dabbing her eyes and trying to make light of it. 'The stupidest things seem to set me off.'

'It's hardly surprising you're tired and emotional. You've had half the bloody world on your back these past few weeks. I mean, I've worked on some big cases in my time, but I've never had the President of the United States personally intervene on one,' said Janani, pulling a face.

'But it's not my case and never was,' Eve protested. 'People just assume it is because of that bloody photo.'

It was Frank Tooley's fault she'd been dragged into the public furore that now engulfed the Becca Farrow murder investigation. Despite Quinn confronting him on the Millennium Bridge that morning, he hadn't deleted all the images he'd taken. When the TikTok video naming Bradley Aspen as Becca's killer had gone viral, Tooley had shared one on his X account, with the following caption:

> *@FranklyTrueCrime SPOTTED! #Novus trial hero Eve Wren in secret meeting with #BeccaFarrow murder cop Alix Quinn on Millennium Bridge. Eve's the #CPS star lawyer who can put #BradleyAspen behind bars! #JusticeforBecca #TheSeven*

Tooley couldn't have been more wrong. Once Bradley Aspen's name had begun circulating online, the media made the collective decision to publish it too, citing public interest. However, that had triggered Aspen to issue a strong-worded statement through lawyers denying he had played any part in Becca's death. He said he had an alibi for the night in question, although he'd declined to give more details. His statement also addressed the death of Nadia Vinke in Prague that the TikTok video had linked him to, saying the Czech police had investigated the incident and concluded it was a tragic accident. Any attempt to blame him for either death was despicable and defamatory. The statement had reiterated that he had familial diplomatic immunity and was therefore not obliged to participate in any police investigation. It ended with him asking for people to respect his privacy as an innocent man.

That final comment had caused uproar. In the weeks that followed, the British media and public had clamoured for the US government to lift Aspen's immunity so he could be questioned by the police and have his alibi double-checked. If he was as innocent as he said he was, why not prove it? But the US government had repeatedly refused, citing the Vienna Convention rules for diplomacy.

Meanwhile, thanks to Tooley's photo, Eve had been viciously hounded online for letting Aspen get away with murder. The attention had been unbearable. She'd had reporters coming to the flat, trailing her to work, and even doorstepping her parents at their home in the Midlands. The only saving grace was that Tooley appeared to have been scared off by the attention. She hadn't seen him since Quinn had confronted him on the bridge and his messages had dried up. But she couldn't shake off the feeling that he was still watching her, lurking in doorways as she passed by, or standing outside her home as she came and went. Her inability to sleep was as much to do with her fear of him as it was the stress of being publicly slaughtered over Bradley Aspen.

Janani tried to reassure her. 'People will get bored and move on to something else now the AG's made a statement.'

The President's Rose Garden outburst did seem to have signalled the end of the matter regarding lifting Bradley Aspen's familial diplomatic immunity. Shortly after his comments aired yesterday, the Attorney General, the UK government's most senior legal advisor, had confirmed in a statement that the President's decision must be respected under the Vienna Convention. The AG made particular reference to the fact there was no physical or circumstantial evidence linking Aspen to the scene of Becca Farrow's death, and that a person could not be prosecuted on the basis of unfounded online accusations.

Janani pointed at Eve's face. 'Your mascara's smudged.'

This time Eve went into the cubicle for toilet paper to wipe her face. As she did, the door to the restroom swung open, bringing a wave of chatter with it.

'She can deny it all she wants, but she's loving the attention,' Ashley could be heard saying. 'First she's hobnobbing with film stars like Madeleine Farmer, now it's the White House—'

A distinct 'sssh' interrupted Ashley's flow. Eve imagined Janani pointing to the cubicle to alert Ashley to her presence.

She wiped beneath her eyes and deposited the paper into the toilet bowl. Then she squared her shoulders and returned to the sink to reapply her make-up. Ashley, who was with her sidekick Sarah, watched her keenly.

'Have you been crying?' she asked.

'No. I'm just tired,' said Eve levelly. 'I've not been sleeping great.'

'You should ask your BFF Madeleine for some sleeping pills. I'm sure she's got a stash to hand . . . Just remember not to take too many at once.'

Even Sarah appeared shocked by the spitefulness of Ashley's comment. Madeleine Farmer had almost died when she'd accidentally overdosed on pain medication during the Novus trial. It was no joking matter.

'Ashley, there's really no need to be so nasty,' Janani admonished her. 'Eve's been through a lot these past few weeks.'

'She brought it on herself when she stuck her nose into an investigation that was nothing to do with her,' Ashley shot back.

That was it. Eve had had enough. She rounded on her colleague.

'None of this is my doing and you know it. I didn't ask to be dragged into the Becca Farrow case. Beverly asked me to talk to the investigating officer as a favour. I didn't volunteer. The video on TikTok that named Bradley Aspen had absolutely nothing to do with me. All the diplomatic immunity stuff that's gone on since has been handled by the international team, not ours. I didn't ask to have my photo taken with DC Quinn and I certainly didn't ask for it to be leaked. Instead, I've had my name and picture plastered all over social media like I'm somehow personally responsible for Bradley Aspen being untouchable. Just because I worked on Novus and just because Madeleine Farmer mentioned my name in a bloody newspaper interview.'

Eve didn't give Ashley a chance to argue back. Cheeks flaming, she gathered up her belongings and stormed out of the restroom. Rather than take the lift down to the exit, she headed to the stairwell, the stomp of her boots against the concrete steps giving her a satisfying outlet for her rage. She was tired of Ashley's snide insinuations that she'd purposely inveigled herself into the case for the plaudits.

But what Ashley and the others didn't know was that she was, despite the backlash, very much involved now. The President's comments and the AG's statement hadn't signalled the end of the matter for Eve or the people she was meeting this evening. They weren't friends like she'd told Janani, but a group of individuals who had secretly been given the same task as her by the Attorney General: find a loophole to bring Bradley Aspen to justice and find it fast.

# Chapter Eighteen

## GEMMA

The guest hadn't even tried to hide the bright-orange curry stain they'd smeared on the bottom sheet. Instead, they'd flung back the top covers so that the mess was on full display, while the empty takeaway cartons had been discarded on the floor. Nose wrinkling at the smell, Gemma bundled up the sheets and stuffed them into the plastic laundry bag, which then she double-knotted and left in the corridor outside the room. The stain had seeped through to the mattress; as she remade the bed with fresh linen, deftly tucking in the corners, she wondered if the next guest would notice the smell of bleach.

Guests behaved like pigs in hotels because they knew they didn't have to clean up after themselves. Like it was their right to soil and stain with no consequence. Gemma knew that some of the bigger hotels on the seafront levied a fee for deep cleaning in extreme cases – usually out-of-control stag parties – but The Compton wouldn't dream of imposing one in case it put guests off staying there.

Right now, however, the hotel was busier than it usually would be for early April. Every room had been occupied over the weekend just gone, and they were at eighty per cent capacity midweek as well, which was unheard of.

The Compton's uptick in business was down to her. Gemma, to her astonishment, was Bridlington's newest visitor attraction: the TikToker who'd outed a killer online. It didn't seem to bother people that Bradley Aspen had denied murdering Becca Farrow or that Gemma was being accused in some quarters of making it up. There were plenty of true-crime fans still keen to spot the teenager at the centre of a scandal so big that even the President of the United States was talking about it, and the media mentions of The Compton had made it the best-known hotel in East Riding. Since being unmasked as @Gemz1026, she'd been getting plenty of media attention too, with one tabloid nicknaming her the Undercovers Agent, which was supposedly a pun on her chambermaid job.

She finished up the room and returned her cleaning products to her cart, which was parked in the open doorway. The laundry man would be round in a bit to collect the bags of dirty sheets she'd left outside every room that she'd cleaned. This room was the last of the day – now she could clock off and go home. She was bone-tired from having to work twice as hard with so many extra guests, and all she wanted to do was post another video then crawl into bed.

Still, at least she was being paid more for her efforts. The Compton's owners had been thrilled to learn of Gemma's involvement in the biggest news story of the year so far, and had sent word from their sun loungers in Tenerife that they were upping her wages to make sure she didn't leave. The whopping fifty per cent increase had been a shock and a godsend: she needed all the money she could get her hands on right now to fight the council in case it escalated its battle to put a stop to Mel's hoarding with an enforced house clearance. It would kill her mum if they did that, and Gemma needed to pay a solicitor to represent them if it came to it.

After returning her cart to the staff quarters, she fetched her coat and bag and made her way along the corridor to the hotel's rear exit, hoping to slip off home without any fanfare. She needed to upload another video as soon as she got in to keep up the momentum. She wasn't the only TikToker calling for justice for Becca now, but as the OG she had the most followers, the most likes. She was desperate to make sure it stayed that way. She also had a growing band of regular followers urging her for more updates.

One in particular – a lad from Birmingham who was nineteen like her and went by the nickname Sponge – had messaged her so frequently that they'd become friends. He nursed a particular hatred for Valerie Aspen for letting her son hide behind her immunity, and they'd spent hours trading messages that ripped her character to pieces.

Reece apparently had other ideas about Gemma going home though, materialising at the other end of the corridor just as she was about to leave.

'Oh no you don't,' he called out. 'I've got some stuff for you to sign.'

'It's gone seven. I'm done for the day.'

'I know you are, sweetie. It won't take long, I promise.'

For reasons she didn't understand, Reece now adopted a sickly-sweet voice whenever he addressed her. Gemma wished he'd stop it. She missed how it was between them before all her TikTok stuff had blown up. They'd banter and have a laugh. Work used to be fun.

'What is it this time?' she asked, as she trudged back along the corridor and trailed him into the small space behind the reception desk.

'New delivery of T-shirts. I think these are the best ones so far.'

They couldn't be any worse than the others, Gemma thought sourly. The first batch had had her photo printed on them with the slogan 'TikTok's No 1 Sleuth', overlaid by a smaller stamp that said 'Made in Bridlington'. Gemma had refused to wear it, but that hadn't deterred Reece from selling them to guests. The second batch wasn't much better: a picture of The Compton, with the same slogan and stamp. This latest delivery, which Reece was unpacking from a large brown box, surpassed them both though. Each T-shirt bore a picture of Becca Farrow cribbed from the internet, with the slogan 'Justice for Becca from Brid' printed beneath it. Looking pleased with himself, Reece flipped one round to show her the message printed on the back: 'The Compton Cares'.

Gemma cringed. 'She wasn't from Brid.'

'Near enough,' trilled Reece. 'Can you sign them?'

'Won't that look daft?' she said. 'I think you'll sell far more if they haven't been scribbled on.'

Reece held the T-shirt up at arm's length and stared at it, head tilted, like he was appraising a work of art. 'I suppose you're right.'

As Becca's smiling face stared back at them, Gemma had an idea. 'Actually, can I take one? I'm shooting another video tonight and I could wear it.'

Reece was thrilled. 'Make sure you put in the comments that they're available from reception here.'

'I will,' she said, taking the top from him. The size was a large, too big for her slight frame, but if she angled her camera right she might be able to keep 'from Brid' out of the frame.

Gemma took her time as she walked home along the seafront. She wanted to script her next video in her head so she'd be word-perfect by the time it came to record. With so many others making videos about Becca and Bradley Aspen now, she could no long risk doing hers on the hoof. Hers had to be better than everyone else's.

Approaching the house, she continued to mutter to herself and didn't notice at first the people sitting on the front wall. Once glance told her they weren't welcome visitors.

For the first couple of weeks after she'd posted Bradley's name and picture along with the footage from Nadia's funeral, Gemma had got used to coming home to find a pack of reporters after an interview. They all wanted to know who had told her about Bradley and sent her the video, but she'd just ignored their questions. She had no idea who @ConcernedCitizen911 was – they hadn't responded to any of her messages since that first exchange. Initially she had been keen to get their reaction to the way the story had exploded in the media, hoping they'd be pleased. Then she'd sought reassurance because people were telling her Bradley might sue for defamation. But no matter how many messages Gemma sent, @ConcernedCitizen911 ignored them all.

Kira Maybank hopped down from the wall. Her gang of acolytes had reduced to a handful since the last time their paths had crossed, but Gemma still felt intimidated by the sight of them.

'There you are,' said Kira. 'We've been waiting for you to get home.'

Gemma frowned. Kira actually sounded friendly for once.

'I've been working.'

'I thought you might have given it up, now you're famous.'

Again, Kira didn't sound like her usual nasty self. Gemma was unnerved. If Kira was being nice, there was bound to be an ulterior motive.

'We wondered if you fancied coming for a drink?'

'With you lot?' Gemma spluttered.

'Don't be like that. I know I gave you a hard time at school but I'm genuinely made up for you now. We all know what a shithole Bridlington is, but you've made it famous in a good way.'

Gemma couldn't have been more shocked than if Kira had just punched her in the face. That she would've expected.

'So, fancy it? We're going to Palmer's,' said Kira, referencing a bar in town.

Gemma stared back at the lass who'd made her life a misery for so long. Instinct told her to run a mile, but a tiny part of her was thrilled that Kira wanted to include her. For so long she'd just wanted acceptance. But she couldn't trust Kira. Not after everything she'd done to her.

'I can't go out tonight. I've got stuff to do.'

Kira's gaze swivelled to the front of the house. Gemma squirmed as she took in the peeling and flaked paintwork on the front door and the yellowing net curtains hanging in the front room window. The small patch of garden next to the drive was as overgrown as the back one.

'It must be hard, having to live with someone who struggles like your mum does. I shouldn't have been such a cow about it at school,' said Kira.

Gemma still didn't trust a word she was saying. 'Why are you being nice to me now? Last time I saw you, you threatened to punch my lights out.'

On hearing that, two of the lads peeled away from the wall. Kira held her hand out to them, like an owner getting their dog to sit. The boys backed off obediently.

'Like I said, you've done a good thing for Brid and my mum reckons you deserve a break. They were best mates once; did you know that? My mum and yours. Me and you used to play together all the time when they worked at the Co-op.'

One of the lads sniggered. Kira silenced him with a look.

Gemma's suspicion deepened. She'd been a pre-schooler when her mum had worked at the Co-op and she didn't remember knowing Kira back then. Her mum would surely have mentioned knowing Kira's mum when she was called into school to discuss Gemma's truanting and Kira's bullying had come to light.

'What stopped them being mates?' she asked.

Kira shrugged. 'Nowt. They just drifted apart after your dad did a bunk. Mum says they always stop for a chat if they see each other in town.'

That bit might have been true, but Gemma still wasn't buying the act. Any moment now Kira would drop the pretence. She curled her fists against her thighs, ready to retaliate for the blow she was sure would come.

'Anyhow, Mum reckons you and me should be friends again like when we were little,' Kira added. 'They always know best, our mums. Mine's always got my back.'

The comment made Gemma snap to. 'What did you just say?'

'That my mum always knows best. She's got my back.'

Gemma's mind sharpened. Kira had given her an idea. Forget the script she'd been practising – she'd just thought of a much better topic for her next video. She inched towards the front gate, long broken away from its hinges, anxious to get indoors to start recording.

'I've got to go,' she said.

'What about drinks on Friday instead?' asked Kira. 'We can fetch you at The Compton. You get off at seven, right?'

Gemma nodded in a non-committal way. She'd rather choke than go for a drink with them. Kira was bad news, and the idea that she'd ever be pleased for Gemma was laughable.

'See you then,' said Kira, grinning.

With that, she and her entourage brushed past Gemma, heading in the direction of town. Gemma shot inside the house and went straight to her room. Instead of doing a general update on Bradley Aspen, she was going to make a video about Valerie Aspen's failings as his mother. What Kira had said about her mum having her back had really struck a chord. By letting him hide behind her immunity, Valerie was now actively covering up her son's crimes. So far, Gemma's videos had focused on the authorities not doing enough to bring Bradley Aspen to justice – now it was his mum's turn to take the blame.

# Chapter Nineteen

## EVE

Despite having lived in London for three years, this was Eve's first time visiting the area the taxi had dropped her off in. The route from Petty France had taken them alongside Battersea Park, through Fulham's nappy valley and then across Putney Bridge, before stopping in Barnes at Beverly's house. Now, listening to the facts of the case being recounted by the person who'd called the meeting to order, Eve wished she'd paid more attention to the bridge when they'd crossed it.

The third known victim's name was Aldana Porras. She'd moved to the UK from Argentina after earning childcare qualifications at college, finding employment with a family in Putney who had three children between the ages of two and nine. The children had adored her from day one, the parents even more so. They'd never had a live-in nanny who'd worked as hard, who so graciously took on every additional or last-minute duty with a smile, who was an unintrusive joy to have in their home.

Seven months ago, on a late September evening balmy enough to be mistaken for summer still, Aldana had gone to visit a friend in Willesden. She didn't have a curfew, but her employers did expect her to be ready to start work at 7 a.m. when the children got up. When morning came round and Aldana still hadn't emerged from her room, the mother went to check and discovered her bed hadn't been slept in.

The family was immediately worried. It was out of character for Aldana to stay out all night. She didn't touch alcohol, so she wasn't the kind to go out partying and not come home. She was also so diligent that if she'd had a problem getting home and needed to stay over at her friend's, she would've let them know.

It wasn't until noon that the family received the terrible news that Aldana had been pulled from the Thames close to Putney Bridge at around one thirty in the morning. The skipper of a multi-cat workboat heading upriver to Purfleet had seen her enter the water. He and his crew had managed to fish her out before the current took her. Unconscious, she had been rushed to the Chelsea and Westminster Hospital across the river, where doctors had decided to put her into an induced coma so she could be monitored for signs of secondary drowning.

Met Police officers stationed at Putney were tasked with investigating the incident. They had two possible theories: Aldana had accidentally fallen from the bridge, or she'd jumped on purpose. Her employers had been devastated by the latter suggestion. To them, Aldana had always seemed mentally robust and happy with her life. Yet her falling in by accident made no sense either.

It was two weeks before Aldana had emerged from the coma to set the record straight. She had not jumped or fallen in error. She had been pushed.

Her account of what had happened began with her having missed the last Tube home because she'd lost track of time catching up with her friend. Anxious to get back to see to the children in the morning, she'd caught various night buses across west London until she reached Fulham Palace Road. From there, rather than catch another bus, she'd decided to walk the last leg across Putney Bridge because it was such a nice night.

She'd been three-quarters of the way across when someone had attacked her from behind. She hadn't heard anyone approaching. She'd tried desperately to fight off her assailant but he was too strong. She had, however, seen his face briefly, half-hidden beneath a peaked cap, in the seconds before he'd heaved her over the side and into the river below.

The glimpse was, by Aldana's own admission, fleeting. But on seeing the captured CCTV image of the man who'd pushed Becca Farrow from Southwark Bridge, she was certain he was the same person who'd attacked her. She then identified the man as being Bradley Aspen after he had been publicly outed in connection with Becca's murder.

'Aldana is certain it's Aspen, because she knows him,' DCI Vince Carroll finished. 'The house where she nannies is six doors down from where his family live. They've passed each other in the street numerous times and also attended a couple of neighbourhood events.'

The stunned silence that fell across the room was broken by Beverly's dog, a short-haired Yorkie, running to the bifold doors to yap furiously at a pigeon that had landed on the patio outside.

As meeting places went, her boss's dining room was a new one for Eve. But this wasn't your typical meeting. Those gathered were the recently appointed members of a secret taskforce set up between the CPS and police, to try to build a case against Bradley Aspen. As far as the rest of the world was concerned, Aspen was untouchable under the rules of the Vienna Convention. His diplomatic immunity could only be lifted by US government decree – and the President's public show of support for him and his mother, Valerie, after they'd denied his involvement had made it clear that would never be given.

It was Beverly who'd persuaded Sol, the DPP, that they shouldn't give up. She'd suggested that he lobby the Attorney General to put together a select group of advocates and detectives to work together to identify any evidence that could be used to get Aspen's immunity lifted. If he had murdered Becca and Nadia Vinke in Prague and got away with both, what was to stop him killing again? The CPS was still being derided for not charging DC Zayn Walker in the Hazel Mackett case; it would not live down Aspen committing further crimes right under its nose.

Beverly's stark warning had convinced the DPP that the taskforce was worth a punt. If they could link Aspen to further murders – or attempted murders like Aldana's – the US government would have to capitulate on his immunity. It could not and should not protect a US citizen suspected of multiple killings from prosecution. The optics would make a mockery of America's standing as a nation that fought for justice, and the sitting President did hate to be mocked.

Sol had selected Paul Ferdie, Chief Crown Prosecutor and Head of International Justice, to co-chair the taskforce, while the City of Police commissioner put forward DCI Carroll from its Major and Complex Crimes Division. Carroll was Quinn's boss and he'd insisted she be on the taskforce because she'd worked Becca's case since the start. Sitting next to Quinn at Beverly's dining table was a detective sergeant named Anthony Cato, the third and final representative for City police.

Across the table from them were Eve, Paul Ferdie and John Horner. Eve had been shocked that the DPP wanted her on the taskforce, given how much negative attention she'd received after Tooley had posted the picture of her and Quinn.

'That's exactly why you need to be involved, Eve,' Sol had told her over the phone. 'You're getting a kicking for something that's not your fault. Just think how satisfying it will be to be part of the team that does bring Aspen to justice. But if we don't manage it, the public will be none the wiser that we even tried.'

The taskforce, he'd assured her, had been sanctioned for operation by the Attorney General. However, for the sake of good relations with the US, she would deny any knowledge should its existence be exposed. Eve still hadn't been convinced she should say yes, until Sol revealed Horner would be on the taskforce too.

'You two did a brilliant job on Novus. I want you together on this,' he'd said.

Knowing Horner was involved had tipped Eve into agreeing. Together with Ferdie, their job would be to stress-test any evidence that the detective trio dug up against Aspen. Their case needed to be undeniable to sway the US government. It was a mammoth task for such a small group and they'd been warned to expect to be in it for the long haul. The group would continue their day jobs alongside it and would meet regularly in secret to discuss developments.

Sol had also told Eve it was the first time such a taskforce had been set up. In previous cases where the UK government had challenged a foreign citizen's diplomatic immunity on its soil, there had been concrete evidence and even admissions of guilt that made pushing for a waiver straightforward. The circumstantial evidence and the President's intervention had made Bradley Aspen a political hot potato that no one could touch – except them.

# Chapter Twenty

## EVE

Beverly was only a spectator tonight. Sol had decided that, as Becca's godmother, she was too close to the case to be an objective participant, but she'd circumvented that by offering her home as a meeting venue. The taskforce needed privacy that it wouldn't get at Petty France or Bishopsgate. Sequestered inside her lovely cottage in Barnes, they could talk freely. She'd also laid on pizza, presuming everyone would be hungry as they'd all come straight from work.

'Aldana's positive ID is a great start,' said Paul Ferdie. 'But what about DNA from the scene?'

The taskforce already knew that Forensics had successfully retrieved DNA from the balustrade Becca Farrow had been pushed over and also from her clothing. Even though she'd been submerged before her body was pulled from the river, epithelial DNA – such as skin tissue from contact – could still survive in water for up to a week, and perhaps longer in winter conditions.

But even though they had a clear sample, it couldn't be tested against Bradley Aspen's DNA because, legally, they couldn't force him to provide a sample. If the DNA from Aldana's clothing matched that taken from Becca's, it would confirm they were looking for the same attacker, but wouldn't allow them to definitively identify Aspen as being that person.

'We're still waiting for the Met to update us on any DNA,' said Carroll. 'We've also been on to the Czech authorities to see if any DNA was taken from the scene of Nadia Vinke's fall. It's a long shot though, given it was treated as an accidental death at the time.'

The Czech police were standing by the outcome of their investigation. However, calls were growing for them to reopen the case after *the Guardian* had got its hands on a copy of the statement given by Leeza van der Kleji in which she'd accused Aspen of deliberately pushing her best friend off Charles Bridge.

'In the meantime, we've noted the physical similarities between Becca, Nadia and Aldana: above average height, long dark wavy hair, all on the curvy side. So, we've been looking at other cases of female drownings with the same victimology that have occurred since Bradley Aspen's been living in London.' He paused. 'We've identified three. Gabrielle Brieley, Shannon Boland and Melis Güler.'

Eve was sickened. Three more women that Bradley Aspen might've killed.

'That many victims would make him a serial killer,' she pointed out.

'It would,' said Carroll soberly. 'These victims were aged between twenty and thirty-five, and each drowned in the Thames during the early hours, presumed to have fallen in from nearby bridges. No witnesses to any of them. None of the victims had a history of depression or mental health issues and there were no suicide notes, but like Nadia they'd all been out drinking beforehand and two of them had traces of cocaine in their systems. Coroner verdict for all three was misadventure,' Carroll finished.

'Which bridges?' asked Eve.

'Kingston, Richmond and Battersea, in that order.'

'All within a two-mile radius of his home. Like Southwark and Putney, these bridges have balustrades above waist height,' said DS Cato. In his thirties, he had a relaxed rapport that was easy to warm to. 'However, the victims being taller than average would've made it easier for him to tip them in. He'd have had to lift a shorter woman to get her over the side.'

'The deaths are going upstream,' Eve observed. 'He started in the suburbs and ended up in central London.'

'What about CCTV for these victims?' asked Horner.

'We're trying to find out,' said Carroll. 'Those three bridges are in the Met's jurisdiction, and it's taking some negotiation higher than my pay grade to get the case files sent over. It might be that we'll have someone from the Met joining us at some point to cover their end of things.'

Eve thought for a moment. 'You said Aldana never touched alcohol – but what about drugs? Did the hospital do a tox screen while she was sedated?'

'That's a good point,' said Ferdie. 'If she was sober, she'd be an anomaly among the victims. Becca and these other three women were in varying states of inebriety, making them vulnerable to attack. He would've taken a big risk targeting someone sober.'

'I can check that,' Quinn offered to Carroll. He nodded, and she scribbled a note to herself on the pad in front of her.

'We're definitely including Nadia Vinke as a victim?' asked Eve.

'I think we should,' said Carroll. 'As it stands, it looks like she was his first.'

'Actually, let's refer to them as possible victims,' said Ferdie. 'We should keep in mind that the cases might not be related.'

'Aspen might not be our suspect either,' said Horner. His comment was met with scowls from the detectives at the table but he ploughed on. 'We can't lose sight of the fact that the person who chucked his name in the frame is a TikToker who lives at the other end of the country. Yes, the video looks authentic and, no, she doesn't appear to have a personal axe to grind to want to get him into trouble, but equally, people only started calling in to say they also thought it was him after it went viral.'

'Aldana has picked him out as the man who attacked her,' said Carroll firmly.

'But again, that was only after his name went viral,' said Eve. 'The defence could argue that Aldana is so desperate for someone to take the blame for nearly killing her that she's picked on Aspen because he's already been linked to a similar case. We also need to consider the physiological and psychological impact of her almost drowning. What if her memory was affected by her being in an induced coma?'

'What about the fact they lived in the same street?' Quinn argued back. 'He could've been stalking her before he did it.'

'If she knew him that well, why didn't she mention him sooner as being her attacker?' asked Horner.

The tension in the room jumped a notch.

'I know it looks like we're just shooting things down, but we have to ensure that the evidence is robust,' Ferdie told the detectives. 'It might not look it at times, but we are all on the same page.'

Carroll nodded. 'It's not you lot I get frustrated with. It's the thought of that lad strutting round my manor like he hasn't got a care in the world. Whoever leaked his name along with that footage of Nadia's funeral knows he did it, and so do I. Copper's instinct.'

Quinn and Cato nodded in agreement but the CPS trio said nothing. Copper's instinct was meaningless to the US authorities.

The meeting continued for another thirty minutes before wrapping up. The group agreed to meet again in a week unless something came up that needed more urgent attention.

Putting their coats on to leave, Quinn asked Eve if she could have a word. After saying goodbye to the others, the pair of them walked to the next street where Quinn's car was parked. Eve checked her phone on the way and blanched. Someone she'd never met or even heard of had taken it upon themselves to email her work address with a volley of abuse, blaming her for letting Aspen escape justice. It was the tenth such message she'd received today. It felt like she was now the subject of an orchestrated campaign of hate, and it shook her to the core.

'Is that Frank Tooley again?' Quinn asked.

'No, I think the media attention has scared him off. This is someone else.'

She passed Quinn her phone. The detective muttered swear words while she scrolled. 'Jesus, Eve, they're saying you deserve to drown too. That falls under a malicious communication if you want to take it further.'

'I know it does, but I'd rather just block them. I know I should be in favour of pursuing prosecutions working for the CPS, but it feels different when I'm the one making the complaint. I don't want to give these people any attention.'

'Make sure you save all the messages, just in case.'

'I already am.' Eve spoke with a conviction she didn't entirely feel. She didn't want to be cowed by the threats, but it was impossible not to be worried by them.

'Good.' Quinn passed the phone back then jammed her hands into her coat pockets. 'This taskforce is a bit mad, isn't it?'

'I was surprised to be asked after Tooley's photo stunt.'

'Me too. Do you think we're being set up as scapegoats if it all goes wrong?'

Eve was taken aback. 'What do you mean?'

'Exactly because of the photo, and how people reacted to us being pictured together because of you and the Novus trial,' said Quinn. 'If anything goes wrong with this taskforce, it's going to be really easy for them to pin the blame on us two. That photo put us front and centre of Becca's case.'

'I can't speak for Paul because I've never worked with him before, but I do trust John not to stab me in the back.' Eve hoped she sounded convincing, because now that Quinn had planted the idea, she wondered if she should be less complacent.

'The thing that gets me about Becca's murder and these other cases is that nobody is asking why,' Quinn continued. 'Why would Bradley Aspen push these women to their deaths from bridges? What's the significance of that? There must be a reason he's chosen that method of killing over any other. It's an MO that comes with a high risk of being witnessed.'

'Maybe that's the point. He gets a kick out of knowing that, even if he's caught, he can't be touched because of his immunity. The thrill isn't the kill, it's evading capture afterwards,' said Eve. 'But right now, the why isn't as important as proving that he's definitely guilty. The why can come later.'

Quinn stared at Eve for a moment, like she was trying to work something out in her mind before she spoke again.

'I've met him.'

'What?'

'Aspen.'

'When?'

'The other night. In a bar.'

'You just happened to bump into him?' asked Eve sceptically.

'No, I followed him.'

Eve exhaled roughly. 'You've had him under surveillance? Does DCI Carroll know?'

'Of course not. I just wanted to get a look at him, to see what he's like. Don't tell me you're not curious too.'

'Of course I am, but you can't just put a suspect under surveillance without authorisation from above—'

Quinn cut her off. 'Eve, don't you get tired of men calling the shots and getting away with shit? Men like Tooley thinking he's got the right to harass you whenever he likes? Men like Bradley Aspen thinking they can get away with hurting women. I'm sick of it.'

Eve knew it was a fair point. Men, also, like her former date, Harry, who thought it was okay to stand her up without a word, and Jamie, Leah's doctor friend, who wouldn't take no for an answer. Since that afternoon in the pub, he'd badgered Eve six times to go out with him again. Each time she'd politely declined – the way he'd reacted to her leaving that day had raised too many red flags for her – but he wouldn't take the hint.

'I get what you're saying, but that doesn't mean you should be off chasing Bradley Aspen on your own,' she said.

'So come with me. I know for a fact he's going back to the same bar tonight.'

'How? Did you talk to him?'

'Say you'll come and I'll tell you.'

Eve floundered. This was a really bad idea. Ferdie and Carroll would be furious if they found out she and Quinn had gone to find Aspen, not to mention Sol and the Attorney General. What if someone recognised them, then posted another photo of them online? Yet she couldn't deny that she was curious to see Aspen in the flesh. If they couldn't successfully build a case against him, she might never get the chance in an official capacity.

'Okay, I'll come,' said Eve. 'But just for a quick look. If I think it's too risky once we're there, we leave, no argument.'

Quinn stuck out her hand to shake. 'Deal.'

# Chapter Twenty-One

## VALERIE

Ask any tourist what they most associated with Regent's Park and their likely answer would be London Zoo, or possibly the open-air theatre. As Valerie turned on to the Outer Circle on the park's border, it struck her that few Londoners, let alone visitors, might be aware that it was also home to the capital's second largest private garden after Buckingham Palace's.

The garden, spanning twelve acres, belonged to Winfield House. Built in 1936 for American heiress Barbara Woolworth Hutton before her marriage to the actor Cary Grant, the Grade II mansion on the park's west side had been home to every US ambassador deployed to London since 1955.

The entrance to the residence could easily be missed if it weren't for the armed guards standing sentry at them. Valerie drove through the gates without stopping. Her arrival was expected.

More guards flagged the driveway leading to the house. Valerie sped on. This wasn't her first visit to Winfield House. Had this been a few weeks ago, she might've feared it would be her last – that she was being summoned there to be fired. But the ambassador, like the

President, had been unequivocal in his support of her since Bradley had been dragged into the Becca Farrow murder investigation.

Valerie and Mark were devastated that their son had been labelled a killer. The leaking of his name, along with the video of Nadia's funeral, had spitefully ensured the public thought he was guilty regardless of actual evidence. Comments posted about him online had made Valerie physically sick. The vitriol was far worse than anything she could've imagined. The masses wanted an eye for an eye and were baying for her son's blood. It didn't matter that he had an alibi – because he had immunity, people automatically assumed he was guilty and trying to hide behind it.

Valerie had done her best to comfort him. She could see how broken the allegations and the exposure had left him. He'd spent the past few weeks locked away in his room, distraught. Yet it was difficult to find the right words when she knew Bradley had been responsible for Nadia's death. Alone in her and Mark's bedroom, she'd watched the leaked funeral footage on repeat; the distraught faces of Nadia's parents and siblings were now seared on her brain. She'd also re-read comments given to one of the broadsheets by Becca's godmother, a woman called Beverly who happened to be a public prosecutor. Beverly wouldn't be drawn on the speculation about Bradley for legal reasons, but instead spoke of the immeasurable loss that Becca's parents felt. Brought to tears every time, Valerie had to keep reminding herself that Bradley had an alibi for the night Becca had died – that he'd been at home, asleep, just across the landing from her and Mark.

She'd become so anxious to quell the backlash that she'd even asked to waive her diplomatic immunity so his could be lifted. Then he could be questioned by the police and clear his name. But the Vienna Convention rules did not allow individuals to relinquish theirs – only the citizen's home nation could make that call. And Valerie had been told in no uncertain terms that the

President would never agree to it. She understood his position in not wanting to set a precedent, but it frustrated the hell out of her that Bradley's reputation was being trashed in the meantime.

She also appreciated the irony that if she'd met with the President in DC as planned and hadn't been spooked by the news report about Becca Farrow, she might've got the job, and then the issue of immunity would no longer be relevant. Her diplomatic status would've ended upon her leaving the embassy, and Bradley wouldn't have become a pawn in an international game of who blinked first.

Tonight was about drawing a line under these events. The ambassador had invited Valerie for a private dinner away from the rumour-mongers at Nine Elms. He was concerned about her well-being. The details of the dinner were being kept off-book to avoid speculation – that was why Valerie was driving herself and not using her assigned mission car and driver. Beside her on the passenger seat was the overnight bag she'd been ordered to bring so she could have a drink and relax and not worry about getting home. There were plenty of guest rooms at the residence that could accommodate her.

Winfield House suddenly loomed before her. It took her breath away every time she saw it. Someone had once told her that it was technically a townhouse, but to her it was a stately home, a thing of extravagant beauty that only the Brits with their rich history of architecture could pull off. Besides having the second largest back garden in the capital, the red-brick and Portland stone neo-Georgian property boasted thirty-five bedrooms, an indoor swimming pool, a tennis court, and a collection of fine art and artefacts worth millions.

Dusk had given way to night on the drive from Putney and the residence was lit up accordingly. There was no danger of it distracting passing motorists though; the vast, tree-lined grounds hid it from the road. You had to know it was there to know it was there.

Valerie pulled up by the front door, which was sheltered beneath a black and white awning. She'd attended numerous functions at Winfield House where a red carpet had been rolled out to greet guests, but tonight there was just a footman waiting to park her car, and the housekeeper welcoming her inside.

She expected to be taken into one of the formal reception rooms, but to her surprise the housekeeper led her into the kitchen, where the ambassador was sitting at a bar stool pulled up to one of the worktops. Laid out on the worktop were various dishes, along with two wine glasses and a bottle cooling in an ice bucket.

'I decided to give everyone the night off,' he said, patting the empty stool next to him. 'I didn't cook though. This is all my chef's doing. I hope you like Greek.'

Feeling apprehensive, Valerie climbed on to the bar stool. She was glad she hadn't overdone it with her outfit – she'd stuck to her fail-safe jeans and blazer combo – as the ambassador was dressed down in matching leisurewear and trainers, his salt-and-pepper hair wet from a shower. It was the most casual Valerie had ever seen him, and this was probably the most laid-back setting they'd ever been in alone together. They'd always enjoyed a professional warmth but Valerie would never have described them as friends.

'White wine?'

'Sure. Thank you.'

'Don't worry, this isn't the only bottle. There's more in the fridge. You hungry? Help yourself.'

Valerie did as she was told, scooping a bit of each mezze dish on to her plate. The food looked amazing but her appetite had deserted her. Now she was here, she suddenly felt nervous that there might be another reason why the ambassador had summoned her to Winfield.

'How's Penny shaping up?' he asked.

Valerie squirmed. 'Okay. She's a hard worker.'

Penny was Langdon's replacement. Triggered by their hostile encounter in the embassy gardens, Valerie had accused him of leaking Bradley's name to the TikTok poster the same day it happened. It was a bruising encounter in her office that had escalated into a screaming match and had ended with him demanding security be called. Adamant he had nothing to hide, Langdon voluntarily submitted all his electronic devices for examination – and there was nothing on them that pointed to him being the leak. Valerie remained sure he was behind it though. Langdon knew about Prague and he would've known how to source the funeral footage. But Nadia's death wasn't a can of worms she wanted to reopen, so she'd issued a grovelling apology for falsely accusing him and Langdon was moved sideways to another department.

'Good. I'm glad it's working out.'

The ambassador forked in a mouthful of feta and chewed, watching Valerie carefully as he did. Once he'd swallowed, he dropped his fork on to his plate with a clatter.

'Jesus, Val, you look like a condemned woman being forced to eat a last meal before she's dragged off to the gas chamber. I thought tonight would be a chance for you to de-stress but I'm not sure we have enough hours or enough wine,' he said, laughing.

Valerie was mid-sip and so taken aback that she almost spat her wine over the worktop, which made the ambassador laugh even louder. Wiping her mouth with the back of her hand, Valerie joined in with the laughter.

'Is it that obvious I'm stressed?' she asked, once they'd both calmed down.

'It's hardly a surprise that you are. I mean, who wouldn't be when their kid is accused like Bradley's been. How's he coping?'

Valerie knocked back more wine. 'He's not. He barely leaves the house. His friends are trying to be supportive, but he won't let them come round to check on him. Mark's away for work tonight and I tried to persuade Bradley to invite them over so he's not on his own, but he refused. I don't know how to help him.' She could feel herself growing teary. 'He's innocent but it feels like we're not being allowed to prove it.'

'Actually, that's the reason I asked you here tonight.'

Valerie stiffened. She knew it.

'There's concern in the White House that this is dragging on. Parsons called me. The attention on Bradley isn't dying down as quickly as they'd like. It's dominating the news agenda.'

Perry Parsons was the President's Chief of Staff. Calls between him and the ambassador were a regularity, but Valerie was mortified he'd called about this.

'I did offer to waive my immunity—'

'Not an option, as you well know.' The ambassador broke off a piece of pitta bread and jabbed it in a bowl of hummus, scooping some up. 'There is a way to prove Bradley was nowhere near Southwark Bridge though. We can triangulate his phone to show he was in bed at your house when Becca Farrow was pushed. Then we leak the data to a friendly journalist along with some comments about how this witch-hunt needs to stop.'

'Do you think that will be enough? I mean, people will say he just left his phone at home.'

'Let them. Once the data's out there, they'll soon find something else to talk about. They always do.'

'I hope you're right.'

'I always am.'

Valerie drained her glass. Without waiting to be asked, she grabbed the bottle from the ice bucket and refilled. The ambassador grinned.

‘That’s more like it.’ Then he added, ‘There is something else you could do to put a stop to all this.’

‘What’s that?’

‘Sue the person who put the video up on TikTok in the first place. If it wasn’t for her, Bradley’s name would never have been linked to the murder. She’s making money off your misery, and off Becca’s family too. She’s relentless.’

The ambassador wasn’t the first person to suggest they litigated. Mark had also wanted to take legal action against the girl. Valerie had refused, however. She feared engaging lawyers would inflame the situation even more.

‘It’s defamation. She’s perpetuated damaging falsehoods about your son and now she’s attacking you,’ the ambassador went on.

‘Me?’

‘Haven’t you seen the latest video she’s posted?’

‘I’ve been avoiding social media.’

The ambassador reached for his phone, which was on the worktop next to the dishes. ‘It went live about an hour ago.’

Bile rose in Valerie’s throat as the video played. The tone was vicious. The girl was accusing her of knowing all along that Bradley was a murderer and letting him get away with it. She’d hashtagged the video #Hismumknows and #Valerieisguiltytoo. It had already garnered tens of thousands of likes.

‘Real nasty stuff,’ said the ambassador. ‘But it’s in your power to stop her. I’ve taken the liberty of getting the embassy counsel to draft a cease-and-desist letter on your behalf. You say the word and she’ll be served first thing tomorrow.’

Valerie desperately wanted to say no, or that she should at least discuss it with Mark first. Even though he was in favour of calling in lawyers, she knew he’d want to be in control of the process.

‘The White House approves this course of action,’ the ambassador added.

Any hope Valerie had of retaining control evaporated like bubbles on the breeze.

'If you think it's for the best,' she said reluctantly.

The ambassador climbed down from his stool. 'I do. Let me go and give counsel the word. I won't be long. Help yourself to more wine.'

As the ambassador left the kitchen, Valerie stared down at her paused screen and the TikTok poster's angry face. Would a cease-and-desist letter really make her stop, or was their nightmare about to get a whole lot worse?

# Chapter Twenty-Two

## EVE

The bar wasn't what Eve had imagined. 'Rough' was the politest term she could think of to describe it. Buried in a side street near Lime Street, the tone was set before they'd even entered – from the bullion windows caked in grime and the dried puddles of vomit beneath them, to the intimidatingly tall and wide security guards manning the entrance. Inside was equally unalluring, with sticky flooring, painted black walls, and lighting so dim that Eve had to squint to see. The clientele appeared to be mostly students.

'Are you sure this is the right place?' she asked Quinn. 'It doesn't exactly scream diplomat's son from the posh end of Putney.'

'Yep.' Quinn scanned the vast bar, eyes narrowed. 'Can't see Aspen anywhere, though. He can't have arrived yet.'

It was already gone ten. Eve hoped he'd show up soon. She was already shattered and even though her sleep would likely be broken again, she was still desperate for her bed.

'Why don't you grab a table and I'll get us drinks,' said Quinn. 'Oh, and let your hair down.'

Eve laughed. 'In this place? I don't think so.'

'No, I mean literally. Undo the bun.'

'Why?'

'You are exactly Aspen's type. Tallish, with dark hair and curves – just like Becca, Aldana and Nadia. I want to see how he reacts when he sees you,' said Quinn matter-of-factly.

Eve was incredulous. 'Are you kidding? You want to use me as bait?'

Quinn shrugged.

'Is this why you wanted me to come with you?'

'If I'd told you back in Barnes, you'd have said no.'

'Too bloody right I would've,' said Eve angrily. 'I can't believe this. I'm going home.'

'Eve, don't. I'm sorry—'

But Eve was already walking away. Reaching the exit, the door suddenly pushed open into her path, almost sending her flying. In front of her appeared a young man.

'Excuse me,' said Bradley Aspen, smiling. Then he walked round her and disappeared towards the bar.

Stunned, Eve turned to Quinn, who was also rooted to the spot.

'It's him,' she breathed.

Quinn nodded. 'I'm going to stay.'

Eve hesitated for a second. Then she reached up and undid her hair, shaking it loose over her shoulders. 'Let's get that drink.'

◆ ◆ ◆

Forty-five minutes later Eve was on her second glass of white wine. Quinn was still drinking the first orange juice she'd ordered. They'd managed to squeeze on to the end of a long table being occupied by a mixed group of students, all talking loudly over the background rock music. Ambient it was not.

Quinn had the better view of Bradley Aspen from where they were sitting. The limited seating meant Eve was awkwardly positioned side-on to him and she didn't want to rouse suspicion by turning round to look every few minutes. Until twenty minutes ago he'd been alone, drinking a pint while glued to his phone. Then two men had joined him, both roughly the same age. The three of them were now deep in conversation at their table, heads close together as they talked. Quinn seemed frustrated Aspen hadn't looked their way once.

'Maybe we should switch seats so you're facing him,' she suggested, not for the first time.

'I'm not being a honey trap,' Eve repeated, but she smiled as she said it. Quinn had apologised for her hair gaffe, saying she'd let herself get carried away because she was so desperate to get something on Aspen that might stick. It hadn't been her intention to use Eve as bait – she just wanted to see if Aspen really did have a type.

Eve quickly glanced toward Aspen's table, then looked away again.

'Who do you think those two are?'

'Friends, presumably.'

'They clearly don't think he's guilty if they're still hanging out with him.'

'A lot of people out there think the same, though,' said Quinn. 'For every hundred people baying for his immunity to be lifted, there are quite a few who think he's innocent and should be left alone. They believe that Nadia's death was an accident and it's not his fault he looks like the CCTV grab of Becca's attacker.'

'If they knew about Aldana as well they might change their minds.'

Ferdie and Carroll wanted to keep Aldana's ID of Aspen under wraps until the taskforce was ready to pass all evidence to the US authorities. The last thing anyone wanted was details being drip-fed via the media.

Eve sipped her drink, then checked out their surroundings again. 'This place really is a bit of a step down from Putney.'

'Maybe that's why he likes it. Let's face it, it's an ideal place to lie low if your face has been plastered all over the internet and media.'

Quinn had a point. Eve could barely make out people's expressions in the low light.

'He's been here five times in the last fortnight alone,' Quinn said.

Eve was alarmed. 'Alix, if you've followed him here more than once, he could've spotted you and realised you're watching him. We could get into serious trouble for this. If he thinks we're harassing him and makes a complaint, we could both lose our jobs. I've already got a strike against my name after being let go from my old firm, and you're still a trainee. They'd kick you off the force without a second thought. We need to leave *now*.'

'He won't have noticed me,' Quinn scoffed. 'He's too wrapped up in himself.'

'I disagree. He's likely to be more on guard because of the attention he's getting.'

'Does he look like he's being wary?'

Eve glanced round just in time to see Aspen throw his head back in laughter. His friends joined in. He looked like he didn't have a care in the world.

'Let's give it a few more minutes,' said Quinn. 'Then we'll go.'

Six minutes later, Eve had finished her wine. She couldn't relax knowing what a risk they had taken just by being there. Quinn should've been honest about the number of times she'd followed Aspen. Eve put the glass down.

'I'm going. We've watched him for long enough.'

'Fine,' said Quinn resignedly. 'Do you want a lift home?'

'Thanks, but my flat's not far from here, so I'm good to walk. Can you watch my bag for a second though? I need the toilet first.'

Inside the restroom, Eve went through the motions like she was on autopilot. She felt drained, anxious, and was so preoccupied with getting home that she didn't immediately notice Bradley Aspen waiting outside the restroom as she left.

'Hello.'

Eve stalled. She looked around, but there was no one else there. He was definitely talking to her. A clammy chill hit the back of her neck. This was bad. 'How's your evening going?' he asked.

Words failed her. She shouldn't be anywhere near him, let alone talking to him.

'Can I buy you a drink?'

Panic caught in her throat. She shook her head.

He seemed a little annoyed. 'What's your problem?'

She swallowed hard. She had to get out of there. She thought for a second, then put her hand in front of her mouth.

'Sorry, going home. Really sore throat from talking over the music.'

Trembling, she went to go past him.

'That's a shame. Are you sure I can't buy you a drink?' He smiled as he spoke, displaying perfectly aligned and preternatural white teeth, yet it didn't quite reach his eyes. He was undeniably handsome, but the way he was sizing her up was unnerving. With a start, Eve realised that up close she could see an even stronger resemblance between him and the CCTV image of Becca's attacker. An involuntary shiver shot through her.

'I'm sure.'

'Maybe some other time,' he said, flashing another half-smile. He stepped back to let her pass, then at the last minute repositioned himself so that their bodies touched. Jumping with fright, she pulled away, then dashed back into the bar to find Quinn.

The detective was looking at something on her phone when Eve reached their table.

'We need to get out of here now,' she said. When Quinn didn't move, she hissed, 'I mean it. NOW.'

They headed outside. Eve didn't look back to see if Aspen was watching them. She did not want to give him the satisfaction. He might have the appearance of someone friendly and unthreatening, but she'd been around enough unsavoury men in her time as a defence solicitor to know there was something very off about him. Call it a woman's instinct.

Quinn's car was parked a few streets away. Eve breathlessly recounted what had happened on the walk there.

'The way he pushed into me as I went past was so creepy. He didn't care that he was invading my space.'

'He got up from his seat the second you got up from yours. It was like he'd been waiting for you to move,' said Quinn.

Eve shuddered again. 'I'm scared.'

'Don't be. He doesn't even know who you are.'

'You've misunderstood. I'm not scared for me,' said Eve. 'I'm scared that if we can't build a case against him, he's going to hurt someone else. He's been accused of murder and everyone knows it, but he's still asking women to have drinks with him. Alix, what if the next woman he asks says yes?'

# Chapter Twenty-Three

## EVE

Quinn dropped Eve right outside her apartment block door and waited until she was safely inside. Inside the unmanned foyer, Eve did her usual checks of the front door to make sure it had closed securely behind her. She tugged hard on the handle and made sure the cameras both inside and out were pointed in the right direction to catch anyone trying to get in.

Darrel the concierge had reassured her repeatedly over the past few weeks that the building's security system was fully operational, but she couldn't go up to her flat until she'd run her own checks. Tonight, she felt even more spooked than usual. Her run-in with Bradley Aspen had shredded her nerves to the point where she felt every inch of her was exposed. She stared through the glass door into the street, imagining Frank Tooley was out there nearby, watching and waiting. Not knowing when he might suddenly reappear was worse than the incessant contact.

Leah was at the hospital on an overnight again, but there was noise coming from inside the flat when Eve let herself in. She paused in the doorway, key still in the lock. It sounded like it was coming from the kitchen. Eve removed the key but left the door ajar in case she needed a quick escape. Then, turning on all the lights as she went, she slowly edged towards the kitchen, her breath shallow with fear.

The kitchen light was already on. On the table was a small wireless speaker tuned to a radio station, and next to it a note.

> *E, thought I'd leave this on so you wouldn't get freaked out by the quiet when you got in. See you in the morning, Lx*

Eve exhaled shakily. The radio had had the opposite impact of what Leah had intended, but she appreciated her flatmate's thoughtfulness. Then Eve noticed the small 'P.T.O.' in the bottom-right corner. She flipped the note over.

> *I've left you a bottle of wine in the fridge. Thought you might need it. Lx*

The tears came quicker than Eve could blink them away. She angrily wiped her eyes. She hated that Frank Tooley had made her feel scared in her own home. This was supposed to be her safe space—

Suddenly she remembered she'd left her front door ajar. She bolted from the kitchen to shut it. Her chest heaved with panic as she double-checked and triple-checked the lock was properly secured. What if someone had slipped inside the flat while she was in the kitchen? She knew she wasn't being rational but she couldn't stop herself. She went round the flat, turning on the lights in her and Leah's rooms, opening both wardrobes and looking under both beds. She even checked behind the shower curtain in the bathroom, though doing so terrified her. She was so sure someone was lurking behind it that she almost screamed as she yanked it back.

Still tearful, she went back to her room, sank down on the edge of her bed and cried. She couldn't carry on like this. She hated how timid she'd become – someone who cried at the drop of a hat and was frightened of her own shadow.

Tomorrow she would speak to Beverly about having cameras and a panic button installed inside the flat like Horner had mentioned. Hopefully their landlord would agree to it. She knew Leah would understand. When Tooley had published the picture of her and Quinn, Eve had told Leah about him tracking her to their address and how the stress had triggered her insomnia. She'd been worried it would frighten Leah too, but she'd been angry on Eve's behalf rather than scared.

Satisfied the flat was empty and secure, Eve changed into her nightwear then pulled her duvet from her bed and dragged it to the sofa. She was exhausted, but she could tell her mind wasn't going to let her sleep any time soon. She was too on edge and needed to calm down first. Leah's wine would help, she decided. She grabbed it from the fridge and took down a large glass from the cupboard, which she filled to the brim. She was about to return the bottle to the fridge when she thought better of it. Clutching both bottle and glass, she returned to the front room. If falling asleep naturally was beyond her, passing out drunk would have to do instead.

Eve was out for the count when the door intercom buzzed the first time, and didn't hear it. The second time it buzzed for a fraction longer, finally dragging her from her dreamless state. Disorientated, she sat up on the sofa, duvet bunched around her. Was it time to get up? But then she realised it was still dark out and when she found her phone on the floor beside the empty wine bottle, it said it was only 4.30 a.m.

She waited for a moment to see if the buzzer would go again. Sometimes drunk people going home on a night out would activate the intercom for fun, or a visitor to one of the neighbouring flats would accidentally press the wrong flat number. When it buzzed a third and fourth time in short succession, she reluctantly went to answer it.

The intercom unit was on the wall beside the front door to the flat. There was a video screen that normally showed who was buzzing to be let in at street level, but all Eve could see when she peered closely at it was the section of pavement outside the building. She waited but there was clearly no one there.

She was halfway back to the sofa when the buzzer went again. Now she was annoyed. Her head was pounding from the wine and all she wanted to do was lie down. She went back to the unit and jammed her finger down on the speaker button.

'Will you bloody well piss off and stop waking me up,' she shouted.

Still the video screen showed nothing but pavement.

Then, in a flash, a man's face suddenly loomed in front of the camera, until the image on the video screen was just a pair of eyes staring right at her. The speaker crackled to life.

'I know you're in there, Eve.'

Finger still on the speaker button, she screamed – then, just as quickly, the eyes and face disappeared from view.

# Chapter Twenty-Four

## GEMMA

For once Gemma didn't have to dig her way through the kitchen to reach the kettle to make herself a liquid breakfast. For the sixth morning in a row, she was enjoying the luxury of a bacon roll and creamy latte from a café round the corner from The Compton. It was all Sponge's doing. In the course of their messaging last week, her new online friend from Birmingham had suggested that she change the settings on her TikTok account to accept tips from followers who wanted to support her content. It had taken some convincing – Gemma hated being seen as a charity case – but she'd relented when Sponge had pointed out that she'd been getting such a positive response to her videos about the Becca Farrow case, why shouldn't she be rewarded for them? TikTok paid its users a certain amount if a video was viewed so many times, but it wasn't as much as she could make herself.

Under Sponge's guidance, Gemma had applied to activate the tipping function, then posted a video thanking her followers for their support with the adage that if anyone wanted to send her tips, she would be thrilled.

The money had started rolling in immediately. By the time her alarm had gone off at seven the following morning, she'd collected two hundred pounds. As the week went on, it continued to roll in. She'd never been so rich. She couldn't believe people actually wanted to tip her because they liked what she was doing.

Sipping her coffee inside the café, she checked her stats on the app. Her latest video attacking Valerie Aspen had gone viral overnight. The #TrueCrimeTokers obsessed with Becca's murder had seized upon Gemma's fresh take on the case, the vast majority agreeing Valerie must have known all along that her son was a killer. Most agreed she should be punished too. But whereas Gemma had called for her to be investigated, a lot of the commentators were baying for Valerie to suffer a worse fate than Becca.

If Gemma was being completely honest, the reaction scared her. What posters had said about Bradley was nothing compared to the hate they were spewing about his mum. Her stance had been that Valerie knew he was guilty and was covering for him. But in the replies, people were saying that she must've done something to him as a child to make him turn out so evil. Even Sponge had posted a comment saying Valerie deserved to die and had received thousands of likes for it. Gemma had messaged him privately saying she didn't like what he'd said, but his response was 'That bitch deserves everything that's coming to her.'

Gemma wasn't the only one worried that the hate and threats were starting to get out of hand. Dozens of people had posted comments urging her to take down the video, saying that it was defamatory and could be seen as inciting violence against Valerie. They said they didn't want Gemma to get into trouble over it. But Sponge, on seeing the comments, had been scathing. 'If they want to ignore the truth, let them,' he'd messaged her. 'You know that Aspen bitch is covering up for her son. You can't stop standing up for Becca now. She deserves justice. This is your brand.'

Gemma had conceded he had a point and let the video stand. But she didn't post another one before leaving for work like she usually did, deciding to let things cool down a bit first.

After breakfast, she left the café and headed for The Compton. She was a bit late but she knew that Reece wouldn't care. The owners had decided to invest in the hotel now it was getting more bookings and they'd taken on a trainee chambermaid to help Gemma with the rooms. They were paying her even more of a pittance than they had Gemma at first, but the girl, Stacie, seemed not to mind. She was only sixteen, straight out of school. Gemma hoped that if she continued to make enough money from her TikToks she could jack her job in and Stacie could be promoted.

She didn't notice the man in the dark suit lingering at the side of the reception area when she walked in to give the counter a dust. Reece drew her attention to him with a sharp nudge of his elbow into her side.

'Ow, what d'you do that for?' she complained.

'That man's been waiting for you,' said Reece in a hushed voice. 'Wouldn't say who he was, but he did say he wasn't a reporter when I threatened to kick him out.'

Gemma's stomach flipped. He must be from the council. They'd finally caught up with her.

The letters had been coming thick and fast in the wake of the one she'd found on her mum's bed. Gemma knew they shouldn't ignore them, but as the letters were addressed to her mum as the homeowner, she couldn't stop her taking them up to her room to hide them. Had the council decided a more direct approach was needed?

Gemma went over to the man, duster still in hand.

'You wanted to see me? I'm Gemma Kirk.'

Unsmiling, the man held out a large brown envelope. He waited for Gemma to take it, then said, 'You've been served. Do what the letter says.' Then he turned on his heel and walked out of the front door.

Reece was at her side in an instant. 'What is it?'

The letter bore a stamp. Harcourt & Swallow Law Ltd. Gemma's breath caught in her throat. It wasn't the council.

She shoved the duster at Reece for him to hold and ripped open the envelope. There was just one sheet of paper, with type on both sides.

'What does "cease-and-desist" mean?' asked Reece.

Gemma's hand shook as she scanned the letter. 'It's on behalf of Bradley Aspen's mum. She's telling me to stop posting videos about them or she'll sue.'

Reece was outraged. 'She can't tell you to do that. What about free speech? It's not you who should be dragged through the courts, it's her and her son!'

Part of Gemma was afraid – she'd never had a letter like it before – but part of her was angry too. She was tired of people thinking they could push her around. She'd had a gutful of it her entire life.

'You can't let her get away with it,' Reece added haughtily. 'It's an empty threat. She won't sue, because if it ever went to court, she'd have to answer questions about her murdering son and she'd be shown up for the liar she is.'

'What do you think I should do?'

'Post another video. Tell the world she's trying to silence you, but you won't let her. She thinks if she can shut you up, people will stop going on about her son.'

Gemma felt uneasy. 'Maybe I should stop. This is a proper legal letter.'

'Valerie Aspen is trying to bully you, Gem. She thinks if she hires some flash lawyer to send you a letter, you'll cave. Don't prove her right.'

'I don't want to get taken to court.'

'It won't come to that. Don't forget, it's not just you saying she's as guilty as her son. She's only coming after you because you've started it all. It's thanks to you that poor Becca isn't being forgotten.'

Slowly, Gemma realised Reece was right. Valerie Aspen was yet another in a long line of people wanting to bully her to keep quiet, be compliant, not fight back. Well, not any more. She'd had enough. This time she was going to stand up for herself.

'Can I take my break early?' she asked.

Reece's eyes lit up. 'You want to do the video now?'

'No time like the present,' said Gemma with grim determination. 'Valerie Aspen needs to know she's just made a massive mistake coming after me.'

'Let me help.'

'How?' Gemma really didn't want him on camera with her.

'I can direct this one,' he said excitedly. 'You do the talking and I'll hold the phone. Between us she won't know what's hit her.'

# Chapter Twenty-Five

## EVE

If Horner was surprised to find Eve sitting behind his desk when he arrived for work, he didn't show it. Instead, he put down his backpack and instructed her to get to her feet.

'I need a strong coffee to get started, and judging by your face, so do you. Come on, let's nip out to the Flat Cap.'

The coffee shop wasn't the closest one to Petty France but that was why they both liked it. They were less likely to bump into or be overheard by colleagues than if they went to one of the chain branches nearby.

In the lift down to the ground floor, Horner peered at Eve through his owlish, large-framed glasses. 'You look like you haven't slept a wink,' he said astutely.

Eve couldn't answer him. She knew that if she did, she'd end up crying again, and she didn't want to do that inside the building. She scrunched up her face to hold the tears back. Horner stared at her, alarmed.

'What's going on, Eve?'

She shook her head frantically. 'Not yet.'

He took the hint and together they left Petty France in silence. In fact, beyond asking her what kind of coffee she wanted, Horner didn't say another word until they had collected their order and settled themselves at a small table at the back of the coffee house.

'Well?'

With a tremulous exhale, Eve told him everything that had happened the previous evening, from her creepy interaction with Bradley Aspen in the pub to someone ringing the flat's intercom in the early hours and scaring the life out of her. She managed to get through it without crying and left no detail out, even though she knew she'd be dropping Quinn in it for her unauthorised surveillance. But she had to give Horner the full story. She needed him to tell her what to do.

Horner listened intently like he always did. When she finished, he had one simple question for her.

'Was it Frank Tooley?'

'Definitely not. He's got a distinct accent and is in his fifties. This person wasn't Scottish and was definitely younger.'

'Could it have been Bradley Aspen?'

Eve nodded. 'I think so. It looked like him.'

'Thinking isn't good enough. Did you call the police?'

'I logged the incident online but I didn't say who I thought it was. I wanted to speak to you first.'

'Have you told Quinn?'

She shook her head.

'Good. Don't tell her yet, I don't want her and Carroll getting carried away. Now, does the intercom record footage?'

'I don't know. It's not like one of those Ring doorbells, it's for the entire building. I can find out though.' She'd ask Darrel.

'Do.' He gave Eve a stern look. 'I don't need to tell you how out of order you and Quinn were for following Aspen. You shouldn't have been anywhere near him.'

'I know, and I'm sorry. We had no idea he'd approach me though.'

'Quinn clearly hoped he would,' said Horner sternly. 'That's why she dragged you along. You are his type to a tee.'

'Are you going to tell DCI Carroll?'

'I should do. Paul needs to know as well.'

Eve sensed the 'but' before he said it.

'But I don't want either of you kicked off the taskforce. So, for now, it stays between us, but if either of you pulls a stunt like that again I'll have to take it further. Do you understand how serious this is, Eve? You cannot interfere with potential suspects or do anything that constitutes tampering with evidence.'

He looked so disappointed that Eve was crushed. His opinion mattered so much to her.

'What if it was Aspen who was at my door?'

'We add it to the evidence pile. If we can get a video recording, that would be concrete proof that he followed someone with the same victimology as Becca, Nadia and the others to her home and tried to intimidate her. But the thing that's bugging me is him saying your name. How did he know it? You didn't introduce yourself in the bar, did you?'

Eve shook her head.

'You said Quinn never referred to your name either, so it's not like he could've overheard it.'

'I don't think she did. My recollection is a bit fuzzy though,' she admitted. The hangover beating a tattoo inside her head didn't help.

'Eve, did the doorbell actually ring? Or did you just dream it?'

The suggestion that she'd imagined it was upsetting. 'It did, and I didn't,' she replied hotly.

'I'm going to say this kindly, and certainly not in a preachy way because I can't talk when it comes to having a few, but if you drank a bottle and a half of wine before going to bed, how can you be certain?'

She cringed. The amount she'd drunk was a lot, and if this was a cross-examination in court, the defence and jury would be right to doubt her account. The wine could've impaired her memory.

'I only drank that much because I'm really struggling to sleep,' she said defensively.

'The stress you're dealing with at the moment would probably be less acute if you took alcohol out of the equation,' said Horner gently.

'I know. I'm fine during the day, it's just at night. I don't feel safe in the flat when Leah's at work. I keep thinking Tooley's going to turn up again.'

'I thought he'd backed off?'

Horner had checked in with her a few times to see if Tooley was still bothering Eve, after she'd told him about the true-crime fan grabbing her in the street and then dropping off the file at her flat. She still hadn't looked at its contents and had no plans to. She didn't want to give Tooley the satisfaction, and while he didn't know it, this was a small victory for her.

'He has. It's been a while since he last got in touch.'

'Is your flatmate on nights at the moment?'

Eve nodded. 'Until the weekend.'

'If you'd like, I can talk to Beverly or whoever to get some extra security measures installed in your flat.'

Eve sagged with relief. 'That's why I came to find you this morning. Beverly's not in today and I didn't know who else to ask.'

'Leave it with me. In the meantime, check to see if there is any footage from your door intercom we can use.'

'What if he comes back?' asked Eve worriedly.

'Do you have any friends you can stay with until the weekend?'

The few she had in London lived in shared accommodation, and she didn't much fancy crashing on their sofas.

'I've got some savings I can use to book into a hotel,' she said. 'I know it's extreme, but if I don't get some sleep soon, I'm not going to be able to function at all.'

'That's a good plan. I also think you should take the rest of the week off. When was the last time you took leave?'

Eve could barely recall. She'd taken time off after the Novus trial last July, then a few days' leave around Christmas to go home to Shropshire. She was long overdue a break.

'I have time owing, but I don't think I'll be able to take it off at short notice,' said Eve.

'Let me clear it with Sol. We need you to be fit and well if you're going to juggle the taskforce with the rest of your workload.'

The thought of four days doing absolutely nothing except catching up on sleep sounded terrific, but Eve wasn't sure how healthy being alone with her thoughts would be.

'If you can stretch to it, book a hotel that's got twenty-four-hour security,' Horner advised. 'A lot of the chain ones don't.'

Eve's savings would stretch to that, but it would put a dent in the mortgage deposit she was trying to save towards. Rubbing her eyes, which were gritty from tiredness, she decided it was a sacrifice worth making.

# Chapter Twenty-Six

## VALERIE

Mark stormed into the kitchen holding his phone aloft like a general bearing a standard. 'That's the fourth one in ten minutes. When the hell is it going to stop?'

'Turn off the notifications,' said Valerie placatingly. 'Then you won't get bothered.'

'I can't turn it off. It's the doorbell. What if someone we know comes round?'

She was on the cusp of pointing out that such a scenario was highly unlikely, seeing as almost everyone they knew was now giving them a wide berth, but stopped herself. This was the most in-depth conversation they'd had since Wednesday, when Mark had found out that a cease-and-desist had been sent on their behalf to the TikToker who'd started all this. Even though he'd been pushing for legal action, he was furious that the embassy's legal counsel had acted without his implicit approval, and incandescent that the fallout had brought a steady stream of reporters to their door in the two days since.

Rather than accept the warning to halt her activities, the TikToker had ramped up her coverage against Valerie. What was more, the letter had triggered a groundswell of support in the girl's favour. Instead of quelling the speculation that Bradley was a killer, it had increased it tenfold.

As though on cue, the doorbell went again. Valerie checked the app on her phone and listened as a young man from *The Times* announced himself. She pressed play on the automated message telling him that they weren't available to answer the door. He hovered for a few moments then rang the doorbell again.

'For fuck's sake, Valerie,' Mark thundered, his face puce. 'This is out of control. Did you see there are also protestors in the street? A group of them, waving placards that say Bradley is guilty and his immunity should be revoked.'

Valerie held her breath. It was hard to believe, but she and Mark had yet to have a meaningful conversation about the accusations made against their son. He'd railed plenty against the media attention and how Bradley's name was being dragged through the dirt, but he wouldn't entertain a conversation about the specifics.

'I guess they're believing what they've read,' she said. 'There's also the CCTV image the police released that's wound everyone up.'

Even Mark had had to concede the man in the image did look a bit like Bradley. Her husband's eyes bored into hers. 'Anyone who believes what's being said about our son is a jerk.'

Valerie swallowed hard. She understood why Mark had dismissed the public outcry and supported Bradley unconditionally, but it left her in a lonely position. She wanted to share the whispers of doubt that were keeping her awake at night, so Mark could reassure her and put an end to them, but she knew he'd be furious if she brought them up. It had been bad enough telling him that Bradley had pushed Nadia after all – the leaked video forcing Valerie to finally confess – and that she had kept it from him. She'd never seen him so angry.

Mark chucked his phone down on the island and began preparing a pot of coffee. Valerie was perched on a high stool beside the island, her laptop open in front of her. She'd been given dispensation to work from home for the next week at least, but her concentration was shot.

She watched and listened as he banged and huffed his way around the kitchen. He slammed a mug down on the side with so much force she was surprised it didn't shatter.

'Mark, can you please stop that. You're going to break something,' she said.

'Stop what?' he challenged.

'Slamming around the place. I get that you're upset, but it's not helping.' She sucked down a steadying breath. 'We need to talk about it.'

'We just have,' came the curt response. 'I told you, I'm sick of people ringing our doorbell.'

'I didn't mean that. I meant what's being said about Bradley.'

He turned to her then, eyes narrowed. 'Meaning?'

Did it really need spelling out? 'That he's been accused of murder, Mark.'

He stared at her for the longest time, until the coffee began to bubble on the stove. He turned off the heat. 'Why did you never tell me about what happened with that girl in Prague?'

'I should've told you. I realise that now and I'm sorry. At the time my focus was making sure Bradley was okay. He was upset his friend had died and then to be accused like that – it was all I could think about. Then, when he told me he had pushed her, I panicked and tried to sort it out as best I could myself. But I should've considered you too.'

'Why change a habit of a lifetime,' said Mark sourly. 'It's always been about what you want, hasn't it, with you dictating our lives and where we live.'

'I thought you were happy with our life. You've always said you were proud of what I did for a living and were happy to support me.'

Mark reacted like she hadn't said anything. 'Poor Bradley has been dragged from pillar to post across the globe from the age of two. You heard what the doctors said back then – all that moving unsettled him.'

Valerie was stung. It had been her idea to seek help for their son when his toddler temper tantrums had morphed into angry outbursts as he'd started school. Thankfully, the battery of experts who'd examined him had collectively ruled out any underlying behavioural issue, saying Bradley was simply struggling to process his emotions. He couldn't relax around his classmates or let his guard down to befriend them because he was always braced for the inevitable goodbye when they moved again. He was angry because he was lonely. Valerie and Mark had been reassured he'd grow out of it as he grew older. And he had done – by his early teens he'd embraced their nomadic lifestyle and was all the more confident for it. By the time of Nadia's accident, he'd been happy and calm and his tempter outbursts only occasional. To have Mark throw all this in her face now was deeply unfair.

'He's settled now, so what's your point?'

'You just don't get it,' her husband seethed. 'I'm talking about the endless disruption to our lives. Bradley having to move schools. Me having to shift my business across continents. It was a struggle setting up again in London but I did it. Except now I find out I never needed to.'

Valerie finally grasped what his complaint was. 'You think we should've stayed in Prague and you're annoyed that I never gave you that choice,' she said flatly.

'Annoyed? I'm fuming. If you'd told me what was going on, we could've dealt with it together. Instead you spun me a load of BS about why we needed to move to London. A move that cost my company big-time.'

Valerie was surprised. 'Did it? You never said.'

'I guess that makes two of us,' he said coldly.

The look Mark gave Valerie shook her to the core. It was like he despised her. Suddenly she felt afraid for their marriage. They'd had their issues – which couple hadn't? – but this was something else.

Then, like a death knell, the doorbell pealed again.

Mark exploded. He snatched his phone up from the counter, but instead of checking the app to see who it was, he marched to the front door. Valerie didn't need to see who it was to tell it was a reporter. The volley of abuse that spilled from her husband's mouth made it clear. He wasn't a curser generally, but the language he let fly was pretty much one long expletive. She might've found it amusing to hear her normally politely spoken husband let rip had she not been so stressed.

When Mark returned to the kitchen his mood was even blacker. 'I seriously cannot deal with any more of this,' he said. 'I'm done.'

Valerie slid from her stool and went across to him. 'We can turn the doorbell ringer off. Or I'll put a sign up saying we're not here.'

'No, that's not what I meant,' he said, shaking his head. 'I'm done being here.'

Valerie's veins turned to ice. 'You don't mean that, honey. Look, why don't we all get away for a few days? I can find us somewhere to stay in the country.'

'Somewhere *you* want to go, presumably.'

'Mark, please. Give me a break. If you and I argue, it just makes things worse.'

Her husband sneered at her. 'You think this situation's going to get better any time soon?'

'Yes, I do. People will eventually find something else to talk about.'

'What if they don't? What if the police never catch the person who killed Becca Farrow, and Bradley spends the rest of his life under suspicion for her and Nadia Vinke?'

'The police will, I'm sure of it,' she said desperately. She could feel Mark slipping away from her. Her not telling him about Prague had broken them.

'I don't share your confidence. You're right about getting away though. I need to get out of here.'

'We'll all go. Me, you, Bradley.'

'No. Bradley can come if he wants to, but not you.'

She choked back a sob. 'Mark, don't do this. Don't leave.'

Ignoring her, he headed out of the kitchen. Scout, who had been asleep in her basket in the corner, bounded after him. Valerie followed her husband to the bottom of the stairs, tears streaming down both cheeks. Mark took the stairs two at a time.

She waited there, Scout beside her, until her husband came back down carrying a suitcase. She had no idea how many minutes had passed. Through her haze of tears she saw it was a small case and felt a stab of hope. If he wasn't planning to return, he'd have surely packed more stuff.

She still had to ask though. 'You are coming back, aren't you?'

'I don't know. I've just spoken to Bradley and he wants to stay put. I'll let him know where I'm staying if he changes his mind.'

Valerie wiped the tears from under her eyes with her fingertips. 'Will you let me know where you are?'

Before Mark could answer, the doorbell rang again. His eyes rolled heavenwards.

'I'll get it,' she said, dashing forward.

This time, however, it wasn't a reporter. Standing on the doorstep, looking nervous as hell, was Valerie's new assistant, Penny.

'What are you doing here?' asked Valerie.

'I have a super-urgent report that you need to sign off and I thought it was quicker to get it done in person. Can I come in?' She glanced over her shoulder to the edge of the driveway, where the reporters who'd knocked throughout the morning were now grouped. 'They were so rude and aggressive. They demanded I told them who I was.'

'What did you say?'

Penny grinned. 'Jehovah's Witness. You asking me in will really freak them out.'

She stepped into the hallway and let out a 'Wow, this is cool.' Valerie decided Penny was one of those women that oozed cheerleader vibes and saw the good in everything. Quite the contrast to Langdon in all his seriousness.

On seeing Mark, Penny marched right up and stuck out her hand. 'Hey. It's good to meet you.'

Mark didn't know who she was though and recoiled from her approach.

'She's not a reporter,' said Valerie hastily. 'This is Penny, my new assistant.' Then she kicked herself for not remembering she hadn't told him about Langdon moving on. She hadn't wanted to because of Prague.

Luckily for her, Mark either hadn't registered the mention or didn't care. He nodded to Penny, walked to the coat stand and unhooked his jacket. Penny must've spotted the suitcase.

'Going somewhere nice?' she asked him.

Mark's eyes met Valerie's. Silently she implored him not to tell the truth. He broke contact first. 'Business trip.'

He gave Valerie a perfunctory kiss on the cheek, picked up his suitcase and left the house. As the front door closed behind him, Valerie caught the clamour of voices from the driveway as the pack of reporters fired questions in his direction.

'Thank God he's gone,' said Penny, shoulders sagging.

Valerie stared at her. 'Come again?'

'I'm here because there's something you need to know and I don't think your husband should be privy to it.'

'You don't have a report for me to sign?'

'God no. I wouldn't have bothered you at home for something like that. I'd have just emailed it. No, this I needed to tell you in person.' Penny looked about the hallway. 'Is there somewhere we can sit down? Cos you're going to need to.'

Rather than take her into the kitchen, which felt too informal, Valerie led Penny into the dining room. She closed the door behind them, then watched, her insides churning, as Penny tugged her laptop from her bag and opened it on the table. Leaning over, she fired it up.

'I'm going to need your Wi-Fi password.'

Valerie managed to recite it from memory.

'Great, I'm in.' Penny pulled two chairs out from the table and nodded to the one nearest Valerie. 'I really think you should be sitting down for this.'

'What's this about?' asked Valerie, now sick with worry.

'Bradley's phone data.' Penny tapped at the keyboard and moments later pulled up a file. But before she clicked to open it, she turned to face Valerie head on. 'You wanted security to pull Bradley's phone data to prove that he was at home in bed on the night of Becca Farrow's murder.'

Valerie nodded. 'The ambassador thought it was a good idea. He thinks that if we release it as proof, all this nonsense might stop.'

'That sounds like a cool plan,' said Penny, her blunt blonde bob swishing as she nodded enthusiastically. 'Unfortunately, we're not going to be able to do that.'

Valerie stared at her assistant with mounting horror, her throat burning from a sudden burst of bile. 'Are you saying that the data from Bradley's phone puts him at Southwark Bridge?'

'Actually, no,' said Penny chirpily. 'It shows that he was here the entire time, exactly where he told you he was.'

'I don't understand then. That's good news, isn't it?'

'It is for Bradley. But you need to read what else security found. They, um, took it upon themselves to run a couple more checks.'

Her cheeks slightly pinked, Penny quickly opened the file, then sat back so Valerie had a clear view to read it.

She couldn't take in what she was reading. 'I never asked for this.'

'I know. Like I say, they checked anyway.'

Valerie stared at the screen, stunned. That couldn't be right.

'Someone's made a mistake,' she said.

Penny pulled a face. 'I thought the same, so I went back to check. They assured me that what you're reading is correct.'

Valerie crowded closer to the screen to read it again. She shook her head. 'This makes no sense.'

'I know, but it's right there in black and white,' said Penny. 'Bradley's phone wasn't anywhere near Southwark Bridge on the night Becca Farrow was murdered – but your husband's was.'

# Chapter Twenty-Seven

## GEMMA

The last thing Gemma had expected was for Kira to keep her word. In fact, she'd forgotten their conversation about going out entirely, distracted by the escalation of her online war against Valerie Aspen. So when Reece stuck his head round the door of the staff quarters on Friday evening just as she was clocking off, to tell her that Kira was in reception waiting for her, it took Gemma a few seconds to register what he was talking about.

'She's here? I thought she was joking,' she said uneasily.

'She said you're off out in town.' Reece looked her up and down. 'You're not exactly dolled up for it though.'

Gemma gave him a quick rundown of her and Kira's history. When she had finished, he pursed his lips like he'd just taken a sip of something acidic.

'No way should you go. You can't trust her.'

'I know. But what am I going to say?'

Reece pulled himself up to his full height, which was a smidge under five foot six. But what he lacked in size he made up for in sheer force of personality. 'Leave it with me. I'll get rid.'

While he was gone, Gemma checked her cart was stocked ahead of tomorrow's morning shift. Normally she would just do it when she arrived, but with bookings up again it would be another busy weekend and every minute counted.

Reece returned with a triumphant grin spread across his features. 'She's gone.'

'What did you tell her?'

He snickered. 'Period pains. I said you'd gone home to lie down with a hot water bottle and a Dairy Milk.'

'Do you think she believed you?'

'With my acting skills? Absolutely. She didn't look best pleased though, the bullying cow.'

Gemma's unease grew. Maybe she should've gone. Kira wouldn't like being cancelled on.

'I'd get off home now if I were you,' said Reece. 'Just in case she decides to do a house call to check up on you.'

Gemma didn't need telling twice. Bidding him a hasty goodbye, she slipped out of the hotel's rear exit. The seafront and her normal route home beckoned, but tonight she headed for the back streets instead. Less chance of bumping into Kira or someone who might tell on her.

Light drizzle dappled the air, so she pulled her hoodie over her head. She planned to film another video when she got home and didn't want her hair to look a state for it. This one was too important. She'd been going over it in her head for the past day, wondering if it was the right thing to do, before deciding it was. It was going to be her last video on the subject of Bradley Aspen. The final say – then she was closing down her account and leaving it alone.

She had to. Things had got out of hand since she and Reece had made that video in retaliation to the cease-and-desist letter. Two days on, she wished she'd kept her gob shut and just gone along with what the letter said. Not because people didn't agree with her, but because too many did. It was #TeamGemz all the way now. But for some of Gemma's followers, led by Sponge, supporting her was just an excuse to attack Valerie, and the threats being left in the comments section were off the scale. People wanted Valerie to get hurt. Like, seriously hurt. Despite her own mum's many failings as a parent, Gemma hadn't grown up around violence, and the idea that people wanted to attack a stranger because of videos she'd posted bothered her no end. Closing down her account would make it stop. It had to.

◆ ◆ ◆

As she put her key in the lock, Gemma heard voices inside the house coming from the hallway. They had a visitor? Gemma couldn't remember the last time someone had come to call who wasn't after a bill being paid. Then she froze, worried that Reece's prediction that Kira might do a house call had been correct. But as she strained to listen, Gemma realised the voice besides her mum's belonged to a woman far older than Kira. Older than her mum, even.

She turned the key and let herself in. Her mum was in her customary spot at the top of the stairs – Gemma guessed she must've retreated there after letting the guest in. Who was, as she'd guessed from her voice, an older woman.

She was dressed in an ill-fitting burgundy suit and clumpy black shoes, a large boxy handbag slung over her shoulder. The woman turned to face Gemma.

'Ah, you must be the daughter?'

She didn't sound particularly friendly. Gemma wondered if she was always like that or whether her attitude had shifted in the time she'd been inside their house. Her mum had a gift for rubbing people up the wrong way.

'Who are you?' Gemma asked.

'My name is Martine Barraclough. I'm—'

'Don't talk to her,' her mum shouted from the top of the stairs. 'She's from the council.'

Gemma's insides somersaulted. Why would the council be doing a house call at nearly seven thirty on a Friday evening?

'I called earlier but your mum told me to come back when you'd be home from work,' said Martine, as though she'd read Gemma's mind. 'Is there somewhere we can sit down?'

'Why are you here?' asked Gemma, ignoring the question because, no, there wasn't.

'We've sent your mother a number of letters about the state of the property following complaints from neighbours.' Martine's tone softened. 'I'm from the vulnerable adults' team. I want to help.'

'We don't need your help,' her mum shouted from her stairs perch. 'Tell her, Gem.'

The hallway suddenly felt even more cramped than usual. Gemma pinched the bridge of her nose, as though trying to ward off an impending headache. Really, she was trying to buy herself some time before answering.

'What kind of help can you give us?' she asked Martine quietly.

The woman flashed her a kindly smile. 'I can start by doing a safeguarding assessment. If that identifies that your mother needs additional support, there are next steps we can take.'

'What's she saying?' her mum hollered.

Martine took a step closer towards Gemma. 'I'm not here to make things worse, only better,' she whispered. 'For you as much as your mum.'

Gemma nodded, the lump in her throat rendering her unable to talk. She couldn't remember the last time someone had expressed concern for her welfare, let alone offered to help.

From the stairs, her mum yelled at Martine to leave.

'I can see I'm not going to get far tonight,' the social worker said to Gemma. 'I do need to come back next week though. What day is good for you?'

'I don't know, I'd have to check with work.'

'Why don't we say Wednesday at nine. If you can't make it, you need to call the office. The number's on the last letter we sent.'

Her mum's shouting grew louder.

'I don't have the letter! Mum has it.'

But Martine was already at the door. 'I'll see you next week. Try not to worry in the meantime.'

*Easier said than done*, thought Gemma.

As she stepped outside, Martine let out a loud shriek. 'What the— Oh my God, that is disgusting.' She turned on Gemma, all warmth gone. 'Do you have a dog?'

'No.'

'Well someone round here does, because they've just let theirs do a shit on your doorstep.'

Stunned, Gemma looked down to see the sole and sides of Martine's right shoe were now smeared with excrement. The smell made her gag.

'Don't just stand there,' snapped Martine. 'I need a cloth, or to run it under a tap.'

Gemma bolted for the kitchen. She couldn't find the roll of kitchen towel among the mess, so grabbed an old duster instead. Martine didn't look impressed when she handed it over.

'This is dirty.'

'It's all there is.'

She gagged again as Martine wiped her shoe clean. Gemma thought she was going to hand the cloth back, but she walked to the bin outside and deposited it there.

'You need to have a word with your neighbours about letting their dogs out,' she said coldly.

As Martine stalked down the path, Gemma stared down at the doorstep. She'd need to boil the kettle to rinse it off. There was no point complaining to the neighbours though, because she knew two things that Martine didn't. First, none of their neighbours owned a dog, and second, she'd changed enough soiled sheets at The Compton to know the difference between canine and human waste. What had been dumped on their doorstep wasn't the former. Someone had left her a message. And she had a pretty good idea who.

# Chapter Twenty-Eight

## EVE

The hotel cost more than Eve had planned to pay, but it was worth every penny she had siphoned from her deposit savings. The minute she'd seen it advertised on the booking website, she'd known she'd feel safe there. Boutique-sized, the building operated like a private residence. It wasn't open to the public to just come and go, meaning the security of its guests was paramount. The room Eve had booked was compact yet stunningly designed, with all mod cons and a huge television at the end of the king-size bed, just in case she couldn't sleep. The hotel itself was on the Pimlico–Belgravia border, an area with a low crime rate and close enough to Petty France if she was needed for an emergency.

The first night, she'd ordered room service for dinner. To her surprise, she'd then fallen asleep with little effort. She'd woken up once or twice in the night but had managed to drop off again. The next two nights she'd slept through. With Sol approving her time off, the daytimes were spent catching up on all the TV shows she'd missed. She ordered salads and other healthy dishes from room service and avoided all alcohol. The hotel had a secret garden that she walked round a few times for fresh air. It was, without question, the perfect bolt-hole.

Checking out Saturday lunchtime, Eve was sad to leave. She felt more like herself than she had in weeks. Her brain was sharper and she could finally think straight. But she couldn't afford to stay at the hotel any longer, and after tonight Leah would be back on days, so she had no reason not to return to the flat. Although not quite yet. Tonight she was staying at Horner's house in Loughton at the invitation of his wife, Lizzy. He'd confided in her what Eve had been going through after their conversation on Wednesday, and she'd called Eve herself later in the day to invite her to dinner at the weekend. Their twins were both going to be at sleepovers, so Eve could sleep in their daughter's room, as long as she didn't mind the mess.

Eve had gratefully accepted Lizzy's invite. Loughton was in Essex, a county about thirty-five miles outside London, while the town itself buffered Epping Forest, a 6,000-acre area of woodland. It would be nice to get out of the capital for the weekend and to spend time with Lizzy, who Eve had got to know after Novus.

'Did you enjoy your stay?' the receptionist asked, as Eve handed over the key card for her room.

'Like you wouldn't believe,' she grinned.

Even the weather had taken a turn for the better to match her mood. Warm and sunny, it was already being trumpeted as the hottest April on record so far. Eve could well believe it as she walked along Lupus Street shouldering her rucksack, sweat sheening her forehead and dampening her underarms.

Pimlico Tube station was up ahead. Eve's insides churned. It would take far too long to travel to Loughton by bus, so she had to get the Tube, even though that meant using an escalator. She was hoping that because it was a Saturday, the station wouldn't be too crowded. Busy times she feared the most, because someone could knock into her and send her flying, which was what had happened to Horner when he'd sustained his head injury during the Novus trial.

As it was, her descent to the platform was uneventful, bar the blood that was rushing to her ears and making her feel dizzy. She clung on to the handrail for dear life until she reached the bottom, leaving behind a sweaty imprint. Stepping off the escalator, she was so giddy with relief her legs almost gave way.

The journey to Loughton took an hour via the Central line. Once the train had passed through Liverpool Street, the number of passengers thinned out and the carriage was almost empty. The final seven stops were above ground, giving Eve time to check her emails. There was one from the management company of their block in Old Street, in response to her request for the video footage from early Wednesday morning. She quickly scrolled through the preamble to get to the answer.

> *. . . unfortunately on the occasion in question no video footage was taken or stored due to a technical hitch. We can assure you and other tenants that this has now been rectified . . .*

In other words, the system hadn't been working, and when they'd been caught out, the management company had scrambled to fix it. Riled, Eve closed down the email. With no footage, there was now no way to determine who had been at her door. She wanted to believe it had been Bradley Aspen, but now that her thinking was clearer, she knew she couldn't be sure. It was more likely someone else in the block who knew her by name. The twenty flats were mostly rented by young professionals like her and Leah, and because they'd been invited to parties in a few of them, she was on first-name terms with a number of other tenants. It was odd that whoever it was hadn't said their name though, or followed up with an apology for scaring the hell out of her.

As the Tube carried her out of the capital, Eve's mind drifted to the taskforce. She'd managed to switch off from work these past few days but now wondered if Horner knew of any developments. She'd seen the media reports that Valerie Aspen had issued a cease-and-desist notice against the TikToker who'd outed Bradley as Becca's killer. The TikToker, whose name was Gemma Kirk, had come out all guns blazing in retaliation, posting video after video claiming Valerie was trying to hide her son's guilt, and her own complicity, behind lawyers. Public opinion now fell firmly on Gemma's side, but it seemed only a matter of time before Valerie would follow through with her threat to sue her.

Loughton was the next station. Eve got to her feet, hitching her rucksack on to her shoulder. As she moved into position in the doorway, ready to disembark as soon as the train stopped, something caught her eye in the next carriage. A man was standing by the window of the interconnecting doors – and staring right at her.

Eve yelped in shock. Slowly, Frank Tooley raised his hand to acknowledge that she'd seen him.

'No, no, no,' she whimpered.

Every fibre of her being screamed at her to get off the train, but it was still travelling at speed. Instinctively she reached for the emergency alarm.

'Don't do that,' admonished an elderly gentleman in the priority seat nearest to her. 'If you pull that we could be stuck for ages. I've got an appointment to get to.'

Trembling, Eve withdrew her hand. She snatched her phone from the back pocket of her jeans and called Horner, who was due to pick her up outside the station.

'You nearly here?' Horner answered. His voice was tinny, like he was on loudspeaker. 'I'm just pulling into the car park—'

'Tooley's on the Tube,' she blurted out.

'What? Are you sure?'

She glanced at the interconnecting door. The window was now empty.

'He . . . he is. In the next carriage along.' She gulped down a sob. The calmness she'd carried with her from the hotel had vanished.

'Try not to panic. I'll see if I can get on to the platform.'

'Hurry, the train's about to stop.'

Seconds later, it slid to a halt. Eve repeatedly jabbed the button to open the door.

'Hold your horses,' said the pensioner, now waiting to disembark beside her. 'The doors are automatic. You pushing that won't do anything.'

Finally the doors opened and Eve half-jumped, half-fell down on to the platform. Horner was waiting for her, panting like he'd run to get there.

'Where is he?' he cried.

She pointed to the next carriage. 'He's in there. He's got grey hair, beard, blue jacket.' It wasn't the same padded winter coat Tooley had worn the first time he'd ambushed her, but it was a similar bright shade.

Horner reached the carriage just as the beeps sounded to indicate the doors were closing.

'I can't see him,' he shouted back to Eve.

The train started to pull away from the platform. Eve had been in the second carriage from the front, Tooley in the third. But as his carriage went past, she could see Horner was right – he wasn't anywhere inside it.

Horner rushed to her side. 'Can you see him?'

Carriage after carriage went past but Tooley wasn't in them. The train was gathering speed.

'Could you have been mistaken?' Horner asked.

Eve was close to tears. 'I don't think so – no, wait! Look, that's him!'

She pointed to the last carriage as it trundled past. There, in the window of the final set of doors, stood Frank Tooley.

'What's he doing?' said Horner.

'He's holding something.'

It was a piece of paper, which Tooley had slapped against the window. Eve strained to see the words on it but it was no good – the train was going too fast. The carriage rushed past her and with it Tooley's message.

# Chapter Twenty-Nine

## EVE

Lizzy put the mug of tea down in front of Eve. Without checking first, she'd sweetened it with two teaspoonfuls of sugar. 'For the shock.'

'Unless you want something stronger?' asked Horner. He checked his watch. 'It's after three now.'

Eve flicked him a wry look. 'I thought drinking made stress worse?'

'I meant drinking during working hours,' he said, matching her drollness.

'Tea first, then we can think about wine,' said his wife. 'You're meant to be cutting back. For the migraines.'

'You got yourself checked out?' Eve asked Horner.

'I did. Everything was clear on the CT scan, but it looks like a consequence of my injury last year is that I'm now susceptible to the odd migraine if I get overtired.'

'His consultant also said he should drink less,' said Lizzy.

'Fine, the wine can wait.' He sounded grumpy, but Eve caught the wink he flashed at his wife as she joined them at the scrubbed wooden table in their vast kitchen. Eve was pretty sure she'd never met any man as devoted to his partner as Horner was to Lizzy. Not even her dad with her mum, and they'd been married for more than thirty years.

It was touching to witness, and the kind of relationship she aspired to have herself. Eve had been engaged before she moved to London, to Nick, but had called off the wedding because she knew deep down that she would be settling. Nick was a lovely man, but he was the wrong man for her.

As she sipped her tea, Eve felt the tension and fear ebb away. It was easy to relax in Horner and Lizzy's presence, and their house was as welcoming as they were. The semi-detached property had been upgraded with a high-spec side return and rear extension, but it was still very much a functioning family home, with piles of shoes by the front door, electronics littering every surface, and a tumble dryer permanently in use in the utility room. Eve loved it.

A large ginger cat suddenly appeared at her ankles and rubbed against them.

'You're not allergic I hope,' said Lizzy. 'This is Creeper.'

'That's quite a name,' Eve laughed.

'It's from Minecraft. The twins chose it,' said Horner.

Now fourteen, Finn and Mia had said a brief hello when Eve arrived then skulked back to their respective bedrooms. Lizzy had shouted a reminder to Mia to tidy her room for Eve, who'd said she'd be fine with the sofa.

'Nonsense,' Lizzy had retorted. 'Her room's actually not too bad, unlike her brother's. You need a hazmat suit to enter and a tetanus shot to leave.'

Creeper had taken a shine to Eve and leapt up on her lap. She felt herself relax even more as she stroked his thick fur and he purred like an F1 sports car.

Horner leaned towards her. 'You ready to talk about it now?'

Eve nodded. She hadn't been ready on the car ride to theirs. The shock of seeing Tooley in the next Tube carriage had left her too rattled to speak. She couldn't believe his brazenness.

'I get that he must've followed me from the hotel to the Tube, but how did he know I was staying there in the first place?'

'He must've been stalking you when you checked in on Wednesday.'

Eve shuddered, close to tears again. The thought of Tooley following her everywhere terrified her. Lizzy reached over and squeezed Eve's hand. 'It's okay. You're safe here, and the police are involved now.'

As soon as they'd got back, Horner had called DCI Carroll from the taskforce for advice. Should they report Tooley to Essex Police, because he'd followed Eve to Loughton, or should they contact the Met because she lived in London? To Eve's relief, Carroll said that even though her Old Street address was outside the City of London Police's parameters, because one of the incidents of harassment had taken place on the Millennium Bridge with DC Quinn as a witness, he'd get someone at Bishopsgate station to deal with it.

Lizzy turned to her husband. 'You definitely couldn't read the note he'd written?'

'No, the train was moving too fast.'

'I want him to leave me alone,' said Eve wearily. 'I hate the thought that he's constantly watching me.'

'If he is, he might have seen who rang your doorbell in the early hours,' Lizzy remarked. Horner shot his wife a look.

'But it was gone four in the morning,' said Eve, horrified. 'He surely wouldn't have been outside my flat at that time?'

Horner spoke carefully. 'It's a possibility, Eve. He had to have followed you from your flat to know which hotel you'd gone to, so he could've been there at other times too. What's opposite?'

Eve had to think for a moment. Even though she would look in that direction dozens of times a week, she never really paid much attention. People often failed to notice what was right under their noses.

'More flats and some offices. There's also a gym on the corner, but it's not open twenty-four hours.'

'He might be Airbnbing somewhere. I'll flag it to Carroll.'

That did it for Eve. It was bad enough Tooley was following her, but the thought he might've set up permanent surveillance across the road was too much.

'The police will make him back off,' Horner reassured her.

'Remind me again why he's obsessed with talking to you?' Lizzy asked.

Eve told her about the file Tooley had dropped off at her apartment block. 'I haven't looked at it. I don't want to,' she said.

'I don't blame you.' Lizzy glanced at her husband. 'Maybe Eve being on the taskforce isn't such a good idea right now. If word gets out, it will put an even bigger spotlight on her.'

'You can step down if you want,' said Horner, nodding. 'No one would blame you.'

'I'm not going to let Tooley stop me doing my job. I want to be on the taskforce. But thank you,' she said to Lizzy. 'I appreciate your concern.'

Lizzy squeezed Eve's hand. 'Any time.' She checked her watch. 'The kids need dropping off at their sleepovers. I'll take them while you two catch up. I'm sure there's some taskforce stuff you need to discuss. But once I'm back, no more work talk, okay? It's the weekend, you should both be switching off.' The sound of her chair scraping back across the tiled floor sent Creeper bolting from Eve's lap.

'Does that mean we can open a bottle now?' Horner asked his wife hopefully.

Lizzy rolled her eyes. 'Go on then. But make sure you save me a glass.'

◆ ◆ ◆

Horner had been busy in the days since Eve had last seen him. While the detective trio, Carroll, Cato and Quinn, were carrying out inquiries, he'd been making some of his own.

Now, spread across the table in front of them were printouts of photographs he'd taken while walking Becca Farrow's last-known route to Southwark Bridge. Next to them was his laptop, opened on a map of the area surrounding the bridge, and two freshly poured glasses of chilled white wine.

'One of the biggest puzzles is how Aspen got off and on to the bridge without being picked up on CCTV anywhere nearby. I think I know how,' said Horner.

He passed one of the printouts to Eve. The photo was of a fairly narrow, nondescript street flanked on either side by office blocks that didn't top more than five storeys.

'This is Queen Street. It crosses Upper Thames Street, then becomes Queen Street Place as it runs down to the bridge.' He pointed to the map open on his laptop so Eve could follow the route. 'Becca was last seen walking along Cloak Lane, so coming down Queen Street is almost certainly the way she came to get the bridge.'

Eve studied the map and the printout. In her mind's eye she could see Becca moving along the route, stumbling and weaving after a night of heavy drinking.

'What else do you see in the photo?' Horner asked her.

Eve looked closely. Nothing seemed out of place . . .

'The bikes,' she said triumphantly, pointing to the row of hire cycles which stretched up one side of the street.

'Correct. Queen Street is pretty much one long docking station.'

'You think Bradley Aspen used one of the bikes?'

'I do. Becca was pushed into the water at this end of Southwark Bridge – why would Aspen risk continuing to cross it where he could be picked up on CCTV cameras? Much safer to double back the way he came and use the back streets to make his escape. See this passage?' Horner pulled forward another printout, this time depicting an even narrower street with barely a metre of pavement on either side. 'When I was looking at possible driving routes, I thought he might've parked down here, but it makes more sense that he used a bike. This passage is a cut-through that comes out at the back at Mansion House. From there he could've gone in any direction.'

Eve studied the row of hire cycles. She'd never used one herself, but knew they were wildly popular in the capital. You couldn't cross a street without seeing one.

'He might not have used one of these,' she said. 'He could've parked elsewhere and walked there or caught a cab.'

'Do you not think a cabbie or Uber driver or the like would've come forward if he'd got in their vehicle? The whole world is aware of this case now. As for driving himself, the only vehicles he has access to belong to his parents, and both have diplomatic number plates. Carroll ran checks and neither was in the vicinity.'

'He could've hired a car.'

'Again, you'd expect that information to have come to light by now,' said Horner.

'He could've used his own bike.'

'That's true, but he chose this bridge for a reason. We know that the lack of CCTV and the height of the balustrade worked in his favour – the access to the bikes could've capped it.'

'Do you think he chooses the bridge more than the victim? I thought we'd decided he had a victimology.'

'I think it's a bit of both. He identifies bridges that make his task easier, then waits for the right woman to come along at the right time. If it wasn't Becca Farrow, it would've been someone else who looked just like her.'

Horner paused for a moment, then shifted awkwardly in his chair. Eve filled in the gap for him.

'Someone who looks like me as well.'

'I didn't say that.'

'You didn't have to. Quinn's already pointed it out.'

'It might not have been him who rang your doorbell, Eve.'

'But it might have. I've been thinking – what if Lizzy is right and Tooley had been hanging around then and saw who it was? He might be able to identify him.'

'That would mean you talking to Tooley to ask him.'

'I know.'

Both paused. Then, in an unchoreographed show of synchronicity, both reached for their glasses of wine at the same time. Horner drank first, then spoke first.

'Confronting your stalker to find out if a potential serial killer is stalking you is a new one on me. I think I should come with you when you go to meet Tooley.'

'You think?' Eve deadpanned.

'It could backfire,' said Horner. 'You could be putting yourself in harm's way.'

'But what if we can get Tooley on the record saying it was Bradley Aspen at my door? It helps our case. Undeniable evidence, remember.'

Horner raised his glass. 'I'll drink to that.'

'I can call him now.'

'Don't. Let him sweat for twenty-four hours. The way it panned out on the Tube might've spooked him, and it could be better to wait so that when you call him it's like the incident's been forgotten.'

'Let him off the hook for freaking me out, in other words.'

Horner looked fretful. 'I don't want to ignore the crimes of one man to catch another for his, but I don't see any other way at the moment. Tooley could be crucial.'

'I agree,' admitted Eve. She raised her glass and clinked it against his. 'But here's to nailing the creep when all this is over.'

# Chapter Thirty

## VALERIE

Every Sunday morning, unless they were away, Valerie rose early to power-walk Scout the one and a half miles from their house to Richmond Park. This morning, her energy low and her mood not much better, she doubted she'd manage more than one lap. But still she pulled on her walking gear, eager not to let Mark's absence sway her from the routine. Besides, there didn't seem much point lying in bed with his side of it glaringly empty.

It was just after six and far earlier than she'd normally venture out. Stealing downstairs, she hoped the early wake-up wouldn't trigger Scout into barking, in case she woke Bradley. He hadn't said much since Mark had walked out on Friday, but she knew he was struggling mentally with his dad gone and the allegations hanging over him, and she wanted him to rest. When she'd passed his bedroom on her way to turn in last night, she was sure she could hear him crying. Maybe it was an outpouring of relief that the phone triangulation data had proved he hadn't been anywhere near Southwark Bridge. She didn't knock on his door to ask though, knowing her son well enough to know that if he wanted to talk, he'd come to her.

She hadn't told him that his dad's phone had pinged near the bridge instead. Valerie remained convinced that it was a mistake and had asked Penny to have the findings wiped from wherever security had recorded them. She was furious that a check had been run on her husband's phone when she hadn't requested it. Mark had been with her all night after going out for dinner with friends – they'd both drunk too much and had collapsed straight into bed on getting home.

Scout wasn't in the kitchen where Valerie had left her last night. Had Bradley come down in the night to take her upstairs? The dog wasn't allowed to sleep on their beds as a rule, but given the circumstances it would be churlish to complain if he'd needed the comfort. But then she heard the faint strain of the television playing in the lounge. Pushing open the door, she found Bradley on the sofa with Scout stretched out next to him. She batted her tail on seeing Valerie enter.

'Morning,' said Valerie. 'Couldn't sleep either, honey?'

Bradley looked up. His eyes glittered red, but she knew he hadn't been crying. It was a sign of something else, something that made her heart sink. 'Have you been drinking?'

'No.'

'Are you high?'

He looked back at the television.

'I asked you a question.'

'Mom, leave it.'

There were no signs of drug-taking anywhere in the front room. It was as she'd left it last night, clean and orderly. She marched back to the kitchen and searched there, even checking in the food waste bin. She grew angrier with every passing second. He'd promised her that he'd never bring drugs into the house again, after the last time. She went up to his bedroom. Bradley must've heard her and followed.

'Stay out of my room,' he snapped.

'My house, my rules. Where's the gear? I want it gone.'

'Mom, you're overreacting. It was just a bit of dope and blow.'

Her cheeks burned red. She pointed to the scar at her throat. 'Overreacting? Have you forgotten what caused this?'

'How many more times? I said I was sorry.'

'Come on, where is it?' she demanded to know.

She went to pull open his clothes drawers. Bradley yelled at her to stop.

'I didn't take it here. I went out.'

'You did what?' she asked, shocked.

'I went out after you'd gone to bed.'

'Where?'

'Into town to meet some friends.'

'Are you for real? You snuck out?'

'Jesus, Mom, you're acting like I'm a kid. I'm twenty-four. I went out, met my friends, had a couple of drinks, did some blow, had a smoke, came home. It's not a big deal.'

'Not a big deal? The entire world thinks you're a killer and you're out getting high like you don't care.'

Bradley reeled back as though she'd slapped him. 'The entire world? So you think it too?'

'That's not what I meant.'

'Yes, it is. You think it. I can tell from your face.'

'That'll be the drugs making you paranoid,' she said witheringly.

'You think I'm capable though. You think, because of Nadia, I killed that other woman.'

It was a surprise to hear Nadia's name leave his lips. He hadn't referred to her by name since that flight back from Prague – not even after Gemma Kirk had posted the video of her funeral on TikTok. Valerie had likened it to not walking on a broken ankle: it felt too painful to even try. Instead, Bradley just called her 'that girl'.

'You told me that was an accident and I believed you,' she said.

'But do you still believe me?'

The CCTV image of Becca Farrow's killer flashed before her mind. *No, remember the phone data*, she told herself firmly.

'I do. I have a question, though.'

'What?'

'Where were you tonight, honey?'

'What?'

'Which part of town did you meet your friends in?'

'Near King's Cross. Why?'

'Just asking.'

Bradley looked baffled for a moment, then his face fell. 'You want to know if I was near the river?'

'You need to stay away from that whole area. If anyone recognises you, they'll jump to the wrong conclusion. I know it's not fair, but just until things die down.'

His eyes glittered even redder, this time with unshed tears. 'It's never going to stop, is it? I'm always going to be presumed guilty, whatever I say or do.'

'It will stop. It has to.'

'Can't you get a job at another embassy? Some tiny obscure country where people don't have the internet?'

Valerie smiled sadly. 'I don't think so, honey. Your dad won't want to move again.'

'Does he get a say if he's not living with us any more?'

'He's just gone away for a couple of days,' she said stiffly.

A shadow crossed Bradley's face. 'You sure about that?'

'Look, we can't move again. We just need to wait this out. The police will find the real killer and you'll be exonerated. It's just a matter of time.'

She wasn't sure who she was trying to convince more, though – him or her.

◆ ◆ ◆

She ended up delaying taking Scout out for her walk until late morning. After a breakfast of poached eggs and avocado on muffins, she packed Bradley off to bed to sleep off his high. Then she spent time tidying up before heading out. The house was already pretty straight, but she wanted it to look good for Mark's return, whenever that might be.

The end of their driveway and the street beyond were mercifully empty. Evidently even reporters and protestors needed a lie-in occasionally.

Valerie set off at a fast pace, Scout at her heel. Usually these morning walks cleared her head, but today she had too many thoughts and worries backed up. She needed help processing them all. Tucking her pods into her ears, she did a quick mental calculation. It was eleven forty-five in London, so it would be six forty-five in the morning in DC. Early, but for her the call couldn't wait.

Glenn picked up just as it was about to go to voicemail.

'You took your time answering,' said Valerie, careful to keep her tone light. She was conscious they'd spoken only three times since her hasty return from Washington. They'd texted, but the messages were brief and lacked substance. What she really craved was a heart-to-heart. 'I know it's early, but is this a good time?'

She couldn't hear any noise in the background. Sunday morning he should be at home with his wife and kids.

'Sure is. I'm on a golf weekend with college friends. I'm just getting ready for a light breakfast before hitting the green.'

'From college? Anyone I know?'

He reeled off a few names she recognised from Chicago. Unlike Glenn, she hadn't kept in touch with any of their fellow alumni. He was the only person she could be bothered with.

'Sounds fun,' she said. 'I won't keep you if you need to eat.'

'It can wait. My waistline will thank me. So, I'm guessing from your tone that you're having a really shitty time still?'

He knew her so well.

'You guessed correctly. I almost don't know where to start.'

But start she did, telling him everything, from Mark walking out to Penny's data disclosure to Bradley taking drugs again. When she finished, Glenn let out a low whistle.

'That is a lot to deal with. How are you coping?'

She slowed her pace to allow Scout to sniff the grass verge. 'Not great. I just want some let-up. Between the reporters, the trolls, the lawyers, and the millions who think I'm a terrible mom, it's all a bit much.' Again, she tried to keep the tone light but the crack in her voice betrayed her. 'Bradley's asked if I can transfer to an embassy in the back of nowhere. Know of any jobs going in the Federated States of Micronesia?'

The Pacific islands, near Papua New Guinea, were one of the remotest countries to have a US embassy anywhere in the world.

Glenn didn't share her amusement though. He changed the subject – and knocked the stuffing right out of her.

'Could Bradley have taken Mark's phone to Southwark Bridge?'

Valerie's mouth dropped. 'Are you serious?'

'Very. Your husband's phone was triangulated near to the scene of a murder that your son's been linked to. You say that Mark was at home in bed with you all night, yet his phone was there somehow, and the most obvious explanation is Bradley had it on him. If he snuck out last night while you were asleep, chances are he's done it before.'

'You seriously think my son's a killer?' asked Valerie, distraught.

'I've looked into Nadia Vinke's death, Val. I've also looked into what happened to her best friend afterwards. I don't think either of them were accidents.'

'You did what? But why?'

'To protect you. I'm worried about you.'

'How is trash-talking my husband and son protecting me?' she exclaimed.

'People think you've known all along that Bradley killed Nadia and Becca. I want to help you prove that you didn't.'

'Isn't my word enough?'

'Not in court. Look, I shouldn't be telling you this, but I'm hearing noises that the President is being leaned on to cut you loose because of all the negative press. If he sacks you, your immunity is lifted. After what you just told me about Mark's phone, the police will have a field day with Bradley *and* him.'

The rush of blood to her head silenced the sounds around her. Of birdsong, of distant traffic, of Scout whining for them to keep walking. 'I can't let that happen,' she said weakly.

The line went quiet, and for a moment she thought it had disconnected. 'Glenn?'

'What if the police find evidence connecting Bradley to more crimes, do you think the President will still fight your corner then?'

'More crimes? Don't be ridiculous. This is my child we're talking about, Glenn. He says he didn't hurt Becca Farrow. Nadia was an accident.'

'What about the girl on Putney Bridge, the one who worked for your neighbour?'

Valerie had forgotten she'd told Glenn about that.

'It was nothing to do with Bradley,' she said unconvincingly.

'If he's innocent, why did you rush back from DC the minute that you saw the news report about Becca Farrow? Why did you tell me that you thought Bradley was in trouble again? Remember?

I asked you what kind of trouble, and you said "the Prague kind". You were the one who made the connection between Bradley and Becca, because you knew he'd killed before,' said Glenn. 'I think deep down you've always believed he's capable of hurting people, but you're desperately trying to be a good mom and protect him. I get that, I really do. I'd do anything to protect my two. But sometimes you just shouldn't. At least two young women have died, Val. What about their moms?'

He was right. She couldn't pretend any longer. This morning had proved that Bradley could lie as easily as breathing. All this time he'd said he'd been too upset to leave the house and see his friends, and all the time he had been sneaking out to get high with them. She couldn't trust anything he told her, and that included whether he'd really meant to hurt Nadia and whether he'd killed Becca Farrow and had tried to kill Aldana Porras.

'What should I do?' she asked despairingly.

'Whatever's necessary to cover your back.'

# Chapter Thirty-One

## GEMMA

There were twenty-six different versions of Gemma's final TikTok on the Aspen case saved on her phone but not one of them uploaded. Preparing to record version number twenty-seven, she wanted to scream into her pillow with frustration. Why couldn't she get the wording right? Or string more than ten words into a sentence without stammering or waffling? She'd spent all day Saturday and Sunday trying to record it, and now it was Monday morning and she still hadn't got it right. Three days was the longest she'd gone without sharing a video; from the messages she was being sent, people were desperate to know why.

She checked the time. She was late leaving for work, and if she didn't nail this version right this second, it would have to wait until tonight. She pressed record.

'Hi everyone. I know I've been keeping you waiting, but I've . . . um . . . well . . . oh, *fuck*.'

Livid with herself, she reached over and turned the recording off. Then she stormed out of her bedroom before she did something she regretted, like smash her phone against the wall in a fit of anger.

In the bathroom she removed her make-up and splashed cold water on her face, and tried not to notice the pile of clothes that had appeared in the bath overnight. Her mum had dumped them there because Gemma had refused her nightly plea to put them in her bedroom. It had taken Gemma an hour to get back to sleep afterwards, and now she was exhausted before the day had even begun. Staring at her pale reflection in the cracked mirror above the salmon-pink sink, a relic from her grandparents' ownership of the house, she decided Reece and Stacie would have to manage without her for once. She couldn't remember the last time she'd thrown a sickie but she didn't have it in her to clean up after strangers today. Not when she had a deadline to sort out her mum's crap.

Martine's planned return had weighed heavily on Gemma all weekend. She'd tried to talk to her mum about clearing up, explaining that the social worker would be assessing the state of the place when she came on Wednesday, but it was like talking to a brick wall. Gemma honestly believed her mum just didn't see mess in the way other people did. It was like her brain had a filter that made the house look spic and span, whereas Gemma's #nofilter saw it for the hoarding it was. It was a form of mental illness, and her mum might never be able to overcome it. Gemma knew that because she'd watched a TV documentary with a presenter whose mum was exactly like hers. She'd cried watching it because she identified so much with the presenter, who hadn't had a normal childhood either because she was too ashamed to have friends visit. In one scene the presenter showed off her own home, and it was so tidy and clean she could've eaten dinner off the floor. It was how Gemma dreamt her own house would be when she was older.

She got her phone from her room, texted Reece to say she was ill, then went downstairs. Her first port of call was the doorstep, to check that no more nasty surprises had been dumped on it. She was ninety-nine per cent certain Kira was behind the shitshow because Gemma had dared to stand her up. It was exactly the sort of disgusting thing she'd do to make a point. Well, not her personally. She'd have got one of her lackeys to make the deposit on her behalf.

The only area of her life that didn't require Gemma to be constantly worried right now was her finances. She had a surplus of cash at the moment, with what was coming in from her TikTok subscribers. With that in mind, she decided to nip to the bakery up the road and buy some fresh bread and a few sweet treats for later. Then she'd take her mum breakfast in bed. Hopefully it would put her in a good enough mood that they could have a conversation about preparing for Martine's return.

Her mum hadn't shut the curtains before going to sleep the previous evening, and her bedroom was bathed in sunshine as Gemma entered. She wondered if she could persuade her to go for a walk later, as long as they stayed down this end of the beach and didn't go near The Compton. Like all seaside resorts, Bridlington came into its own when the sun was out. Even the rundown areas looked lovely.

But first they needed to make a start on tidying up.

Her mum stirred beneath her duvet. Piled on the bed next to her were clothes and books and even some shoes. Gemma kicked aside a box of Christmas decorations to put the tray she was carrying down on the floor. Then she gently shifted the clothes and other items on to a chair at the side the room, reassuring her mum the entire time.

'I'll put them back as soon as we're done eating, Mum.'

Mel pulled herself upright and leaned back against the headboard. She studied the empty space beside her, then nodded. 'Once we've eaten.'

Gemma put the tray on the bed, then asked if it was okay to sit down now. Her mum said yes, so she climbed on to the bed beside her, resting against the headboard too.

'This is lovely, Gem. What's the occasion? Is it your birthday? Did I forget?' her mum asked fretfully.

'There's no reason. I've got the day off and thought it would be a nice treat.'

Gemma didn't tell her she was pulling a sickie. Her mum would spiral with worry and there'd be no hope of them talking sensibly about Martine's visit.

The tray was laden with butter, honey, jam, chocolate spread and half a farmhouse loaf, toasted. Gemma knew her mum often forgot to eat, and when she did it was mostly snacks, so she was pleased to see her wolf down four doorstep slices. She managed two and a bit.

'I thought we could do something together today,' she said, as they sipped tea.

'Like what?'

Gemma had thought long and hard about how to frame it so her mum didn't feel pressured. 'Do you remember I had that cash register when I was small, with the little plastic coins and paper money? I was wondering if we could find it.'

'Why?'

'A friend of mine has a little girl who wants one,' she lied. 'They don't have any money though, so I thought I could lend it to her.'

Her mum's brow furrowed. 'You want to give it away?'

'No, it would be a loan. Like I say, they don't have any money and I was really lucky when I was little. You and Dad got me everything I asked for.'

Her mum visibly flinched at the mention of Dennis.

'The girl's dad has walked out too, so I feel sorry for them. You and me know what that's like.'

'We certainly do,' her mum bristled.

'So I was thinking,' Gemma went on carefully, 'that I could let her play with the cash register and maybe a few other toys?'

She watched her mother carefully for signs of distress but, remarkably, her mum seemed okay with the idea. Of course, a bag of children's toys was barely going to make a dent in the hoarding but it was better than nothing. If she could show Martine that, with some gentle persuasion, they could throw stuff out, her mum might get some mental health support. What she needed was counselling to unpick why she hoarded in the first place.

'How about I take the tray downstairs and you get dressed? You're really good at finding stuff so I know it won't take us long to dig the cash register out.'

Leaving the bedroom, it wasn't lost on Gemma that she spoke to Mel like a mother would her child, rather than the other way round. Sadness coursed through her. She'd give anything to just be the kid sometimes, to have no responsibilities, no worries, and for someone to make *her* breakfast.

Her mum followed her downstairs a few minutes later. Together they went into the front room. Gemma's phone vibrated in her back pocket. More notifications. The buzzing had become incessant, online and in her head. She'd do a bit of tidying with her mum then have another crack at recording her last video. She just wanted it done and over with.

'Where shall we look first?' she asked her mum.

Mel scanned the room, her expression joyful. Gemma could see the mess didn't bother her at all. This was Aladdin's cave to her, each item a treasure lovingly hidden away.

'It's in one of those crates beneath the window.'

Gemma dutifully went behind the sofa to where the bay window was. She was careful not to brush against the foot of the net curtains, which had blackened over time with mould. She should probably get them washed before Martine's visit, or even replace them now that she had the money.

'It's the second crate along,' her mum called out.

Gemma crouched down – just as there was an almighty crash right above her head. The net curtains billowed as glass rained down on her. Too stunned to move, she screamed for her mum. But Mel acted like she hadn't heard her.

'My things!' she shrieked.

Heart pounding in her chest, Gemma slowly straightened up. Behind her, the lower-middle pane of the bay window was smashed in. She brushed fragments of glass from her hair and shoulders. Her mum was still wailing.

In the middle of the room lay a brick. It had landed on the crate containing her old Barbie dolls, cracking the plastic lid. Hand shaking like a leaf, Gemma picked it up. It was a standard red house brick with no discernible markings. Her mum's shouts subsided.

'What is that?'

'It's a brick, Mum. Someone threw it at our window.'

Her voice didn't sound like it normally did to her ears. It was shaky and feeble and scared. If this was Kira's idea of more revenge for being stood up, it was way too much. If she hadn't been crouching, the brick would've hit her.

'Call the police, Gem. Tell them what happened. Someone attacked my things!'

Gemma's spirits sank lower. She could've been seriously injured, but all her mum cared about was her hoard. 'Sure. I'll call them now,' she said.

She took her phone from her back pocket and pretended to dial the emergency number. She wasn't really going to ring. No way was she going to tell the police about Kira. It would only make it worse.

'It's ringing now,' she whispered to her mum. 'I'll take it outside to talk to them, so they can hear me better.'

She went into the back garden and gulped down fresh air to calm herself. She'd get the window fixed and hopefully Kira would soon find someone else to torment. Until then, Gemma would stay the hell out of her way.

She was about to put her phone away when a message popped up from Sponge. She groaned. She was not in the mood for his rantings right now. But the message had a video attachment with it which made her curious, because he never recorded his own videos. He just liked to comment on hers.

The video was of a residential street. It looked way posher than any of the houses in Bridlington. Suddenly Sponge's smiling face loomed into view. 'Guess where I am, Gemz?' The camera swung round to focus on a street sign. She didn't recognise the name but beneath it, in capitals, was the word 'Putney'. Gemma gasped. That was where the Aspens lived. The camera landed back on Sponge. 'You've been bang on all along, Gemz. That lying bitch Valerie Aspen needs to pay for covering up for her murdering bastard son. So I decided to jump on the train from Brum and do it myself.' His smile grew wider. 'Wish me luck, Gemz. This one's for you.'

# Chapter Thirty-Two

## EVE

The meeting place was of Eve's choosing. Outdoors, next to the Tower of London and in front of Traitors' Gate, through which centuries ago prisoners were transported into the tower by barge. Busy, noisy, and surrounded by what felt like thousands of other people.

Frank Tooley was not impressed. 'This is hardly conducive to conversation,' he complained, surveying the crowds streaming past them.

*Good*, thought Eve.

There was nowhere for them to sit down either. Again, all part of the plan. She didn't want him to think this was a relaxed situation where they'd be having a cosy chat on friendly terms. She wanted it to be as awkward as possible. Her skin crawled just standing close to the man.

'I'm fine with it,' Eve said, keeping her gaze trained across the river on HMS *Belfast*, the naval frigate turned tourist attraction. Further along the waterfront on the same side as her was Horner. He'd kept to his word to accompany her to the meeting, even though it had meant them both ducking out of work early. From here, however, they were headed to another meeting of the taskforce.

Despite it being less than a week since the last one, DCI Carroll had called Paul Ferdie requesting to meet because his team had uncovered a significant piece of evidence and needed the CPS to see it. Ferdie said Carroll had been beside himself with excitement on the call, so it must be a breakthrough. Eve couldn't wait to find out what it was.

But first, Tooley.

Her instinct was to berate him for frightening her on the Tube. He didn't have children of his own but he might have a sister or a niece – how would he feel if a man twice their age was stalking them? But she didn't, because it would more likely empower than embarrass him. Men like Tooley liked having the upper hand and Eve wasn't prepared to give it to him.

'You held up a note to me on the Tube but I couldn't read it. What did it say?'

'Have you bothered to read the file I left you?'

Horner had remarked to Eve on their way to meet Tooley that he would ask about the file. Mentally she kicked herself for not thinking ahead and checking its contents.

'I haven't, I'm afraid. I've been busy with my current cases.'

'Trying to prosecute that diplomat's son? I thought that one was dead in the water, so to speak.' Tooley chuckled at his own joke.

Eve was infuriated. Had he forgotten it was him who'd stirred things up by posting the photo of her and Quinn on social media? She tried to steer the conversation back.

'Was the note a reminder for me to read it?'

'Would you have read the file if it had been?'

Irritated, Eve suggested he told her what was in the file, rather than waste even more time.

'I can do better than that. I brought a copy with me for you to read, just in case.'

Eve's heart sank. She had hoped this would be a quick conversation. She held her hand out. Tooley pulled the file from the supermarket carrier bag he had with him.

'I think you'll find it interesting reading,' he said.

She'd be the judge of that.

'You might recognise the names, in fact.'

Eve's head snapped up and she looked Tooley in the eye for the first time since he'd arrived. 'What's that supposed to mean?'

'See for yourself,' he said smugly.

Eve opened the file. She didn't have to read far to realise she did recognise the names. Very well, in fact. The case had been one of her first crown court experiences.

In July 2018, a man named Stephen Sheridan had gone on trial at Wolverhampton Crown Court for false imprisonment of a minor. The victim was a ten-year-old called Albie Marsh who lived in a neighbouring street. Eve, working for a private law firm in the Midlands, had been part of the team tasked with building Sheridan's defence.

The prosecution claimed that Sheridan, who had learning disabilities, had snatched the boy from the street and held him in the cellar of his home for thirty-six hours. Sheridan denied the charges, maintaining the boy had entered his house willingly and stayed because he hadn't wanted to go home. The fact Albie's disappearance had gone unreported by his neglectful parents for almost twenty-four hours because he often stayed out for long periods with his friends went in Sheridan's favour.

What muddied the defence team's case, however, was a recorded history of hostility between the victim and the accused. Sheridan had made multiple complaints to the police that Albie and other neighbourhood kids would stand outside his home shouting names and throwing things at his front door. When questioned by the prosecution, he admitted that he would scream and make threats in retaliation, including the implicit warning he 'would get' Albie.

On the witness stand – hidden from the rest of the court by a screen – Albie did not deny tormenting Sheridan on previous occasions. However, he claimed that on the day in question he'd simply been walking past Sheridan's house on his own when the man had grabbed him and bundled him inside.

Based on the history of threats and the boy's compelling and often tearful testimony of being held captive, the jury convicted Sheridan by a majority verdict and he was sentenced to nine years' imprisonment.

Eve finished reading. 'Why are you showing me this?'

'It is my view that a gross miscarriage of justice was committed when Stephen Sheridan was imprisoned, and I want your help in overturning it, seeing as you helped precipitate it.'

Eve held her nerve. 'We did our best, but the evidence against Stephen was substantial and proven. He kept Albie in his cellar against his will for almost two days.'

'No he didn't. Marsh went there willingly, just as Stephen said. He stayed in the front room, sleeping on the sofa, and spent the time watching telly, playing computer games, and eating junk food. He only went into the cellar when the police came looking.'

'That's what Stephen said, but there was no DNA evidence to show Albie had been anywhere else in the house other than the cellar.'

'You know as well as I do that Stephen told the court he'd cleaned up before the police arrived because Marsh had told him the place was a mess. Marsh knew what he was doing.'

The prosecution, however, had successfully argued that Sheridan had deliberately covered his tracks when he'd dusted, mopped and scrubbed the place from top to bottom. Eve said this to Tooley, but he had an answer for that too.

'What if I told you we now have proof that Marsh lied to the police and then again in court?'

'We?'

'Stephen Sheridan's mum read my true-crime blog and contacted me.'

Eve remembered Mary Sheridan well. She'd been a sweet soul, like her son, and simply wanted to be left alone to live a peaceful life. But Stephen would regularly get into rows because he lacked the ability to process anger. Mary had been away visiting her sister when he'd imprisoned Albie. It had been gut-wrenching to see him sent to prison, but Eve understood why the jury had seen fit to convict him. Still, she was curious to find out more from Tooley now.

'What's this proof?'

'The boy took photographs during his stay and shared them with his friends.'

Eve was stunned. There had been no mention of this anywhere in the police investigation or during the trial. 'How do you know that?'

'Marsh is seventeen now and an even bigger troublemaker than he was back then. He was overheard in a pub boasting that he lied in court by a parent of a boy he'd hung around with at the time of his so-called kidnap. The dad then spoke to his son and he admitted it was true. Marsh had shown his gang pictures of him eating pizza and crisps and watching telly on Stephen's sofa.'

'Does the friend have copies of the photos?'

'No, but he believes Marsh still has them. He told his dad who told Stephen's mum that Marsh would've held on to them for – what do they call it? Oh yes, bragging rights.'

Eve felt sick to her stomach. If this was true, Marsh had perverted the course of justice. She closed the file and handed it back to Tooley. 'If what you're saying is true, it could be construed as a miscarriage of justice. But I can't help you with that. I work for the CPS now. You could try taking this to my old firm in Shropshire who oversaw Stephen's defence, but without the pictures you don't have proof that Marsh lied.' She crossed her arms. 'Right. Now we've discussed the file, I need to ask a favour from you.'

Tooley looked affronted. 'That's simply not good enough, Ms Wren. You have a professional responsibility to help Stephen Sheridan.'

'I work for the CPS now,' she repeated. 'I cannot help with any appeal against a conviction.'

'No, but you can re-examine the evidence, like you did with the Novus trial.'

'Even if I could do that, which I can't, it falls under a different CPS division. West Midlands would be responsible. But there's no point them reviewing the evidence that exists, because the incriminating photos aren't part of it. You're talking about new evidence. Until you have the actual proof, an appeal will get nowhere.' Her mind landed on Stephen Sheridan and the memory of how distressed and scared he'd been when she'd seen him for the last time in the court cells after his sentence was handed down. 'I really am sorry. I hope the photos are found because it would force the police to reopen the case.'

'I don't believe you cannot help, Ms Wren. You're choosing not to.'

He was really irritating her now. 'What would you like me to do? Go round to Albie Marsh's house and demand he hand the photos over?'

Tooley didn't take well to her show of temper. 'There's no need to be rude. Of course I don't expect you to confront him directly. But there must be something you can do. You owe it to Mr Sheridan and his mother for failing in your duty to present all the facts in your defence.'

'That's not fair.'

'Isn't it? Mr Sheridan knew Marsh had taken photos. He even posed with Marsh in a couple of them. Yet you, his solicitor, were unaware of this crucial fact.'

Eve's mouth went dry. 'Stephen said that?'

'Yes. I went to see him in prison. I asked him why he never told you about the photos and he said he thought you knew.'

'I – I didn't. I mean . . . if I had . . .' She trailed off. How could she have missed something so vital? She thought back over the many interviews she'd conducted with Stephen before the trial. He'd been so adamant Albie Marsh had been in the house willingly – why hadn't he told her about the photographs?

*Why hadn't she asked Stephen if there was more proof that Albie had been there willingly than just his word?*

Suddenly Horner appeared in her peripheral vision. He tapped his watch face. Eve checked hers. They needed to leave or they'd be late for the taskforce meeting.

'I have to go now,' she told Tooley. 'I'm late for my next appointment.'

He crossed his arms huffily. 'Fine. Go.'

'Look, I do want to help. But without those photos, I don't see what any of us can do. Not my old firm, the CPS, the police, or you. We can't base an appeal on something someone overheard in a pub.'

Tooley seemed to like that she'd lumped him in with the various law enforcement agencies. 'I will do my best to get hold of them.'

'Don't do anything to put yourself at risk,' warned Eve, then regretted it immediately. Tooley's face brightened on hearing her express concern. *You idiot*, she berated herself. *Now he thinks you're worried about him*. It was time to set him straight.

'Now that we've talked about Stephen's case, I'd like you to stop calling me and following me. Is that okay?' she asked politely.

Tooley stared at her impassively. Eve ploughed on, hating that she had to indulge him like this.

'I did wonder, however, if you happened to see someone ringing the bell to my flat repeatedly in the early hours.'

Eve cited the date and time. Tooley broke into a broad smile, and by doing so confirmed he had indeed been watching her flat at all hours. It took every ounce of self-control not to lose her temper with him.

'I did see him, yes.'

'Who was it? I need to know.'

'I'm happy to tell you. The person I saw outside your flat in the early hours was . . .'

He took a dramatic, lengthy pause. Eve could almost hear him doing a mental drum roll.

'. . . the man who flagged you the taxi on the Strand the evening you and I first met.'

'Jamie?' she asked, shocked.

'If that's his name, then yes.'

'Not Bradley Aspen?'

Now it was Tooley's turn to look surprised. 'Why would he be bothering you at your home?' The surprise turned to excitement. 'Is Bradley Aspen stalking you? Is it because he knows you're the lawyer trying to put him behind bars?'

Eve finally lost her cool. 'No. The only person who's been stalking me is you, Mr Tooley. Thank you for telling me it was Jamie you saw outside the flat in the early hours. The fact that you were there too is not okay. Hassle me at my home again and I'll have you arrested.'

She walked away to join Horner. Without a word, the pair of them set off in the direction of Tower Hill. Glancing behind, she saw that Tooley looked lost for words for once. Then he turned on his heel and went in the opposite direction, swallowed up by the passing crowds.

# Chapter Thirty-Three

## EVE

Horner shared Eve's disappointment that Bradley Aspen hadn't been her early-hours caller. It would've been compelling evidence to use against him if he had. It unsettled her to know it was Jamie though. He hadn't contacted her since she'd declined his last invite for a drink, and she had hoped that was the end of it. Him turning up at her flat like that was creepy.

'Who is this Jamie bloke?' asked Horner, as the two of them walked away from the Tower of London.

Eve filled him in. 'I presume he knows our address because of Leah. He looks quite a bit like Aspen. If you met him, you'd see why I mistook him.'

She made a mental note to tell Leah what Jamie had done. She suspected, given the late hour, that he'd been passing by chance after a night out and had been off his face when he'd rung their bell. That didn't let him off the hook though, and Leah having a word when she saw him next at St Bart's wouldn't hurt. He needed to promise never to do it again.

They were headed along Minories on foot. Carroll had arranged for them to meet at a venue a twenty-minute walk from

Traitors' Gate, a factor in why Eve had chosen to meet Tooley there. The DCI didn't fancy schlepping across town to Barnes again, apparently. Horner told Eve that Beverly was put out because it meant she couldn't eavesdrop on the meeting. It was on a need-to-know basis, and she didn't qualify.

Horner used his phone map to follow Carroll's directions. The route cut across Aldgate High Street into an area dwarfed by tower blocks.

'It's along here,' he said, taking them on to a cut-through called Gravel Lane. Just shy of the road's end, he indicated they should turn left.

Eve stopped. 'Really? In here?'

Horner checked. 'That's what it says.'

Ahead was a housing estate, in the middle of which loomed a high-rise.

'Middlesex Street Estate,' Eve read aloud from the sign outside.

'Carroll says we're to go to the foot of Petticoat Tower.' Horner looked skywards at the high-rise. 'I'm guessing that's it.'

A few minutes later, they reached the meeting point. Quinn was waiting for them. 'Good, you're here. We're on the nineteenth floor,' she said, nodding up at the high-rise. 'The DCI knows the owner of a flat and they've kindly said we can use it for the meeting.'

Eve baulked. 'The nineteenth?'

'Yep. The views across the city are amazing. Oh shit, I forgot. You don't like heights, do you. Look, once we're inside, I can close the curtains, so you can't see out. Will that help?'

'It might.' Eve felt embarrassed her phobia was even an issue. 'Let's just go up. I'm sure I'll be fine once I'm inside.'

She wasn't, but she tried not to show it. Following Quinn and Horner into the open-plan flat after a jerky ride in a lift that made alarming grinding noises, she was confronted by a balcony that looked out over the west of the capital. Even though there were glass patio doors between the balcony and the front room, Eve swayed on the spot, her fight or flight response urging her to run back to the lift and return to safer ground. Instead, she gritted her teeth and took a seat on the sofa furthest away from the patio doors. She hoped none of the others could see how much she was sweating.

Carroll and Cato were already there. Paul Ferdie was absent, but apparently only five minutes away. Carroll said to wait. He had the impatient air of a man with news to impart but he wanted a full audience for it.

As the others chatted, Eve took in her surroundings to get her mind off the fact she was nineteen storeys up. The flat had the feel of an older person's abode. The sofa was upholstered in corduroy chintz. The two armchairs, occupied by Quinn and DS Anthony Cato, matched it. Beside the one Quinn was sitting in was a nest of small tables, and on the top one someone had left a glasses case and a book of crosswords. The television in the corner was tiny by today's flatscreen standards, while the bookcase in the corner was crammed with a full set of Maeve Binchy along with various porcelain ornaments.

She caught Quinn's attention. 'Whose flat is this?' she mouthed, not wanting Carroll to hear her.

'The DCI's mum's,' Quinn mouthed back.

Eve grinned. 'Thought as much. Where is she?'

'At a neighbour's.'

There was a sharp rap on the door. Cato sprang from his armchair to answer it. He returned seconds later with Paul Ferdie in tow. He didn't have a chance to apologise for being late before Carroll clapped his hands loudly.

'Thanks for coming, everyone.' He surveyed the room, a wide smile splitting his face. 'I'm just going to come out and say it. I think we've got the bastard.'

Quinn and Cato grinned like they already knew how. Eve felt a spike of excitement. This had to be good, judging by their reactions.

Carroll was holding a foolscap folder. 'It was John who set us on the right path when he flagged the hire bikes. Turns out each one is tracked by GPS, so lost or stolen ones can be recovered. On the night of Becca's murder, a bike was returned to the rack next to Southwark Bridge at two minutes past two. The GPS shows it was ridden there from Putney.'

Horner broke into a smile, but Carroll wasn't finished.

'That's not all. At two seventeen, a different cycle was removed from the rack. It went along Skinners Lane and up Garlick Hill to Mansion House.'

Eve noted it was the same route Horner had predicted Bradley Aspen had taken.

'From there it went west to Queen Victoria Street. However, the GPS recorded the cycle as stopping for a six-minute period at the junction of Lambeth Hill. So, naturally, we had a look at the CCTV round there, because that junction is teeming with TfL cameras. Look what we found.'

He took a sheet of paper from the folder and passed it to Horner. Ferdie closed in for a look. Both did a double take.

'Is that who I think it is?' asked Ferdie incredulously.

'It certainly is. Guess whose credit card was used to hire both bikes as well?'

Horner, slack-jawed as he stared at the image, looked up. 'Seriously?'

'Yep,' said the DCI, who was clearly enjoying every second of his ta-da moment. 'We've had it confirmed by the bike hire people and the credit card company.'

Eve shifted eagerly on the sofa. She was dying to snatch the printout from them. Quinn had noticed and laughed.

'Let Eve see it too,' she said.

Horner's eyes met Eve's. His shone with anticipation. 'You're not going to believe this,' he said. Beside him, Ferdie was still dazed. 'It's really both of them?'

Carroll chuckled. 'It really is.'

Eve stood up to take the printout from Horner. She could feel all eyes on her as she examined the image on it. It showed a clear view of a road junction, with only two cars passing in the background. Clearer still, in the foreground, sitting astride a hire bike, was Bradley Aspen.

And standing next to him, looking animated, was his father, Mark.

# Chapter Thirty-Four

## VALERIE

Theirs was a neighbourhood so safe that women could walk alone at night and not worry. At least that was what the realtors selling the multimillion-pound houses there, and the people who bought them, liked to boast. Valerie was more circumspect. Their slice of the capital was no more immune from crime than any other area. So, when Scout began whining at the front door at 11 p.m., the time Mark usually took her for one last wheel around the streets to do her business, she knew to pack her personal alarm alongside the poo bags.

The temperature had cooled considerably now the dark had swallowed the sun. Valerie shivered. She should've worn her coat rather than a gilet over her thin cotton top. The top had long sleeves, but it might as well not have.

She let Scout dictate the route. Together they ambled up the street in the direction of the playing fields. Was this the way she and Mark always went during their evening walks? Valerie had never given much thought to why her husband relished taking the dog out before turning in, but he always came back in a better mood than when he'd left. It really was relaxing: the streets were still and calm, the only sound the squeak of her trainers and Scout's gentle panting as she strained at the leash.

Valerie was glad she'd left her phone at home now, so the peace couldn't be shattered by Mark texting again. He'd messaged her eight times this evening already and multiple times throughout the day, even though he'd been at work. Until her phone call with Glenn, it had been her chasing him all weekend, begging to know where he was and if they could talk. He'd ignored each and every heartfelt plea. So, after Glenn's warning about White House support for her slipping, she had taken a step back and ceased her beseeching. Her sudden silence had lit a fire under Mark, because God forbid that she should seize control of the situation.

Scout had found something worth sniffing on a grass verge outside a stunning detached house that made their rental look shabby. After checking it wasn't anything like a discarded chicken bone that could harm her, Valerie stood back and let the lead go slack.

She loved Mark. She really did. But she also recognised that, sometimes, she felt diminished around him. That who she was outside the family home counted for nothing inside it. Her, the high-flying career woman – she'd always hated that label but had never managed to come up with a better alternative – with the job that had whisked them all over the world. A job she loved as much as him. A job that had formed her identity even when it had been a pipe dream in her back pocket at college. A job that, like her identity, was seriously at risk.

As a mother and wife, she wanted to do everything in her power to protect her family. But there also had to be a cut-off, no? A cut-off where it was no longer all about Bradley and Mark, and where her needs went to the front of the queue for once. That cut-off had now been reached. Talking to Glenn on the weekend had made her realise it. Because he was right. The anomaly over

Mark's phone being pinged at Southwark Bridge and Bradley's lies meant she could no longer not consider herself in all of this. The drip-feed of evidence could become a tsunami that wiped out all trace of what she'd achieved in her life.

How to extricate herself was the question she now grappled with. She could not, and should not, continue to cover for them both—

Scout's head shot up. A low growl vibrated in her throat and her lips curled back to bare her teeth. Valerie tightened her grip on her lead.

'What is it, girl?'

The punch came from behind, hitting Valerie square between the shoulder blades. She pitched forward, stunned.

'What the hell . . .' she gasped.

She turned to confront her assailant – and that was when she realised it wasn't a fist that had hit her. A searing heat burst across her shoulders, and with it a pain like nothing she'd ever felt before. Scout let out a volley of barks, darting past her legs to get to whoever was behind her. She felt another punch, not as hard as before, but the pain that followed was even more excruciating. She doubled over.

'That's for Becca,' hissed a male voice in her ear.

Valerie could feel blood oozing down her back. Scout was still barking and growling and snapping at her attacker. She wanted to scream but couldn't make her mouth obey. She groped in her pocket for her personal alarm but didn't have the strength to press it. Then she heard footsteps, the hard slap of trainers against concrete, loud at first then receding into the distance.

Sobbing now, she dropped to her hands and knees on the grass verge. Scout whimpered and tried to shove her snout into Valerie's face. When Valerie slumped over on to her side, the dog began to bark again and didn't stop.

A few minutes later, the front door to the detached house burst open. Valerie, barely conscious, heard a woman's voice coming down the driveway.

'Whose dog is that barking? It's woken my kids up – oh God, oh God. SIMON! Call an ambulance! A woman's collapsed – I think she's been stabbed!'

Those were the last words Valerie heard before her world went dark.

# PART III

## NINE WEEKS LATER

# Chapter Thirty-Five

## EVE

Eve watched the performance from across the street. Ashley, surrounded by reporters, holding court. Eve could tell she was trying to maintain a serious front as she delivered the pre-planned statement, but her lips kept tugging upwards. The way Ashley was milking her moment in the spotlight made Eve cringe. Her colleague had even had her hair blow-dried specially.

She waited until the reporters had finished their questions and began to disperse. Then she crossed the road to where Ashley stood checking her phone.

'Got the message across, did you?' Eve asked her.

Ashley looked her up and down like Eve had been dragged to the Old Bailey's entrance rather than walked there. 'What the hell are you wearing?' she asked.

Eve was in denim shorts, a white T-shirt and silver Birkenstocks. 'It's my day off,' she said defensively. 'It's also thirty degrees.'

After a so-so May, June was heating up to near-unbearable levels. The city in a heatwave was sticky and sweaty, and Eve was glad her week off had coincided with this one. Ashley's cheeks were even pinker than usual as she perspired in the suit she'd picked out for court.

'If you're not working, why are you here?'

Eve shrugged. 'I just wondered if we were definitely going through with it.'

Ashley threw her hands up. 'For crying out loud, Eve. You know we are. Gemma Kirk needs to be held responsible.'

'She. Wasn't. Even. There,' said Eve through clenched teeth.

Eve had been appalled by the decision to charge Gemma with the attempted murder of Valerie Aspen under secondary liability – more commonly known as joint enterprise. As the law stood, a person could be jointly charged with the crime of another if it was determined that they could've predicted the other person was likely to commit that crime and intended to encourage or assist them. The case against Gemma was based around the videos she'd posted on TikTok and the messages she'd traded with a young man called Kenny Nasser – known to his friends and online associates as Sponge.

In particular, it centred on a private video message that he'd recorded and sent from near Valerie's home in Putney hours before he tried to kill her, when he'd told Gemma that he was doing it for her. Secondary liability meant Gemma didn't need to inflict the stab wounds herself to be convicted and sentenced. She didn't even have to be present at the crime scene. The CPS had decided there was still a case to answer, and Ashley was the advocate now overseeing it.

Yesterday was Sunday, and Gemma had spent hers being transported down to London from Yorkshire, where she'd been on remand since her first court appearance before magistrates. She had been held overnight at Bishopsgate police station. In the next hour or so, she would appear before a judge inside the Bailey's Courtroom Number Seven, where it was expected she would be remanded in custody. Nasser, arrested trying to board a flight at Birmingham Airport two days after the stabbing, would be in the dock with her.

'Her videos are the reason Valerie Aspen was stabbed and left for dead. Your reaction to this, and to the Hazel Mackett charging decision, makes me think you're not cut out for prosecuting, Eve,' said Ashley imperiously, flicking her newly straightened hair over her shoulder. 'You should go back to the other side.'

It was a question that Eve had pondered a lot during the past few weeks, since word had come down from the DPP that Gemma's culpability needed to be examined. It felt wrong for them to be prosecuting a young woman who hadn't even been present when the crime was committed. Eve's instinct was to defend her.

She pointed to the vast stone archway above their heads. Engraved across it was a motto.

'"Defend the Children of the Poor & Punish the Wrongdoer",' she recited. 'This case makes a mockery of that. Gemma Kirk's facing years behind bars if convicted, while Bradley Aspen walks free for multiple murders.'

'I'm with you on the latter,' said Ashley. 'It makes me sick that we can't touch him.'

Eve searched Ashley's face for signs she was being disingenuous, but it was obvious they were on the same page. Everyone in their division had been shocked and dismayed by the order from high up within the government to leave Bradley Aspen alone after his mother was stabbed and left for dead. The US administration, led by an irate President, had been vociferous in its condemnation of the British authorities. It laid the blame for the murder attempt firmly at their door, saying steps should've been taken to stop the online witch-hunt of the Aspen family.

In an attempt to pass the buck, the UK government had then condemned social media providers in equally strong terms for promoting hatred and violence on their platforms – which was when the legal focus had shifted to Gemma, the TikToker who had led the charge in blaming Valerie for her son's alleged crimes.

The order to leave Bradley Aspen alone was only the official line, however. Behind closed doors it was a different story. The Attorney General – supported by cabinet colleagues – had made it clear to the DPP that the secret taskforce inquiry was not only to continue but to step up its evidence-gathering. Extra resources had been made available, including an offer of surveillance support from M15 if needed.

It was why Eve and Horner were suddenly both on a week's leave at the same time and she was standing outside the Bailey, as it was known in legal circles, dressed like she was ready for the beach. Her confronting Ashley was part of the carefully constructed story they were spinning to explain their time off: Horner was off sick, while Eve had been ordered to take time off because she was so upset about the decision to charge Gemma. Horner's excuse was a lie, hers wasn't. She *had* been kicking off in meetings about Gemma. She'd come to the Bailey to confront Ashley ahead of the hearing knowing full well she'd tell everyone back at Petty France, exactly like Eve wanted her to.

'Any word on how Gemma's doing?' Eve asked. The journey from Yorkshire to London in a sweatbox – the nickname given to prison vans – must've been hellish in this heatwave.

'She's distressed,' said Ashley uncomfortably. 'You would be too.'

Eve's eyes narrowed. 'You don't agree with the decision to charge her either, do you? You're just parroting the company line. Christ, Ashley. You'd rather take the fifteen minutes of fame than take a stand against something you disagree with.'

Ashley's cheeks blazed scarlet. 'I want those who've committed crimes brought to justice too. Do I agree with Gemma being charged with attempted murder? No. I think it should be a lesser charge, like incitement. That's out of my hands though. I mean, it's even out of the bloody DPP's hands,' she exclaimed. 'But here's the thing, Eve. Gemma did stoke unbelievable online hatred against Valerie Aspen, and it was one of her followers who attacked her. Valerie almost died. A few millimetres to the right and her spinal cord would've been severed. Whatever you might think about her son, doesn't Valerie deserve justice for that? The jury will ultimately decide whether Gemma's guilty, but it's in the public interest to charge her and bring her to court.'

◆ ◆ ◆

Eve had arranged to meet Beverly in a café round the corner from the Bailey. Their catch-ups had become a regular occurrence over the past few weeks, because even though Beverly had returned to work at the CPS following her compassionate leave, she wasn't being kept in the loop regarding the taskforce, to maintain its secrecy. So she'd asked Eve to update her where she could. It had put Eve in the awkward position of not wanting to refuse her boss, but fortunately Beverly had made it clear she wouldn't push her on anything she was reluctant to share. She simply wanted reassurance that the taskforce was doing all it could to expose her goddaughter's killer.

Normally they'd meet after work, but Beverly had suggested taking advantage of Eve not being in the office to meet for brunch. But she wasn't waiting inside the café for Eve as usual. She was stood outside talking to an older man in a light-grey suit. As Eve approached, she could see the conversation was less than genial – both of them were gesticulating angrily. Eve was immediately intrigued; Beverly had a reputation within Petty France for not being easily cowed, but the stranger looked like he was giving as good as he got.

Reaching them, Eve cleared her throat. The conversation abruptly halted.

'Ah, Eve, there you are,' said Beverly. Her voice was oddly stilted.

The stranger looked her up and down, brow creased. 'Eve Wren?'

Eve nodded. To her surprise, his expression mellowed and he held out his hand. 'Pleased to meet you. I'm Cliff Daniels. I read about your work on the Novus trial and it was very impressive.'

He had a Yorkshire accent to match Beverly's. Eve returned the handshake and thanked him for the compliment. Beverly continued to look distinctly uncomfortable.

'Are you a lawyer too?' Eve inquired politely.

'I am. I'm based in Leeds but I'm down here for a case and I just happened to bump into Beverly on my way to court. This is the first time we've seen each other in years,' said Cliff. He glanced at Beverly, but she remained stony-faced. 'It must be nearly thirty years in fact. We started our careers around the same time at a practice in Bradford.'

He seemed far friendlier talking about Beverly than to her. Seconds later, Eve discovered why.

'I was just telling her what an appalling decision the CPS has made in charging my client Gemma Kirk.'

'And I was telling you that I cannot discuss it,' Beverly snapped, visibly angered. 'Other than to say it wasn't a charging decision I was privy to.'

They both looked at Eve expectantly, as though she could settle the argument for them. She groped for something to say that wasn't contentious. 'Isn't the hearing due to start shortly?' was the best she could come up with.

Cliff plucked back his left suit sleeve to expose a wristwatch. His skin was slick with sweat. Eve wondered if it was the heat causing it, or nerves.

'You're right,' he said, reading the time. 'I best get going.'

'How's Gemma doing?' Eve asked, hoping the question wouldn't get her into trouble with Beverly. But she had to ask.

'Not great. She's a poorly educated and vulnerable nineteen-year-old with a chaotic home life and limited prospects. Exactly the kind of young person the legal system screws up and spits out,' said Cliff bitterly. 'Charging her on the basis of joint enterprise is a joke, frankly.'

Again, Eve didn't know how to respond. But it seemed her expression had done it for her because Cliff softened again.

'It's good to see someone from the CPS understands where I'm coming from. Thank you, Eve.'

Without another word to either of them, he walked off in the direction of the Bailey.

Beverly watched his retreating back then exhaled. 'God, that was horrible. Cliff's a really decent man, and in any other circumstance I'd have loved catching up with him. I'm so pleased Gemma Kirk's got him on her side. He'll do right by her.'

Astonished, Eve stared at her boss. 'Are you saying you don't agree with us charging her either?'

'For attempted murder? No. It should've been incitement, if that. I hope the jury makes the right decision and acquits.' Beverly regarded Eve for a moment, then lowered her voice. 'You know what I keep thinking? The best thing that could happen for Gemma and your taskforce is that Bradley Aspen tries to hurt someone else. Don't look at me like that, hear me out,' she protested, catching Eve's look of horror. 'The last thing I want is for another family to suffer like Becca's is. You know how much I want the bastard caught,' she added, her voice catching. 'But right now, public opinion is tipped in Valerie's favour because she's the victim. People are conveniently overlooking that all this started because her son was named as a suspect in Becca's murder. Meanwhile, my poor goddaughter has been completely forgotten. But if Aspen attempted to kill again, it would validate what Gemma has been saying online and the US government would have to lift his immunity. The fallout would be too great if they didn't.'

'It would only work if he was caught in the act though,' Eve pointed out. 'It wouldn't be enough for him to just be suspected of another attack.'

Beverly nodded. 'Yes, he'd have to be. Then Gemma's defence could use it to argue that she never intended Valerie to get hurt, she was just campaigning for Bradley to be brought to justice before he struck again. Crazy as it sounds, Bradley Aspen could actually be the person to save her.'

# Chapter Thirty-Six

## GEMMA

The holding cell at the Old Bailey was cooler than the van that had brought Gemma to court. Although barely bigger than a toilet cubicle, it was painted cream and separated from the outside by metal bars, like prisons in old films. It was nice to be able to see out after two weeks in a cell where the door was solid metal, but she was still too hot. Making her stay in prison-issue grey joggers when the south was baking in a heatwave seemed cruel. She'd asked for something cooler to wear at the police station she'd been held in last night, but the custody sergeant had just laughed at her. 'This isn't TK Maxx, love.'

It didn't help that she couldn't sit still. The more she fidgeted, the more she sweated. She just wanted this over with. Her solicitor had talked her through what would be happening at today's hearing. They'd be making an application for bail and were hopeful they could successfully argue her case for it. She'd have to accept bail conditions, like abiding by a curfew and reporting to her local police station every day, but it would mean she could go home for now.

The solicitor's name was Cliff Daniels. Gemma liked him because he didn't talk down to her. He'd been assigned to represent her on the day of her arrest, and had travelled to London overnight to instruct the barrister who'd be speaking for her in today's hearing. Both lawyers were now waiting in the courtroom along with everyone else.

Gemma shook her head as she paced. What was happening to her was madness and she couldn't believe no one was stopping it. How could she be charged with trying to kill someone when she'd been 250 miles away? Even Cliff couldn't really explain it, other than to say she was being made an example of. After the initial shock of being arrested – which was a massive understatement, because she'd never been as frightened in her life – and appearing before magistrates for a box-ticking hearing, Gemma had been sent to HMP New Hall near Wakefield. To her surprise, she didn't mind it as much as she'd thought she would. It wasn't nice being locked up, but in prison she had no responsibilities, which made a change from being the one who took care of everything. Prison was orderly compared to her life outside. She had a cell to herself but could socialise on the wing, which she quickly learned was mostly populated by inmates like her, on remand and awaiting trial. She'd even made friends with a couple of girls her age who worked out she was the TikToker that had exposed Bradley Aspen and thought she was cool for doing so.

There had been a couple of hairy moments – one inmate had kicked off at another during communal television time, and others had waded into the punch-up – but on the whole Gemma had coped. Now she needed to get bail and head home, because her mum was doing the opposite of coping without her. During the few calls they'd had since her arrest, her mum had cried non-stop, and it worried Gemma how hysterical she'd been. She dreaded to think what state the house was in without her there to manage the worst of the hoarding. Martine from the council had visited a couple of times before Gemma's arrest and her mum had been slowly opening up to the idea of accepting outside help. But with her on remand and unable to facilitate more visits, Gemma knew her mum would have backed off from dealing with Martine and resorted to her old habits.

The court officer supervising the cells approached the bars. 'You're up.'

Gemma's insides turned to liquid. She hadn't heard of the Old Bailey until two days ago, when Cliff had informed her that her case had been sent straight there to be dealt with, bypassing crown court. Because of the joint enterprise, the CPS wanted her and Sponge tried together, and the Old Bailey, the nation's most prolific court, was its preferred venue because of the heightened national and international interest. Cliff said it wasn't worth trying to block the venue move. Better to play nice and get bail.

The officer unlocked the cell and led Gemma along the corridor and into the courtroom via some stairs. Her stomach churned, but she tried not to let her nerves show, keeping her expression passive and her posture rigid.

In the dock already was Sponge. He tried to catch her eye.

She ignored him and sat down.

Twenty minutes later she was back in the holding cell sobbing her heart out. Cliff sat awkwardly beside her on the narrow bench.

Bail denied.

'You said I'd be going home,' Gemma cried, tears and snot wetting her face.

'I'm as shocked as you are,' said Cliff, and he sounded it. In a faltering voice, he told her that her barrister had said all the right things, but the judge was unwilling to separate her actions from Sponge's, who had proven himself to be a flight risk when he was arrested trying to board a flight to Turkey. 'The attention surrounding the case clearly hasn't helped either. There's a lot of political pressure in play too.'

'I'm from Bridlington,' she wailed. 'I don't know anything about politics.'

'I know,' said Cliff wretchedly.

Gemma remembered that at their first meeting, Cliff Daniels told her he had a daughter the same age as her. She wondered if he was imagining how he'd feel if she was the one locked up.

She wiped her nose and cheeks on her sleeve. 'Can you get the judge to change his mind?'

'We will of course make another application for bail, but I'm afraid it won't be dealt with today. There will be another hearing in a few weeks.'

Gemma exploded. 'I can't wait that long. I need to get home to Mum. She needs me.'

This had been said in court by her barrister. But the one speaking on behalf of the prosecution somehow knew all about Martine and her visits, and how Mel was now in the adult social care system, as if that alone would help her.

'I'm sorry, Gemma, but we are constrained by court procedure. We have to wait until the next hearing.'

'So I just rot in New Hall until then?'

Cliff looked uneasy. 'Actually, no. I've been told you're being taken from here to HMP Bronzefield instead.'

Gemma was horrified. 'Where's that?'

'In Surrey. It's about twenty miles away and is the closest women's prison to London. It makes more sense if you're standing trial here,' he said apologetically.

'But what about Mum? She won't be able to afford to come all that way to visit me. I need to see her. She doesn't have anyone else, and there's been some trouble, from some locals. She needs protecting.'

Cliff frowned. 'What kind of trouble?'

'There's this girl, Kira, who used to bully me at school. She wanted to be friends again but I didn't meet up like I said I would, and since then she's had it in for me. Someone took a dump on our doorstep and put a brick through our window. Then after that I got a few crank calls at work, saying Mum had been in an accident, and they also faked a picture of me naked and put it on one of those sex hook-up websites with my mobile number so I had pervs ringing me up at all hours.'

'Have you reported any of this to the police?'

Gemma looked at him as though he'd sprouted two heads. 'You want me to make things worse? You don't know Kira like I do. She's the nastiest cow you'll ever meet, and she holds grudges for years. I'm worried she'll go after Mum if I'm not there.'

'I can't promise anything, but I'll see what the firm can do to help,' said Cliff.

'Will I be able to ring Mum before I go to – where did you say it was again?'

'Bronzefield, in Surrey. You'll be able to call her once you arrive.'

'Can you speak to her before that? I don't want her seeing on the telly that I've not got bail and not understand what's going on. Can you do that for me please?'

'I can. Is there anything else I can do for you in the meantime?'

Gemma's voice cracked. 'Make the police and CPS see that it's wrong that I've been charged. I never wanted Valerie Aspen to get hurt. I didn't plan it, I didn't tell Sponge to go for it, I didn't even know he had a knife with him in the video he sent me. For Mum's sake, please make them see it wasn't my fault.'

# Chapter Thirty-Seven

## VALERIE

There was a bench ahead, shaded beneath an ancient oak. Valerie leaned heavily on her cane for the final stretch. Clover kept pace alongside her, offering words of encouragement.

'You're nearly there,' she told her. 'Just a few more steps.'

Reaching the bench, Valerie was damp with sweat from the exertion. Her instinct was to sit down quickly, but instead she did as Clover had instructed her on day one and gingerly lowered herself on to it. Slow and steady was Clover's mantra, and now Valerie's too.

The view from the bench was worth the effort though. It never failed to impress her. Fields as far as the eye could see, not a cloud in the sky, and today it was so warm that the horizon was simmering.

'That was a nice stroll, wasn't it,' beamed Clover, sitting down next to her.

'Less stroll, more stagger,' said Valerie, leaning her cane against the seat.

'From my viewpoint you carried yourself well. The back exercises are helping.'

Clover was the resident physiotherapist at Dalewood House, a privately run clinic in Kent that specialised in injury rehabilitation. Valerie had been staying there for the past three weeks, since her discharge from hospital.

The injury to her back had been severe. Two stab wounds. The first one had missed her spinal cord by just a few millimetres. The second one had punctured her lung. The loss of blood from both had triggered a cardiac arrest, and the paramedics had worked for forty minutes to stabilise her in the street before she was taken to hospital. The first few days she had been heavily sedated, flitting in and out of consciousness.

'How was the pain last night on a scale of one to ten?' asked Clover. She asked the same question of Valerie every morning while on their walk around the grounds.

Every morning Valerie lied. 'It was bad, at least an eight. I woke up a few times.'

Truth was, she'd had a terrible night's sleep, but not due to the pain. That was gradually diminishing thanks to the intense physical rehabilitation she was getting. Instead, she'd endured another endless scroll of nightmares. One into the next the bad dreams had crashed, wrenching her awake. At five in the morning, she had given up trying to sleep and read a book instead.

She lied because she didn't know if she was being monitored at night. If they were looking in on her, she'd rather blame her thrashing around in bed on pain than admit to having nightmares. She wasn't a child.

'That's a worry,' said Clover, her brow furrowing. 'Let me talk to Dr Athwal about reassessing your night-time meds. Your body needs to rest at night or your recovery will take longer. But don't worry, you will get better.'

Valerie nodded, then trained her gaze on the horizon. She'd never recover from this. Her body might, but her mind wouldn't.

It wasn't the horror of being stabbed that would haunt her until she died – although that would take time to come to terms with – but the fact that she couldn't remember anything concrete before it. Her memories were like wisps of smoke that appeared and vanished before she had a chance to hold on to them. Her hospital consultants and now the staff at Dalewood House agreed it must be a response to the major trauma. Her mind had shut down to protect her.

She knew why she'd been stabbed, of course. The police had told her, with Mark filling in the gaps. She was aware that her attacker had been an online troll who believed Bradley was responsible for pushing a young woman to her death from Southwark Bridge. All because he looked a little bit like a grainy CCTV image of the suspect.

'Are you ready to go back inside?' asked Clover. 'I'm burning up out here it's so hot.'

'I am. A nice cold drink would go down well.'

The walk back to the main house took them ten minutes. A fit person would've done it in less than two.

Dalewood House itself was a large, detached property that wouldn't be out of place in Putney. It had twelve bedrooms and therefore only twelve patients being treated at a time. Valerie had got to know a few of them during her stay, and one of the younger ones, Leo, greeted her in the foyer as she and Clover came in.

'Afternoon, Val. How are you feeling today?' he said, swinging his wheelchair round to face her. He was in recovery from a lower leg amputation. He'd been knocked off his jet ski while on holiday in Costa Rica and thrown into the path of a passing speedboat. Like Valerie, he was lucky to be alive.

'You know. Getting by. You?'

'Me? I'm off clubbing later. Wanna come?'

Like Val, Leo was American. Dalewood House was as renowned across the Atlantic as it was in the UK. It was why her embassy colleagues had suggested she come here to continue her recovery.

'Much as I'd love to, my husband's supposed to be visiting later.'

Mark came down twice a week, but she hadn't seen Bradley since her hospital discharge. Mark felt it would be too much for her for them both to come.

'Bring him along. You too, Clover,' Leo cried. 'We can do a club takeover!'

Clover pulled a face. 'Shouldn't you be in the hydro pool now?'

'Guilty as charged, ma'am. I'm on my way.' He raised his hand in a salute then shot off down the corridor. For someone who'd only been in a wheelchair for a few weeks, he was already remarkably nimble in his. Valerie adored his can-do spirit. It hadn't escaped her attention that he couldn't have been less like Bradley, who went through life wanting everything handed to him on *her* plate.

'You fine to see to yourself from here?' Clover asked her.

'Yes, you get on. I need to speak to Abigail.'

Abigail was the manager of Dalewood House. Valerie had a pressing request for her.

'She's probably in her office,' said Clover. 'See you later.'

While Clover disappeared in the other direction, Valerie pushed through the door that led to a small collection of offices housing the admin support, business team and Abigail herself. She knocked on her office door, leaning on her cane as she did.

'Come in,' came the answer from within.

Abigail Huntley reminded Valerie a lot of herself. Always professional, but always approachable. Similar age too. She greeted Valerie from behind her modest desk.

'Good morning, Mrs Aspen. What can I do for you today?'

Valerie had told her multiple times to call her by her first name, but Abigail wouldn't. She didn't mind the rest of the staff being informal with guests though.

'I'm here about my cell phone again. I want it returned. I need to be able to contact my staff. My assistant Langdon must be wondering why I haven't bothered to speak to him since I've been out of hospital.'

'Mrs Aspen, as I told you last time you asked, and the time before that, we don't have your phone. Your husband has it.'

'Tell me again why he doesn't want me to have it? I can't remember.'

'It's his belief that you shouldn't have any online access during your recovery because it could be traumatic to read about the attack on you. Dr Athwal and your therapists do support that approach from a clinical perspective.'

'Don't I get a say? I'm a forty-eight-year-old woman, not a kid that can't be trusted.'

'Mrs Aspen, you're fifty-eight,' said Abigail gently.

'That's what I meant,' she snapped.

'I understand your frustration. I really do. You're welcome to use our telephones for any calls you need to make, like when you call your husband.'

'But not the embassy.'

Abigail frowned. 'I don't see why not.'

'Mark told me I couldn't call from here because the line needs to be secure.'

'I'm not sure that's the case if you're just calling your office. Perhaps you could call the embassy's main switchboard and see what they say?'

Valerie perked up. She'd been desperate to call Langdon for a catch-up. He might need a steer on work matters in her absence.

'Can I use your phone?' she asked.

Abigail rose to her feet. 'Come through to Jane's office and use hers. She's running an errand right now.'

They went into the empty office next door. Valerie faltered.

'I don't remember the number.'

'Wait here, I'll look it up for you.' Abigail went back to her office, then returned with a scrap of paper a minute or so later. 'Here you go. Press nine first for an outside line.'

Valerie sat down carefully in Jane's chair and dialled the number. The call connected to an automated message read by a woman who spoke with a cut-glass British accent. She waited for the instruction to enter a five-digit extension number and entered Langdon's, which thankfully she did remember.

A young woman answered. Her accent was American. 'Good morning, you've reached the office of Valerie Aspen. How may I assist you?'

'This is Valerie Aspen. I'd like to speak to Langdon please.'

There was a long silence. 'Valerie? It's me, Penny. Oh my God, it's so good to hear your voice. How are you?'

Valerie was disconcerted. 'Where's Langdon? I need to speak to my assistant, please.'

'Um, Langdon isn't your assistant. I am.'

'Don't be silly. I think I would've remembered Langdon leaving.'

'He did though,' insisted the young woman. 'He transferred to a different department a few months ago. I've been working for you ever since. Well, give or take a week. It all happened quickly so there wasn't time for a full handover.'

'That can't be right. I would never have let Langdon quit.'

Penny sounded hurt. 'You said you were happy with me being his replacement.'

Without warning, an image popped into Valerie's head. A woman with a blonde bob, in her hallway.

'Did you come to my house in Putney?'

'I did,' said Penny triumphantly. 'Right before . . .' She trailed off. 'Your husband did say the trauma was affecting your memory.'

'You've spoken to Mark?' asked Valerie sharply. Why would her husband be calling up her assistant – if that was who this woman really was.

'Only the once. He called to update me on how you were and to say that I mustn't try to contact you either at the hospital or when you came out. It is so nice to speak to you directly again.' Valerie could hear the emotion in Penny's voice. 'We've all been so worried.'

'Well, I'm getting better and I'm coming back to work.'

'Oh, I'm so stoked to hear that. When?'

'I can't say for sure, but soon. I'd like you to come and visit me first.' A wisp of memory fluttered at the edge of her consciousness. 'Isn't there something I need to be signing off for Luxembourg?'

'That project's been put to bed, but there are plenty of others we can discuss. Where are you staying at the moment?'

Valerie recited the address from a brochure that was on the desk. 'When can you come?' she asked.

'Whenever works for you.'

Valerie had another flash of memory. Something on a laptop. Something to do with Mark. Penny was there.

'When you came to my home, what was the purpose of your visit?'

Penny sounded guarded. 'To tell you something.'

'What was it?'

'I don't think I should repeat it over the phone. I don't want to stress you out.'

'It's work-related?'

'You could say that.'

'Can you get here tomorrow afternoon?'

'Sure, of course. Is three o'clock good for you?'

That was the time she had her afternoon nap, but she could skip it for this. 'It is.'

'I'll message you when I'm leaving,' said Penny.

'Actually, don't. I – I don't have a cell phone at the moment. The police have kept it.' It was easier to lie than try to explain that Mark was withholding it from her.

'Oh, right.'

Valerie's mind prodded her again. Not a memory this time, but an instinct.

'Don't tell anyone that you're coming. Just make up an excuse that you need the afternoon off. Understood?'

'Yes. It'll be really good to see you,' Penny finished.

Valerie wished she could say the same, but it was hard to get excited about a visit from someone she could barely recall.

# Chapter Thirty-Eight

## EVE

The taskforce had stepped up its meetings since the attack on Valerie Aspen and were due to catch up again that evening. Eve spent the hours beforehand not enjoying the sunshine but sitting in her stuffy bedroom, fan on full blast, researching legal precedents around diplomatic immunity. She had to be sure they hadn't missed anything. She knew Horner and Ferdie were doing the same.

Depressingly, she'd come up blank again. She couldn't find any cases where an initial refusal to revoke immunity had been overturned. Her research showed that, time and time again, diplomats accused of serious crimes in the UK would be recalled by their home nation to avoid a criminal investigation. It had made her wonder why the US authorities had never suggested Bradley Aspen return to their shores, but she presumed it was because they didn't want it to be seen as an admission of guilt.

She welcomed Leah interrupting her mid-afternoon.

'I'm heading off for my shift now,' said her flatmate, standing in the open doorway, dressed for work. 'How are you getting on?'

'Still coming up blank,' Eve sighed.

Leah's gaze strayed to the far-right corner of the bedroom. Attached to the ceiling was a surveillance camera the CPS had arranged to be installed because of Frank Tooley. There was one by the front door too. It felt more precautionary than necessary now though. Tooley had left a few voicemail messages on her line at Petty France, but he hadn't tried approaching Eve again in the nine weeks since she'd met him by Traitors' Gate. His messages were solely about Stephen Sheridan and his tone was no longer aggressive.

Tooley's latest voicemail had said he was still getting nowhere trying to get hold of the photographs that Stephen's accuser allegedly took. There was nothing Eve could do, so she ignored the message and hoped Tooley would continue to keep his distance. She could no more force Albie Marsh to hand over the pictures – if they even existed – than he could.

'Is that one filming all the time?' Leah asked.

'Apparently.'

'Aren't you bothered you're being constantly watched?'

'Not if it means I can sleep at night.'

'Talking of stalkers, I saw Jamie at the end of my shift yesterday. He said sorry *again*,' said Leah.

Eve rolled her eyes. 'He needs to let it go now. I have.'

Leah had confronted Jamie at St Bart's after Tooley told Eve it was Jamie who'd rung her doorbell at four thirty in the morning. Jamie insisted he hadn't planned to do it – he'd walked past by chance after a night out and had been too drunk to think how upset Eve might be. He'd left a voicemail apology on Eve's phone after

Leah had confronted him, which she'd ignored, but it seemed he was still mortified by his behaviour.

'Yeah, I'm going to tell him it's getting annoying if he says it again. See you later.' Leah blew her a kiss and shut the door behind her. Above Eve's head, the camera whirred.

Eve stopped work at six and had a quick shower, her second of the day thanks to the heatwave. Dinner was a pre-packed salad with a can of drained tuna mixed in. Then, at six fifty, she set off for Petticoat Tower again.

Her fear of heights hadn't eased, but she'd got used to the high-rise setting, their regular meeting place now. Carroll's mum, Kathleen, had shown herself to be an exemplary host, with a steady supply of cups of tea and home-made cakes, hence the salad beforehand.

By the time Eve arrived, a third shower felt in order. The temperature had nudged upwards again as the day stretched to its end, and the heat pressed down hard on the city and its streets. Far from revelling in it, most people that Eve passed on her way there looked like she felt – irritated and drained.

Thankfully, she wasn't alone in arriving at the meeting a sweaty mess. Carroll's face was the colour of a ripe tomato. Quite the contrast to his pale, chunky legs, which he showed off in a pair of beige shorts. The others looked hot and bothered too. Kathleen had opened the glass sliding doors between the front room and the balcony though, allowing the slightest of breezes to waft through the flat. Eve was so grateful for it that for once she didn't sit in the furthest seat. She just made sure not to look outside.

Carroll called the meeting to order, then went first. His update was a blow. The Home Secretary had refused their latest request, made again by MI5 on their behalf as per procedure, for a warrant to tap the Aspen family home, under Part II of the Regulation of Investigatory Powers Act 2000. The taskforce believed – and M15 agreed – that with Valerie out of the way in injury rehab, father and son might openly discuss why Mark had been with Bradley near Southwark Bridge on the night Becca Farrow was murdered. The Home Secretary, however, wasn't convinced.

'She doesn't want us intruding on their privacy because of the row it would trigger if the Americans found out. MI5 did warn us that could be the case. They're now saying that because it's the third time they've asked and the third time it's been refused, they can't try again unless we present new evidence.'

Around the room, shoulders visibly sagged, Eve's included. In the nine weeks since Carroll had presented them with the shocking CCTV image of the father and son, it felt like scant progress had been made. They'd all hoped that this time the Home Secretary would say yes.

'I'm sorry it's not better news,' said Carroll.

He proceeded to recap what they'd gathered so far. Top of the list, and most promising, was a DNA match between a sample taken from the coat Aldana Porras had been wearing when she was attacked and a sample taken from the scene of Becca Farrow's murder. They hadn't been hopeful of the coat yielding anything significant, but the fact Aldana was in the Thames for only minutes before being rescued meant that the DNA had survived. They were all expecting both samples to match Bradley Aspen's.

Getting a sample from him would be a different matter, however. Obtaining DNA without consent was illegal under the Human Tissue Act. If a suspect refused to give a sample, the police could ordinarily ask a judge to grant a compulsion order that forced them to agree. But no judge would grant one in Aspen's case while he was protected by diplomatic immunity.

They also had a new statement from Aldana. The hospital tox screen had confirmed there had been no trace of drugs or alcohol in her system to impair her recollection, and she was now even more certain Bradley Aspen had pushed her in the river. She'd been able to provide the taskforce with a clearer picture of the attack itself and had also explained how her and Aspen's paths had crossed a few times before, making her identification of him even more conclusive. The most significant meeting was at a midsummer's barbecue hosted by one of their neighbours the year previously. Bradley had been drinking heavily and had made a pass at her, but she'd rejected him – the same scenario that had occurred between him and Nadia Vinke before her death in Prague.

The police trio had also spoken to two more friends of Nadia's who'd been on Charles Bridge in Prague that night. They too believed Aspen was capable of killing, but neither wanted to go on the record because of what had happened to her best friend, Leeza van der Kleji. Neither believed the hit-and-run that killed her was an accident.

'What about the other cases you identified at the start?' asked Paul Ferdie. 'Any luck with CCTV matches in the vicinity, or DNA?'

He was referring to the three women pushed from London bridges who had the same victimology as Becca, Nadia and Aldana.

Gabrielle Brieley. Shannon Boland. Melis Güler.

'It's like pulling teeth trying to get anything out of the Met at the moment. They're too busy crowing about charging Gemma Kirk. Her arrest has made them look good for once,' Carroll grumbled.

'Not to everyone. Half the country is outraged she's being scapegoated,' said Eve. Horner stared at her pointedly, which she ignored. 'It's probably more than half now, after she was denied bail today.'

'We're not here to talk about Gemma Kirk, Eve,' said Ferdie bluntly. 'It has nothing to do with why we're here.'

'It has everything to do with it. Bradley Aspen killing Becca and getting away with it is the reason she's in the trouble she's in.' Silence fell across the room. Eve knew they couldn't argue with her. 'We all know he did it, and so does Gemma. Yet she's the one locked up.'

'If only we could bloody well prove it was him,' said Quinn sullenly.

DS Cato raised his hand. 'I've got something to share.' He turned to Carroll. 'I meant to call you on the way here to tell you first, boss, but I was following up a lead and ran out of time.'

'Don't apologise if you're bringing us good news,' said Carroll.

Cato pulled a laptop from his leather messenger bag. The rest of them watched intently as he raised the screen to reveal an Instagram grid. Eve didn't recognise the woman who was the main focus of all the images.

'This is Shannon Boland's account. It's been kept up as a memorial to her.' Cato pointed to the word 'Remembering' next to her name and explained that Instagram added it to profiles of people who'd died, at their family's request. 'We've been looking for a link between Gabrielle, Shannon and Melis besides their shared victimology, and I've found one. Here's a photo that was taken on the night Shannon died. She was in a bar with friends. She'd been drinking and had also taken drugs.'

This was not new information. All three women had been drinking, while Shannon and Melis had consumed cocktails of booze, MDMA and coke.

'The bar Shannon went to that night had a guest DJ. Not run-of-the-mill stuff but dancehall and reggae sounds. Very loud, very high-energy. The DJ is top-flight in his field.' Cato clicked on a post on Shannon's grid. 'This is a video that she posted in the hours before she died. Listen.'

He punched the volume up to max. The flat was suddenly filled with a throbbing bass and rhapsodic beat that was instantly catchy. Eve felt it pulsate through her nerve endings, sending a message to her feet to get up and dance. She curled her toes against the soles of her sandals to stop her feet jiggling.

'I did some more digging and found out that Melis was also at a dancehall and reggae gig the night she died,' said Cato. He closed down Shannon's grid, then opened a saved page from TikTok. The same music filled the room again. 'This is from the account of the bar that Melis went to. Different bar, but the same DJ.'

Carroll's eyes gleamed. 'What about the night Gabrielle Brieley drowned?'

'I haven't found any images or videos of Gabrielle because all her socials have been taken down, but I have found a list of the DJ's gigs for that month – and he was slated to play in the bar we know she went to that night. The reason I ran out of time to call you, boss, is that on my way here I went to the bar to check that the gig had gone ahead – and it had.'

Eve held her breath. Could Cato have struck even more gold?

'Bradley Aspen's socials are set to private now, but that doesn't stop him getting tagged in other people's pictures. I've found fifteen images of him taken at gigs where this DJ has headlined, including at a couple of festivals. I think it's safe to call him a fan.' Cato surveyed the group. 'We now have a confirmed link between Aspen and those three victims.'

# Chapter Thirty-Nine

## EVE

The room erupted with excited chatter. But while the other four congratulated Cato on the breakthrough, Eve had a question for him.

'What about the bar that Becca Farrow was at the night she died? Was the DJ playing there?'

The chatter stopped abruptly as Cato shook his head. 'No, it was a regular bar. No live music or DJ.'

'He must've changed his MO,' said Carroll firmly. 'Aldana hadn't been at a bar at all, but he still attacked her, don't forget. What we need now is to place Aspen in those three bars on the same nights as the victims. It would be great to get a CCTV match to the image we've got of him on Southwark Bridge the night Becca died.'

'It's doubtful the bars will have kept CCTV footage going back that far,' said Horner.

Gabrielle had drowned in 2021, while Shannon and Melis died at the opposite ends of 2023.

'What about outside on the street?' queried Eve.

'We can check,' said Carroll, nodding.

Quinn addressed Cato, raising her voice to be heard. 'Sarge, were any of the tagged photos of Aspen taken on the nights the victims died?'

'Unfortunately not.'

'Aspen's not stupid,' said Carroll. 'If he was planning an assault, he'd be careful to not pose for pictures that could put him in the same venue at the same time.'

The question of premeditation hadn't been discussed much while they focused on gathering new evidence. Becca Farrow's murder had felt spur-of-the-moment, but what they'd learned since – about Nadia, about these other three victims – indicated that thought and planning had gone into the attacks. Aspen appeared to have selected his victims not only because they fitted his type, but because they were inebriated enough to be easy pickings. Sober Aldana was the anomaly.

Eve had an idea. 'How many venues are we talking about in the tagged images?' she asked Cato.

'Let me check.' After a quick count he said six. 'Not including the festivals.'

'Can you talk to all the bars to ask if they remember seeing Bradley at this DJ's gigs? We've got the advantage now that people know who he is, because his face has been everywhere,' she said.

'Wouldn't they have already come forward to say so?' asked Kathleen, who was listening by the door to the kitchen. None of them minded her eavesdropping or chucking in the occasional question. Sometimes it was nice to have an outsider's perspective.

'No one knows that Aspen has been linked to these other deaths, though,' her son pointed out.

'If I remember rightly, one of the tabloids speculated early on about other unsolved river deaths, but once the embassy's legal team issued the cease-and-desist on Valerie Aspen's behalf, the media backed off,' added Horner.

Quinn was checking something on her phone. 'The DJ is due to play in a club near Embankment this Friday.'

The five of them, and Kathleen, stared at her.

'That's in the Met's jurisdiction,' said Carroll bluntly.

Ferdie shook his head. 'I can't see Aspen going to a gig, let alone planning another attack, when all eyes are bound to be on him.'

'I wouldn't be so sure about the former,' said Cato. He pecked at his laptop's keyboard, pulling up one IG profile after another on the screen. 'Here you go. Two of the friends who previously tagged him have shared flyers for Friday's gig and say in the comments that they're definitely going. So he could be attending with them.'

Quinn peered over his shoulder. 'Eve, those are the two blokes we saw him with that night,' she said excitedly, before stopping dead. Her cheeks blazed red.

'You did what?' asked Carroll. His tone was ominous.

Eve was cringing at Quinn's gaffe, but she wasn't going to let her confess alone.

'We were at a pub where Aspen was meeting his friends. This was back in April, after the first taskforce meeting.'

She shot a glance at Horner and hoped it conveyed that she'd keep him out of it. Carroll and Ferdie didn't need to know that he already knew and had kept quiet to protect them.

'Whose bloody stupid idea was that?' Carroll thundered.

'Mine. I wanted to see what he was like close up and I begged Eve to come with me,' said Quinn sheepishly. 'She didn't want to.'

'But I'm glad I did.' Eve took a deep breath. 'Aspen intercepted me coming out of the toilets and made it clear he wanted to get to know me. I'm obviously his type.'

Carroll and Ferdie stared at Eve as though they were seeing her for the first time.

'You do look like Becca Farrow,' said Ferdie wonderingly. 'And Gabrielle, Shannon and Melis.'

'Don't forget Aldana and Nadia,' said Quinn.

Eve could almost see the wheels turning behind Carroll's stare. Then he snapped to.

'What time's this gig starting?' he asked Cato, who still had the flyer up on his laptop screen.

'Nine, but I don't imagine it gets going until later. There are a few warm-ups before the DJ headlines.'

Horner and Ferdie exchanged startled looks. 'You're not sending Eve in case Aspen turns up,' said Ferdie. 'Absolutely not.'

Carroll held firm. 'She wouldn't be on her own. My two would be with her.'

'It's out of the question,' said Horner. 'You're not using Eve as a honeytrap. You can't put her in danger like that. Plus anything that happened would be inadmissible in court and could jeopardise the case. We don't want another Colin Stagg situation.'

Colin Stagg was the young man who had been wrongly suspected of killing Rachel Nickell on Wimbledon Common in 1992. To push him into confessing, the Met had deployed a female undercover officer to fake sexual interest in him. Stagg had spent a year on bail before the case against him was thrown out on the grounds of entrapment and a lack of evidence, and the Met was later ordered to pay him £700,000 in compensation for wrongful arrest and imprisonment. In 2008, a man with diagnosed paranoid schizophrenia called Robert Napper was convicted of Rachel's manslaughter on the grounds of diminished responsibility. At the time of his conviction he was being held at Broadmoor high-security psychiatric hospital for a previous murder and serial rapes.

'You're forgetting that Stagg was innocent. Aspen isn't. Besides, presenting the case in court isn't our priority, is it?' said Cato. 'It's finding evidence to force the US government to lift Aspen's diplomatic immunity so he can be fully investigated.'

'Anthony is right,' said Carroll. 'This isn't about collecting convictable evidence. We're not asking Eve to pursue Aspen either. We just want to see if he takes another shine to her. Then he might just be stupid enough to implicate himself.'

'A minute ago you were saying he wasn't stupid,' Ferdie shot back. 'Sorry, but I am not risking Eve's safety by using her as bait.'

'I agree,' said Horner. 'It's not happening.'

Kathleen piped up from the kitchen doorway. 'Instead of all you men huffing and puffing and deciding for her, why don't you ask Eve what she's happy to do?'

Quinn tried to suppress a laugh but failed. Carroll glared daggers at his mum.

'It should be her decision,' Kathleen added.

They all stared at Eve.

She took a moment before answering. The past few months had been tough on her. She'd been put through the wringer by Frank Tooley and had no intention of making herself vulnerable again for the sake of a case. But this wasn't just any case. There was so much at stake. Justice for Becca and the others – that was six victims that they knew of. There could be more. Meanwhile, Gemma Kirk faced a lengthy prison sentence because she'd taken a stand online about Aspen being protected because of his mum's job. Was it really her fault that someone else had escalated into violence? Beverly's words from earlier came back to Eve in a rush.

*'But if Aspen attempted to kill again, it would validate what Gemma has been saying online and the US government would have to lift his immunity. The fallout would be too great if they didn't . . . Then Gemma's defence could use it to argue their case that she never intended Valerie to get hurt, she was just campaigning for Bradley to be brought to justice before he struck again. Crazy as it sounds, Bradley Aspen could actually be the person to save her.'*

'Eve?' nudged Quinn.

Eve's gaze settled on Horner. She could tell from his expression that he was deeply worried. But Kathleen was right. This was her call.

'I'm in,' she said.

Ferdie tutted, and Horner swore. Carroll beamed like Christmas, his birthday and the yearly golf trip with the lads had all come at once.

'But we do it properly,' Eve added. 'We've got from now until Friday to come up with a plan, and I want more backup on the night than just Quinn and Cato. Will that be a problem if we're in the Met's jurisdiction?' she asked Carroll.

'Crossovers happen all the time. I'll talk to our commissioner. She'll know how best to approach it.'

'I think you're too high-profile to do this, Eve,' said Ferdie unhappily. 'You've already been publicly linked to the case and now you're chasing him around clubs? His defence will argue entrapment.'

'But as Anthony said, that's not what we're aiming for here. Me going to the club is about provoking Aspen into saying something that we get on record to push the US to rethink its decision. Once his immunity is lifted, we run his DNA against the physical evidence taken from Becca and Aldana for a match. That's what will convict him, not me talking to him,' said Eve. 'It's just a shame we don't have physical evidence for the others.'

It was a source of frustration that no DNA could be recovered from Shannon, Gabrielle and Melis. With their deaths investigated and concluded as not suspicious, no forensic tests had been run on their clothing. It was going to be harder to make charges stick relating to their deaths.

'But we do have the DJ and bars link now,' said Quinn. 'That is compelling circumstantial evidence.'

Eve fixed her gaze on Horner again. 'I'm okay doing this. I want to do it.'

'I know. Doesn't mean I have to agree with it though.'

She hated that he was disappointed by her decision. Ferdie, on the other hand, seemed to be coming round.

'Any sign of trouble and you are straight out of there, no arguments,' he said.

'I understand. I'm not going to do anything silly.'

Her comment hung in the air for a moment. Kathleen broke the spell.

'Now that's settled, who's for another cup of tea?'

# Chapter Forty

## VALERIE

The following afternoon, Valerie was waiting impatiently for Penny to arrive at Dalewood House. She wasn't happy. Mark had never turned up the day before, citing a work deadline. He then refused to discuss returning her cell phone to her when she'd brought it up during his call. He refused to explain why not, just that she couldn't have it. Valerie was furious at him for infantilising her, but even gladder she hadn't told him her assistant was making the trip from London for a catch-up.

She shifted position on the bench to ease the stiffness in her back. It was another hot day, and she thought Penny might appreciate sitting outside in the shade after her journey. She'd arranged with the chef and his staff to bring out a pitcher of iced tea and some snacks in half an hour when Penny was due. For now, Valerie was content to just sit there and soak up the view – and to try to remember.

Her sleep the previous night had been less fractured, but the nightmares were more intense. She'd relived the moment she'd been stabbed, the sensation of the blade slicing into her back horribly vivid. Then, after waking briefly, she'd dreamt of being on a bridge surrounded by people and yelling for help. Then she was in water, but it was so murky she couldn't see anything. She'd kicked with all her might trying to reach the surface, but it was like her limbs had turned to stone. Just as she was about to give up and let herself sink, she'd reared up and suddenly she was on the bridge again, and standing there, looking furious that she'd survived, was Mark. That was when she'd woken and realised it was morning.

Recalling her nightmare was the most remembering Valerie had done in weeks. It felt like a cog had turned inside her head and finally her memory was easing back into motion. The brief wisps from the period leading up to her attack felt more solidified today. Not quite the full picture, but substantial enough snatches that, put together, formed a highlights reel, like a movie trailer.

She suspected her row on the phone with Mark yesterday had triggered it. She now remembered that he'd walked out on her the weekend before she was attacked. It was after he'd got angry about reporters ringing the doorbell. She also remembered that Glenn had urged her to put herself first but still couldn't quite recall why he'd been so adamant.

She'd give anything to talk to Glenn now, but Abigail, Dalewood's manager, had made excuses when she'd asked to call him after breakfast. 'Later,' she'd said. 'After your morning therapies.'

When Valerie had finished all those and went to find her, she was told Abigail had left for an external meeting and wouldn't be back until the evening.

Penny was ten minutes early. Escorted outside by one of the admin staff in Abigail's absence, she appeared emotional as she crossed the lawn.

'It's so good to see you,' Penny said, on reaching the bench. 'I've been so worried. Hey, don't get up, I'll come to you.'

To Valerie's surprise, Penny leaned down and hugged her. Part of her felt the level of contact was inappropriate from her assistant, but the rest of her relaxed into it, welcoming the young woman's comforting embrace.

Hug over, Penny sat down beside her. She looked immaculate in a sleeveless white silk blouse, black pencil skirt and heels. Her blonde bob had been gelled off her face and secured in a chignon. Valerie suddenly felt self-conscious of her own attire – an oversized white T-shirt and creased olive-coloured linen trousers that Dalewood House had provided. She'd asked Mark to bring her some of her own clothes from home, but every time he visited, he claimed to have forgotten.

'How are you healing?' asked Penny.

Valerie liked that she'd asked her that and not how she was feeling. She was tired of having to answer that question. She'd been stabbed. She could've died. How did they think she was feeling?

'My back's healing well according to my surgeon and the doctors here. The physio to strengthen the muscles the blade went through is really helping . . . and my walking is improving each day,' she said. 'They've actually been more concerned about my heart than the stab wounds, after I went into cardiac arrest. But all the scans and tests I've had done are showing no permanent damage. I got really, really lucky.'

'I still can't believe anyone could hurt you like that. Thank God the police caught them.'

Valerie frowned. 'Them? There was only one person there. One of the few things I do remember is that there was only one set of footsteps running away.'

'You haven't heard? The police have arrested the TikToker who posted all the videos about you and Bradley. She's been charged under what's called joint enterprise because it was her content that got people riled up, and the person who stabbed you was her friend. So she's going to be standing trial with him.'

Valerie jolted as a flood of memories returned with a whoosh, punching the breath from her lungs. The TikTok videos saying it was her fault . . . the ambassador at Winfield House, telling her the White House was getting antsy . . . the cease-and-desist letter she hadn't wanted to send. One big domino effect that had resulted in her being stabbed.

'What's the charge against her?' Valerie asked weakly.

'Attempted murder, same as the man.'

'Can they do that? She wasn't there when it happened.'

Penny shrugged her delicate shoulders. She had the build of a ballerina. 'Apparently they can. She deserves it too. Her trolling got you stabbed. I hope she gets the maximum jail time.'

'How long would that be?'

'Um, it could be as much as life, I think. But don't quote me on that. Oh, how nice. I love iced tea.'

One of the kitchen staff had arrived bearing a tray with the drinks and food that Valerie had ordered. He also had a small folding table with him. The two women waited quietly while he set everything up and left.

'Can I give you your present now?' asked Penny.

Valerie was touched. 'You didn't have to bring me anything.'

'I know, but I figured you needed this. Sorry I didn't have time to wrap it.'

From her bag Penny pulled out a box holding the latest model of iPhone. She handed it to Valerie.

'It's fully charged and set up. I transferred everything I could from your cloud storage, but I'm afraid you've got a new number temporarily. We can figure out getting your old number reinstated once the police give us the all-clear,' she said.

Valerie decided now was not the time to explain that it was actually Mark who was withholding her old phone, not the police.

'I hope you didn't pay for this yourself,' she said.

'No, it's from work. Not all your contacts transferred for some reason, so I've taken the liberty of pre-programming some numbers that were missing, like my personal cell,' Penny added. 'You've also had quite a few calls to the office from a Glenn at the State Department in DC. He left a cell number so I've saved that too. I hope that's okay.'

'Of course it is. Thank you so much for doing this. I've really missed having a phone,' said Valerie, clutching the box to her chest like it was gold bullion. 'Glenn is my best friend from college. He must be wondering where I am.'

Penny seemed surprised by that. 'He doesn't know you're here?'

'If he's been ringing the office, I guess not. Mark's been very protective of me since the attack.'

'I see.'

The shift in Penny's demeanour couldn't have been more obvious than if she'd held up a sign. At the mention of Mark's name, her expression tightened and her eyes flickered downward to a spot on the floor by her feet.

'Do you have a problem with my husband?' Valerie asked her bluntly.

Penny looked her square in the eye. 'You asked me on the phone yesterday why I'd come to your house that day. It was because I had something to tell you about Mark.'

Valerie scrunched up her face as she tried to remember. 'Was it something to do with a laptop?'

'I did have one with me, yes, to show you what I needed to tell you.'

'That sounds like embassy double-speak,' said Valerie wryly. 'What was it you needed to show me?'

'Phone data from the night Becca Farrow was murdered.'

Valerie was taken aback. It had been a while since anyone had dared to say Becca's name in front of her. They tended to skirt around it, referring to her as 'the victim on Southwark Bridge'. Like it was somehow Becca's fault for all this, and not her son and husband's . . .

She let out a little cry of shock.

'Jesus, I remember now. You had data that showed Mark's phone had been triangulated near Southwark Bridge when Becca died. I thought it must've been a mistake and told you to wipe the data.' Then another memory shot forward, so strong it ricocheted like gunfire against the inside of her skull. 'I don't think Mark was in bed with me all night.'

'Sorry?'

'I thought the data had to be wrong because Mark had been in bed with me all night. But I don't think he was. I woke up at some point. We'd been to a dinner party the evening before. I'd drunk a lot, and I woke up thirsty.' She closed her eyes for a second. 'There was a glass of water on my nightstand. But when I rolled over to go back to sleep, Mark's side of the bed was empty.'

'Perhaps he'd got up to use the bathroom? Or was downstairs getting a drink himself?'

Valerie shook her heard. 'Mark has the constitution of a camel. He never gets up in the night to pee. He barely stirs. I'm certain as I can be that he wasn't in bed with me the entire time that night. Which means he could've been somewhere else.' She stared at Penny, her mind racing. 'I think the data was right. My husband really was at Southwark Bridge that night.'

# Chapter Forty-One

## VALERIE

Valerie's mind felt clearer than it had in weeks. 'My friend Glenn told me I should stop protecting Bradley because I've known all along what he was capable of. But he's wrong. It's not Bradley I should be focusing on. I have to speak to Mark right now,' she said firmly. 'Help me switch this on so I can call him.'

She thrust the iPhone box back at Penny, whose fingers fumbled as she lifted off the lid and prised the device from its cardboard moorings. She powered it up then handed it back.

Valerie dialled her husband's number from memory. She turned to face the other way as the call connected.

'Hello?'

'Mark, it's me.'

Silence, then a greeting so effusively false it made her skin crawl. 'Honey, this is a lovely surprise. Is everything okay?'

'We need to talk.'

Another pause. 'Why are you calling me from a cell? I don't recognise the number.'

'I have a new phone. I got tired of waiting to get mine back.'

'Who got it for you?' Mark's voice was as hard as granite.

'That doesn't matter.'

'I think it does. You're not meant to be having any access to online.'

'Don't worry, it's a dumb phone,' she lied. 'Anyhow, that's not why I'm calling. We need to talk about *your* phone, and why it was pinged near Southwark Bridge on the night Becca Farrow was murdered.'

'What? That's crazy.'

'I don't think it is. I've seen the triangulation data that puts you near the scene.'

'Valerie, do you have any idea how insane you sound? I had nothing to do with that woman being killed. I think I need to speak to Dr Athwal. You don't sound at all well.'

He sounded genuinely worried but Valerie was undeterred. 'It's called being a suspicious wife,' she deadpanned. From the midst of her trauma she could feel her old self crawling to the surface. 'There's something else I've remembered. You weren't in bed with me the whole night.'

Mark reacted furiously. 'How dare you accuse me of lying. I have done nothing but support you and protect you and you come out with BS like that?'

Valerie held her nerve again. 'Did you, or did you not, get out of bed and go to Southwark Bridge on the night that Becca Farrow was murdered?'

'This . . . this is insane,' he spluttered. 'Val, why on earth would I do such a thing?'

'I don't know,' she admitted. 'But you're involved. I know you are.'

'This is your memory playing tricks, or else someone's been filling your head with crap. Who got you that phone? I want to know.'

In-control Mark was back, but Valerie wasn't bowed. 'It's none of your business.'

'That's it. I'm driving down to see you. I'll speak to the manager—'

'Hang on, I thought you were too busy with work to visit.'

'I am. The business is hanging by a thread like you wouldn't believe. I'm having to fight to keep clients. They all want to cancel their contracts because of Bradley.'

'Is there a clause for that? "We may rescind our business in the event of the company boss's son being accused of murder."'

Beside her, Penny shifted. Valerie turned to see she was gathering up her bag. 'Please stay. I really need you to. I won't be much longer.'

Penny nodded.

Still on the other end of the line, Mark demanded to know who she was talking to.

'A friend. So you don't need to come. I am fine.'

She was more than fine, in fact. She felt more assured than she had in years. Like she was emerging from a fog and everything was pin-sharp again.

'Bradley meant to kill Nadia Vinke when he pushed her,' she said simply. 'He also killed Becca Farrow and tried to kill Aldana Porras. I just need to work out where you fit into it all.'

'Aldana who?'

'Oh, come on, Mark. Don't pretend like you don't know who she is.'

'I don't.'

'Aldana was the Smiths' nanny. The same Aldana who Bradley tried it on with at the midsummer barbecue last year. The same Aldana who was pushed into the Thames off Putney Bridge two weeks after she'd turned him down at that barbecue.'

Penny did a bad job of stifling a gasp, while Mark filled the line with protests. Valerie talked over them both.

'I think I've always known it. I just didn't want to believe it. No mother wants to think their child is capable of hurting someone, let alone killing them, but we both know what Bradley is. The signs have always been there. What I don't get is why you were there that night too. Were you trying to help him on Southwark Bridge? Not to help him murder her, but to protect him, to save his next victim. Is that what happened, Mark? Were you trying to stop him but you were too late?'

The silence stretched out like elastic. Then, 'I'm getting in the car now. I'll be there in—'

Valerie hung up. She turned to Penny, who looked shaken.

'I need your help. I want to discharge myself and I have approximately forty-five minutes to do it in. That's how long it'll take my husband to get here from Putney.'

'But what about your treatment?'

'It's just a few exercises. I can do them in the hotel room.'

'You want to go to a hotel?'

'Yes. One that's discreet and where Mark won't be able to find me. Can you arrange that?'

Penny nodded. 'I know a great place.'

'Good. You do that while I sort out the discharge.'

They both got to their feet. Valerie winced, stiff from sitting still for a period, but she also felt energised. She hadn't worked out what her next steps should be, but getting out of here felt like the first one in the right direction.

'Do you think the clinic will be okay with you wanting to leave?' asked Penny, as they walked towards the main house.

'They can't keep me here against my will. But if they try, I'll threaten to call the media and tell them I'm being kept hostage. Pretty sure they won't want to risk that.'

Penny gave her an approving smile, then it faltered. 'I'm sorry, but I couldn't help overhearing. Do you really think your son hurt those women?'

'I think he is capable, yes. I can't pretend any longer, and it's my job as his mother to make sure he's stopped.'

'Shouldn't you call the police?'

'They won't do anything because of his immunity. I need to sort this out myself.'

She could see Penny was troubled.

'You're not implicated in any way by this conversation, or by assisting me in getting out of here,' Valerie reassured her. 'Don't forget, working directly for a senior diplomat, you have immunity too. No matter what happens to me in the next few days, you'll be protected, I promise.'

# Chapter Forty-Two

## GEMMA

It took a day for Gemma to settle in at HMP Bronzefield. Not because it was a better prison than the previous one, but because all the fight had gone out of her. She was too numbed by the judge's decision to deny her bail to protest about her new home, or to feel scared, to be intimidated, even to cry. She was a model prisoner in every respect: accepting of her fate, docile as a dormouse, compliantly doing everything she was told, keeping her head down and avoiding trouble. She was so good, in fact, that she was moved straight off the induction wing into her assigned houseblock. One of the induction wing guards had jokingly called her Zombie Girl on account of how catatonic she was.

This was her third morning waking up in Bronzefield. She didn't need to open her eyes to be reminded of where she was. The noises told her. Voices baying for the 8 a.m. unlock to hurry up and happen. When the guards finally did the rounds, her cellmate, a woman ten years older called Rhonda, bounded out into the corridor like a hare released from a trap. The women only had half an hour to shower and eat breakfast before they were expected to present for their assigned jobs. Rhonda worked in maintenance.

Gemma hadn't been assigned a job yet, nor was she hungry, so she stayed where she was, on her bunk, curled up on her side.

At eight thirty she was locked in again. Just for half an hour while the inmates with jobs went to their workplaces. Gemma took the time to enjoy the solitude of a cell to herself. She washed her face in the small basin and tried to make herself look a bit more presentable. Tomorrow she'd have to get up and shower – it had been almost five days since her last and the heat had made her skin and hair feel grimy.

When unlock came round again, she decided to go to the library to see if there were any newspapers to read. She had learned from her stint at the previous prison that papers were brought into the prison usually two or three days out of date; as it was Thursday now, there might be papers from carrying reports about Monday's remand hearing. She was desperate to know what was being said about her.

She was also desperate to hear how her mum was doing. She'd used the phone provided in their cell to ring the house a few times yesterday but her mum hadn't answered. In the end, Gemma had contacted her solicitor Cliff Daniels and begged him to go round and check on her mum, which he'd promised he would do at the weekend if Gemma hadn't spoken to her in the meantime.

Rhonda had told her she'd find it easy to make friends on the wing, and that all the women were supportive of one another. But Gemma didn't have it in her for chit-chat with strangers at the moment. She wasn't rude, or unfriendly, she just couldn't bring herself to engage. A couple of the older women seemed to recognise that she was lost in her own head, and had taken her to one side at yesterday's association to say they'd be happy to listen when she was ready to talk. Take your time, they'd said, you're not going anywhere so there's no rush. Well intentioned, but that had made her feel even worse.

She was slowly making her way to the library when Sandra accosted her. Sandra was another inmate and also the peer worker assigned to help Gemma settle in and ease her through the induction process.

'Hey, did you manage to get some sleep last night?' Sandra asked.

'A bit.'

'Good. I've been told to let you know that your education assessment is going to be this afternoon at three. It shouldn't take that long, so you'll be back on the block well before association and dinner. I can come with you if you want.'

Gemma nodded. 'I'd like that, thanks. What happens at the assessment?'

'It's like they want to check if there are any gaps in your education that might be partly to blame for you ending up in here, to see if they can help you when you get out. Like, lots of the girls end up studying for GSCEs, or you can learn new skills.'

'I won't be here long enough to sit a GCSE,' said Gemma. 'I'm not guilty.'

Sandra gave her a sympathetic look. 'I know it's difficult, but try not to think about that for now. Focus on settling in and finding your feet.'

One of the guards, a woman in her forties called Tracey with dyed blonde hair and a kindly manner, interrupted them.

'The governor needs to see you, Gemma.'

'Now? I was going to the library.'

'Sorry, but I'm to take you there immediately.' Tracey appraised Sandra. 'You're her peer worker, right? I think you should come too. She might need support.'

That alarmed Gemma. 'Why? What's happened?'

'The details are above my paygrade, love,' said Tracey. 'I'm just under orders to get you there pronto.'

The walk to the governor's office seemed to take forever. Gemma was grateful Sandra was with her. She kept up a steady stream of chatter about prison life and what Gemma could expect in the coming weeks, and how once she got a job and could start earning for spends, she'd find it more bearable. Friends and family could send her money too, up to fifty quid a time. Tracey let Sandra ramble on, but every now and then would smile at something she said.

Outside the door to the governor's suite, Tracey paused. 'I'll be waiting out here for when you're done.' Then she knocked loudly and opened the door to let them in. Gemma let Sandra lead the way. Her legs were shaking so much she thought they might not hold her up. She could think of only two reasons the governor would want to see her suddenly: that somehow Cliff had managed to get a new bail application before a judge and she'd been granted it, or the police wanted to charge her with something else.

It was only when she stepped in front of the governor's desk and saw his grim expression that a third option occurred to her.

*Mum.*

'What's happened?' she blurted out.

'Please sit down, Gemma.'

'No, just tell me.'

Two men were seated next to his desk. One rose to his feet. His expression matched the governor's.

'Hello, Gemma. My name is Detective Inspector Brian Sullivan.'

She recognised his accent as being local to hers. 'You're from Yorkshire?'

'Hull, originally. Been down south for twenty years now.' He appeared on edge. 'I'm very sorry to have to tell you this, Gemma, but there's been a serious incident at your home in Bridlington.

There was a fire last night, and I'm afraid it's caused considerable damage to the property.'

Shock punched any hope of a reply from Gemma's throat. Sandra grabbed her by the shoulders to hold her upright.

'Your mum was in the house when the fire started, upstairs in her bedroom,' DI Sullivan went on, his voice strained. 'The fire service did everything they could, but the way the fire took hold meant they couldn't get to her in time. I'm so sorry to have to tell you this, Gemma, but your mum is dead.'

# Chapter Forty-Three

## EVE

By the time the taskforce gathered at Petticoat Tower mid-afternoon on Thursday, they had all seen the news that a fire had destroyed Gemma Kirk's home overnight. It was headlining everywhere. The name of the person who'd perished in the blaze wasn't being released until a formal identification had been made, but reading between the lines it seemed clear the victim was Gemma's mum, Melanie.

Eve felt a profound sorrow for Gemma and expressed it vociferously.

'I can't begin to imagine how she must be feeling,' she said to Quinn, as they discussed the incident. The others listened as they helped themselves to the tea and biscuits Kathleen had provided.

'There's no knowing if it would've happened had she been at home on bail, but you have to wonder,' said Quinn.

A local news source – reported online and now parroted by the nationals as fact – said the fire was being treated as arson. According to an unnamed neighbour quoted in the original piece, a downstairs front window boarded up with plywood after a previous incident had been drenched in petrol and set alight sometime after midnight. Gemma's mum was a hoarder, according to the neighbour, so the house was packed to the gills with flammable material. 'It went up like a Roman candle,' they'd said.

The report also speculated that Gemma had been the victim of a vendetta that wasn't related to her TikTok activities or the Valerie Aspen stabbing. The police had arrested a nineteen-year-old from Bridlington in connection with the fire, but no further information was available.

'Will it have a bearing on whether she gets bail now?' Quinn's question was for Eve and the other two CPS advocates present.

'I doubt it,' said Paul Ferdie, half-eaten digestive in hand. 'It's tragic but it doesn't change that Gemma is still facing a serious charge. It also makes it more complicated that she no longer has a home address she can be bailed to.'

Photographs of Gemma's burned-out home were circulating online; a smouldering, charred wreck that looked beyond repair.

DCI Carroll stuffed down a third biscuit then rubbed his palms together to rid them of crumbs. 'Right, let me make the introductions. Everyone, this is DCs Matt Keane and Paulina Oteh. They'll be joining Eve, Alix and Anthony tomorrow night inside the bar. Matt, Paulina, this is Eve Wren, Paul Ferdie and John Horner from the CPS.'

There was a flurry of handshaking and hellos. Eve could see why Carroll had picked the newcomers for the op. Both looked incredibly cool, like they belonged on the club scene. Paulina's hair was cropped to the scalp, but she had the striking features needed to carry off such a severe cut. Eve felt like an awkward adolescent in her presence.

'Obviously the commissioner is aware we're planning this recce, but it's still strictly off the books,' said Carroll.

'Same with our chief,' chipped in Ferdie.

Eve wondered which chief he was referring to: the Director of Public Prosecutions or the Attorney General. Or was it someone even higher up than those two? 'Recce' also implied they'd only be watching Aspen inside the club, when they all knew surveillance could mean more than that.

'What's our actual objective tomorrow night?' said Horner. He was het up, drumming his fingers against his thigh as he spoke. 'We need to be clear so that once we've achieved it, Eve can get the hell out of there.'

She was touched by his concern. It was also a good point.

'We've already agreed that our priority isn't evidence to present in court, although if we can get that, great. We're looking for leverage to get the immunity lifted. Eve will be fitted with a recording device that the rest of us can listen in on,' said Carroll. 'We're not expecting a full confession, but we can assume Aspen isn't aware that anyone's joined the dots on the other cases because there's been no mention in the media or online. So, Eve, I want to see what he says when you bring up Gabrielle, Melis, Shannon and Aldana. Not straight away, obviously, but when the moment's right.'

'I'll do my best, but what if he doesn't want to talk to me?' asked Eve.

'Make him,' said Carroll bluntly.

Horner didn't look impressed by that, and nor did Ferdie.

'Only do what you're comfortable with, Eve,' Ferdie said sharply.

'We either try to nail him or we don't,' said Carroll.

It was the first time Eve had felt a fissure between the taskforce. It made her nervous for tomorrow night. She needed everyone to communicate properly and be on the same page in case anything went wrong and she needed to get out of harm's way.

'We wouldn't have spent the last couple of months meeting in your mum's front room if we didn't want the same outcome,' said Ferdie.

For a second it looked as though Carroll might react negatively to that, but Kathleen intervened before he could.

'He's got a point. We might be high up here, but my sofa is about as low-tech as you can get.'

A ripple of laughter ran round the room. Carroll grudgingly joined in. Then he turned to Eve. 'Do what you're comfortable with.'

'Thank you,' she said. 'How big is this recording device?' she asked Cato. 'I need to make sure that whatever I wear can hide it.'

'It's very small and can lie flat against your skin beneath clothing.'

'It's going to be really noisy in the club,' Horner pointed out.

'Tech will be able to isolate dialogue afterwards,' replied Cato.

'Alix also checked out the club and knows where the quiet areas are that I can steer Aspen to,' said Eve. 'We've talked it through.'

'I've thought of something else,' said Quinn. 'It doesn't need to be Eve though – any of us inside the club could do it.'

'What's that?' asked Ferdie.

'Get Aspen's DNA. If he's drinking from a glass or beer bottle, try to pocket it. Or if he touches any of us, make sure we preserve our clothing.'

'I don't need to point out that collecting his DNA by subterfuge would be both illegal and inadmissible,' said Horner sternly.

'Again, collecting evidence for court is not our goal tomorrow. But if we do happen to get a positive match between Aspen and the DNA samples recovered in Becca and Aldana's cases, the US authorities will have to act,' Carroll finished. 'Once they lift his immunity, we can get a legitimate sample.'

Would they though? Eve wished she shared the DCI's confidence. It was also time she asked the question that had been fermenting at the back of her mind ever since Quinn had brought it up after the very first meeting of the taskforce, in Barnes.

'What if Bradley realises who I am and makes an official complaint?'

'I'm more concerned that someone else in the club will recognise you because of the previous publicity, and put your face all over social media again,' said Horner. 'This is why I really don't want you to do this. You don't have to go along with it, Eve.'

It was the first time he'd said it aloud. Carroll huffed, clearly exasperated, but Horner ignored the interruption.

'It's not just your neck on the line either. People won't believe you're at the same club as Aspen by coincidence, and they'll realise we've had him under surveillance. The US will be furious and our government will deny all knowledge of this taskforce ever existing. It could end badly for all of us, but especially for you, Eve. You'll be the scapegoat.'

'If you're not onboard, there's the door,' said Carroll, gesturing angrily.

'I'm staying because I want to make sure Eve's safe tomorrow night,' Horner shot back.

Ferdie tried to calm the room. 'None of us will be hung out to dry, least of all Eve. This might be off the books but there's still a paper trail regarding the taskforce. I've made sure of it.'

Carroll waved his hand dismissively. 'No point worrying about anything unless it happens.'

'I think Eve deserves more reassurance than that,' said Horner, still het up.

'That's all she's going to get, because we're wasting time going over something that might not happen,' said Carroll. 'Look, this is our last chance. I didn't want to say anything before, but the commissioner wants us to wind the taskforce down on our side. We've got one more week and that's it, she's pulling the plug.' The others reacted with shock, even Cato and Quinn. Carroll clearly hadn't forewarned them. 'With Gemma Kirk and Kenny Nasser standing trial for Valerie Aspen's attempted murder, people don't care what her son's been accused of now. Plenty feel sorry for him, in fact, thinking it's been a witch-hunt and that the allegations are false and his poor mum almost got killed for it. The commissioner thinks because of that we've reached the end of the road. So unless we make one last-ditch effort tomorrow night to nail him, he's going to get away with it. It's now or never.'

# Chapter Forty-Four

## VALERIE

Valerie had just finished showering when there was a knock on the door to her suite. Unnerved, she wrapped the complimentary bathrobe tight around her middle and secured the sash with a double knot. She hadn't ordered room service – hadn't requested any service, in fact – and the only person who knew she was at the hotel was way across town at the embassy. Had Penny sent something over but forgotten to tell her? It was unlikely, she decided. Her new assistant was even more organised than Langdon, and he'd written the rulebook on time management and efficiency.

She went to the door, her bare feet noiseless on the luxuriantly thick carpet pile. But before she could answer it, there was a second rap of knuckles on wood, louder this time. Followed by a voice so familiar she was stunned to hear it.

'Val, it's me.'

She yanked the door open. 'What are you doing here?'

Glenn never arrived in London unannounced. He always let her know ahead of time. He looked her up and down with a grin. 'Have I interrupted something?'

'Wipe that mind of yours. I've just showered.'

His grin grew wider. 'Nope, still thinking it.'

Laughing, Valerie beckoned him inside. He pulled a cabin-sized carry-on behind him and let go of the handle to give her a hug.

'Ouch, careful,' she said. 'My back's still tender.'

He broke away, shaking his head. 'I can't believe you got stabbed. I'm so sorry, Val.'

'I'm not gonna lie – it's been tough. But I'm doing much better now. Come in and sit down.' She was aware her voice was an octave too high to sound natural, but she wanted to keep the mood upbeat, like she always did with Glenn. He was her escape from the serious stuff.

She led him into the suite's seating area. He flopped down on the sofa next to her like all the stuffing had gone out of him. She lowered herself slowly.

'When did you get in?' she asked.

'About an hour ago. I came straight here.'

'How the hell did you find me? I know Penny wouldn't have told you and no one else knows where I am.'

'I called in a favour. It's easy to trace someone when you know how.'

It was then she noticed he wasn't making eye contact. His focus appeared to be on a spot on the wall above the television. She gently pushed his shoulder with her fingertips.

'Glenn, why are you here? Is it because of that last phone call we had before I was attacked? I'm not angry with you for what you said. You were right, I need to do what's necessary. That's why I'm hiding out in this hotel suite, trying to figure out the best course of action. Because if the President won't accept my resignation, I'm—'

She stopped, astonished. Glenn was crying. In all the time she'd known him, she'd never seen him shed a single tear outside of his parents' funerals.

'What's wrong?' she asked, panicked. 'Is it Claire? The kids?'

'No, but I have something bad to tell you, and I didn't want to do it on the phone. I felt I owed it to you to tell you in person,' he said.

'Now you're really scaring me. Tell me what? Are you sick?'

He shook his head. 'No. I came to tell you that it's my fault you got stabbed and that I'm so, so sorry, Val.'

'How could it possibly have been your fault?' she asked, bewildered.

The tears flowed as fast as Glenn could wipe them away. Valerie waited, on the edge of her seat, for him to compose himself. It would be useless trying to pump him for an answer when he could barely get his words out.

Eventually, he calmed down and sucked in a deep, shuddering breath. 'I told Claire what Bradley did in Prague.'

Valerie stared at him, horrified.

'I didn't think it would be a big deal. I made it clear it was an accident. But when you cancelled your meet with the President and rushed back to London from DC, she worked out Bradley was in some kind of trouble again. Then she caught me reading the reports about the woman being pushed off Southwark Bridge and she put two and two together. She asked me if it was connected, so I told her.'

Valerie recovered her voice. 'I told you that in confidence,' she hissed.

'I couldn't keep it a secret from her.'

'You damn well could've. I'm your oldest, closest friend. I can't believe you broke my trust.'

'Val, Claire's my *wife*. I'm not going to lie to her.'

Call it arrogance on her part, but it had never occurred to Valerie that Glenn might confide in Claire the same way he did her. Theirs was the deeper connection, she'd always thought, based on decades of friendship. It was built on shared secrets, mutual respect, and a profound understanding of what made the other one tick. Claire was just his wife.

What a fool she'd been.

'Did you tell her about Mark's phone being triangulated on Southwark Bridge?'

He said no, but his expression gave him away. Fighting to hang on to her temper, Valerie asked Glenn to explain why her being stabbed was his fault.

'Claire was appalled that you were letting Bradley hide behind his familial immunity. I kept telling her it wasn't that simple but she wouldn't listen.'

'I wasn't allowed to quit. Once the President got involved and spoke out publicly on Bradley's behalf, it was out of my hands,' said Valerie defensively. 'This is bigger than me. It's bigger than Bradley. It's politics, pure and simple.'

Glenn shook his head. 'Val, a woman's been murdered. If you really wanted to, you could find a way to get the immunity lifted. That's what Claire was trying to get you to do.'

Valerie stilled. 'How?'

'I didn't know until after you got stabbed, I swear. If I'd known what she was doing, I'd have put a stop to it.'

'What did she do?' she asked again through clenched teeth.

Glenn looked like he might need another moment to compose himself. Instead, he took Valerie's hands in his. She wanted to pull away to show him that she couldn't be so easily won over, but felt too weak to do so. She had a feeling this might be the last time they ever talked like this.

'It was Claire who messaged the TikToker with Bradley's name and sent her the footage of Nadia Vinke's funeral.'

Valerie wrenched her hands from his grasp. She stood up and backed away, the pain in her back forgotten. She clutched her right hand to her throat and the scar that marked it.

'Please tell me she didn't,' she heaved.

'I'm so sorry. She felt really strongly that Bradley should face justice. She wasn't thinking what it might unleash.'

'That's bullshit and you know it. She did it to ruin my life. Claire's never liked me and she's always been jealous of how close we are.' Valerie swayed on the spot, light-headed from shock. 'I can't believe this. How did you find out?'

'She was being secretive with her phone, and I was worried she was hiding something from me. I confronted her and that's when she told me what she'd done. She'd set up a TikTok account using an anonymous name. She did it out of concern.'

Valerie scoffed. 'Concern? Is that a joke? Where was her concern for me when she was firing up the public to make threats against my life? Or is she happy that someone tried to murder me because of what she did?'

'Hey, don't pretend like this is all Claire's doing,' said Glenn, getting to his feet also. 'Your son started this when he pushed Becca Farrow off a bridge for kicks.'

Valerie reared up. 'You've changed your tune. A minute ago, you were crying and telling me that it was all your fault I got stabbed and how sorry you were.'

'Of course I'm sorry. I should never have told Claire about Prague, I accept that. And she should never have contacted that TikToker. But don't you dare act like you bear no responsibility here. You could've saved Becca's life.'

'What? How?'

'By making Bradley face up to what he did to Nadia Vinke.'

'He said it was an accident.'

'You don't believe that any more than I do. I can see it in your face. Bradley's been violent since he was a kid and it got worse when he started taking drugs. *You* told me that, after he pushed you and gave you that scar. He meant to hurt Nadia. You've known all along, and so has Mark.'

'That's where you're wrong. Mark didn't find out that Nadia fell because Bradley had shoved her until your wife supplied that video for the world to see and I had to tell him.'

'That's not possible.'

'It is. I never told him the full story. I didn't want to worry him.'

Glenn paled. 'Val, Mark knew before he left Prague and joined the two of you in London.'

'No he didn't.'

'You think George Stow kept what happened to himself? Of course he didn't. When you called him about Bradley's confession, he took action to suppress it – but he didn't do it alone. Right before he joined you in London, Mark was involved in the negotiations to pay off Nadia's family.'

Valerie trembled. 'He can't have.'

'It's true. How do you think I know all this? Because there's a trail. There's always a trail, Val.'

Defeated, she sank back down on the sofa. 'So George told Mark what really happened?'

'No. Bradley told him the truth before the two of you flew to London. George just confirmed it.'

Valerie was dumbfounded. All these years she'd lived with the heavy burden of keeping her son's secret, thinking it was hers alone to bear. The upset and distress that came with it grinding her down. Yet Mark had known first. Bradley had trusted his father to deal with the practicalities while forcing the emotional responsibility on to her. Mark had known that, and he'd still let her shoulder it alone for years. She had never felt so betrayed.

'I'm sorry, Val. I thought you knew Bradley had told Mark.'

Her mind rambled with more questions.

'How did Mark even know George to work with him to pay off Nadia's family? I don't think they'd ever met.'

Glenn shrugged as he sat down again. 'I don't have all the answers. I only found out myself a couple of weeks ago. I contacted someone I know in Prague after the attack on you because of what you told me about Mark's phone being pinged at Southwark Bridge. I had a hunch he got involved behind the scenes in Prague and I was right.'

'What about Nadia's best friend? Did Mark take care of her too with the hit-and-run?'

'That did cross my mind, but I checked it out. There's nothing linking Mark directly to what happened, or George.'

'They still could've arranged it,' Valerie shot back.

'I think it's best you chalk that one up to a tragic coincidence.'

Valerie dropped her face into her hands. She couldn't believe what she was hearing. Mark had colluded to protect Bradley in Prague and he'd colluded with him again on Southwark Bridge. She played back her husband's reaction to her mentioning Aldana Porras, the neighbour's nanny who was pushed off Putney Bridge: his denial of the incident and of even knowing her was patently false.

She felt Glenn's hand rub her shoulder and pulled away roughly. She turned to face him. 'Does Claire know about Mark working with George in Prague?'

'No.'

Her eyes raked his face for signs he was lying, then she realised she could no longer trust her own judgement.

'Glenn, I need you to be honest with me.'

He crumbled quicker than a sandcastle at high tide. 'She does.'

'Why hasn't she shared what she knows?' Then the dime dropped. 'Oh, because the TikToker got arrested for my attempted murder and can't access her account in jail. What a blow for your wife,' she said sarcastically.

She gingerly got to her feet again.

'I'd like you to leave now.' When he didn't budge, she raised her voice. 'Glenn, get the hell out or I will call the police.'

He scrambled to his feet. 'I understand you're angry, Val, but let's not leave it like this.'

'I'm not angry with you. I'm angry with myself. I've spent too long listening to men telling me what to do. You, Mark, Langdon, the ambassador – hell, even the President thinks he can control me. I am going to fix this mess, but I'm going to do it on my terms. Not on anyone else's, and certainly not on Claire's.'

It was one thing for her to be seen protecting her son against false allegations. But if it got out that she knew her husband had been involved in covering up his crimes, she'd be finished. She might even face jail time for assisting a felon.

'You can tell Claire she doesn't have to worry any more, you and I are done.'

'Val, please—'

She went to the door and held it wide open. 'Get out.'

Glenn wearily took hold of his carry-on and wheeled it past her into the corridor. Then he stopped. 'Can we please just—'

She slammed the door shut before he could finish. Then she called Penny and told her to drop everything and get to the hotel. They had work to do.

# Chapter Forty-Five

## GEMMA

Gemma clutched the receiver to her ear and listened intently while her mum told her she couldn't get to the phone right now, so leave a message and she'd call back when she had a second. Gemma waited until she'd finished speaking, then dialled the number again.

*'Hello, this is Mel, I can't get to the phone right now . . .'*

Rhonda came over and pressed her finger down on the call end button. 'If you keep ringing her phone, you'll fill up the voicemail and then it won't work.'

Gemma dropped the receiver back in its cradle. 'I just wanted to hear her voice.'

Rhonda squeezed her shoulder. 'I know, mate. Come on – the others are waiting for us. Breakfast started five minutes ago, and you need to keep your strength up for seeing your brief.'

Cliff Daniels was coming in to see her at ten.

Concerned about her state of mind, the governor had wanted to send Gemma to the hospital wing in the wake of her mum's death, but she'd refused to go. She'd also turned down support from the prison chaplain – she hadn't been religious before and wasn't about to start now. She had all the support she needed right here on the block. On hearing her mum had perished in the fire, the women had thrown a protective ring around Gemma, taking turns to listen when she wanted to talk, to hug her when she cried, to cheer her on when she ranted. Most sympathetic were the long-termers who'd also experienced losing a loved one while they were behind bars. It hollows you out, they'd told her, not being able to say goodbye properly and not being able to grieve alongside the rest of your family. You just have to take each day as it comes, they advised. With Sandra's help, Gemma had submitted a request to attend the funeral and was waiting to hear if she'd be allowed.

Breakfast was usually a small bag of bland cereal, like Rice Crispies or oats, with UHT milk and two slices of bread. Rhonda had offered to fetch Gemma's while Sandra and the others made room for her at the table. She liked that they didn't ask how she was, they just shuffled up and absorbed her into their conversation. But when Rhonda returned and placed a tray in front of Gemma, she did a double take.

'Coco Pops?'

The chocolate cereal was a rare treat. But it wasn't just one small box waiting to be opened – there were four of them.

'On us,' said Zena, from along the table.

Gemma looked at her friends' trays and saw that some of them only had bread to eat.

'I can't take your breakfasts.'

'Yes, you can. Now eat up before it gets cold,' Sandra joked.

Gemma was overwhelmed by the gesture. These women had shown her more kindness in a few days than anyone had shown her in years. She blinked back tears. Rhonda, now sitting next to her, wrapped her arm around Gemma's shoulders.

'We've got your back, kid.'

◆ ◆ ◆

There were rooms set aside for inmates to talk with their legal representatives without being overheard. Cliff Daniels had made the long drive down from Leeds overnight and was already seated at a table inside one when Gemma was taken to meet him, papers spread out in front of him. It was only Monday that she'd last seen him, but it felt a lifetime ago. She'd been sent to a new prison halfway across the country and had lost her mum, her home and everything she owned, all in the space of a few days. She couldn't begin to get her head around the speed at which her life had been turned upside down.

Cliff started by expressing his sympathies for her loss and telling her that the police investigation into the arson was continuing.

'It was definitely done on purpose?' she asked, now seated opposite him. The guard who'd escorted her to the room had left them to it.

'The fire service investigators have confirmed it. There's evidence an accelerant was used to set fire to the boarded-up window at the front. The police arrested Kira Maybank after I told them how she's been targeting you, but as of last night she's been bailed pending further inquiries.'

'She won't have dirtied her hands to do it herself. One of her idiot gang will have done it for her.'

'That's for the police to establish, which I'm sure they will.'

'How bad is the damage?'

'Very bad. It will take extensive repair work to put it right, but your insurance should cover it.'

She let out a hollow laugh. 'Insurance? Don't be daft. We couldn't afford that.'

'You had no buildings or contents cover?'

Gemma shrugged. 'We were skint and had other bills to pay.'

'Were you renting?'

'No, Mum inherited the house from her parents.'

'That's something, I suppose. If you had a mortgage outstanding on the property, the lack of insurance would've invalidated it and the provider could've called in the loan. Look, this isn't my area of expertise, but I can ask one of my colleagues in our conveyancing department to go through your options.'

The bricks and mortar and the ownership of the house were of no concern to Gemma now. It was what was inside that mattered – and now that was all gone. They could bulldoze the place to the ground for all she cared.

'Would it have been quick?'

'The fire taking hold? Probably.'

'No, I mean Mum dying. Would it have been quick, or would she have suffered?'

Cliff looked pained to be asked. 'My guess is she'd have been rendered unconscious by the smoke first,' he said carefully.

'Can you still feel things if you're unconscious?'

'I don't know, Gemma.' He let out a little cough. 'Um, shall we talk about how we're going to approach the next bail hearing? We've managed to get you before the judge on Monday because of the special circumstances. You won't have to appear in person, it can be done from here, by video link.'

'Cancel it.'

'I'm sorry?'

'I don't want bail now. I'm fine to stay here.'

Cliff grew flustered. 'But Gemma, you don't deserve to be in here, and in the light of your mother's death it's right that we should ask again for bail.'

'You're my solicitor, right?'

'That's correct.'

'So you have to do what I instruct you to do?'

'Well, yes, technically, but it's my ethical and professional responsibility to advise you when I think a course of action isn't appropriate.'

'You're doing a great job of advising me, Mr Daniels. I promise I'll tell anyone who asks that you are. But I don't want you to apply for bail.' She paused. 'I think I also want to plead guilty at my trial.'

Starting at his chin and working upwards, Cliff's face went puce. 'Gemma, you can't give up. We have a really strong case to fight this.'

'It's what I want. I've got nothing to get out for.' For a second, she thought she might break down, but fought to compose herself.

'That's not the point. You'll be pleading guilty to a crime I don't think you're guilty of and I believe a jury will agree with me. You deserve the chance to defend yourself,' he said. 'Look, I understand that you have experienced the most awful trauma this week, and that's going to take time to process. But try not to let your grief cloud your judgement. Let us go before the judge on Monday and get you out of here. Then you can be with your friends and other family on the outside while you deal with what's happened.'

'Friends and other family? The only mate I've got is the manager of the crappy hotel where I work, and he's only interested in making money off me at the minute. I don't have any other family. Mum's dead, my dad's dead, all my grandparents are dead, and the only living relative I know of is an uncle in Sheffield I've not seen for years and wouldn't recognise. I have online friends, but I couldn't even tell you their real names. I didn't know what Sponge's was until they said it in court. I don't have anyone on the outside waiting for me.' She exhaled shakily, trying not to let the emotion get the better of her. She wanted to stay strong like the other women on the wing. 'But I have got friends in here. People who really care about me.'

Cliff looked dubious. 'You've only been in here since Monday.'

'Ever had a friend give you their Coco Pops?' The solicitor stared at her blankly, patently baffled. 'No? I had four give me theirs this morning. That means something in here. I've also got a roof over my head. Where am I meant to go if I'm bailed? I've got no home to go to since the fire and no way of getting it sorted. I've got no money to rebuild a house; my crappy earnings won't touch the sides of what's needed. I suppose I could stay at the hotel but I'm not sure my bosses would like it being used as a temporary bail hostel. Mr Daniels, I appreciate you trying to look after me, but I really am better off in here for now.'

He sighed unhappily. 'Okay. We'll withdraw the bail application. But please, please think again about the plea. I don't want to see a girl your age locked up for something that I'm confident we can fight in court and win.'

Gemma went through the motions of nodding and promising not to do anything hasty, but deep down her mind was made up. There was nothing for her on the outside, not in Bridlington or anywhere else. Bronzefield was where she belonged now, and if pleading guilty to attempted murder meant she could stay there, that was what she'd do.

# Chapter Forty-Six

## EVE

The heatwave decided Eve's outfit in the end. By Friday evening the temperature was pushing a sweltering thirty-four degrees, and the thought of getting dressed up to go to a club made her sweat even more. Panicked that nothing in her wardrobe was suitable, she'd borrowed a sleeveless cotton khaki jumpsuit from Leah, which she'd teamed with wedge sandals. Not the kind of thing she'd normally wear unless on holiday, but cool enough for her to make it through the evening without keeling over from heatstroke. It also had lots of pockets in which the matchbox-sized recording device could be concealed. The tiny microphone was attached to the inside of her lapel, while tucked discreetly inside her right ear, masked by her dark hair, was an earpiece the others could talk to her through. DCI Carroll was parked a few spaces down from the club's entrance. Ferdie and Horner – who it had been agreed should play no active role in tonight's operation – were listening in from a nearby café.

DS Cato had fitted Eve with both the earpiece and recording device at a pub near Trafalgar Square before they made their way to the club. Quinn had arrived separately from her fellow DCs, Matt

Keane and Paulina Oteh, and the three of them were now separately staking out the venue, pretending to sip from bottles of beer.

The club was a step-up from the seedy pub Eve and Quinn had previously tracked Aspen to. Three times the pub's size, the walls were painted a deep orange, the floor was fashioned from reclaimed wooden boards, and chairs and tables in various shades of blue lined the sides of the vast space. It was also far busier, at least five deep at the bar. It took Eve almost twenty minutes to get to the front to order a drink; now she was wedged in so tightly between the other punters that she couldn't even raise her hand to get the bar staff's attention, much less reach into the pocket where the recording device was primed to be switched on. DS Cato was waiting for her towards the rear of the club, using the vantage point to scan who came in. They knew there was no guarantee that Aspen would show with his friends, but they were optimistic.

The music suddenly cranked up in volume. The bass was so loud that Eve felt it thumping in her chest. The DJ wasn't due onstage for another hour though – how much louder could it get? She was worried it might be impossible to find a quiet space to chat even if she did engage Aspen in conversation.

She suddenly felt a sharp pain in her ribs. The man standing next to her had elbowed her trying to get his phone from his back pocket.

'Sorry, didn't mean to hit you— Oh. Hello, Eve.'

She did a double take. It was Jamie. Her heart sank. Wedged in on both sides and from behind, there was literally no getting away from him.

'Hello,' she replied, her tone cool.

'It's good to see you. How have you been?'

She wanted to laugh at his brazenness. Despite what he'd said to Leah, nothing in his reaction now suggested he was contrite for ringing her doorbell in the early hours and scaring her. She wouldn't give him the satisfaction of showing she was bothered though, and mirrored his nonchalance.

'I'm really good, thanks. You?'

'Same. Work's good. Everything's good.'

Eve nodded like she was interested but kept her gaze trained on the bar staff as they skilfully juggled orders of multiple drinks. She wasn't going to miss her turn because of him.

'I didn't have you down as a fan of dancehall,' he said.

'Likewise.' A thought occurred to her. 'Did you follow me here?'

Jamie laughed. 'No, I came with some mates.'

She didn't know whether to believe him.

'You look really good, Eve,' he was saying now, as he pressed into her side a bit harder than necessary.

She didn't return the compliment.

'We should go out for a drink again sometime,' he added.

She couldn't keep her composure. 'Are you kidding me?' She laughed in his face. 'I don't think so.'

'Is this because I came to the flat? Don't be like that. It was just a bit of fun.'

'I think recollections may differ,' she quipped. Turning back to the bar, she silently urged the staff to hurry up so it was her turn next. She couldn't wait to get away from him.

Undeterred, Jamie rested his hand on the small of her back. Eve tried to shift position but there was no space to pull away from him. He leaned in so his mouth was against her ear, and she squirmed.

'I have said sorry, Eve. You're taking it far too seriously.'

Eve seethed. His arrogance was staggering. 'You knew I was feeling stressed because I was being harassed by Frank Tooley but you still thought it was okay to do what you did. You must've heard on the intercom that I was getting freaked out but you kept pressing on the bell anyway.'

'Okay, I get it. My bad. Let me take you out to say sorry properly.'

Quinn's voice suddenly sounded in Eve's earpiece. 'Is that bloke bothering you, Eve? I can see him leching from here.'

Eve nodded. Unfortunately, Jamie thought she was responding to him and moved even closer.

'You look bloody amazing tonight,' he whispered in her ear.

Eve's skin crawled as Jamie's gaze settled on her cleavage. She tried to pull away again but his hand slid slower down her body.

'Get off me,' she snapped.

He flashed her a smarmy smile. 'You don't mean it.'

Before she could retort, Jamie appeared to lose his footing, and a gap suddenly appeared between them. A man with a shaved head had put himself between them, his back to Eve. Pinned in again, she couldn't hear what was being said but she saw Jamie's expression contort before he started backing away from the bar. The crowd parted to let him through. Eve was pleased he'd been seen off, but when the man turned round, she gave a start. He was wearing thick-framed black glasses, but there was no mistaking Bradley Aspen up close.

He smiled. 'Hello. I hope you didn't mind me stepping in, but I was standing right behind you, and I could see the man was being an idiot.'

Eve tried to hide her shock. Had the others recognised him when he arrived? From afar it might be hard to tell who he was because he looked so different. His American accent was barely discernible as well, like he was trying to disguise that too. Heart pounding, Eve flashed him what she hoped would be a grateful smile and mentally scrabbled for a way to make him stay put. She had to alert the others to his presence without him catching on.

'I don't mind at all. He was being a dick. Um, can I buy you a drink to say thank you? I might get served any day now.'

Bradley chuckled. 'Sure. A Peroni would be great.'

As they waited, Eve asked where in London he lived. 'Not far from Finsbury Park, in a flat share.' Not a single second of hesitation as the lie slipped out, Eve noted. 'What about you?'

If he could lie, so could she. 'Tooting. I'm Leah, by the way.' Tonight she was borrowing her flatmate's jumpsuit and her name.

'Pleased to meet you, Leah. I'm Mason.'

*Like hell you are.*

'So, you're a big fan of dancehall and reggae?' she asked, hoping the others might've noticed them talking and realised he was Bradley.

He shrugged. 'I've seen the DJ a couple of times before but I'm not really feeling it tonight. It's too hot in here.'

He wasn't wrong. It could've been nearing forty degrees inside the club.

'Are you here with friends?' he asked.

'Just one. She's chatting to some guy. They're over there.'

Eve gestured towards a table at the side of the room where she'd last seen detectives Keane and Oteh doing a good impression of a couple engrossed in conversation. Now she couldn't see them over the many heads in the crowd. Could they see her still?

'Why don't I find us somewhere to sit as well while you get the drinks?' Bradley suggested. 'There's a quiet area at the back of the club.'

She nodded. 'Good idea.'

She waited until he'd stepped away, then lowered her chin towards the microphone in her lapel so the others would hear her clearly. She spoke hurriedly, anxious Bradley might come back and hear her.

'He's here. We've just spoken. His head is shaved, he's wearing glasses, dark frames, and he's calling himself Mason. He's dropped the American accent too.'

Cato's voice filled her right ear. 'Understood. We'll try to get eyeballs on him, and you. The place is heaving though. I'm jammed in near the DJ booth.'

Quinn, Keane and Oteh echoed his reply. They were all struggling to make visual contact with Eve.

Beer bottles in hand, Eve pushed her way through the throng to find Bradley, shoving past people to reach the rear. The club must surely have been at capacity, but it looked like they were still letting people in. Then someone on a microphone introduced a warm-up act and an ear-shattering cheer went up and the crowd surged as people began to dance. Eve was shoved from side to side but kept pushing her way towards the back of the venue. She hoped the others had been able to spot her looking for Bradley in the horde, but it was so packed now she feared it would be impossible.

She found him next to a fire exit that had been propped ajar with a beer barrel to let some air in. There was a bouncer right outside, presumably to stop people trying to sneak in without paying. They were surrounded, but everyone had their backs to them, their focus on the front of the club and the booth where the warm-up DJ had started his set.

Eve handed Bradley one of the bottles, but he declined to take it, folding his arms across his chest.

'I'm not thirsty now,' he said, shouting over the music.

'Oh. Um, I guess I can put it down here until you're ready,' she bellowed back. She rested the bottle on the floor beside the barrel.

He beckoned her towards him, gesturing that he wanted her to hear him. His mouth was almost against her ear when he said, clearly, 'I'm not picking it up. I'm not stupid. I know what you're trying to do.'

'What?'

Quick as a flash, he reached forward and plucked the listening device from her ear. Eve was so shocked she froze – giving Bradley the vital seconds he needed. He grabbed her upper arm to hold her still then yanked the microphone from her lapel. Then he stamped on it, crushing it to pieces. The others wouldn't be able to hear a thing now.

'You should've hidden the mic better instead of putting it in the most obvious place a man would look, Eve.'

Oh God. He knew her name. Her arm stung where he'd pinched the skin.

'I – I . . .'

Still gripping her arm, he pulled her closer so she could hear him again. Her legs buckled and she prayed the others were already making their way to help her.

'Don't even try to pretend, Eve. I know who you are and what you're doing.' His accent was back to normal. 'Your friend Quinn isn't very discreet for a cop. I followed her and her colleagues all the way here from the subway and she talked the entire time about her plan to get my DNA.'

Bradley aimed a kick at the beer bottle, sending it flying through the gap in the fire door. The bouncer outside reacted angrily when the contents sprayed the bottom of his trousers. He burst through the gap to remonstrate with them.

'I'm so sorry,' said Bradley, his voice raised. 'My girlfriend knocked it over. She's had too much to drink already.'

'No I haven't, and I'm not your girlfriend,' Eve protested, but to her horror she realised she sounded drunk. Why were her words slurred? And why was the room starting to spin? She rubbed the top of her arm, which still stung. Then, to her horror, she realised the sting had been a needle going in. 'What did you give me?'

'Don't be silly. You're drunk because you sank a bottle of prosecco before we came out,' Bradley said, rolling his eyes at the bouncer for effect.

'You need to get her out of here,' the man replied loudly, unimpressed.

'I know. I really apologise that she got beer on you. Can we get out this way?' Bradley asked him.

The bouncer stepped aside and pulled the fire exit wider for them to pass through. Eve struggled to walk – it was like her legs were wading through slurry. Bradley hooked his arm around her waist as he dragged her away from the club.

'I'm going to take such good care of you, Eve,' he hissed in her ear. 'How about we take a nice walk by the river?'

# Chapter Forty-Seven

## EVE

Eve tried not to panic. The others would realise they'd left and would catch them up. But it was a struggle to stay calm the further Bradley walked her away from the club, and from where Carroll was parked. The club was on the Strand near the Adelphi Theatre and it would take them only a few minutes to reach Waterloo Bridge.

She still felt woozy, but as they walked, she could feel her limbs regaining sensation. Whatever he'd stuck in her arm couldn't have been a strong dose, but did he know that? Eve tried to think as rationally as her fogged mind would allow. Her instinct was to scream for help and get the hell away from him, but she also knew this might be their only opportunity to get the truth. Her phone was in the thigh pocket of the jumpsuit but the volume was off because she hadn't wanted to be disturbed in the club. If she could get to it, she might be able to record everything he said.

But first she had to play along. Eve pretended to loll against him for support. 'Is this how you got the others to go with you?' she asked, drawing out her words for effect.

'I didn't need to. They were already drunk. But you're a special case, Eve. I knew I'd need that something extra.'

'How did you know I'd be at the club?'

'I've been waiting for you to show up again ever since that first time in the pub in Lime Street. I knew exactly who you and Quinn were that night. Such a pathetic attempt to spy on me,' he sneered.

'You recognised us? How?'

'I saw the picture of you two on the Millennium Bridge. What can I say? I like reading my own press.'

Neither she nor Quinn or any of the others had considered that Aspen might have seen their picture. How stupid of them not to think of it. Eve's panic raised a notch.

They were crossing the Strand now. Bradley tried to pull her along faster but Eve turned her ankle stepping off the pavement, unsteady on the wedge sandals. She yelped and bent down to rub it. Bradley frowned.

'You felt that?'

'No, my ankle just feels weird,' she lied. 'My legs are like jelly. What did you give me?'

'Just a sedative to take the edge off.'

Eve let out a fake moan and fell heavily against him again. She had to keep up the pretence. Bradley pitched sideways in his effort to keep her upright. Eve seized on the moment to reach into her pocket for her phone, but she wasn't quick enough. Bradley saw what she was doing and grabbed the phone from her. Then he dropped it down a drain at the side of the road.

'Nice try.'

Eve recoiled. If they couldn't ping her location, how would the others find her now?

◆ ◆ ◆

Eventually they reached Victoria Embankment. Traffic streamed past on both sides. Directly to the left was Waterloo Bridge and

Eve could see the Thames below it, the river's surface glittering like a mirror ball where the setting sun bounced off it. She felt a surge of hope.

'You won't push me in like Becca,' she said. 'It's still light. People will see us on the bridge.'

Bradley hesitated for a moment, like the thought hadn't occurred to him. Then he grasped her upper arm tighter. 'No, what they'll see is me fighting to get away from the CPS lawyer who's been obsessed with proving I'm guilty since day one. Whose meeting with DC Quinn helped fuel all the online hate that got my poor mom stabbed. Who tricked me into meeting her and then attacked me when I tried to get away from her. The CPS lawyer who sadly lost her balance and fell in.'

'People won't buy that story for a second,' said Eve.

'I still won't get arrested though. I'm untouchable, don't forget.'

Finally she succumbed to panic. 'You won't away with it. We know Nadia was your first victim but Becca wasn't your next. There was Aldana, Shannon, Gabrielle and Melis too. Anything happens to me, those cases become public knowledge.'

Bradley was thunderstruck. 'You're bluffing.'

'Why would I know their names? How would we have known to come to that club tonight when that DJ was playing? We've worked it out, Bradley. Me and my colleagues and the police. We know you killed them too.'

For a second Eve thought he was going to bolt. But instead, to her surprise, a slow smile spread across his face.

'You can't prove it though, can you? If you could, you wouldn't be staking out the club like a bunch of morons, waiting for me to make the wrong move. You'd be presenting your evidence to the US government to get my immunity lifted. But you can't do that because you can't make the evidence stack up enough.'

Tears streaked down Eve's cheeks. 'Please don't hurt me.'

'Too late for that. You shouldn't have tried to set me up. You've left me no choice.'

She started to protest but was cut short by a volley of beeps coming from Bradley's phone, which was in the back pocket of his trousers. Holding Eve tightly with one hand, he fished it out with the other. He opened one of the messages he'd been sent, then gasped loudly.

'What the— No, she can't have. She wouldn't.'

Eve leaned over to see what he was reading. The headline made her gasp too.

> *DIPLOMAT VALERIE ASPEN IN SHOCK RESIGNATION STATEMENT: 'MY SON IS A KILLER AND I WON'T PROTECT HIM ANY LONGER'*

There was a video with the story. Bradley pressed play. Valerie, sitting in what looked like a hotel room, filled the screen. She spoke directly to camera.

*'My name is Valerie Aspen and this is my resignation statement. I refuse to collude any longer in being a performative pawn for politicians who value politics more than they do the lives of young women. I am standing down from my position at the US Embassy in London with immediate effect, and if the President has even one cent of conscience, he will accept my resignation without question.'*

There was a pause while Valerie looked down for a moment to compose herself.

*'My resignation means my son Bradley Aspen is no longer protected by familial diplomatic immunity and can be brought to justice for the murders of Nadia Vinke, Becca Farrow and for the attempted murder of Aldana Porras. There may be others. My heart goes out to the families of his victims and I am truly sorry for not speaking up sooner. I am*

*a mother who loves her son more than anything in the world, but I cannot protect him any longer. He needs to face up to what he's done.'*

The video ended. Eve turned to a shell-shocked Bradley.

'I can't believe she's done this,' he said, his voice hoarse.

'It's over,' said Eve. 'You'll be arrested now.'

He stared at her, wild-eyed. 'No. No. That's not happening. I won't let it.'

'Bradley, it's over. Either give yourself up or the police will come for you.'

'I'm not going to jail. I'd rather die first.'

Panic caught in Eve's throat. 'What do you mean?'

His features twisted menacingly and he pulled her towards the kerb.

'This ends when I say it does.' Gripping her upper arm, he pulled her across the two lanes of Victoria Embankment, weaving deftly in and out of the traffic. There was a cycle lane on the river side and both jumped as a rider streaking past yelled at them to get out of the way. His grip loosened for a second and Eve twisted on the spot to pull away, but he grabbed her tighter again. He didn't care that he was hurting her. All he cared about was getting her up on that bridge. Nothing and no one would stop him.

# Chapter Forty-Eight

## EVE

In the split second after Bradley and Eve had plummeted backwards off Waterloo Bridge, he'd clung to her, as though hoping it might save them both. Then their bodies spun apart. Screaming, Eve slammed into the river on her left side. Pain shot through her arm and shoulder. Then she was under, trying to hold her breath as her body was buffeted by the current. The water was so dark it was almost black but she could see lights above her and kicked towards them. Her left arm was too painful to raise but she clawed frantically with her right until, finally, her head broke the surface. She could hear yelling and screams. Someone shouted 'There she is', but the current was too fast to tread water in. She was being dragged down again and felt powerless to stop it.

Suddenly there was a splash beside her, followed by an even bigger one.

'Grab hold, Eve,' shouted Frank Tooley. To her shock, he was bobbing in the water a few metres away from her. Of all the people. He was the person who had tried to talk Bradley down on the bridge after appearing from nowhere, and now he was trying to rescue her from drowning. 'It's right behind you.'

She looked and saw there was a lifebuoy floating a couple of metres away. She kicked furiously towards it, reaching out with her good arm. Three times it flipped out of her grip, the water making it slippery to handle, but the fourth time she managed to hook her arm over it. As she did, waves broke over her head, making her choke again.

The waves were from a lifeboat speeding towards them. The current had carried Eve away from the bridge and into the middle of the river. She looked round for Aspen but couldn't see him. Tooley's face was purple from the effort of staying afloat. She tried to kick towards him, but she was too far away. As the lifeboat slowed its approach, she watched him go under. She screamed his name but then hands grabbed her from behind and pulled her out of the water. She collapsed in the bottom of the lifeboat, exhausted and shaking.

'You have to help Frank,' Eve croaked. She tried to add 'he saved me' but her lungs suddenly seized, and she began choking. Seconds later, her body went limp.

# Chapter Forty-Nine

## VALERIE

The knock on the door was far gentler than she had expected. A soft rap of knuckles on wood. One-two-three. This was a hotel though, so a rain of fists and a battering ram like cops used on TV shows might be too much for the other guests. If this were her home, she doubted they'd have been so polite.

Valerie rose to her feet, every inch of her hurting. The events of the past couple of days meant she'd neglected her exercises and her back screamed in protest every time she moved. But she pushed the pain down and focused on her steps to the door, because where she was going, she'd have to learn to live with the pain. Hydro pools and hands-on physiotherapy would not be easily accessed in jail.

Another knock. Slightly harder, louder, but still not with the urgency she'd been expecting. Valerie tried to move faster. She could no longer avoid the inevitable. Penny had alerted her by text to the breaking news bulletins and she'd watched for hours, horrified, the scenes on Waterloo Bridge on a loop. Every time they showed the clip of a body bag being loaded into an ambulance and said it was a man who'd drowned, she'd cried. This was her doing. In trying to do the right thing by posting her resignation video, she'd got it so very, very wrong.

Now it was time for her reckoning.

She peered through the spyhole, did a double take, then yanked the door open.

'What are you doing here?'

Mark slumped against the doorframe. He'd aged a decade since she'd last seen him. His shirt was crumpled and untucked and, glancing down, she saw his trainers didn't match. One was a dark blue Nike, the other a black.

'Bradley.'

She held her breath, braced for the confirmation.

'He's not dead.'

It was her turn to slump. Her heart jack-hammered against her ribcage. She was so sure her son had died in the river. 'But the body – I've seen the news.'

'Not his. Someone jumped in to save the lawyer. Whoever it was didn't make it. Bradley got rescued.'

The delicate skin beneath Mark's eyes was red raw. Valerie fought an impulse to reach out and touch his face to comfort him. Instead, she kept her hands by her sides.

'Well, now you've told me, you can go.'

Mark looked crestfallen. 'That's it? You don't want to talk?'

'We shouldn't discuss anything. The police will be here soon to arrest me and they'll be looking for you too.'

'Arrest you? What for?'

'You're really asking that? I harboured a felon, Mark. I knew Bradley pushed Nadia to her death in Prague and I did nothing. Then Aldana was attacked, and I knew it could be him but again I kept quiet.' She paused. 'I also harboured you. I know you were with him the night he murdered Becca Farrow.

The phone triangulation proves it. I imagine by now the police know it too.'

'I was trying to stop him,' said Mark wretchedly. 'I also suspected he'd attacked Aldana but when I asked him, he denied it. So I decided to keep tabs on him to stop him doing it again. I even installed a tracking app on his phone, but I think he must've got wise to it, because he started leaving his phone at home on purpose. That night, I didn't check on his whereabouts like I usually do. Do you remember? We went out for dinner then came home and went straight to bed. I think that's why he chose that night to attack again, because he knew I was out of it. But I woke up about an hour after we'd gone to bed and that's when I saw he'd slipped out.'

'What made you wake up?'

Before he could answer, a door abruptly slammed closed further down the corridor. They both jumped at the interruption.

'Can I come in?' asked Mark. 'I don't want to be talking out here where people might be listening.'

Valerie reluctantly stepped aside. It wasn't going to help their cases if the police found them together like this, seemingly colluding, but he had a point about being overheard.

'Did Penny tell you where I was staying?' she asked, as Mark crossed the suite and sat down on the sofa.

'No, she refused to. Told me to get lost. So I called Glenn. I figured he'd know, like he always does,' he said tightly.

She ignored the dig. 'What woke you up that night?' she asked again.

'Bradley used my credit card to hire a city cycle. The notification buzzed my watch.'

That made sense. They both had set up their devices so they would be informed of every single transaction made on their credit cards after Bradley had previously racked up huge debts without them knowing.

'Why didn't he use his own card?' Valerie asked. To encourage better habits, they'd given Bradley a pre-loaded credit card that they topped up occasionally. Any other spending was on him.

'I don't know. Maybe it was maxed out.'

'That still doesn't explain how you knew to follow him to Southwark Bridge. It could've been any bridge.'

'I checked his search history on his laptop. Southwark was all over it. He knew there was no CCTV on the bridge itself, that's why he chose it.' Her husband's face crumpled. 'I was in a taxi by Mansion House when I saw him on the bike coming in the opposite direction, away from the bridge. I jumped out to confront him but I was too late.'

Mark suddenly leapt to his feet and gripped his wife's shoulders. 'I'm done for, Val. I know it and I accept it. I covered for our son knowing full well he was a killer. But you didn't know. You believed Prague was an accident because he told you that. So both Bradley and I will tell the police you knew nothing. George Stow is long dead so there's no danger of him saying the wrong thing.'

The part of her that still loved her husband fiercely was touched by his eagerness to protect her. But she shrugged off his hands and shook her head. 'I'm afraid it's not as simple as that.'

In a faltering voice, she told him about Glenn's wife, Claire, working out the truth, and how Claire had been the person responsible for the TikToker outing Bradley. By the time she had finished, Mark was ashen.

'Even if you and Bradley swear blind that I knew nothing, she knows enough to condemn me,' said Valerie. 'I think it's pretty clear based on her actions so far that she wouldn't think twice about it either. And you know what, she'd be right to do so. I should've acted sooner to stop him.' Her voice broke. 'He's my son and I love him, but I was wrong to protect him. We both were.'

This time she let Mark embrace her. They both cried. This was the end and they both knew it. There was no immunity to protect them or Bradley now, no President in their corner. Valerie pulled away first.

'I think we should hand ourselves in. If we wait for the police to come to us, it'll just be a horrible media circus. Let's try to do it with what little dignity we have left,' she said, smiling sadly. 'Do you know which police station Bradley's been taken to?'

'I don't. On the news they just said a central London one. I guess we could go to the nearest one?' Valerie's hideaway was a tiny boutique hotel in Farringdon. Mark searched his phone. 'Bishopsgate station is the closest. It's a half-hour walk or a nine-minute cab ride.'

Seeing him on his phone suddenly reminded Valerie of something.

'Why did you refuse to give me my cell back at Darwood House?'

'I didn't want Bradley bothering you when you were trying to recover. He's put you through enough already.'

Valerie's eyes brimmed with fresh tears. 'Am I a bad mom? Is it my fault because we moved around so much?'

'I should never have said that to you. Your career did not make Bradley the way he is. You did not make him a killer. Neither of us did.'

'But kids are a product of their upbringing, isn't that what everyone says?'

Mark choked. 'We loved Bradley from the minute he was born and he never wanted for anything. If that's us being bad parents, then millions of kids all over the world would be killers as well, but they're not. It's who he is.'

'Something must've driven him to do it, though. There's always a reason.'

'I did ask him why, after Becca's murder, but he couldn't or wouldn't give me a straight answer. My guess is that once he got away with Nadia's death and knew he could hide behind his immunity, it was the thrill of escaping punishment.'

After a few moments they both wiped their tears away. Valerie nodded towards the door. 'Shall we go?'

'Yes.'

They made it as far as the ground floor. Stepping out of the lift, Valerie and Mark were instantly surrounded by uniformed police officers. A young woman in plain clothes stepped forward, her expression stern.

'Valerie Aspen, I am arresting you on suspicion of perverting the course of justice. Anything you do say . . .'

The rest of the caution blurred. Valerie screamed as her wrists were cuffed behind her back and her spine spasmed excruciatingly. 'Please, it hurts,' she cried. Mark, also cuffed and being led away, shouted over his shoulder, 'You don't need to restrain her. She was just stabbed, for crying out loud.'

The female officer ordered Valerie's cuffs be removed. 'Let's go easy on her,' she told her colleagues. 'She's not going to make a run for it in her condition.'

Flanked on both sides, Valerie was escorted from the hotel. It was late now, gone midnight, but the heat of the day hadn't dissipated, and the warmth enveloped her like a hug as she stepped into it. She'd never felt less comforted though.

There was a line of marked police cars parked at the kerbside. In her peripheral vision Valerie saw Mark being placed in the back seat of the vehicle behind the one she was being escorted towards. Then, to her shock, Penny suddenly appeared in front of her. She was dressed casually in a short white linen dress, her usually immaculate blonde bob plastered to her face in sweaty tendrils, but she looked determined. She raised her ID badge.

'I am here as a representative of the US Embassy,' she barked at the female officer. 'Where are you taking her? Our legal counsel needs to know.'

The officer was flustered. 'Bishopsgate station.'

'Fine.' She turned to Valerie. 'We'll be right behind you. You'll be released within the hour, I promise.'

Valerie wasn't sure if she should say anything after being cautioned but decided she had nothing to lose. 'But I don't work for the embassy. I quit, remember?'

Penny smiled triumphantly. 'You're in your notice period and the ambassador wants to hold you to it. You're still covered by immunity, Valerie. This isn't over.'

# Chapter Fifty

## EVE

It was three days before Eve could make sense of what had happened. The first two had passed in a blur of tests, visitors and questions. She'd been taken by ambulance from Waterloo Bridge to St Thomas's Hospital and was still there. Like Aldana Porras, Eve was at risk from secondary drowning, a complication that could occur after water entered the lungs in a near-drowning, and she needed close monitoring.

On the third morning of her admission, she awoke feeling physically better, but mentally her mind was shot to pieces. Frank Tooley was dead because of her. He'd jumped in to save her but had been dragged down by the current.

It was only by luck that there was a RNLI lifeboat station on the bank next to Waterloo Bridge and someone had alerted them to Bradley Aspen pulling Eve off the bridge into the water. But while their prompt dispatch had ensured Eve and Aspen were quickly brought to safety, the crew hadn't been able to save Tooley as well.

Over and over, she replayed the moment Tooley had tossed her the lifebuoy and told her to grab it. She should've swum towards him then, so he could've held on too, but her shoulder had dislocated hitting the water and she didn't have the strength. She had watched him go under but done nothing. She had let him drown.

The tears that threatened to fall again were interrupted by a nurse, Lisa, needing to take Eve's blood pressure. Apparently satisfied with the result, she removed the cuff and offered a smile. 'Someone called Nick rang the nurses' station just now to check how you were. He said he was your ex-fiancé.'

Eve was startled. Contact with Nick after she'd ended their engagement and moved to London had been limited at first, and then non-existent. She'd even fallen out of the habit of stalking his socials to see what he was doing, and with who. She was touched that he'd sought to find out how she was.

As Lisa left her bedside and went to the next patient, Eve wondered if he'd tried her phone first. He'd have had no luck though – Bradley had thrown it down a drain and it was now lost somewhere in its murky depths.

She wondered if Nick had contacted her parents, too – for a while after their break-up he'd remained close to them, helped by the fact he lived close by in Shropshire. She'd ask when they visited again later. They had rushed to London and her bedside after the police had contacted them to tell them what had happened, and were staying in a hotel a few streets away from St Thomas's.

She called out politely to Lisa, who'd just finished up with the other patient. 'What time is it now?' She had no phone and no watch now.

'Five to eleven.'

'Thanks.'

Carroll and Quinn were coming to see her at eleven. She had yet to be formally interviewed but this visit wasn't it; other detectives not connected to the taskforce would do that in the next couple of days. So far, from what Horner had shared with her during his couple of visits, the existence of the taskforce remained a secret and the narrative was that Eve had been in the club with friends by sheer coincidence when Aspen targeted her. It was a flimsy account that invited scrutiny because of who Eve was though, and none of them knew how long it would hold. She was worried she would be scapegoated by the powers that be and hoped Carroll and Quinn might have some reassurance for her when they turned up.

The room she was in held four beds and was set off the main ward. Her parents had pushed for a separate room, but Eve had shot down the suggestion. She didn't want the solitude, nor did she deserve it. It was better for her to be alongside others and where she could be distracted by the clamour that never abated in hospitals, not even at night-time. The whirr of machines and the low hum of voices, like the two she could detect now coming down the corridor towards the room's open doorway.

Carroll and Quinn.

It was the first time she'd seen either of them since the incident. Both looked exhausted as they pulled chairs up to sit beside her, Quinn asking to borrow a spare one from the patient in the next bed. They exchanged a few pleasantries, then Eve updated them on how she was feeling. Carroll shook his head forlornly.

'I'm really bloody sorry, Eve,' he said. 'I never thought Aspen would go that far.'

'It's not your fault. I knew the risks and I knew what he was capable of.' She didn't want to dwell on what he'd put her through. She wasn't ready to discuss it. 'What's the latest with him?'

Quinn, who'd worn a stern expression since sitting down, broke into a smile. 'The US has confirmed his immunity has been lifted. An hour ago he was charged with Becca's murder and for the attempted murder of you and Aldana. He'll be appearing in court first thing.'

Far from being happy, Eve was panicked. 'I don't want him charged for what he did to me. I don't want to go to court.'

Carroll frowned. 'He tried to kill you.'

'But we all know what will happen when I'm on the stand. We can't suppress any evidence about why I was really at the club and who else was involved, so the defence can argue it was entrapment. It'll be bad for all of us.'

Quinn threw a look at Carroll. 'She's got a point.'

'I don't see how the charge relating to you can be withdrawn though,' said Carroll grumpily. 'Everyone's seen what he did to you because of the footage.'

Members of the public who'd been on the bridge had captured Aspen dragging Eve over the side on their phones. At least six different videos had circulated online since.

'It's not like you can't cooperate either, working for the CPS.'

Eve knew Carroll was right. It hardly gave out the right message if she refused to support the prosecution.

'With a bit of luck, he'll plead guilty to avoid a trial,' said Quinn.

Eve hoped so, too. But Patrick Nye and the Novus trial had taught her that even the guilty liked to have their day in court.

'What about charges relating to Melis, Shannon and Gabrielle?' she asked.

'There isn't enough evidence at the moment.'

'What about Aspen's parents?' She knew from Horner's updates that Valerie and Mark Aspen had been arrested for perverting the course of justice. 'What's happening with their immunity? I mean, she's resigned her position, so presumably it no longer applies to either of them as well. I watched the video.'

Eve shuddered as she said it. It was seeing the video of Valerie quitting her embassy role that had triggered Aspen into dragging her off the bridge.

'Valerie Aspen has kept her immunity because she's technically still an employee of the embassy. You remain covered even in your notice period, apparently. The husband's had his revoked because of the CCTV image of him and his son near Southwark Bridge on the night Becca was killed, but he's not been charged with anything yet and has been bailed while inquiries continue,' said Carroll, clearly peeved. 'According to our commissioner, back-channel discussions are going on between the US government and ours to keep Valerie out of court in the light of her stabbing, and because there's no proof that she knew anything about her son's murders until just before she recorded the video resignation that guaranteed he'd face justice. They're going to protect her, and I think she'll be whisked back to the States any day now. Just you watch.'

# Chapter Fifty-One

## VALERIE

It took forty-eight hours, in fact, before Valerie was whisked away.

While Eve was being discharged from hospital, Valerie was packing two suitcases to fly back to the States that evening. Both cases were hers. Mark's bail conditions meant he was unable to leave the UK. He would stay in the house in Putney with Scout until his case was resolved.

Dog and husband were sitting on the bed watching her squeeze as many clothes and personal items as she could into the cases. Scout never liked it when she went away, and she could see from the dog's mournful expression that this occasion was no different. Mark's expression was even worse. He understood why Valerie's legal team had told her it was prudent that she return to the US, but he felt he was being abandoned to his fate, by his wife and by his home nation.

'I don't understand why you can't stay,' he was complaining again.

'You know why. It's about averting a diplomatic crisis.'

She left the vagueness of the statement hanging in the air. There was no pending crisis. Valerie couldn't bring herself to admit the truth, but it had been her idea to leave. She was running to save herself. The embassy's legal team was on the fence, thinking that with her diplomatic status intact, she should wait it out. Word had trickled down from the White House that her notice period would be extended indefinitely if that was what it took. People believed that she hadn't known what Bradley had done and there was a groundswell of support for her because of the stabbing. Mark, however, was a different prospect, and so it had come down to a choice: him or her.

She'd chosen herself. She doubted their marriage would survive their son being convicted as a serial killer, and without it, all she had left was her career. She still had a few years left to give and she couldn't let her legacy be this. At least, that was what the ambassador had said to her when they'd spoken on the phone after her short-lived arrest, echoing what Glenn had also said.

Penny had once again proved herself an exemplary assistant, sorting out all the travel arrangements to expedite Valerie's escape. In the short term, Valerie would be based in DC – it seemed wise to be close to the White House and the Hill while she was in favour there. After that, who knew. She had a skill set that could easily transfer to a Dow Jones company, or she might even try her hand at college lecturing.

Placing some socks inside the second suitcase, Valerie swallowed down the wrench she felt at leaving without saying goodbye to Bradley. She hadn't seen or spoken to him since his arrest and her lawyers had advised her to maintain her distance. She had never imagined a day might come when she would turn her back on her son, but this Bradley wasn't her boy, not really. He was a stranger to her, and a cold-blooded killer.

A mother's love for her child was supposed to be unconditional, but Valerie now knew that wasn't true. The love she had was seeping away the more she learned of Bradley's crimes: the police had confirmed they were investigating at least three more murders they believed were committed by him. Three more young, vibrant women with the world at their feet, who he'd pushed off bridges and left to drown.

Mark looked like he was on the verge of launching into another pitiful diatribe when the Ring app on his phone pealed. Scout shot off the bed and ran downstairs, barking.

'I bet it's another reporter,' said Mark furiously. There was still a steady stream of them coming each day. He activated the microphone. 'What do you want?' he snapped.

The reporter at the door introduced herself as being from the *New York Times*. Valerie recognised her name as one of the paper's heavyweight investigative journalists. The woman had covered the #MeToo scandal among other major stories. Why had the *NYT* sent her all the way to London for a quote in person?

'I'd like to talk to Mrs Aspen about a serious allegation that's been made against her regarding the cover-up of her son's murder of Nadia Vinke that she orchestrated in Prague with a man named George Stow.'

Valerie's stomach plummeted to her feet. How did this journalist know about George?

'My source is on the record and happy to be named,' the woman continued. 'Mrs Aspen knows him well, in fact. It's Langdon Clarke, her former assistant. So, is she there? Can I speak with her?'

'No you damn well can't,' said Mark. He ended the conversation and closed the app. Immediately the doorbell pealed again.

Valerie sank down on the edge of the bed next to him. 'It's over,' she whispered, tears streaking her face. 'They'll lift my immunity now.'

Mark grabbed her hand. 'Your flight is in four hours. I can stall the reporter long enough for you to get on it.'

'How?'

'If she thinks she's going to get an interview with you, she'll hold off contacting the embassy. You can get to the airport in the meantime.'

'She might have done that already.'

'If they knew, we'd know. Penny would find out and tell us.'

Valerie was doubtful. 'I don't think she's privy to everything.'

'She knows plenty, and something this big would've got back to her. Let me handle it, okay? I'll buy you the time.'

He activated the microphone again on the Ring app. 'Are you still there?'

'I am, Mr Aspen.'

'Can you come back in a few hours? I've spoken to my wife and she's willing to talk but she's resting right now. She's still recovering from being attacked.'

'Sure. Can you give me a definite time?'

Mark glanced at his watch. 'It's four p.m. now, so how about you come round at eight, if that's not too late? She's ready to give her side of the story. We both are.'

Valerie's flight was scheduled to take off at seven thirty from Heathrow.

'That works for me,' said the reporter. 'I'll be back then.'

The two of them watched on the app's video function as she walked away from their property. There was a small Fiat parked in the road that must've been a hire vehicle, because she got into it and drove away.

'Good, she's not hanging around. That means she won't see you leave in a taxi. Let's finish getting you packed,' said Mark decisively.

Valerie was overcome. 'You'll get into even more trouble for assisting my departure. I can't let you do that.'

'Val, we can't both go down for what Bradley did. You only sought help from George because you thought Nadia had slipped and fallen and Bradley was being unfairly blamed, because that's what Bradley told you. You shouldn't be punished for acting with the best intentions with the knowledge you had at the time.'

'I doubt anyone will believe that once Langdon's spilled his guts,' she said bitterly.

'It won't matter by then because you'll be home. Plus, you can deny everything and say he's an aggrieved former employee trying to make capital from the murders of these poor women. The only person who can corroborate it is George, and he's dead.'

'You think I should definitely catch my flight, even after this?'

'Even more so. If you don't leave the UK now, you might not get another chance.'

# Chapter Fifty-Two

## GEMMA

Cliff Daniels was already waiting as Gemma was escorted into the room at Bronzefield where inmates could appear in court by video link. He had an air of impatience about him, jumping to his feet to greet Gemma with an effusive handshake as she entered the room. The guard who'd escorted her there retreated to the corridor outside.

'I have two bits of very good news,' said Cliff, smiling widely. 'The first is that the CPS is dropping the attempted murder charge. You'll face a lesser charge of incitement in relation to the videos you posted on TikTok, but you should be released on bail today. I've already made the application to the court and this hearing will rubber-stamp it. A few more hours and you'll be free to leave.'

Gemma's face fell. 'But I don't want to leave. I like it here. They look after me. I've made friends. I don't have anyone on the outside.'

'You can't stay in prison, and nor should you want to, Gemma,' said Cliff gently. 'Once you're home, you'll realise that.'

'Home? And where exactly is that, seeing as my house burned down?'

'I meant home as in Bridlington. We'll help you find somewhere to stay for the time being, and there are charities and organisations that can help someone in your situation too. They might be able to give you some advice on what to do about the house. The house and the land it's on are still yours.'

Gemma was wracked with frustration. He just didn't get it. Being at Bronzefield had been the happiest she'd felt in a long time. Well, not happy as such, because her mum had just died and she couldn't be happy about that – but secure. Nothing bad could happen to her in the prison because the bad stuff happened on the outside. The other women looked out for her in a way her mum had never been able to do. Gemma finally understood what it felt like to be mothered.

'Why have they dropped the attempted murder charge?' she said, flopping down into a seat across the table from Cliff's.

'They've decided it's not in the public interest. It basically means they know it's unlikely they'll secure a conviction.'

He started to tell her that Valerie Aspen had fled the UK and something about a newspaper story, but Gemma tuned him out. She didn't care about any of that. She was only concerned about her own situation.

She cut short his flow. 'You said there were two bits of good news?'

'Ah, yes. It's about the fire. Kira Maybank and two others have been charged with arson. If they're convicted, they'll be jailed for life.'

'Life? What, be in prison forever?'

'Yes. It's the maximum sentence for arson where loss of life has occurred. My understanding is the police have uncovered substantial evidence that points to their guilt.'

But Gemma wasn't listening. Her mind was in overdrive. There was her wanting to stay in prison, while Kira was going to get banged up whether she liked it or not. It wasn't fair—

She sat up straight. She knew exactly what to do.

'How long would Kira get if Mum hadn't been killed?'

'It depends, but had that been the outcome I would still expect a custodial sentence of up to eight years, because there was high culpability,' said Cliff. 'That means there were significant factors at play, including the fact an accelerant was used, it was a revenge attack, and there was an obvious intention to cause serious harm to property and a high risk of injury to persons.' He paused. 'I'm truly sorry that wasn't the outcome.'

Gemma nodded, swallowing down the lump in her throat that always formed when someone said a nice thing about her mum. She then smiled at Cliff. 'Okay. I do want bail, and I want to go back to Brid.'

He looked relieved. 'Good. I know things will be tough for you with your mum gone and the house in the state it's in, but you're not alone, Gemma. We'll get you all the help you need.'

Gemma continued smiling, which Cliff clearly took as her agreeing with him.

If only he knew. She was happy to go back to Brid now, but not for the reasons he thought. They'd probably call hers a revenge attack too. They'd say she did it for her mum. An eye for an eye and all that. But she'd make sure Kira's mum was out and the house was empty first. She wasn't daft. She might not end up back in Bronzefield either, but it would be another prison where she could feel safe again. And when her time was up there, she'd just find another way to stay.

# Chapter Fifty-Three

## EVE

Eve carried the two mugs filled with tea from the kitchen. She had a little time to spare before her parents arrived to drive her to Shropshire, and Beverly had come round after work to see her off. It was the first opportunity they'd had to catch up since the events of the previous week, and while it felt a little strange to have her boss making herself comfortable on her sofa, Eve was glad to see her.

Beverly accepted the tea with thanks. She'd brought Eve some wrapped chocolates for the car journey, but on sitting down beside her, Eve decided to open them now. Within a few minutes they'd demolished a third of the box.

'What time are your parents picking you up?' asked Beverly.

'At nine, so in about an hour. We should get back to Shropshire by midnight.'

'Why so late?'

'Dad hates driving in London during the daytime. Says it's too manic.'

She was going to stay with her parents for a couple of weeks so they could look after her while she recovered. Her arm was in a sling to support the shoulder that had been dislocated, but other than that her body was healed. There were no signs of secondary drowning and no other injuries. Her mind, however, would need a longer recuperation. Counselling was being arranged for when she returned to London.

She tried to unwrap another chocolate with her free hand but couldn't manage it.

'Here, let me,' said Beverly, taking it from her. 'How long do you need to wear the sling for?'

'I've got an outpatient's appointment in three weeks, so I guess until then.'

Beverly handed her the chocolate, paused for a beat, then cleared her throat.

'I just want to say . . . I can't – I can't thank you enough for what you did for Becca. Her parents have asked me to pass on the same. Your bravery means Bradley Aspen will be sent to jail for life for what he did to her.'

Eve could see her boss was on the verge of tears and was touched. 'I think it was more stupidity than bravery, but I'm glad we nailed him.'

'I also want you to know that I am making sure you are protected from any comeback, and Sol has expressed the same. As far as we're concerned, you acted with the best intentions to help bring a killer to justice.'

A fierce public debate had been raging online about Eve's presence on Waterloo Bridge and whether it was police-sanctioned entrapment, but the furore had started to die down since Aspen had been formally charged. It was hard for anyone to argue that he hadn't deserved to be caught by any means necessary when he stood accused of hurting so many women.

Eve was mollified to know she had the backing of the DPP as well as Beverly, but it didn't quell her concern. 'I'm worried about giving evidence against Aspen at the trial and what the reaction will be when people find out we set up the taskforce.'

'I've got good news on that front. Even if it's mentioned in court, the media can't publish anything. A DSMA-notice has been sent out.'

Previously known as D-notices, these were issued to the media by the government when it wanted to prevent certain information being made public, in order to protect the nation's interests. Eve could see why the taskforce would qualify for one – ministers wouldn't want the Americans to know the secret steps the Attorney General had sanctioned to pressure them into lifting Bradley Aspen's immunity.

'I'm really relieved to hear that,' she said.

'It won't necessarily stop the conspiracy theorists speculating online, but it means no media outlet can confirm the taskforce existed,' said Beverly.

Both sipped their tea in silence. After the lull, Eve asked after Becca's parents.

'They're doing okay, all things considered. Losing a child is a grief like no other though. It destroys you. Every day you have to remind yourself to keep breathing and putting one foot in front of the other.'

Something in her expression made Eve wonder if Beverly was talking from experience. Her boss quickly gathered herself.

'And how are you really doing, Eve? Because I think you're doing an excellent impression of someone who's pretending they're fine when they've just very nearly drowned.'

Now it was Eve's turn to tear up. She shook her head, unable to answer.

'You will get through this. I know you will,' said Beverly. 'Getting back to work will help.'

Eve did not share Beverly's optimism, but her future at the CPS was a discussion for another day.

Time to change the subject.

'I got my replacement phone today. Before you arrived, there was a breaking news alert about Valerie Aspen, but I didn't see the rest of it.' For the sake of her sanity, Eve was staying off news sites for the time being. She didn't need to know what was being written about her. 'What's happened?'

'You know she got on a flight to the US just as the *New York Times* was set to publish an investigation into her covering up Nadia Vinke's death in Prague? Well, the story just went live.' Beverly pulled a face that showed how unimpressed she was. 'If it's true, it looks like she's played everyone, including the President, who's not happy about the flak he's getting for standing by her. She's also abandoned her husband in London to take the rap for her. He's been charged with perverting the course of justice by us, and the Czechs are now calling him a person of interest in Leeza van der Kleji's hit-and-run.'

Eve was shocked. 'They think he's the one who ran her over?'

'No, but they think he had a hand in arranging it.'

'Crikey. So what about Valerie now – is she going to be extradited to the UK?'

If Mark Aspen had been charged with perverting the course of justice, the chances were that Valerie would be too.

'That's for others to decide.' Beverly unwrapped another chocolate and popped it in her mouth. 'It's good news for Gemma Kirk though. The attempted murder charge has been dropped and she's been bailed. There's no public interest in prosecuting her for that now. She may still face a charge of publishing material intended to incite violence, but the DPP has ordered a case review first. My gut feeling is that it won't come to court.'

'That's what I said all along should happen,' said Eve hotly. 'Even if she had faced the lesser charge straight away, it's doubtful she'd have been remanded for it, so she would've been at home when the fire started. She might've saved her mum.'

'Or she could've died alongside her,' said Beverly gravely. 'I feel the same about the charges, Eve, but I don't know if it's helpful to speculate.'

'It's up to Gemma to decide what's helpful. She's the one who's lost everything. Is she back in Bridlington now?'

'I believe she's on her way. The latest bail hearing was earlier today.'

Eve made a mental note to drop Cliff Daniels a line to see how Gemma was. After meeting him by the Bailey that day, she doubted he'd mind her approaching him in private. His client didn't deserve to be in prison, and Eve hoped the girl never had to set foot inside one again.

'What have you got planned while you're at your parents'?' asked Beverly.

'Rest, mostly, but I should see my sister and her family and my brothers if they can be bothered to come round. Some friends have asked to visit too.'

Eve felt her cheeks warming and hoped Beverly wouldn't notice. One of the friends was Nick, her ex. He had contacted her parents, as she'd rightly surmised, and at her mum's invite was due round tomorrow night for dinner. Far from being nervous about seeing him after so long, Eve found she was looking forward to it.

'Good. The break is exactly what you need,' said Beverly, getting to her feet to leave. 'Then you'll come back refreshed and ready to dive into new cases.'

Once again, Eve wished she could share her boss's enthusiasm. The mention of new cases did remind her that she had something to ask Beverly though. In front of her on the coffee table was the Stephen Sheridan file that Frank Tooley had given her. She picked it up.

'This is what Frank Tooley was so keen to talk to me about. It was one of my first crown court cases as an instructing solicitor.' Quickly she explained about the photographs Albie Marsh had bragged he'd taken that might exonerate Stephen. 'I don't know how we can get hold of those photos, but I was hoping you could read the case file while I'm gone to see if anything else stands out that might help?'

Beverly took the file from her. 'Of course. I'd be happy to go through it.' She gave Eve a searching look. 'It's not your fault he died. You couldn't have stopped it.'

'Yes, I could,' said Eve, fighting back tears again. 'I know he went about it the wrong way, but if I'd given Frank just five more minutes of my time to discuss the case, he wouldn't have kept hassling me, he wouldn't have been on Waterloo Bridge that night and he wouldn't have drowned jumping in to save me. I owe him this.'

# ACKNOWLEDGEMENTS

*The Bait* is my second thriller with Thomas & Mercer and I am once again indebted to my editor Victoria Haslam and everyone at Amazon Publishing for making this the most brilliant publishing experience. You are all superstars! Particular thanks go to Russel McLean, Sadie Mayne and Gemma Wain for doing such a meticulous job on the edits. Thanks also to Dan Mogford for yet another amazing cover design.

Another million thank-yous again to my agent Marilia Savvides for the unequivocal support. I'm so proud to be a part of The Plot Agency and to watch it grow. Thanks also to Alexandra Cliff and Charlotte Bowerman at RML.

A lot of research went into *The Bait* and I must thank Julie Seddon, Brian Price, Neil Lancaster, Amelia Holgate at TfL, Tony Kent, Dr Lucinda Gabriel and Merilyn Davies for answering all my questions. Any errors are mine alone! I'm equally grateful to John Marrs and John Russell for all the brilliant advice, and to everyone at the Tandem Collective for the support.

I'd also like to express gratitude to my friends and family for all the encouragement and enthusiasm, especially Rory and Sophie. As always, I couldn't have done it without the two of you. I love you so much. Same goes for our newest addition, Scout – yes, she is a golden retriever too! – who has turned out to be the best writing companion ever.

Finally, thank you to all the readers and reviewers who got behind *The Seven* after it was published. I hope you enjoy Eve Wren's second outing as much as her first! Being able to share my stories with you really is the best job in the world.

# ABOUT THE AUTHOR

Robyn Delvey is a pseudonym for critically acclaimed and award-winning writer Michelle Davies. She is the author of several previously published novels and has worked for some of the most successful brands in UK magazine publishing, including *Grazia* and *Stylist*. She trained in journalism and for a period was court reporter on an award-winning weekly newspaper in Buckinghamshire, covering trials at both magistrates' and Crown courts. She now lives in north London with her partner and their daughter.

## Follow the Author on Amazon

If you enjoyed this book, follow Robyn Delvey on Amazon to be notified when the author releases a new book!
To do this, please follow these instructions:

### Desktop:

1) Search for the author's name on Amazon or in the Amazon App.
2) Click on the author's name to arrive on their Amazon page.
3) Click the 'Follow' button.

### Mobile and Tablet:

1) Search for the author's name on Amazon or in the Amazon App.
2) Click on one of the author's books.
3) Click on the author's name to arrive on their Amazon page.
4) Click the 'Follow' button.

### Kindle eReader and Kindle App:

If you enjoyed this book on a Kindle eReader or in the Kindle App, you will find the author 'Follow' button after the last page.